TAMLIN USKEVREN

Tamlin looked at the master keys.
There were only seven on an undecorated electrum
ring. Four of them, Tamlin knew, would together open
all of the mundane doors to Stormweather Towers.
Another unlocked the treasury, while the sixth
granted access to Thamalon's desk in the library.

The seventh was the mystery key.
As a boy, Tamlin had pestered his father about it,
but the Old Owl had only shrugged.
It had been dug up from the ruins of the previous
Stormweather Towers, he'd explained,
so whatever it had once opened must have perished in
the flames. He kept it as a remembrance
of his own father, Aldimar.

THE LAST PERSON YOU EXPECT

Alas, thought Tamlin, the truth to any mystery
is always far less exciting than the
speculation it inspires

SEMBIA:
GATEWAY TO THE REALMS

LORD OF STORMWEATHER

SEMBIA

GATEWAY TO THE REALMS

BOOK
VII

DAVE GROSS

To Ed Greenwood,
for the Whole Wide Realms.

Sembia: Gateway to the Realms, Book VII
Lord of Stormweather

©2003, 2008 Wizards of the Coast, Inc.

Published by Wizards of the Coast, Inc. FORGOTTEN REALMS, WIZARDS OF THE COAST, and their respective logos are trademarks of Wizards of the Coast, Inc., in the U.S.A. and other countries.

Printed in the U.S.A.

Cover art by Raymond Swanland
Map by Dennis Kauth
First Printing: March 2003
This Edition First Printing: February 2008

9 8 7 6 5 4 3 2 1

ISBN: 978-0-7869-4786-7
620-21629740-001-EN

U.S., CANADA,
ASIA, PACIFIC, & LATIN AMERICA
Wizards of the Coast, Inc.
P.O. Box 707
Renton, WA 98057-0707
+1-800-324-6496

EUROPEAN HEADQUARTERS
Hasbro UK Ltd
Caswell Way
Newport, Gwent NP9 0YH
GREAT BRITAIN
Save this address for your records.

Visit our web site at www.wizards.com

THE
MOONSEA

THE VAST

THE DALELANDS

SELGAUNT

CORMYR   SEMBIA

SEA OF
FALLEN
STARS

THE DRAGON COAST

THE VILHON REACH

AMN

TETHYR

THE LAKE OF STEAM

CALIMSHAN

CALIMPORT

N

W   E

S

TASHALAR

0   450

MILES

CHAPTER 1

11 Alturiak, 1373 DR

Tamlin soars through the thunderous clouds. Lightning sears his naked skin as the storm-god Talos scratches at the flea that dares crawl in his beard.

He spreads his arms to catch the wind, heedless of the torment of his body. Above the clouds there is something he must see, a revelation of arcane wisdom.

The gale beats him down, and he tumbles through the cold mist. His arms find no hold in the empty air. To fly, he needs magic, but he does not have the words to call it. He opens his mouth to shout a half-remembered phrase from youthful fantasy.

But the words have no power, and the storm sucks the breath from his lungs, hollowing him but for the leaden fear that rolls in his stomach, weighing him, bearing him down, down, and down. . . .

Tamlin awoke in darkness, reeling from his vision. He was numb, astonished.

Tamlin Uskevren had not experienced a flying dream since he was ten years old. At twenty-eight, he'd all but forgotten there was anything but oblivion in slumber.

That wasn't quite true, he realized. While a thousand forgotten dreams blazed like stars in his memory, he knew a host of vague illusions had taken their place over the years. Those mornings he woke befogged with imagined fumblings in linen closets with the comeliest of serving wenches—those were forgeries of his idle, conscious mind. They weren't true dreams.

They were nothing like flying.

Before he had time to ponder the meaning of their return, his tender body demanded his full attention. His head throbbed, dull and toxic from a night of . . . he couldn't remember exactly what. Wavering visions of dancing girls merged with a violent struggle in a black alley, and both gave way to the remembrance of soaring through moonlit clouds. Clenching his teeth, he rejected all of these thoughts as the reality of his present circumstances came into focus.

Rather than the comforting eiderdown quilt of his bed, Tamlin felt cold, damp limestone against his cheek.

He turned his head slightly, but that was enough to summon an overwhelming wave of nausea. A thin, hot stream of bile surged up to burn his throat before leaking out of his cracked lips. He felt it run down his chin to join a clammy mass of vomit clumped beneath his cheek. The stink revolted him, but he had not the strength to lift his head away from it.

Tamlin had been hung over many times before, but never so miserably. His normally silken voice was as rough as charcoal and weaker than a moth's fart when he called out, "Great . . . hopping . . . Ilmater . . ."

The martyr god was forever the subject of Tamlin's exclamations, but thus far the deity had never deigned to answer his profanity.

"Es?" he croaked. "Escevar?"

No one answered, but he wasn't surprised. Neither his henchman nor his bodyguard were nearby. He was alone. A sudden weight of despair pulled on his heart, and he feared he might never see them again. He remembered Escevar shouting for help just before . . . the rest was still a confusing vortex of memories.

He knew somehow that he'd lolled insensate for days, but how many?

Dripping water counted long seconds nearby, and the only other sound was a faint scrabbling near his feet. When he pushed himself up on one elbow, pain gripped his spine and squeezed hot tears from his gummy eyes. Blinking, he strained to perceive the faintest blur of yellow light emanating from the crack beneath a door. Except for the silhouettes of a few vertical bars, he could make out no other features of the room.

"Hello!" he called. He cleared his throat. "A spot of help, if you don't mind. Much appreciated, I assure you."

No one answered. Briefly he thought he sensed a presence, someone standing silently nearby.

"Hello?" he ventured meekly.

Still there was no answer. He tried to shake off the feeling of being watched by praying aloud once more.

"Blessed Beshaba, how have I offended thee?"

The goddess of ill fortune had rarely cast her gaze on Thamalon Uskevren II, but she had her place in the temple gallery of Stormweather Towers.

"Tymora, I beg you. Talk some sense into her."

The goddess of luck wasn't known for her power to persuade her twin sister, but she smiled on brash fools from time to time. Tamlin hoped he'd been sufficiently brash lately—the fool part he'd long since mastered.

"*Ow!*"

Whatever rustled at his toes had finally bitten through his doeskin boots. He kicked, and intense pain shot through his spine, but he was rewarded by an indignant squeal.

"Great god of rats and mice!" Tamlin yelped. "Whatever your name, lay off!"

His sight had returned just well enough that he could make out the vague shape of a large rat perched just beyond the reach of his pointed boots. Careful of his back, Tamlin pushed himself into a sitting position, swallowed hard to suppress another bout of nausea, and peered into the gloom.

Between him and the light under the door was a wall of bars. He reached out to feel them and discovered cold iron. Beyond that barrier, he saw a cracked stone floor. An elaborate design sketched in chalk curved between the bars and the door. Its perfect arc implied a circle around his cage, and its white lines glowed faintly brighter as he stared at them.

Tamlin knew at once that it was a magic circle.

Despite a summer's tutelage with a wizard, Tamlin had never shown an aptitude for the Art. After three months, he couldn't so much as ignite a candle with a lump of sulfur and coal, so gradually his passion for things arcane dwindled into a quaint but thereby acceptable superstitious streak.

His lack of talent was disappointing, but where skill was lacking, wealth could often suffice. Tamlin's collection of magical charms was the most extensive among his cohorts, some of whom teasingly called him "the sorcerer" behind his back.

He didn't mind the jest, at least not from those whose favor he desired, but he preferred the nickname "Deuce," a reminder to all that he was Thamalon Uskevren *the Second*, heir to one of the most powerful merchant Houses of Selgaunt's Old Chauncel.

So long as Thamalon the elder lived, he was known beyond his most intimate circles simply as Tamlin. In truth, and none too secretly, he preferred to remain "Deuce" and "the younger" for as long as possible. As the heir to Stormweather Towers, he enjoyed all the benefits of wealth and power with precious few of the responsibilities.

Not that any of those benefits was helpful at the moment.

Tamlin tried standing but found that his cage was only five feet high, forcing him to stoop like a hunchback in one of his brother's ridiculous plays. Rather than endure that indignity, he sat down once more, careful to avoid the mess he'd made.

His fingers took an inventory of his attire. He still wore the woolen hose and fashionably high boots, but the slender dagger was missing from his hip. No surprise, that. His cloak was gone, but he retained both the quilted doublet and his fine silk blouse, though he planned to burn them both once he found clean garments. It was one thing to blanch at some revolting beggar in the gutter, but to offend himself with such a stink—it was beyond endurance!

His new hat was gone, as were his jewels, which was a pity, for most of his charms went with them. At last he touched his collar and found a pair of pins his captors had overlooked. One enhanced virility while muting fertility—a popular item among those who could better afford charms than bastards—and the other was a ward against pickpockets. The witch who sold them to him had thrice sworn to their efficacy, though he supposed he couldn't complain. Neither was purported to foil kidnappings.

The inquisitive rodent crept closer, smelled the rebel contents of Tamlin's stomach, and made a lapping sound. The noise would have made Tamlin vomit again if he'd had anything left in his stomach. Briefly, he pitied the rat, but then pain wrenched his stomach. He'd never before felt anything quite like that dry, taut ache, and he wondered whether he'd contracted some disease in his crude prison, wherever it was. He needed the ministrations of a cleric, but first he had to find a way out of his cage.

Therein lay the rub.

"How did I get into this mess, Ratty?"

The rodent paused briefly in its disgusting feast, then resumed slurping.

Even if the rat could speak with all the wisdom of

Elminster the Sage, it didn't matter. Tamlin was already beginning to recall the events of the hours preceding his current disgrace, and he knew that he had no one to blame but himself.

"Let's get out of here, Deuce."

Even in adulthood, Escevar had an impish array of freckles across his pug nose. Combined with his russet hair, they gave him a mischievous air that Tamlin appreciated in part because standing beside Escevar made him look more mature.

"I am not afraid of Mister Pale," said Tamlin.

He smiled, thinking he sounded brave by saying it aloud. The smile turned into a wince as another wave of his hangover crashed against his brain.

Perhaps I should have retired before dawn, he thought.

"I don't know. He wouldn't have ushered you out of the meeting without the Old Owl's nod," said Escevar, looking up toward Vox for support.

Vox stood a head taller than Tamlin, and his brutal features—those not obscured by his wild black beard—suggested he was not wholly human. His wide, crooked nose and heavy forehead with its single eyebrow suggested ogre ancestry. He wore his hair in a thick braid curled around the left side of his neck. Tamlin had seen the ugly scar it concealed and knew it was a legacy of the wound that stole the man's voice.

"You agree that I should stay and apologize," said Tamlin. "Don't you, Vox?"

The big man replied in the private language he and Tamlin had devised, a quick series of hand gestures, *Better to be out of his sight for a while.*

"Far be it from me to ignore the advice of my bodyguard," said Tamlin, hoping to sound reluctant.

Secretly, he was glad to escape. It had been a long time

since he'd made his father this angry, and all over a slip of the tongue.

He nodded toward the grand stairway, and Vox led the way. As the three men passed through the halls of Stormweather Towers, servants stepped aside and bowed, tiny bells tinkling on their turbans. As they approached the grand front entrance, Tamlin ordered the doorman to summon a carriage, and allowed the man to wrap him neatly in his fine ermine coat.

They stepped outside, into the bracing Alturiak morning. A light snow covered the cobblestone drive, while drifts of a foot or more still lingered in the corners of the courtyard from a recent snowstorm.

Before the frozen fountain stood one of the four House carriages. Escevar instructed the driver as the footman lent his arm to help Tamlin mount the step before nestling into the cushioned seats. Vox joined the footman on the rear step of the carriage, while Escevar joined his master inside. The coachman slapped the reins, and they rode through the gates and into the streets of Selgaunt.

"We should stop at the Green Gauntlet," said Tamlin. "I could use a few drinks to smooth the corners."

"That's in the wrong direction," said Escevar. He produced a slim pewter flask from a pocket within his thigh-high boot. "This should help us reach the festhall in comfort."

Tamlin took a long pull from the flask. The brandy performed its magic, warming his throat and soothing his troubled stomach.

"This is the one with the Calishite girl you were telling me about?"

"The Djinni's Pearl." Escevar leered. He'd been buzzing with gossip for a tenday about the exotic new festhall dancer.

"She is undoubtedly still asleep at this hour."

"I suspect the proprietors will be glad to accommodate a special performance."

"I hope you brought another purse," said Tamlin, rubbing his sore neck. "And another flask."

❂ ❂ ❂ ❂ ❂

The additional funds proved unnecessary once the bare-chested doorman heard the name Uskevren. Within moments, musicians arrived and filled the parlor with the sour strains of desert music. Tamlin and Escevar lounged on fringed pillows, while Vox squatted behind them, leaning on his war axe.

The place had seemed empty when they first arrived, but with a few claps of his hands, their host conjured a trio of serving wenches wearing gossamer harem pants and a few ounces of cheap jewelry. They were obviously local girls, matched in the predictable blond, brunette, and redhead combination that panderers all thought was sure to please. They brought the men wine-drenched dates and took turns feeding them first to Escevar, who tasted everything before it was fit for his master, then to Tamlin.

"Perhaps we should have waited until evening," said Tamlin. He yawned into his fist. "It's more fun with a crowd."

"Boy!" called Escevar. A pasty Sembian lad ran to their low table. His gaudy fez and vest looked as though they'd been stolen from a performing monkey. "Your best wine."

Vox touched Tamlin's shoulder with two fingers, then pressed a third before tapping all three once, sharply.

"Relax, Vox," said Tamlin. "Have a date."

He flipped one of the dark fruits over his shoulder in the general vicinity of the big man's mouth. Vox snatched it out of the air with a huge fist, sniffed it, and took a bite.

Tamlin drank wine and watched dully as the local girls danced to the Calishite music. Despite the pleasant undulations of their bodies and the very nearly artful gestures of their hands and chins, he couldn't stop thinking about the morning's gaffe. As much as he wanted to blame his father for unreasonably ejecting him from the meeting, he realized the failing was his own. A slip of the tongue, Tamlin had called it. A drunken obscenity, his father had thundered.

Tamlin drained his goblet and held it up for a refill.

The remainder of the afternoon was hard to recall. Tamlin remembered asking after the Djinni's Pearl, and he had a dim recollection of assurances that she would rise with the noon sun. Would he care for some grilled lamb?

At some point he insisted that Vox join them in a drink. The brooding bodyguard no doubt protested. Tamlin didn't remember for certain, but that was the way Vox usually behaved. Dutiful to the end.

The one clear memory of the last minutes in the festhall was of stumbling into the nearby alley to be sick against the wall. The stench of garlic in his vomit remained pungent even days later, as he wallowed in fresher stinks. He retained a vague impression of Vox's strong hands on his arms, then a sudden fall to the moist ground. The sounds of blades drawn from their sheaths . . . a painful cry from Escevar, abruptly silenced . . . sudden darkness as a big body crashed to the ground beside him . . . and a series of stunning red impacts to his skull. . . .

CHAPTER 2

COLLECTIONS

"Sometimes I despair of that boy," said Thamalon Uskevren to his seemingly empty library.

"Yes, my lord," replied Erevis Cale, startling his master but sparing him again from the embarrassing habit of talking to himself.

The Lord of Stormweather Towers didn't turn, comfortable in the knowledge that he was never safer than when his most trusted servant stood just behind his left shoulder. Despite the twelve years he'd known his butler, Thamalon was still surprised when Cale suddenly ap-peared out of nowhere. The tall, bald man had a knack for invisibility that had nothing to do with wizardry, and the children used to jest that "Mister Pale" was thin enough to slip under doors. Thamalon knew that Cale had other dangerous talents, and he trusted his servant well enough not to inquire too pointedly about them.

"How does he expect to learn how to lead the family if he can't be bothered to attend our conferences on time?"

Cale didn't answer. He was an excellent butler.

"And that 'lesser Houses' remark, oh, that was calculated, I tell you. No slip of the tongue, that. He purposefully sabotaged that meeting, and for what? Why, for no reason at all, I say. He is full of wanton mischief! By the time I was his age, I was already— What is this? Who put this here?"

Thamalon's antique globe of Abeir-Toril had been moved to make room for a cedar easel. On it was a wide frame covered with a fringed curtain, complete with tasseled pull-cord for a grand unveiling.

"A gift from Master Tamlin."

"If that boy believes that he can smooth over this morning's debacle with a gift . . ." Thamalon felt the vein in his right temple begin to pulse. He dismissed the painting with a backhanded wave. He'd retreated to his library to escape the day's events, not to reexamine them. "Bah!"

Thamalon sat in his great manticore-hide chair and immediately noticed that someone had left several tomes open on his desk. The vein throbbed again. Sometimes it seemed that only he of the entire household held books in their deserved reverence. He grimaced at the carelessness, but before he could utter a ripe curse, Cale was already tidying the mess.

"Leave it," said Thamalon, spotting an interesting chapter title. "*Mysteries of the Moon Cults*? That's not one of mine. Is it?"

He knew perfectly well it wasn't, for he held the catalogue of his entire collection in memory, and he'd not yet grown as forgetful as other men his age.

How would I remember if I had forgotten? he asked himself, considering the joke about memory being the second thing to go. The thought made him scowl.

Approaching sixty-six, Thamalon was enjoying an unexpected revival of romance with his wife Shamur, who was still as lively as a colt at a scant forty-nine. Their marriage hadn't been a happy one until recently, and their conjugal catching-up had made Thamalon more keenly aware than ever of the difference in their ages. More specifically, it reminded him of his own age. He was far older than his father or uncles were when they died. Despite the illusion of youth that Shamur's new affections granted him, he felt the weight of years more with each passing day.

"I suspect Master Talbot left those," said Cale, "but perhaps you will ask him. He should be arriving directly."

"How do you know?"

"It is my duty to know, sir."

Thamalon clucked at his butler's uncharacteristic formality. Cale had long been more a confidant than a servant, but lately he'd seemed aloof. The narrowly averted war with the elves of the Tangled Trees had set everyone on edge, and the Uskevren family had suffered more than its share of crises in the past few years. Through it all, Cale had remained a bastion of calm. He seemed distant, more like a stranger than a trusted friend. Perhaps it was because the household had changed so much in recent months, especially with Thazienne's extended absence. Thamalon still worried about his daughter, though less so than before he commissioned the auguries that pronounced her safe. Even so, her departure seemed to mark the beginning of Cale's gloom.

Before Thamalon could broach the subject of his butler's distraction, someone thumped on the library door.

"That would be Master Talbot," said Cale as he went to the door.

When he opened it, Talbot Uskevren entered carrying a large coffer.

"May I take that, young master?" offered Cale.

"Better let me," said Talbot, hefting the box.

The dull clank of coins sounded from within the container. Cale arched an eyebrow but stood aside to let Talbot pass.

A few months shy of his twenty-second birthday, Thamalon's

younger son was somehow still growing. He loomed over Cale, who was notable throughout the city of Selgaunt for his height. Yet where Cale was lean as a scarecrow, Talbot was built like a dock porter. He also dressed like one, with rough leather trousers and a homespun shirt with the sleeves rolled up.

Fresh paint stains on his clothes showed that Talbot had come from the Wide Realms Playhouse, where he served as actor, manager, and general handyman. Thick black hair curled on his arms and chest, and his whiskers looked three days old, though Thamalon had seen him clean-shaven just that morning.

There were days when Thamalon might have doubted he had sired the boy, except that he saw his wife's gray eyes beneath his own strong brow on Talbot's face. While he didn't look much like his elder brother, Talbot strongly resembled both his great-uncle Roel and Thamalon's late brother Perivel, another big man who moved with unaffected, predatory grace.

Talbot set the coffer on the floor before the desk. Thamalon felt its heavy impact even through the sturdy floor.

"I don't recall your being in trouble," said Thamalon, "and you have missed my birthday by seven months. What is this gift?"

"It's the loan," said Talbot.

Thamalon started for the second time since he'd entered his library, which he'd once considered his sanctuary from unpleasant surprises. With a glance, he dismissed the butler. While Cale was privy to all household business, the loan was an unusually personal matter. Cale slipped silently out of the room, and Thamalon knew the butler would stand guard against further interruptions until he and Talbot were finished.

Thamalon left his desk and beckoned his son over to the chessboard, where they settled into the matching chairs. They hadn't played in over a year, but the proximity of the board was a reminder of one of the few things they enjoyed together.

"You have until Tarsakh to make the first payment," said Thamalon. He tried to strike a jolly tone. "You are far more prompt than most of my debtors."

"It's the full amount," said Talbot. His eyes flicked over the mahogany and ivory chess pieces.

"What about your—?"

"It didn't work out," said Talbot.

"They wouldn't resurrect—?"

"They couldn't."

"But the High Songmaster assured me—"

"Yes, well, he was mistaken."

"Damn it, Talbot, stop interrupting me! And look at me when you speak to me."

Talbot was only a mediocre actor, despite a talent for mimicry. Thamalon saw anguish beneath his son's barely composed expression.

"The clerics couldn't even contact his spirit?"

Talbot shook his head.

"I am truly sorry, son," said Thamalon, because it was true.

He'd never liked the idea of spending so much Uskevren gold to resurrect Chaney Foxmantle. The gods granted clerics such power only for the most divine purposes, and Thamalon felt that mortals had no business making a business of restoring life.

For months after his friend's death, Talbot bargained without threatening, pressed without cajoling, and finally won a compromise from his reluctant father. On condition that High Songmaster Ansril Ammhaddan approve the casting, Thamalon agreed to lend Talbot the coin with the Wide Realms playhouse as security. Father and son drew up a private contract and agreed upon a modest interest and payment schedule based on future playhouse profits.

Still, despite his best efforts to teach his offspring the principles of sound financial dealings, Thamalon knew that coin meant nothing to this boy who'd lost his closest friend. The dark intrigue that had cost Foxmantle his life had still never been explained to Thamalon's satisfaction, and he was sure that Talbot harbored a few more secrets about the affair. Cale had suggested a few possibilities based on street rumors, but Thamalon found them too fantastic to accept.

A werewolf, indeed.

Father and son watched each other a while in silence, and Thamalon's eyebrows leaped as he combined those rumors with the titles of the books he'd just seen on his desk.

"Werewolf?"

Talbot nodded with a sad smile and a little snort, as if to say, *What took you so long?*

Thamalon took several long moments to form his next questions.

"You don't . . ."

"No."

"So you . . ."

"It's under control."

"Ah," said Thamalon. "That's good."

He couldn't think of anything else to say while his mind still reeled with the absurdity of the revelation. Best not to think on it too hard, he decided.

They sat silently a while longer. Thamalon entertained a feeble hope that he was the brunt of some preposterous joke that would be explained later, perhaps over a bottle of Usk Fine Old.

He set aside the revelation to concentrate on the matter of Talbot's unseemly mourning, but he knew there were no words to soothe the loss of a beloved companion. Forty years after Nelember's death, Thamalon still quietly mourned his own best friend. The prim old tutor had been the first to perish in the assault that razed the first Stormweather Towers. The old clerk had done more to nurture and shape Thamalon than had his own father, Aldimar.

Suddenly Thamalon feared that he'd worked so hard to avoid Aldimar's obvious vices, such as piracy, he'd fallen prey to his more insidious faults, like siring bastards and treating his children with biting contempt.

"A man needs a friend he can trust," Thamalon offered. "I am grateful that Chaney was there to watch my son's back."

Talbot's eyes glimmered, but he opened them wide to let them dry before tears could form.

"Thanks."

"I mean it, Talbot," said Thamalon. "Sometimes I wish I had been a better friend to you."

"Only sometimes?"

"Not very often, mind you. You must admit, you have only lately become interesting."

As he'd calculated, the remark surprised his son into a genuine laugh.

"Well," said Talbot, "I could use some help painting the back-drop for *The Happy Bachelor* before tomorrow's rehearsal."

It was Thamalon's turn to laugh. Still, he wouldn't be diverted from his argument.

"Seriously, my boy, I have begun to realize just how much time I have devoted to the House—and how little I have devoted to those within it."

"Now, just because you and mother keep sneaking into the linen closet doesn't mean you have to go all soft on the rest of us."

"Have done! I won't have you talking about the lady of the house that way." He laughed. "That reminds me, whatever became of that fetching young country girl? What was her name?"

"Feena." The name was a charm to dispel Talbot's brief cheer. "She had to go home."

"I thought perhaps you and she—"

"Yeah. So did I."

Talbot's eyes wandered once more, this time to the gently twirling wings of an elven glass sculpture suspended from the ceiling.

"So why did she go?"

"Since her mother died, her village was without a cleric. She had to look after her people."

Thamalon paused before asking, "Why didn't you go with her?"

Talbot looked up and said, "Because I have to look after mine."

"Mm," grunted Thamalon. He knew that Talbot had many friends at the playhouse, but he wondered just how familial his loyalties ran.

"Will you be a friend to your brother?"

"Oh, come now, dear chap, you can't seriously mean that," drawled Talbot in a parody of his elder brother's voice.

The imitation was surprisingly good. Thamalon had once overheard the boy mimicking a wrathful Erevis Cale for an audience of giggling chambermaids, but he had no idea his son's repetoire was so wide.

"I'm afraid I do," said Thamalon, refusing to lighten his tone. "I know you two have never been the closest of siblings."

"That's putting it mildly. The only reason he survived to adulthood is because he's had that great lumbering ogre to protect him."

"Tamlin will inherit Stormweather Towers one day, and all the holdings of House Uskevren."

"I know," said Talbot, "and he's welcome to it."

Thamalon bristled. Talbot noticed.

"You know what I mean," said Talbot. "I have the playhouse, and Tazi is a free spirit. Besides, neither of us would dream of challenging your will."

"That isn't good enough." Thamalon slapped his hand on the table. "Tamlin will need your help one day. I want to know that you will support him, as a brother should."

"I don't like him very much." Talbot sighed. "There are days when I still want to throttle him."

"You must learn to suppress that desire."

"Oh, I am well practiced at that," said Talbot.

"Then I can trust you to watch his back?"

Talbot flinched at the phrase used earlier to describe his only true friend, but he nodded and said, "Why all this talk now? You sound like a man who— You're not ill, are you?"

"No, no, nothing like that," said Thamalon. "Perhaps I grow maudlin in my dotage. Maybe your sister's long absence has made me more keenly aware that you three must look to each other one day, when I have gone peculiar and need help eating my porridge. Or perhaps your mother's attentions have indeed made me soft. Why, just last evening she surprised me in the kitchen with a great spoonful of cake batter, and—"

"Have done!" roared Talbot in excellent imitation of his father's voice. He leaped from his chair and bolted theatrically toward the door with his big hands over his ears. "I won't hear you talk about the lady of the house that way!"

Thamalon laughed so hard he almost added incontinence to his roster of infirmities. He was still chortling when Cale peered into the room. Helpless with laughter, Thamalon dismissed his butler with a friendly wave.

When he recovered from his mirth, Thamalon realized that Talbot had left without a receipt for the returned loan. As much as he was coming to like his son as a young man, he couldn't understand how his three children could be so blithely unconcerned with matters of business.

Unlike his son, Thamalon couldn't bear to relax before business was done. He made a little space amid the clutter of his desk and wrote a bill of receipt in his meticulous hand. He spilled a handful of fine sand to dry the ink, blew it off, and fixed his seal to the document just below his signature before leaving it atop a neat stack of Talbot's books.

Alone at last, Thamalon luxuriated in the privacy of his library. Though it was open to all members of the household in his absence, including those servants who wished to better their positions through study, he still considered it his sanctum. It was there that he kept his most prized artifacts—sculptures, paintings, and art objects from all over the vast reaches of Faerûn. Elven works were prominent, causing a mild scandal among those few outsiders who'd visited the library, for elves were not well loved in Sembia, even before the skirmishes of the past summer.

The misplaced globe crowded a small area devoted to some recent astronomical acquisitions. Thamalon had purchased them only a few days earlier, when Cale introduced him to a man called Alkenen, a street peddler whom Thamalon still suspected was more properly called a "fence." Regardless of the man's propriety, he offered an astonishing lot of curiosities to the amateur sky gazer. The centerpiece was a fine orrery that Alkenen swore had been made by artisans of the far isle of Evermeet.

The model of the planets had come as part of a small collection of astronomical oddities. Thamalon had hoped to spend a relaxing evening examining them at leisure, but Tamlin's ill-timed gift was sitting right in the middle of it all. He started to move the painting aside, but curiosity got the better of him. He pulled the ridiculous little tassel and unveiled the painting.

He couldn't have been more shocked had he revealed a nude portrait of his daughter. The swirling, monochromatic image fairly screamed "Pietro Malveen." The youngest son of the disgraced family was popular among the rebellious youth of Selgaunt's artistic community. No doubt because owning one of Pietro's paintings was just scandalous enough to be fashionable, Tamlin had purchased nearly a dozen of the impressionistic works to bestow as gifts.

What Tamlin didn't realize—or so Thamalon prayed—was that the Malveens were likely the source of at least one attempt on his brother's life, though Thamalon hadn't entrusted his children with that knowledge. There was no proof of the first attempt, only rumor passed from Cale's mysterious cousin, who walked the darker lanes of Selgaunt.

More damning was the circumstance of Talbot's adventure of the past year, which ended in the immolation of an old converted warehouse that had once been Malveen property.

Ever since that time, the famed swordsman Radu Malveen had been missing, leaving only his elder brother Laskar and their younger brother Pietro to carry the family name. Their sisters had wisely married away from their family's notorious reputation.

Despite Tamlin's ignorance of the recent offenses of the Malveen men, Thamalon was still irritated. The quality of the gift was one thing, but to think it would absolve him of his irresponsible behavior was so blatant a ploy as to be insulting.

Perhaps an insult was exactly what Tamlin intended, thought Thamalon. He was by far the most sophisticated of the children, but perhaps his courtesy was a mask for contempt.

The damned vein began to pulse again, and Thamalon breathed deeply to still it. He looked more closely at the painting.

There must have been a sale on brown paint, he mused. Malveen had used little else in depicting the dark edge of a forest looming over a hunting lodge. Flecks of red showed where the frightened inhabitants had lit torches against the darkness, but the flames dispelled no shadows. Instead, they picked out the glittering eyes of grotesque beasts creeping out from the forest. Their bodies were all rough knobs and acute angles, as were the trees, which leaned and swayed as Thamalon peered at them.

He tried to blink away the illusion, but some intangible force had locked his gaze upon the canvas. The movement was no illusion, as the brush strokes swirled and converged in a spiral that pulled Thamalon toward the painting.

That wasn't quite right.

The vortex was drawing him *into* the painting.

He struggled to turn away, but the only movement he could muster was a weak wave of his limp hands. Briefly he thought he must look pathetic staggering around in his housecoat and slippers. He didn't like to think he looked like one of the feeble old drunks who stumbled about the waterfront begging for charity from superstitious sailors eager to buy good luck for a few copper pennies.

The painting pulled him ineluctably closer. Thamalon could smell the pigment—earth and blood and dung. He could almost taste it as the dark colors flooded over and through him.

His feet left the floor. He felt his body drawn apart.

In that last frantic instant, Thamalon Uskevren ceased to exist.

CHAPTER 3

ASSIGNATION

The stench of dung and urine soured the air, but neither of them smelled it. Steaming warmth from the sewage stream provided respite from the winter chill, but neither of them felt it. Any ordinary man in those wretched tunnels would have yearned to scramble back onto the streets, but not these two.

An assassin and a ghost skulked through the vaulted sewers of Selgaunt.

The living man strode along the cobblestone walkway, his steps no louder than the shadow of an owl's wing. The stiff collar of his cloak was laced up just beneath his eyes. The rest of his face hid behind a white enameled mask attached to a steel half-cap protecting his forehead. Behind the cap, a black shower of hair spilled down past his fine shoulders.

The man's shadow crooked upon the walls as he passed each of the eldritch lamps ensconced within its alcove. Eight other shadows rose and fell in turn behind him. Where they oozed along the walls, they left a clammy glimmer on the stones.

"Make a dog," said the ghost. He looked like nothing at all, and his voice echoed only within the assassin's head.

The man said nothing, didn't even break his stride except to slap the edge of his supple leather cloak behind the scabbard at his right hip. The hand that struck the fabric was gnarled and sclerotic beneath a calfskin glove.

"*Rrruh! Ruh ruh!*" barked the ghost. "Come on, here comes another lamp. You can make a *wolfhound.*"

The man turned and stared at the point from which he must have imagined the voice emanated. In the flickering green light, the black spots of his eyes seemed to swallow up all the whites.

"Still a sensitive subject? I thought you'd moved beyond recriminations, Radu. After all, it's not as if *he* disfigured you so. You managed that *handily* enou—"

"Be silent."

Radu Malveen's voice was the sound of a dry wind shaking shattered reeds. It might have been a human voice, once.

"There was a time, of course, when you could have silenced me with a look. What a scary bastard you were, even before you killed me. Ah, my material days. Still, there are advantages to this ethereal existence. That time you dossed down near the festhall, I had just enough room to slip through the wall and peek in at the new talent."

Radu lowered his head but kept his eyes focused on a spot very close to the point from which Chaney perceived the world. Chaney smiled, imagining the assassin's whitening lips, then remembering that Radu no longer had much in the way of lips. That thought made him smile even more.

"If I still had a life to lose, I might think twice before crossing the dread Radu Malveen, prickly, conceited, criminally insane killer from a House of raving no-doubt-on-account-of-profound-venereal-disease lunatics greatest swordsman in Selgaunt. Oh, and pathetic cripple. Mustn't forget the profound and unmanly injuries."

The quick snap of his cloak was the only warning that Malveen had moved. Before an eye could capture the blur that was his single liquid motion, he completed his lunge, extending his slender blade through empty air. While he saw nothing there, something caught his eye from below.

Radu looked down into the sewer water and saw the reflection of his blade passing through the specter of Chaney Foxmantle.

The ghost was almost as slender as Radu, but he was less than half past five feet tall. His fair hair was colorless in death, but some faint blue spark danced in his eyes. Maybe it was the last ember of hope. Maybe it was malice.

Chaney whistled. He looked down at the blade and measured its distance from the place his heart had been.

"Even though I assumed you couldn't hurt me, Seven Sisters and Hopping Ilmater, that was exciting! Good to know for sure, though, don't you think?"

"Foxmantle," warned Malveen, "your insipid rem—"

Radu's eyes darted, seeking something moving out of synchronicity with the ripples of the dark water. He crouched low to view the reflecting water at a sharper angle, watching Chaney's ghost.

There, seven dark figures stood silently in the water, the foul vapors of the sewage mingling with their own indefinite forms. Two looked like street toughs, one a bony old crone, one a dwarf with hairy shoulders, the others middle-aged noblemen of no remarkable features. Their exposed hands were the color of oysters, as were the points of their chins. They hung their heads so low that their damp black hair covered the rest of their faces.

"Who are they?" whispered Radu.

"It certainly took you long enough to notice them. Don't you ever look in a mirror?" Chaney paused for dramatic affect.

"What am I saying, of course you don't look in—"

"Who are they?" Radu's voice was full of razors.

"Don't you recognize them?"

Radu's narrowing eyes showed that he did. "They don't look the same as you."

"No, but they died *after* your rather ignoble defeat, didn't they?"

Radu stared at the shades a moment longer, then he raised his head as if in understanding. He sheathed his sword and strode briskly away.

Chaney chuckled as he watched the man retreat, then gulped as he felt the invisible bonds that kept him within thirty paces of his killer drag him along in his wake.

Radu came to an intersection where three brown streams converged into the wider flow he'd been following. Chaney peered around the corner and saw the amber light of a pair of lanterns twenty feet down one of the passages.

Radu moved silently to the edge of the light.

A well-fed nobleman stood between the lanterns. His velvet gown was heavy with gold thread and tiny jewels, except where sewer mud covered his back and left sleeve. Behind him was a wooden ladder, its second rung freshly broken.

Chaney recognized the fat man as Thuribal Baerodreemer. A generation ago, the Baerodreemers had been among the coalition that brought down House Uskevren, the most powerful of House Foxmantle's allies and the family of Chaney's best friend. Chaney had little use for a Baerodreemer and hoped the man did something to irritate Radu. That could prove entertaining.

"Ah!" Thuribal clutched at his chest as he suddenly noticed Radu's arrival. "You come upon our appointment most stealthily, sir!"

Radu said nothing.

"That is . . . I mean, naturally you would move with the utmost discretion, a man like you, after all . . ."

"*Boo!*" said Chaney. "Come now, Radu. Give the jellyfish a

bit of a spook, will you? Humor me, and I'll let you sleep an hour or two tonight."

"It is d-done, then?" said Thuribal. He couldn't hear the ghost's words.

Radu inclined his head slightly.

"Of course it is, of course, of course!"

Thuribal's face was beaded with sweat. He fumbled at his purse and produced a small velvet pouch, which he held out at arm's length. Immediately realizing the rudeness of the gesture, he withdrew it an inch or two for courtesy.

Radu placed his petrified right hand beneath the pouch. Carefully, Thuribal placed it between Radu's curled fingers.

"I assure you, they are of the finest quality, as you required. In the unlikely event you find them wanting—"

"I know where to find you," whispered Radu.

"Er, ehm . . ."

"Not bad," said Chaney. "Still, I'd like to see him fall down again."

Radu began to withdraw into the shadows.

"Wait!" Thuribal called, stepping forward and slipping in the muck. Chaney almost got his wish. "I, ah, took the liberty of bringing you a new client."

"What?" hissed Radu.

"I know, I know," Thuribal said, hastily waving down Radu's objection in a futile effort to regain his own nerve, "but this is a most special customer, one I am sure you will be glad I brought." He glanced upward and called, "Drakkar?"

A cloaked figured descended slowly through the sewer hole. The top of his deep blue hood was dusted with snow, as were his wide but shallow shoulders. When his feet met the floor, Chaney saw that the man stood as tall as Radu, but his cloak obscured all of his features except for a single brown hand clutching a knotty length of bloodwood. Black thorns studded the crimson surface of the staff, spiraling up from the tip to form a wicked crown of spikes at the head.

"Who's this, then?" asked Chaney.

Radu ignored the ghost's question, as usual. Chaney's gaze fixed upon the shadow beneath the newcomer's hood, and he thought briefly of pushing his own face inside to take a look.

"I thought it would be more convenient for everyone," said Thuribal. "No sense wasting time arranging for another rendezvous, yes?"

The interloper pulled back his cowl. His face was as dark as oiled oak. Fine creases around the black pearls of his eyes spoke of both mirth and cunning. He must have had at least fifty winters, but his hair was as black and wavy as that of any youth. His beard might have been drawn with a pencil, its spare geometry bracketing a strong pointed chin in the Cormyrean fashion.

Drakkar rested his staff in the crook of an elbow and produced a velvet pouch from beneath his cloak. He plucked its strings to reveal the diamonds within.

"I desire a proof," he said.

Radu drew his sword and stepped toward Thuribal.

"What are you doing?" sputtered Thuribal. "I—"

"Oh, no!" said Chaney, clutching his intangible stomach. "You just did one!"

The first thrust came from above. Chaney turned away, but he still heard the sickening clatter as the steel blade smashed Thuribal's teeth. The sword must have severed the man's tongue and jammed it down his throat, for the only sounds Chaney heard from him afterward were muted chokes.

Chaney instantly regretted his earlier wish for Thuribal's misfortune. He sat and hugged his knees.

After the crippling blow, Radu took his time killing the man, far longer than Chaney had observed in any of the man's previous murders.

When the killing blow finally came, Chaney dared to look once more at Radu. The killer had already wiped and sheathed his blade.

Drakkar glanced at what was left of Thuribal. "This is not

what I had hoped to see," he said. "I require an *irreversible* killing."

Radu leaned against the sewer wall. His posture seemed insouciant, but Chaney knew better. He hugged his ghostly knees all the tighter, bracing for what was to come.

The corpse of Thuribal Baerodreemer turned white as ash, clothes and all. Seconds later, it disintegrated into fine powder. Before the stuff could melt into the sewer, a silent wind swirled it up into a grotesque, friable mannequin. Chaney guessed the phantom was invisible to mortal eyes, but there had been no other witness to Radu's previous killings.

None who lived, that was.

As if reading the ghost's mind, Drakkar sketched a shape in the air and ran two fingers over each eyelid. His black pupils flashed viridian, and his eyes widened as he detected the dusty specter.

"Ah," he said in the confident tone of a man who doesn't fully understand what he sees but wishes his audience to think otherwise.

Thuribal's phantom twitched, its hands clawing at the air, head straining to turn away from its killer, mouth yawning wide as its face turned inexorably back toward Radu. Its granular form thickened and flowed, wavered one last time, then cascaded into Radu Malveen.

Radu shuddered and turned his head slowly to the side until his neck popped. With the collar hiding his mouth, the only reaction Chaney and Drakkar could see was the flicker of his black eyes. The three tiny moles beside his left eye briefly converged into one dark blot.

Chaney felt the same bone-hollowing ache that followed each of Radu's murders, and he heard the liquefying howl of the other ghosts join his own involuntary wail. Most of all, he felt the rapturous agony of life suffusing Radu's body, bolstering his unholy continuation.

The first time Chaney had felt the euphoric torment was when he died upon Radu's soul-devouring bone blade.

Moments later, Radu turned the blade on his own brother rather than let him confess to their enemies. Stannis Malveen was already undead, however, a sea-rotted vampire whose infernal essence shattered the bone blade, spraying its shards into his killer's body. Since then, the voracious power resided in Radu, consuming the souls of his victims no matter what weapon he employed.

When it was over, Chaney saw an eighth spectral figure join the undead procession behind Radu. Thuribal's ghost looked up at Chaney, astonished at its fate.

"I'm sorry," Chaney said quietly.

Thuribal lowered his gaze to the shadows at his feet, unmoved by the sympathy of his fellow spirit.

"Perfect." Drakkar smiled, raising a hand to draw a glyph in the air before Radu. "Now, after I cast a few spells on you to verify—"

Radu parted his cloak to show the hilt of his sword.

"Or perhaps you prefer not," said Drakkar, lowering his hand and backing away. He made a taut smile, the practiced gesture of a man used to accepting corrections from a superior. He carefully proffered the pouch of diamonds. "Let us agree upon the time for another meeting."

When Radu inclined his head in agreement, Chaney stared at the other ghosts and sadly shook his head.

CHAPTER 4

A SOUND OF THUNDER

"Where is Lady Shamur?" demanded Erevis Cale.

A trio of chambermaids stared at him dumbly, their mouths forming fearful little moues. Cale knew his bearing could awe the staff of Stormweather Towers, and usually he was glad of it, but he had no patience for hesitation in a crisis.

"Speak, one of you!"

The eldest of the three found her voice. "She left her chambers in search of Lord Thamalon."

"Where?"

The maid shrugged, then saw the danger in the butler's eyes.

"Upstairs," she blurted. "Perhaps the solar?"

Cale dismissed the servants with a chop of his hand, and they scurried away, the tiny bells on their turbans tinkling. The sound was meant to warn when a servant approached, so one could still a conversation or pull one's trousers up, but that night Cale found the jingling more irritating than practical.

Minutes earlier, a terrific peal of thunder had shaken Stormweather Towers, and lightning momentarily blinded all of its inhabitants. Strangely, nothing was burned, and the guards stationed outside reported no unseasonable weather. They had seen flashes only from *within* the mansion windows.

Such a magical effect was unlikely unless an intruder had penetrated the House defenses. Cale lamented once more the death of Brom Selwyn, the house mage who'd given his life in defense of the family a year earlier. He'd advised Lord Thamalon that a replacement was imperative to House security, but even he had to agree that contracting a trustworthy spellcaster could be a long and difficult process.

If one of the Uskevren's many rivals had found a way past the wards. . . .

Cale set aside the speculation. He was searching for the master of the house, whose own thunder he'd expected but not heard since the lightning. Once he conferred with Thamalon, he could do more than order the house guard to seal the mansion.

He passed through the front hall in two dozen long strides, then climbed the grand staircase three steps at a time.

Cale picked up the lamp always left beside the glass doors and raised the wick. He lifted his light and entered the solar.

It was a vast garden chamber filled with burlbush, honeyvine, and lady's promise, among dozens of other varieties transplanted from forests both near and remote. From pots suspended from the ceiling spilled still more flora, interrupted here and there by bright petals nurtured unseasonably beneath glass windows. Amid it all stood a great fountain, its water trickling down huge chunks of basalt sheathed in Lady's Lace moss before flowing away in a serpentine stream filled with silvery blue fish.

"Lady Shamur?" he called, knowing there would be no answer.

He silently scolded himself for following Lady Shamur rather than trying to go directly to Thamalon. Why had he done that?

He answered his own question as he picked up the lamp and stormed to the last place he'd seen the mistress of the house.

Earlier in the day, Cale had overheard Lady Shamur ordering the maids to tidy mistress Tazi's bedchamber. It was unlikely she intended a guest to inhabit her daughter's room, so Cale suspected she had reason to believe her errant daughter's return was imminent.

If so, why had Cale not already known? Apart from his many contacts among Selgaunt's thieves' guild, he might have expected a message from Tazi herself. Since the young woman had left Stormweather months earlier, Cale had received no word from her.

That silence cut him to the heart, for he had once, perhaps foolishly, believed he meant something to her.

Whatever good is in me exists because of you, he'd written to her, before adding in Elvish: *Ai armiel telere maenen hir*.

You hold my heart forever.

When he wrote those words, Tazi lay on the edge of death, and he'd sworn to avenge her.

In the days that followed, he forsook his hopes of leaving his past behind him and once more donned the leathers of his former profession. The killer in Cale not only fulfilled his promise to Tazi but also discovered that his future portended to bring him as much darkness as his past held.

Cale returned to Stormweather Towers as a newly awakened cleric of Mask, the Lord of Shadows. While he'd eliminated the current threat to the Uskevren, doing so had required him to delve so deeply into the machinations of the Night Knives that he knew he would never escape his bonds to the dirty underworld of the city—not while he remained in Selgaunt.

After Tazi at last recovered from her soul-shattering injuries, she'd made no acknowledgement of Cale's letter. Whether she rejected his feelings or was simply waiting for the right time to speak of them, Cale could only guess. He longed to resume their late-night conversations and the secrets they shared about their mutual avocation.

When she left the city to pursue an enemy of her own, he realized he couldn't force her to accept his help, even if he wasn't already sworn to serve her father. He could only abide and hope that one day she would speak to him. Cale realized that day might never come. He'd had his chance to ask her about her feelings, and without taking it he watched her leave Stormweather Towers.

The most he could hope for was word from her mother that Tazi had finally returned home. If so, then he would soon have the chance to ask his questions—if he dared.

Another flash of light seared Cale's vision, and he felt the floor rumble beneath his feet. He dashed toward the grand stairway.

At the mouth of the east wing, he encountered a trio of house guards. They saluted briskly and awaited his orders. Since the death of their captain, Jander Orvist, Cale had been their commander. He meant to appoint a replacement, but Thamalon insisted that the men would continue to look to Cale for orders despite any promotions among their own ranks. To tell the truth, Cale enjoyed his interaction with the soldiers. It made him feel more a part of House Uskevren, not a solitary figure whose best work was done at night.

"The east wing is clear, sir."

Cale nodded. "I will check the library. You check the kitchens, then the stables."

"Yes, sir!"

The guards hastened toward the stairway, their hands over the hilts of their long swords.

The library was dark, as it should never have been. Even when the occupants desired low light, a dozen lamps of continual flames normally flickered around the walls—just one of the late Brom Selwyn's lingering contributions to Stormweather Towers. Cale noticed that the hall sconces nearest the library were dark, but those ten feet or farther away still flickered in their glass receptacles.

Cale frowned at that. It meant there was definitely destructive magic at work.

He paused at the entrance, straining to sense any intruder. He heard nothing unusual, but he smelled lamp oil. After an instant's consideration, he set his own lamp on a hall table and plucked one of the functioning magic lights from its holder. Despite the orange flames within, the glass was cool to the touch.

Cale slipped into the library, crouched low and balanced to change course in an instant. His lanky limbs moved as smoothly as river reeds in a breeze. Soon he discovered the source of the odor.

Near Lord Thamalon's writing desk, upon the fine carpet, a dark stain was still spreading from the ruins of another ordinary lamp. Beside the spill, a small table lay overturned, its contents scattered on the floor along with the painting Master Tamlin had sent his father. There was one other strange addition: a white length of exquisite Sembian lace.

Lady Shamur's evening shawl.

Cale had never stopped listening for intruders, and he held his lamp high to spot further signs of a struggle. One of the fallen objects glittered in the dark.

It was a gray crystal sphere slightly larger than his fist. Hundreds, perhaps thousands of points reflected the lamplight through the globe's translucent body. Many of them glittered like silver filings, while others were luminous spots of color. At its center was a tiny dark sphere, its details invisible in the orange light.

Cale wasn't certain, but he thought he might have glimpsed the object among the astrological oddities his master had recently acquired. Still, there was something interesting about the sphere. Whatever it was, it probably wasn't urgent or relevant to the immediate problem. He dropped it into the side pocket of his coat.

He lifted Lady Shamur's shawl from beneath the painting. Oil had stained its edge, but Cale was relieved to see no further mark of violence upon it. Cale set it on the desk and carefully lifted the painting. There was nothing else beneath it, and it seemed undamaged. He propped it against the side of the desk and crouched for a closer look.

While Cale hadn't enjoyed the privileged upbringing of the Uskevren, he considered himself educated and not entirely untouched by culture. Still, he couldn't imagine anyone who could appreciate this unsettling landscape. The artist had skill and energy, but he must have been the very caricature of the tortured artist to produce a vision of such striking ugliness.

Still, the work was oddly compelling. Cale found himself examining its vague details for some clue . . . about what, he couldn't say. It was foolish to think the painting would reveal where his lord and lady had gone.

Too late, Cale sensed the danger. It was the painting that had taken Shamur and Thamalon, and it was planting some obsession in his own mind. He tried to look away, but all he could manage was to turn his chin while his eyes remained locked to the image, which began to sway.

He should have armed himself immediately upon hearing the first thunderbolt, he realized. Without his dagger in hand, he struck out at the painting with the continual flame lamp. The glass broke upon the picture frame, and Cale slashed at the canvas with the broken shards. A black line appeared on the painting, and for an instant Cale thought he'd broken its spell.

Then lightning flashed for the third time that night in Stormweather Towers, and Cale fell helplessly out of the world.

CHAPTER 5

TRANSFORMATIONS

Tamlin moaned as he awoke.

"Bleeding dark blasted damned bloody, bloody, *bloody!*" he croaked. He was still in the disgusting cell, and he'd been much happier about his predicament while asleep.

He'd been dreaming again, this time more pleasantly. He remembered squinting into the morning light reflected off a thousand burnished shields. He admired the deep red glow of his soldier's armor from a high palanquin, where he reclined with three fragrant maidens veiled in gossamer-thin silks. A cool breeze thrilled his skin, lifting the fine hairs on his naked legs.

In the waking world, his throat was rough and dry, and the memory of sipping cool nectar from an ivory cup did nothing to assuage his thirst.

"You wouldn't happen to have a wee little flask stashed somewhere, would you, Ratty?"

The rat had crept outside the cage. Tamlin watched as the animal sniffed cautiously at the chalk circle before recoiling. Tamlin's eyes had become accustomed to the darkness, or else the ring's faint luminescence had increased. Either way, he could make out the edges of a few barrels on one side of the chamber, as well as the outlines of what might have been a garbage chute before it was boarded shut.

The rat rose up on its hind legs, crouched, and leaped nimbly over the chalk line. Safely on the other side, the rodent scurried away.

"Clever lad," said Tamlin.

He mused for a while on the rat's powers of perception. Was the creature the familiar of his kidnapper? Was it a polymorphed incarnation of the mage himself?

Or herself, Tamlin amended.

Apart from the recently deceased Stormweather house mage, Brom Selwyn, the first three wizards Tamlin could name were all women: Helara, and the albino sisters, Ophelia and Magdon, of the Wizards' Guild. Any of them might devise a spell—or in Magdon's case, a magical gadget—that could free him from his prison for a price.

Hiring a wizard was no small expense. On the other hand, kidnapping was cheap enough and often quite profitable.

Tamlin had been kidnapped twice before. The first kidnappers lost their nerve while debating who would deliver the ransom demand to Stormweather Towers, leaving the teenaged Tamlin to be rescued a few hours later. The second group held out until the ransom arrived, then they released their captive. The villains enjoyed two nights and a day spending their coin before the Uskevren House Guard and a furious Vox caught up to them. Those who survived arrest were still rotting in the dungeons of Selgaunt's prison.

Neither of those groups had enjoyed the advantage of magic, and Tamlin imagined the expense would compound their ransom demand many times over. Despite his father's great wealth, he feared the Old Owl would think twice before paying for Tamlin's return, especially considering the terms on which they'd parted.

"Mother will make him pay," Tamlin reassured himself.

Shamur Uskevren had always doted on her children, and where Thamalon deplored his indolence, his mother adored her firstborn's easy charm and social grace. While she didn't play favorites—not obviously, anyway—Tamlin was certain she'd always loved him best of her three children.

Tamlin rose and immediately planted his elbow in a bowl of something lukewarm and wet. He tasted it on his fingers—a bland gruel bolstered with chunks of salt pork—and realized why the rodent had fled upon his waking.

Tamlin hesitated only briefly to weigh hunger against his disdain for peasant fare. Worse still, Tamlin hated to eat anything Escevar hadn't tasted for him. It was a habit born as much from superstition as from fear of poison. He'd read somewhere that wizards often cast spells on the food of their enemies.

"To the hells with it."

Tamlin spooned up the glob with two fingers. The stuff didn't taste as bad as he'd feared, but Tamlin cringed to imagine how he must look in his miserable cell with his fine clothes soiled, slurping from a bowl like some beggar. If the six dozen young women vying for his attentions in the spring socials could see him in such a state, they might prefer to marry a Baerent, a Foxmantle, or—gods help them—even a Toemalar.

Tamlin thought of the rat's whiskered snout rooting around in the food before him. While that wasn't enough to quell his famished stomach, it did give him an idea.

"*Psst*, Ratty," he hissed, scraping the bottom of the bowl against the stone floor.

He clicked his tongue as he used to do to summon his gyrfalcon, Honeylass. The beautiful creature had perished almost a year earlier in yet another attack on the Uskevren family.

Like Honeylass, the rat seemed more perceptive than the rest of his kind. Unlike the loyal bird, though, the rat had not been trained to trust a human master. It remained warily outside the magic circle.

Tamlin set the remains of his meal aside. If he could lure the rat back to the cage, he thought he might be able to tie a note to the creature. Assuming he emerged to scavenge on the streets at night, perhaps a passerby might spot the message and take it to Stormweather—

"What am I thinking?"

The absurdity of his plan struck Tamlin like a splash of cold water. Even if he could manage to capture the suspicious rodent, somehow manufacture writing materials, and tie a message to the squirming beast, the thought that someone would actually find it was—

"Preposterous," he muttered.

He shook his head in despair. Moments later, he brightened under a variation of his wretched plan. If he could attach a bit of the meat from his gruel to a string, then toss it across the magic circle, maybe he could erase a span and break the spell.

He tried tearing a strip of fabric from his blouse, but it was tougher than it appeared.

"I shall have to thank my tailor," he sneered. "If I ever get out of here."

He plucked the fertility fetish from his collar, hoping it could serve as a crude knife. Unfortunately, one glance at the ornament confirmed what he had feared. It was as dull as a spoon.

If it would not serve as a cutting edge, then perhaps the pin could become a lockpick. The silver charm consisted of a pair of blunt arrows—or what Tamlin called arrows when his more respectable acquaintances inquired. He carefully bent them apart, leaving them attached at the base and straightening them to form a more slender and fragile length of silver.

He felt outside the cage for a keyhole, then grinned when he discovered he could insert his little finger almost to the first knuckle into the opening.

"This will be easy."

Probing the lock was indeed no great challenge, but Tamlin soon discovered four different places where his makeshift pick could move some mechanism inside the lock. The problem was in moving more than one at a time.

Briefly he wished his sister were present. Since childhood, Tazi had had a talent for escaping her bedroom despite the vigilance of the staff. Tamlin had always been jealous of her ability to scale a seemingly sheer garden wall or to tease open a drawing room lock with a few hairpins.

Within a few years, Tazi gained notoriety among the household for her "wildings," nights on which she would escape the confines of Stormweather Towers for the dangerous freedom of the Oxblood Quarter or the docks. In the beginning, Tamlin would try to follow her with Vox and Escevar in tow. Even then, it didn't take Tazi long to shake her hecklers, and it had been years since they could follow her trail.

When Shamur Uskevren revealed her own secret past as a daring burglar, the rest of the family nodded and sighed, as if heredity explained it all. What it didn't explain was Tazi's sudden disappearance months earlier. At first frantic, Shamur and Thamalon calmed themselves after Songmaster Ammhaddan assured them that their daughter remained alive and free, if beyond their protection. Thamalon had wanted to launch an expedition to recover his wayward child—and Tamlin had hoped for command of the venture—before a long, private discussion between husband and wife concluded that Tazi would return on her own, when and if she willed.

Tamlin felt another pang of jealousy at his sister's freedom. If only he'd been similarly bold and had struck out on his own, he wouldn't be in his predicament.

He worked at the lock for what felt like an hour. Even on such a dull tool, he somehow managed to prick a thumb and two fingers, and his neck throbbed painfully. His cage door remained smugly fast.

Tamlin sighed heavily. He was too tired to muster a good curse. Instead, he lay back on the floor for a rest. Soon his eyes fluttered, and he teetered on the edge of sleep before a faint clicking arrested his attention.

The rat was creeping toward his cage again.

Tamlin feigned sleep. He had so much practice, he felt it was a special knack of his to keep his breathing slow and steady until a pesky servant finally gave up waking the young noble and left him dozing in his great bed. Tamlin hoped the rat wasn't much harder to trick.

When he heard the porridge bowl rock under the rat's weight, Tamlin rolled quickly over both rodent and dish. The rat wriggled and squealed, but Tamlin held it to the floor with his body while he snaked his hands under his chest to get a grip on some toothless and clawless region of the creature's body. Soon he had one hand firmly around the rat's throat and upper paws, while its lower claws made bloody stripes on his wrist.

"Loviatar's kisses!" hissed Tamlin.

Evoking the goddess of agonies made Tamlin wonder just how cruel his captors might be. He'd never understood the masochists who surrendered themselves to the Mistress of Pain, but those who inflicted her tortures on the unwilling seemed monstrous and unknowable.

He held the rat to the floor to keep it from attacking him. Though he had the thing, he wasn't quite sure what to do with it. He looked at the bowl and considered using it as a rat-sized version of his own prison. The rat might not even mind, if there was enough food left inside.

Before Tamlin decided, old iron hinges creaked, and the heavy door to the dark room opened. A pair of guards in shabby black tabards stood outside. Bits of thread curled at the outlines of emblems that had been torn from their breasts. One of them held a torch whose flame snapped like a flag. The breeze that shook the fire brought a sewer stench into the already noisome chamber.

A tall man in a long green cape swept past the guards, then gestured to them to shut the door. When they obeyed, the man unsheathed a brightly glowing glass wand.

Tamlin didn't recognize the man, but immediately knew he was a noble. He had the bearing of one who is accustomed to respect without asking for it. His golden-brown hair fell in ringlets to the shoulders of his fine linen cape, which was clasped with twin bronze raven medallions—a common icon among Selgaunt's merchants. Beneath the cape he wore a white linen doublet without ensign. The man's high boots and woolen hose were fashionable but not distinctive.

The visitor had dressed for anonymity, so Tamlin assumed his face was magically disguised as well. It wasn't unhandsome, lined by fifty years or more, and familiar to none of the famous Houses of Selgaunt. Even the man's amused smile gave Tamlin no clues as to his identity.

"My dear boy," he said with a nod toward the squirming rat. "If you are still hungry, I will have one of the men fetch you another bowl."

"Oh, do not trouble yourself," replied Tamlin. "It's just that it has been so long since I was last hunting. . . ." He shrugged in lieu of a wittier riposte.

His captor laughed with surprising warmth. "You have always been such a charming guest, Young Master Thamalon. I hope you shall be my guest again soon, under more pleasant circumstances."

"I shall look forward to it," said Tamlin. "Yet perhaps next time I shall be your host."

"Perhaps," said the stranger. He gave Tamlin a curious look, as if suspecting his prisoner knew something more than he let on.

Tamlin wished he knew enough to take advantage of his captor's uncertainty. For lack of a clue on which to build a bluff, he asked the obvious question.

"As much as I appreciate your kind hospitality, may I inquire as to the length of my stay?"

"Ah, to the point then," said the man. "Therein lies the trouble."

At first, Tamlin didn't rise to the man's unspoken invitation to inquire. The rat spoiled his cool appearance by biting the fleshy web between his thumb and forefinger. Tamlin hissed in irritation.

"Don't tell me you sent the ransom demand to Argent Hall," he said. "Last time it took forever for my cousins to redirect the messenger."

"Droll," said the man.

He raised the glowing wand for a better look at his captive. Tamlin saw a green stone glitter on the man's finger. While nothing else about the man was familiar, Tamlin was certain he'd seen that ring before.

"Please," the stranger said, "do release that vermin. You are liable to catch some dreadful disease if it keeps biting you."

"If the Old Owl balks at your price, send your man to my mother."

Tamlin tried to smile to smooth over his hasty words. Like most of the Old Chauncel, he much preferred to talk around a subject than plunge into it, but he was sick, injured, hungry, disgusted, and disgraced beyond all tolerance. Even so, he kept his grasp on the increasingly frantic rat. If its screams annoyed his captor, so much the better.

A petty revenge is better than none, Tamlin thought. *More importantly, irritation might prompt the man to reveal a clue.*

No, he seems too clever for that sort of ploy. If nothing else, maybe I could throw the rat in his face.

The thought pleased him, though a fleeting pity for the animal gave him qualms.

"The ransom is considerable, but not unreasonable," said the man. His brow creased in irritation. He couldn't keep his gaze from Tamlin's hands and their unwilling occupant.

Tamlin felt relieved that his kidnapper wanted gold after all. The Old Owl might balk at political extortion, but Tamlin was sure he wouldn't be niggardly with the safety of his heir.

"Perhaps my father is distracted by business matters," suggested Tamlin. "If you were to send a discreet inquiry to my—"

"I told you to let go of the Cyric-bedamned rat!" snapped his captor.

Stunned by the man's sudden hostility, Tamlin's mind raced for a disarming reply. Before one materialized, the man pulled an elaborate brass wand from his sleeve. Demonic bats and lizards crawled across its surface, and its head was an ivory skull of some tiny fanged mammal.

The man aimed the tip of the wand at the rat, and Tamlin knew better than to hold on to the struggling animal. He released the rodent and pushed as far away as the cage bars would let him. He moved just in time, as a crooked shaft of sickly yellow light shot through the bars to envelop the rat. The magical beam left a pale afterimage, like the path of lightning burned onto the eye for an instant after its strike.

The rat squealed louder than ever, writhing on the cell floor. Gleaming black buboes formed on its skin, bursting through its gray pelt to form new, wet appendages on its shoulders. Its head grew longer and thicker, and the new limbs spread wider to form translucent, batlike wings.

In seconds, Tamlin realized, the rat would be too big to escape the cage. His fear of remaining trapped with this transfigured vermin overcame his revulsion, and he lunged at the monster, pushing it out through the bars of the cage. The rat-thing screamed again, this time a deeper, more violent sound. Its black claws hooked the bars and pulled, trying to catch hold of Tamlin's flesh.

The man laughed heartily and returned the wand to its secret pocket. "We should perform this trick at the Soargyl's ball next month."

The monster was no longer recognizable as a rat, except for

its naked, ringed tail. Tamlin held its body outside the cage as it continued to grow. It tore at his arms, shredding the sleeves of his doublet and tearing ghastly rents in his skin. The pain was awful, but Tamlin was afraid to release it until he was sure it could no longer squeeze between the bars.

"Enough," said Tamlin's captor. He lifted a finger to point to the top of the cage. "Up you go!"

The beast flapped its dewy wings once, then perched atop Tamlin's cage. Its black eyes reflected red in the light of the glass dagger. It stared down at Tamlin as it shifted its weight from one leg to the other and back again. It looked hungry.

Tamlin hunched down as low as he could. The wounds on his arm began burning, and he knew they would soon itch with infection, if not poison.

"You should be more careful, young master," said the man. "It might take us quite some time to find someone who finds your release valuable."

"Just tell my father I'm wounded!" Tamlin was dizzy with anger. For a hot moment, he wished more for a knife and the key to his cell than he did for ransom. "If you continue to mistreat me, he will make you wish you were dead."

"Now you have put your finger on the problem," said the man. "You see, it is your father and mother who are dead."

CHAPTER 6

When Thamalon was six, he twirled himself dizzy in the grand courtyard of the first Stormweather Towers. His father's guards watched patiently as the five-year-old second son of Aldimar Uskevren fell laughing on the cobblestones. Thamalon was delighted at his new trick until he tried to stand. His legs seemed to bend like rubber, and he went sideways when he wanted to go forward. He reeled and wobbled until he fell down again, and this time one of the guards snickered until the captain rapped his helmet with a truncheon.

Thamalon couldn't stand up. He felt helpless and sick, and—worst of all—he knew he'd done this harm to himself. From that day, Thamalon knew that the worst thing in the world was feeling helpless.

On the night Stormweather Towers fell to an

alliance of the family's rivals, he saw once more that the world turned to chaos when one failed to control it personally. Ever after, he strove to remain the master of his fate.

Also, he never, ever twirled.

Fifty-nine years later, the vertigo of falling *up* out of his own home reminded Thamalon of his youthful resolve and its futility. No matter how much a man, even a strong one, tried to control his fate, there was always some unanticipated factor that could hurl it out of control. The secret at those times was to regain control and turn circumstances to one's own ends.

Thamalon's fall through the painting at first seemed to spin him up toward the stained glass windows of his library. Lightning flashed and thunder slapped him down, away from his former trajectory. An irresistible grip squeezed him tightly enough to make his ribs creak, and Thamalon's body jerked back and forth like a hated doll in the clutches of a lunatic child.

Oddly, he felt himself falling in two directions at once, though neither of them was anything like "up," "down," or even "sideways" anymore. Just when he felt that the competing forces would divide him into halves, one prevailed.

Where—? his lips moved, but before he could complete the thought, much less the word, he crashed.

A thick, moist carpet softened the blow to his head, but his hip cracked against something hard, shooting red lances of pain down to the bone. It was dark, but he smelled spring grass and flowers.

His first thought was that he'd fallen just outside Stormweather Towers, perhaps into the gardens.

A queer squeaking drew his attention upward. There he saw a swarm of bright blue jellyfish hovering over his head. At his gasp, their translucent bodies pulsed, and they shot away as a swarm.

Thamalon realized he was *far* outside of Stormweather Towers.

He stood, gingerly favoring his bruised hip. He said a

brief prayer of thanks to Tymora and Ilmater for sparing him a worse injury. Konnel Baerent had broken his hip the past winter, and his servants carried him about in a chair ever since.

Konnel was almost ten years younger than Thamalon.

"I'm getting too old for this," he muttered.

His robe and slippers were damp with dew, though it was still too dark to see, so he realized he'd moved through both distance and time. He knew he could be halfway around the world from home.

The thought that he'd been transported hundreds or thousands of miles away irritated him. Unfortunately, it seemed more and more likely as the twilight faded and the first echoes of the sun warmed the clouds. Beneath the clouds lay an alien landscape.

Thamalon stood near a deep blue-green forest whose trees were unlike any he'd ever seen. Black trunks rose straight up for perhaps twenty feet, only to splay out in all directions. Their leaves were as broad as lily pads and unusually bright even in the murk. They looked like the leaves in a child's painting of a tree.

A child's painting was a thought to ponder later, preferably when Thamalon could dispatch his guards to "invite" Pietro Malveen to Stormweather Towers for a private discussion.

Thamalon walked carefully beside the woods, exercising both his bruised hip and his imagination. Why did Tamlin give the enchanted painting to Thamalon? Revenge against an authoritarian father? Too petty. Ambition? The boy had never seemed to have any. Treachery? Did Pietro bribe him to do it?

Thamalon couldn't imagine any of his children, however disaffected, turning against the family. He might not have been a warm father, but he couldn't conceive of his children hating him enough to betray him.

Pietro must have used Tamlin's interest in art to strike at Thamalon. What little he'd gleaned about the past year's attacks on Talbot led him to believe that some members of House Malveen still held him to blame for the fall of their family. Because Aldimar had trafficked with them freely, some of the Malveens held it as a betrayal for Thamalon to turn his back on his father's former partners in crime.

Even this theory struck Thamalon as improbable. Laskar Malveen had always appeared to be Thamalon's sort of fellow, an honest man striving to repair the failings of the previous generation. Perhaps he was a consummate actor, as were many of the Old Chauncel. Foxes and weasels, most of them were, and far better at feigning their emotions than any of the players at Talbot's Wide Realms playhouse. Thamalon preferred to think of himself as a lion among the jackals, fearsome to his enemies while defending his pride.

Thamalon filed investigation and revenge in the library of his memory and looked away from the woods, across a rolling plain interrupted here and there by thick copses and blankets of wildflowers where the morning light grazed the hilltops. The nearest flowers seemed even more foreign than the trees, for they were large and heavy upon their stems. Their yellow, pink, and orange skins seemed less plantlike than fleshy.

Another thought to file for later, Thamalon decided, mostly because it gave him the shivers. He enjoyed exotic flora, but he would have preferred to examine it in the safe confines of the solar back home.

The blue creatures he'd surprised upon his arrival floated nearby. He had briefly hoped they were a trauma-induced delusion, but he saw that they were far from the only strange wildlife. Large, birdlike creatures wheeled in the distance, likely circling above some unseen carrion on the ground, and the whistles and deep hoots from the forest indicated a teeming population.

Far above the carrion eaters, a bank of huge clouds drifted slowly from the east. They were uniformly lozenge-shaped, like finless porpoises, and their advance was so regimented that they held his attention until Thamalon realized they weren't clouds but enormous creatures. Judging from their gradual motion, they must have been miles distant. If so, they had to be at least the size of war galleys. The distance made them ethereal, or perhaps their skins were gossamer thin, like those of the jellyfish creatures he'd seen earlier.

Whatever they were, their strange beauty delighted his heart.

Thamalon slapped his hip and realized he hadn't so much as a dagger with him. He also realized he'd better not slap that hip again soon. It was still limber, but it would have a deep bruise soon.

From where the sun breached the horizon, he oriented himself: forest north, plains south. He briefly wished he'd snatched up the astrolabe from his new collection just before he was swept away from home. While the Uskevren had avoided direct dealings with the shipping business since old Aldimar had been brought down for piracy, Thamalon remembered a few lessons on navigation from his childhood. When night returned, he could tell by the constellations whether he was anywhere near Selgaunt, Sembia, or even Faerûn for that matter.

A distant clamor of voices from the woods jolted Thamalon from his thoughts. Before he could identify the language, a burst of red flame erupted amid the trees, smothering all other sound.

Thamalon crouched low and ran along the forest's edge, looking for a spot that served both as vantage and shelter. His hip complained, but he ignored the pain.

From behind a rotting deadfall, Thamalon spied the source of the fire.

Teams of six-legged reptiles led a pair of armored wagons through the forest. Thamalon briefly feared they were basilisks but then realized the creatures' eyes were not hooded, and the drivers were not harmed by their gaze.

The wagons were massive cylindrical vehicles supported by wide, ironclad wheels. Along each side hung a pair of hooded, armored baskets fitted with cross-shaped archery slots. From the openings, bolts flew up toward the trees at such a rate that Thamalon guessed each cramped shelter must contain at least two archers.

Three stout figures stood in the driver's basket of each wagon, neither of them more than five feet tall. One goaded the beasts forward, while his companions fired heavy crossbows at unseen assailants in the trees. On the broad back of each wagon, an armored figure aimed a sort of metal ballista at the trees. Their faces were concealed behind full helms with bulging glass hemispheres over the eyes, but judging by the thick beards curling beneath their visors, Thamalon presumed they were dwarves.

Arrows rained down from the trees, glancing off the dwarves' armor and the heavy plates of their vehicle. The drivers goaded and shouted at their mounts, but the cold-blooded beasts plodded steadily forward, seemingly oblivious to their peril. The lead team suddenly veered from the path, despite the frantic yells of its driver.

As Thamalon watched, the weapon atop the second wagon belched forth another gout of flame. The guards in the driver's basket fired into the flaming boughs, and one was rewarded by the fall of a slender burning figure from the high branches.

Beating the lead lizard's head with the goad, the driver of the errant wagon finally forced the beasts to return to the path. They were less than thirty yards away from the edge of the forest.

They didn't see the mass of choke creeper that awaited them.

Thamalon had studied the dangerous plant the previous summer, when the elves of Tangled Trees and the armies of Sembia teetered on the brink of war. The elves had used the vines as a weapon against human trade caravans.

Thamalon stood to reveal himself. He regretted knowing so few words in Dwarvish.

"Beware!" he shouted, pointing to the treacherous patch.

The vines had already begun reaching out toward the reptiles' legs. "Bad there!"

A flurry of arrows shot toward him. Thamalon dropped behind the hollow log. An arrow had pierced his robe and hung there just under his left armpit. He felt the burning edge of the arrowhead against his ribs and hoped it was only a light graze.

"Do you speak the trade tongue?" called a gruff voice from the wagons.

The dwarf's Common was far better than Thamalon's six or eight words of the dwarven language. Moreover, the sound of his native tongue gave Thamalon hope that he wasn't so far from Sembia as he'd first feared.

Two more arrows pierced the rotting bark of his shelter and sank into the ground near Thamalon's feet. He shouted back without rising, "There's choke creeper between you and the clearing! Your front wagon is nearly in the stuff!"

The dwarves shouted in their own language, and Thamalon heard another great *whoosh* from their flame projector. It sounded like thunder amid the downpour of arrows striking the armored dwarves and their wagons.

He dared another glance above the log. Luckily, the unseen attackers concentrated all their fire on the draft beasts.

Fortunately for the caravan, the lizards' hide was as tough as the dwarves' armor. Only a few arrows stuck in their skin, and those sank only an inch or two into their targets.

Unfortunately for the lizards, the tough green vines had already slithered up and around their short, elephantine legs. Thamalon knew how tenacious the creeper was. It could strangle a strong man to death in a matter of minutes.

The two guards in the lead wagon dropped their crossbows in favor of sharp axes and leaped to the ground. There they hewed like harvesters, chopping the lively vines as near to their beasts' feet as they dared. The reptilian creatures plodded forward against the vines, the only indication of their panic a steady, lowering moan.

The fire-throwers covered their companions' actions with a series of short bursts. Despite the dwarves' restraint, the boughs above them crackled with flame. Blackened limbs began to droop precipitously over the wagons.

One of the dwarves on the ground shouted a familiar-sounding epithet. The vines had encircled both of his legs and was pulling him away from the struggling lizards, toward the squirming center of the patch.

"I am *definitely* too old for this," muttered Thamalon.

He ran toward the fallen dwarf, crouching low to present as small a target as possible to the unseen archers. His injured hip gave him a horrendous limp that might have looked comical in other circumstances.

The vines stripped the dwarf's axe from his hands and drew him deeper into their tangled mass, leaving the weapon behind.

"Roendhalg!" the dwarf's companion called, turning to cleave a path through the wriggling vines between them.

Arrows spanked off the back of his steel armor, but one found the gap between his helmet and his back plate. The dwarf reeled forward, clutching awkwardly at the arrow in his neck. The vines reached for his legs.

Thamalon snatched up Roendhalg's axe and chopped at the vines encircling the other dwarf's ankles. Three strokes was all it took to free him that far from the center of the creeper. The freed dwarf backstepped and fell as the shock of the arrow wound struck him fully. Thamalon dropped the axe and grabbed the fallen dwarf. He was heavier than he looked, even considering the armor.

"Get away!" shouted the dwarf atop the wagon.

He finally turned the flame weapon toward the creeper. The monstrous plant had already plucked the captured dwarf's helmet from his head and was peeling off his armor. Beneath his black beard, the dwarf's face was red from throttling, his eyes bulging, tongue distended.

Thamalon dragged his charge back toward the wagon. He

heard a hiss as the dwarf atop the wagon squeezed the lever for his flame weapon.

"Wait!"

Heedless of Thamalon's shout, the dwarf unleashed a tremendous burst of fire upon the creeper and its captive. The vines thrashed as the flame blasted away their leaves, leaving nothing but the blackened stems and the immolated corpse of their last victim.

"Lift him up!" yelled the driver. He reached down to receive the lolling body of his wounded guard. Immediately after, he offered his arm to Thamalon. "Up you come!"

Inside the basket, Thamalon knelt beside the wounded dwarf while the driver once more took up his goad. While he was no battlefield surgeon, Thamalon knew the basics of tending a wound. Careful not to bump the driver as he beat and cajoled the draft beasts, Thamalon gently removed the wounded dwarf's helmet and began unbuckling his armor. He left the arrow in place. It had pierced the thick muscle of the dwarf's neck about a handspan away from his spine. Thamalon shrugged off his robe and tore a sleeve from his linen shirt to staunch the bleeding.

Behind them, someone in the second wagon blew a staccato blast on an iron horn. The wagons lurched forward as the reptiles slowly but steadily left the forest and their arboreal attackers.

Only after they were out of range of the arrows did Thamalon realize sadly that their attackers had almost certainly been elves. While he had no elf blood, Thamalon had always felt an affinity with the fair folk—so much so that he had sired a pair of twins with an elf woman named Trisdea, even after his marriage to Shamur.

"How fares Grunlaern?"

The driver's question spared Thamalon from further uncomfortable introspection. He glanced only briefly at Thamalon before returning his attention on the path ahead.

"It is a dire wound," reported Thamalon, "but not mortal, I

think. As soon as we can stop, someone should cut out the arrowhead and bandage this properly."

They halted the caravan half an hour later, when the wagons were well clear of any trees. While one of the dwarves tended Grunlaern, the other examined the damage to their wagons. They plucked a few dozen arrows from the wagons, murmuring appreciatively when they saw none had penetrated the armored flanks.

"Well met," said one of the dwarves who'd operated the flame weapons. He carried his goggled helmet under one arm as he walked toward Thamalon. The dwarf smelled faintly of candied almonds. He clasped Thamalon's forearm in a gloved hand. "I am Baeron Longstrides of the Deepspire Miners, son of Hurglud of the Keen Nose, subcommander of the *throbe* caravans."

"Well indeed," said Thamalon, returning the grasp. He'd already decided that he didn't wish his true identity known until he was sure he was among allies. "Call me Nelember the Far-Traveler."

The dwarf's eyes narrowed as he considered the introduction, but he slowly nodded. Thamalon had offered a sufficiently polite disclaimer that he wasn't sharing his true name.

"In fact, I am so far-traveled," added Thamalon, "that I have completely lost my way. Is your destination near?"

"Three days," said Baeron. "We owe you a service. If you wish it, you may ride with us."

Thamalon nodded. "I will. Perhaps there I can recover my bearings."

"No doubt of it," said Baeron. "For we travel to the greatest of all human bastions. We go to Castle Stormweather."

CHAPTER 7

Chaney clambered up the outer wall of the Hunting Garden. How his spectral hands could grip the fine crevices between the granite blocks he still couldn't fathom. For some reason, the phenomenon seemed more paradoxical than the question of why he didn't sink into the ground when he walked, yet he could thrust his face through a wall and peer into the room beyond. He could see and hear, though he could no longer smell or taste, and he could barely feel.

The bodiless existence was full of conundrums.

Briefly he considered letting go to glide along in Radu's wake as the assassin spidered up the wall. It would be fun, unless he was pulled through the stone as Radu leaped down the other side. The sensation of passing through solid objects was unlike anything Chaney had experienced in life. It was an uncomfortable, disorienting numbness. It didn't hurt so much as it made him queasy and fearful of a sudden agony.

Besides, Chaney liked imitating an action that had been so familiar in life. The ghost smiled as he recalled a few of the windows through which he'd crept as a mortal man. He wished regretfully that he'd slipped through a few more before his life had ended.

Radu had tied his boots together and slung them over his shoulder. He had no special knack for climbing apart from his infernal strength and alacrity, but for this occasion he'd purchased a battery of spells from a Thayan witch.

Back at her waterfront shop, the dark-tressed woman had seemed well accustomed to anonymous customers, even masked swordsmen.

"Well met," Chaney had said to the woman. "I'm his haunting."

As Chaney expected, she didn't mark his presence.

Radu explained his needs, showed the woman a pair of tiny diamonds, and surrendered a third at her insistence. The witch took one of the gems and crushed it in an enchanted mortar. When she turned back to Radu, her dozen bracelets chimed as she raised her hands to pluck magic out of nothing.

Even through his high collar and mask, Radu could barely disguise his contempt for the spellcaster—or for himself, for needing her Art. Nevertheless, he stood motionless as she incanted her spells, fed him a spider squirming in bitumen, blew a pinch of cat's fur into his masked face, scattered the glittering dust of the crushed diamond over his shoulders, and finally snapped her fingers on her own eyelash rolled in a bit of tree gum. After the resultant flash, Radu faded from sight, even from Chaney's spectral eyes.

While the witch worked her magic, the shadowy ghosts that stood behind the assassin moaned and swayed like old willow trees on a dry creek bank. Chaney saw Radu's head turn slightly, as if the man noticed some distant sound but couldn't identify it.

Silently, Chaney applauded the unhallowed choir. Anything that disturbed Radu Malveen was a delight to his heart.

The witch bowed her head as the remaining two diamonds appeared in her open hand. An instant later, Chaney felt the tug of his mortal anchor as Radu left the shop.

From the docks, Radu had run north across Sarn Street, where the moon shadows mingled with those cast by the flickering street lamps. Selûne's reflection and those of her trailing tears rippled on Selgaunt Bay, where the black silhouette of the boaters formed a tiny, ragged village between the docks. There the city's cutthroats, thieves, and smugglers made their deals in vessels lashed together to form a community each night. At dawn, they would cast off again, only to join with different neighbors the next night.

After they scaled the outer wall of the Hunting Garden, Radu dropped into the rough brush of the Hulorn's Hunting Garden. Ostensibly private, the place was constantly invaded by teenagers dared by their peers to crawl through the sewers and return with a rare flower as proof of their trespass.

Chaney himself had slipped inside once, with his best friend, Talbot Uskevren. Once within the walls of the gloomy place, Chaney tried spooking Talbot with the story of a girl who'd slipped into the Hunting Garden a few years past, never to be seen again. He succeeded only in frightening himself, and in the end he was the one who bolted first, cutting his chin in the rough sewer grate as he fled a sudden hooting, certain it was the girl's spirit luring him to his doom.

He touched the scar on his chin and imagined he could still feel it. Ten years later, he was the only ghost who haunted the tangled woods—he and his eight inarticulate fellows, who'd fallen back into their customary silence.

At least, he *hoped* they were the only inhabitants of the garden. Something rustled at the edge of the wood, and all the fireflies hid their glowing bellies as the assassin and his ghosts approached.

Radu kept to the deep shadows until he came to the western

barrier of the Palace of Beauty. Chaney could hear the faint strains of a zulkoon from beyond the wall. The eerie sound grew louder as Radu ascended the wall, his bare hands and feet clinging to the stone.

At the top of the wall, they looked down upon the ill-named Palace of Beauty. It was a grotesque edifice of spiraling towers and arches, ranks of balconies, a parliament of gargoyles, and garishly glowing windows. Unlike the similarly eclectic Stormweather Towers, Chaney thought the palace looked like a feverish child's vision of a fairy castle.

It was to this monument to the Hulorn's poor taste that Radu had followed Drakkar for the past two nights. For a wizard of some power, Drakkar was surprisingly oblivious to being followed.

He was also a creature of habit. In just two nights, he'd demonstrated a banal routine beginning with a visit to the Hulorn's palace and ending in one of the city's less savory festhalls.

"There he is," said Chaney.

He slapped his forehead when he realized he was helping Radu. With no other company in his long months of phantom existence, Chaney felt his chatter slipping from the spiteful annoyance he intended to the friendly banter to which he'd grown accustomed in life. He wasn't beginning to like Radu Malveen, for there was nothing remotely likeable about the cold and silent man. The truth was he was lonely, and there was simply no one else to whom Chaney could talk.

Chaney consoled himself with the thought that Radu could see him no better than he could see the invisible assassin. Nevertheless, Radu must have spied Drakkar's dark blue cloak as it crossed the courtyard. Rather than join the audience at the amphitheater, he went directly to the main building. The guards nodded respectfully as he passed.

Radu moved toward the palace, carrying the ghosts in his wake. Chaney hurried to keep up and avoid being dragged through a wall or a guard tower. Even while invisible, Radu radiated a cold, dark presence that guided Chaney across the walls and rooftops, past the unwitting guards.

Chaney held his breath as Radu sneaked past a pair of sentries wearing the Hulorn's red-and-black livery. Fortunately for them, they didn't hear the faint padding of Radu's naked feet, and Chaney was spared another horrid rush of death. A moldy taste still lingered in his mouth from the most recent murders.

While the killings made Chaney feel sick, they filled Radu with vigor. For days after a killing, he enjoyed inhuman strength and speed. Since the recent double-murder of Thuribal Baerodreemer and his hated rival, Chaney could see a faint white aura around Radu. At first it was more brilliant than the corona of an eclipse, but gradually it would fade to a milky halo then to nothing.

Radu visited each of the lighted windows on the north face of the palace in turn, clinging like a beetle to the wall. At last, he came to an open balcony through which Chaney saw what could only be the Hulorn's private gallery. As a twig on one of the least prominent branches of the Foxmantle tree, Chaney had never been invited to tour the private wings of the palace. From what he'd heard from those who had seen it, he'd never regretted missing the experience.

Beyond the balcony, the gallery spread out in the shape of an amputee starfish. The floor was a vast chessboard of crimson and green tiles. Near the center its squares were perfect, but they turned trapezoidal and finally shapeless near the ends of the five short arms of the chamber. One arm housed the balcony, while the others ended in huge doors of various shapes.

Two dozen statues in as many different materials stood among the room like pawns in an unfinished game. They ranged from classical nudes painted in bright hues to abstract collisions of glass, bronze, and driftwood.

The paintings for which the gallery was infamous floated above their own illuminated tiles. Some hovered still, while others drifted slowly on their own, uncertain axes. Most were strange portraits, the most pedestrian of which resembled famous and infamous lords and ladies caricatured with the features of one or more animals. Chaney recognized Presker Talendar's head on the body of an elegant white cat lapping blood from the street. Others were so abstract as to bear little resemblance to anything human. These were the ones that made Chaney feel as though centipedes were crawling in his stomach.

Chaney heard a hiss and thought it came from Radu.

"What is the matter?" he said.

Radu didn't reply, but Chaney felt the killer's presence like a winter shadow.

"What?"

Chaney realized he would have no answer then, so he decided to ask later. In the meantime, he moved into the gallery, where he discovered that even the worst of the paintings was less obscene than the gallery's sole occupant.

The man lay on the floor, gazing up at a slowly spinning painting. He wore the familiar purple doublet and black hose of Andeth Ilchammar, the Hulorn, but otherwise he bore only the roughest resemblance to the man the public knew as the Lord Mayor of Selgaunt. His skull appeared to have been crushed and remolded by a blind and palsied sculptor. While the right side of his face seemed human—if one could overlook the fang jutting up over his mustache—the left was black and as scaly as a constrictor's hide. His sinister eye bulged with a slitted pupil.

The man drummed his fingers on the floor as he regarded the painting. Chaney flinched to see that one of the man's hands was a birdlike talon except for its soft, wormy fingers. The other hand looked more human but for its patchwork skin. Upon his furry forefinger he wore a massive gold ring, while his feathered ring finger bore a brilliant green emerald.

A bell rang outside one of the doors. Andeth rocked back onto his shoulders and rolled forward to stand. A moment later, a servant opened the pentagonal door.

"My lord, he has arrived," said the servant, keeping his gaze on the floor.

Andeth murmured a few arcane words and mimed the act of washing his face. Where his mismatched hands passed over his visage, his features transformed into those familiar to the citizens of Selgaunt. As he completed the gesture, there was no sign remaining that he was anything other than a neatly groomed merchant lord.

"Let him come," said Andeth.

The servant withdrew. With a wicked smile, the Hulorn slipped a wand from his sleeve and shook it three times at the door.

In rapid succession, three small brown clouds appeared, each punctuated by a nasty, wet popping sound. The smoke dissipated to reveal a trio of huge rats. Their eyes burned with infernal light, and their slavering lips trembled and dripped steaming spittle. As one, they looked to their summoner.

Andeth waved once to either side of the door, and the abyssal vermin skittered out of sight just as the visitor arrived.

Drakkar strode purposefully through the door. Chaney thought the tension in his neat jaw was obvious, but the man's expression did nothing to dim the Hulorn's mischievous smile. As he came near the Hulorn, Drakkar looked up and saw the man's mirth—too late. Andeth snapped his fingers and beckoned his rats.

"Beggar!" spat Drakkar.

He whirled to face the vermin, his long dark fingers plucking a thorn from his staff. He hurled it at the rats.

As it left the wizard's fingers, the thorn turned into a burning black spot of energy. It sizzled and split into five individual points, three of which shot into the body of the nearest rat. The creature's momentum hurled the three messy pieces of its body to flop at Drakkar's feet.

The remaining missiles diverged, each striking one of the other attackers. One of the rats screeched like a crow and veered away. The other fearlessly charged Drakkar and climbed straight up his cloak toward his face.

"Dark!" cursed the wizard, beating at the rat with his thorny staff.

"Serves you right," laughed the Hulorn. "No direct spells. You know the rules."

His face twisted in revulsion, Drakkar seized the dire rat with his free hand. The creature sank its teeth into the man's wrist, evoking a shout before Drakkar flung it away.

"Mad Andy!" he shouted. "The children are right to call you that, you barking lunatic. Enough of these ludicrous games!"

Andeth clucked his tongue and held the surviving rats at bay with a gesture.

"Such rough words to a patron who has shielded you from so much harm," said the Hulorn. "If I were truly deranged, would you dare to speak in such a manner?"

Drakkar clenched his teeth so hard that Chaney could see the muscles working beneath his narrow beard.

"If I practice an antic disposition, my friend, you know the reason. Those who think me mad think me harmless, and you of all people should know that I am not in the least fraction *harmless*."

A tic leaped beneath Drakkar's right eye, then leaped again as he relaxed his expression with a supreme effort.

"You hardly need practice this facade," said Drakkar. "You have well mastered it."

Andeth's laugh was full of friendly warmth. "Bravo! Do you see? Even you can be subtle in insult. That was far more civilized, especially for one whose natural charms are so limited by drow blood."

Drakkar betrayed the truth of the Hulorn's accusation, for his arched brows appeared distinctly elven in their vexation. Other than his fine cheekbones and jaw, nothing else betrayed his mixed parentage.

"What do you know?" Chaney remarked, as much to himself as Radu.

The assassin remained undetectable in his silence, though Chaney knew he couldn't have roamed far without tugging at his ghost.

"Now, finish the game," commanded Andeth, "and to business."

Drakkar pulled another thorn from his staff, wetted it on his tongue, and threw it to the ground. He grasped a small pouch at his belt and shouted a quick barrage of arcane syllables.

A pool of fire opened like an eye on the floor before Drakkar, its glow making a demonic mask of the wizard's face. From the flames, a massive black form slowly rose until, blowing and stamping, a huge black stallion appeared. Its mane was a fiery bough, its tail a river of fire.

Drakkar pointed at the rats, which squealed in terror, and said, "Kill them."

The nightmare danced forward and stamped one of the rats into a bloody stain. It tossed its head and threw the other rat high into the air. As the vermin fell, the nightmare caught it in its teeth, gnashed them thrice, and swallowed.

Sneering over his easy victory, Drakkar turned to Andeth. The Hulorn scowled back at him.

"Get it out of here," Andeth said, slapping at the thick, choking smoke. "It stinks of brimstone."

Drakkar intoned the words, performed the gestures, and sent the nightmare back to the Abyss before he turned to smile triumphantly at the Hulorn.

"Very poor form," admonished lord mayor. "That was your problem last year as well. You must learn to employ the razor, not the club."

"As you say, my lord," said Drakkar, sounding anything but chastised.

Andeth sighed again. "Well?"

Momentarily confused, Drakkar stared blankly before he remembered his business.

"I have instructed the guards to behave as we discussed," he reported. "Your visit to the cell was well done, but I still believe we should have employed actors as the guards."

Andeth shook his head. "Too much chance the brother would have known one of them."

"Still, it is crucial that the boy be convinced."

"That will not take much doing," said Andeth. "He is a conceited lush. We might as well have given him a puppet show."

"I am less concerned about him than his retainers," said Drakkar. "Should Larajin become—"

"Spare me," said Andeth, strolling toward the balcony. "Your infatuation with that serving wench is unseemly in a man of your station."

Drakkar followed the Hulorn, and Chaney followed them both, hoping Radu was doing the same.

The wizards stood side by side with their hands on the marble rail, gazing out over the thousand lights of Selgaunt. Chaney leaned back on the rail between them, smiling as he poked his fingers into their eyes. As expected, neither of them noticed, but he kept at it, hoping for at least a blink.

"She is more powerful than you acknowledge," ventured Drakkar.

"I shall consider your warning, my friend."

"And do not underestimate the brother," said Drakkar. "You should allow me to teach you the silverbonds spell."

Andeth shot Drakkar an irritated glance and said, "It does not interest me."

"I realize it is a difficult enchantment to master, but—"

"Enough of that," said Andeth. "Do not practice too many subtle insults in one evening. Not on me."

"My lord," said Drakkar, "speaking as your friend, I encourage you to rely less on those wands and more upon your own ability. One day you may face an opponent who . . ."

The Hulorn gazed at Drakkar through cool, hooded eyes. His expression was enough to put an end to the topic.

"Here," said Andeth, twisting the big green emerald from his finger. "Find a convincing place to return this."

"Simplicity itself," said Drakkar, taking the ring and securing it in a pouch. "A simple suggestion spell, and Presker's butler will discover where his master dropped his favorite jewel while visiting Old High Hall yesterday, but if Thamalon the Lesser is as stupid as you believe. . . ."

"Then we will have someone give him a suggestion as well, shall we not? If not empowered by magic like yours, it should be no less effective," the Hulorn said. "Speaking of which, it is time I recovered our little gift from Stormweather Towers. By now our friend should have removed it from the library."

"Who is it?" asked Drakkar in the crooning voice of a child who had been denied a secret.

"The last person he would suspect," replied Andeth. He wiped his eye with his little finger. Emboldened, Chaney poked at him again, to no effect. "But we cannot allow any single element of our scheme to be crucial. Should one action fail, we must have an alternative."

There was an inquiry in Andeth's tone, and Drakkar heard it.

"I have found the assassin we heard of," he said. "His services are dear, but his power seems genuine."

"Seems?"

"The Waukeenar were utterly unable to contact Baerodreemer's spirit at sunset."

"And the clerics of Oghma?"

"The Namers experienced the same result this morning, my lord."

"Excellent," said Andeth. "After you return from the Talendar, fetch me this killer."

"And, what?"

"And, my friend, we shall put him to work."

CHAPTER 8

BLOSSOMS

At first Cale tensed, then he relaxed his body as he fell. He raised his arms to protect his head and tried not to think of the inevitable impact when he struck bottom.

Assuming there was a bottom.

Once before, Cale had tumbled through a gate between worlds. That had been a markedly different experience, like piercing a thick membrane and entering an airless room. This time, it was gravity itself that changed, tilting him from one reality to another.

"Mask, let it not be the Abyss this—"

The impact crushed the prayer from his lips.

As Cale hit the ground, he saw daylight all around him, blue sky above, brown earth below. He rolled, trying to get his legs under him to stand, but he had arrived on a rough hillside. At first he tumbled painfully amid the scree, but he turned to roll smoothly. A sharp rock raked at his ribs, but he kept his arms protectively over his bald pate.

At the base of the slope he fell on soft grass that slowed him enough to roll at last up to his feet. He wished again that before searching for Thamalon he had taken the time to fetch a weapon or to don the leathers he kept hidden in his bedchamber. Instead he crouched unarmed and unarmored, turning swiftly to scan in all directions.

The first thing he noticed was that he could breathe the air, and apart from the rough landing, he felt reasonably hale. At least this place was more hospitable than the plane he'd last visited.

Atop the rocky hill he spotted a cluster of weird trees bending gracefully against the rising sun. The wind whistled mournfully through their tubular fronds.

On all other sides rose great black tree trunks whose boughs spread out in all directions to form a dense, flat canopy. Above the forest wheeled a flock of long-necked lizards, gliding back to their perches after a brief panic.

Cale hoped it was his own sudden arrival that had startled the creatures, not the approach of some other predator.

To the southwest, the bright green meadow sprawled for about forty yards before succumbing to the forest. Here and there were patches of strange wildflowers, their petals brilliant orange, white, lime, yellow, and blue. Cale recognized none of the flowers, and he had a suspicion that no sage in Faerûn had ever seen them, either.

Not ten feet away, a cluster of cerulean blossoms the size and transparency of water bottles bowed in the breeze. They formed an almost perfectly circular patch around a mossy tree stump. Their thick red stems rose waist-high before bending under the weight of their massive heads, a few of them so heavy they touched the ground. Inside the translucent walls of their petals stirred the vague shapes of fetal sleepers. As the rising sun touched the flowers, their occupants grew restless.

One of the flowers shuddered, and its surface breached. Syrupy purple liquid spilled from the flower head, and a pale white proboscis emerged from the rent. Soon after, the rest of a slender head and neck emerged. Twin lumps on either side of the head appeared to be closed eyes.

Cale realized he was staring open-mouthed at the sight. He surveyed his surroundings again. Reassured that nothing approached the birthing flowers, he moved closer to observe the bizarre process.

Over the course of twenty or thirty minutes, a tiny winged reptile emerged from the sagging petal. As it struggled and finally escaped its crèche, the creature clambered awkwardly over the too-green grass. Its eyes never opened, and Cale saw that there were no slits for eyelids. Was the creature deformed? Or were those bumps some other form of sensory organ?

Cale brushed a finger upon the newborn's back. It felt as cool, smooth, and soft as a rose petal, and he realized it was no lizard after all. Its flesh was that of a plant, not an animal.

"*Srendaen*," murmured Cale.

Of all the languages he'd mastered, Cale loved the poetry of the Elvish tongue not only for its lyrical sound but also for its endless synonyms. The word he used for "beautiful" would never apply to a person, only a thing of luminous, natural beauty.

Led by instinct, the flower-bird began the arduous journey up the steep hillside. Cale thought how piteous it looked, how easy it would be to carry the thing to the crest of the hill. Like all living things, however, it needed to struggle to grow strong. To help it then would be to make it weak later.

Back at the flower patch, another few blossom-sacs were bursting open, while half a dozen more had finally drooped to the ground.

Cale followed the first-born up the hill.

He wasn't so fascinated by the alien creature that he forgot his duty. Mounting the hill would give him a better view of the surrounding territory. Assuming the enchanted painting had captured Thamalon and Shamur before Cale discovered it—and Cale considered that a safe assumption—he had a better chance of spotting them from a high vantage. Finding a way back to Selgaunt would be another challenge, but he could consider that problem later.

Cale remembered something else about his previous journey beyond the material plane. He imagined himself back inside the halls of Stormweather Towers, among the anxious guards. He thought of the bright tapestries in the grand hall, the polished oak tables with their gold candelabras, even the annoying tinkle of the servants' belled turbans . . .

Nothing changed. He remained in the strange new world, and no amount of his wishing would change that reality.

"Worth a shot," he said.

Briefly he wished Jak Fleet was with him. Together they'd escaped the ashen plains of the Abyss, and Cale was certain his halfling friend would be of help again.

"Trickster's Toes," Cale said, smiling ruefully. If nothing else, he could always count on Jak's exclamations to dispel the gloom that seemed naturally to settle around Cale at times. Times when those he'd sworn to protect were in peril.

But Jak wasn't there. Cale was on his own.

He patted the pockets of his long jacket and felt the hard edges of the keys to Stormweather Towers and the soft folds of a black mask he kept with him at all times. It was the eponymous symbol of his patron god.

Little more than a year had passed since Cale first learned of Mask's interest in him, and in that time he'd only just begun to explore his new faith and the powers it granted him. He'd finally, reluctantly embraced his role as a champion of the Lord of Shadows, but resentment over the god's manipulations of his mortal servant still lingered in his heart. Sometimes he felt like a pawn from one of Thamalon's chess armies. At other times, he suspected the god's favor granted Cale that much more power over his own fate.

At the crest of the hill, the flower-bird spread its fragile wings. They were so delicate that Cale feared the slightest gust might tear the creature to shreds, but instead the first breeze lifted the bird and carried it out over the meadow, where it floated like a tiny kite.

From that height, Cale could see for miles in every direction, for all the good it did him. The forest seemed endlessly vast. Squinting into the sun, Cale perceived the faint violet silhouette of mountains. He couldn't begin to guess how distant they were. Too far, was his conclusion.

He heard the dull twang of a bowstring.

Cale tumbled forward and rolled to the left. He came up running away from the arrow that quivered in the ground where he'd been standing.

Sibilant voices called to each other from the trees. It was a strange dialect, but Cale recognized the words as Elvish.

"You have the eyes of a mole!"

"Shoot! He's escaping."

Before him stood the dark shelter of the trees, but Cale knew there was no safety in them for a city man hunted by elves. The slope behind him provided absolutely no cover. Even were he armed with a sword, he could never close with the unseen archers before they feathered him with arrows.

He'd have to rely on his only remaining weapon.

"Wait!" he called in Elvish. "I am a peaceful traveler lost in your lands."

The elves didn't reply at first. Cale imagined they were creeping silently to better positions from which to shoot him. He hoped instead that they were considering his words and finding them worthy of parlay.

Cale remained still, awaiting the verdict.

A slim, brown-skinned elf slowly emerged from the morning shadows. He wore supple breeches and boots the color of the surrounding tree trunks. He held a gracefully curved bow.

With slow deliberation, the elf drew the bow and aimed at

Cale's breast. At less than twenty yards distance, Cale knew he had virtually no chance of dodging the shot.

Cale showed his empty hands. He slowly turned around once to prove that he was unarmed.

"I wish only to find my master and return home," he said.

Two more hushed voices called down from the trees. They were just quiet enough that Cale couldn't make out the words. The elf menacing him nodded once, and he shook his head.

"Where is your home?" he asked.

"Far from here, in a land called Sembia."

The voices conferred once more.

"Who is your master?"

"Thamalon Uskevren." Cale held a hand at nose level and said, "He stands so tall, and his hair is white. Like me, he comes unarmed and means no harm to elves."

A familiar figure silently emerged from the shadows behind the elf. She raised a finger to her lips but didn't spare a glance at Cale. Her gaze was locked on the back of the elf's neck.

Cale wanted to warn her away, but he feared what the elves might do in their alarm. Instead, he kept his expression neutral, his eyes focused upon the bowman's face.

With fluid grace, Shamur Uskevren closed with the elf, drew his knife from its sheath, cut his bowstring, and held the sharp blade to his throat.

"Wait!" Cale cried to the elf's unseen companions.

He waved urgently to beckon Shamur and her hostage out into the open, and an arrow blurred out of the trees and sank deep into Cale's thigh. He felt the arrowhead exit the back of his leg, but the shaft remained stuck.

"It is a misunderstanding!" he shouted to the elves. The pain cracked his voice, but he held it at bay with a grimace. In the common tongue, he called to Shamur, "Quickly, get behind me with him."

"Release him, or we will kill you both!"

"No," said Cale. "First you must understand that we didn't intend to harm him. This is Shamur Uskevren, wife of my master Thamalon. She doesn't understand your tongue and thus didn't know that we parlayed."

Shamur glanced at Cale when she heard her name and that of her husband. She still wore the pleated blue gown she'd worn the day before, but it was limp with dew, and gone were the lacy sash and shawl. Her ash-blond hair was disheveled, and her face was bare of rouge and kohl. Cale supposed that she'd just begun preparing for bed when the thunder shook Stormweather Towers.

While her attire reflected her station as one of the grand dames of Selgaunt, Shamur's demeanor was that of a warrior. She held the elf by his long black ponytail, keeping the knife pressed firmly to his throat. Using him as a shield, she side-stepped out of the shadow of the trees and into the open beside Cale.

"Please, my lady," said Cale. "Behind me."

The elves didn't reply to Cale's explanation, neither with words nor more arrows.

Shamur didn't budge, either. "Tell them to throw down their bows," she said. "I counted at least two others, but I suspect there's a third."

"My lady—"

"Just do it," she said.

Cale had witnessed this mood before, and he knew there was no point to further discussion.

"Throw down your bows," he called to the elves. "And show yourselves."

Two arrows buzzed through the air and sprouted in the ground less than foot before Cale and Shamur.

Shamur drew an inch-long slice upon her captive's skin.

"No!" screamed Shamur's captive. "Great mother!"

"She does not wish to kill him!" shouted Cale. The cold shock of his wound was beginning to give way to a red-hot pain, but he tried to keep anger out of his voice. "But she will do it if you don't throw down your bows."

"Do it!" wailed the hostage.

Cale could smell the elf's fear. Somehow he'd retained the childhood fancy that elves were far finer creatures than humans, but they stank just as badly when frightened.

Without the faintest rustling of foliage, a pair of elves dropped lightly from the trees and emerged from the forest shadows. They set their bows carefully on the grass and stepped away from them.

"And the other one," Cale said with a nod toward the trees.

One of the newly revealed elves puffed his cheeks with a resigned sigh and said, "Come, Kayin."

The third elf emerged from behind a tree and set his bow gently against the trunk.

"All of you," said Cale. "Come here and sit with us so that we may talk."

Reluctantly, the elves complied. Cale knelt painfully on his right knee, holding his injured leg out to the side.

"Ready?" he asked Shamur.

She nodded and said, "Tell him to stay close to me. I still don't trust them."

Cale relayed the message to the captive, who nodded dumbly. Shamur removed the blade from his throat, and the elf sat cross-legged on the ground.

"Let us talk," Cale said to the elves, "but first, will someone please help me get this damned arrow out of my leg?"

Cale and Shamur briefly exchanged their stories. As he'd guessed, Shamur had fallen victim to the enchanted painting shortly before he found her shawl. Since they arrived in the strange land so near to each other, he assumed Thamalon couldn't be far away.

Cale explained their story to the elves in the simplest terms: An enemy wizard had transported them away from their home, and they wished only to return. First, they had to find Thamalon.

The elves reacted with skepticism, then growing curiosity. Cale's command of their language, albeit with a strange accent, was a matter of great interest to them. While they'd learned the common tongue long ago, they'd never encountered a human who spoke their language.

Moreover, the elves seemed impressed by the restraint Cale had shown when injured, as well as the stoicism with which he bore the wound and the painful process of removing the arrow.

An hour later, Cale felt they'd established enough of a rapport that he could leave Shamur with the elves for a few moments. Pleading a need to relieve himself, he limped into the woods and found privacy amid the trees.

Shamur had torn strips from her skirt to make a bandage for his wound. Cale stripped off and discarded the sodden fabric nearest the wound. Briefly he worried that he looked ridiculous with one leg of his black trousers cut away to reveal his long, pale leg. Contrary to gossip among the Uskevren servants, Cale didn't actively cultivate his fearsome image. He did, however, appreciate the added authority his forbidding appearance lent him when dealing with incompetent or lazy house staff.

With a last glance ensure that Shamur and the elves remained in the clearing, Cale tied the mask to his face. It felt comfortable, even natural to have it there.

"Mask," he intoned, pressing a palm to both the entry and exit wounds, "Lord of Shadows, heal your servant."

A cool rush of power filled his body, surging through his veins to culminate at his hands. There, the coolness turned to tingly warmth and suffused his damaged flesh. He felt the divine energy travel through the ragged length of the wound, rebinding sinew and skin until they were whole. When he took away his hands, he saw a round pink scar where the arrow had struck him.

Cale removed the mask and put it back in his pocket. He stood, testing the strength of his leg. Despite a slight weakness from blood loss, he felt hale as ever.

He paused before returning. If the relationship with the elves soured, it would be an advantage for them to think he was still injured. Also, Cale didn't care to invite inquiry about his powers, even from those who knew him.

Perhaps *especially* from those who knew him.

He replaced the bloodied bandage on his leg and returned to the others, affecting a slight limp.

"How is your leg?" asked Shamur.

"Better than it looks."

"Do you have any idea where we are?"

"Far from Faerûn," said Cale.

"Everything looks so peculiar here," Shamur added. "Those trees, the flowers, the birds . . . even the grass seems an odd color. On the other hand, our new acquaintances seem quite similar to the elves of the Tangled Trees."

Cale nodded and said, "And the sun looks the same, as do the sky and the clouds."

The elves watched as the humans conversed in their own tongue.

Cale said to them in Elvish, "We wish to leave you in peace. Can you tell us the way to a human habitation?"

"Human territory lies many days to the south," said the leader of the elf scouts.

His name was Muenda, and his companions were Amari and Kayin, the latter of whom still seemed awed by Shamur's ability to surprise him.

Cale didn't like the prospect of traveling for days through unknown wilderness, especially through a forest of elves hostile to humans.

"Are there human traders among your people?"

"We have had no peace with the humans for more than ten summers," declared Muenda.

Cale considered the diplomacy of the situation before asking his next question. "Would the humans to the south welcome strangers like us?"

Muenda sighed as if he had expected the question. "Yes," he said, "but you will win no friends among the elves if you go there."

"We would prefer to remain on friendly terms with your people," said Cale. "Will you help us search for my master?"

Muenda nodded and said, "If he is within our domain, we will find him. However, it is possible he will be mistaken for an enemy scout or spy."

"As were we," said Cale.

Muenda agreed, and a flick of his eyes showed that he still didn't trust the humans—especially Shamur.

"Very well," said the elf. "We will take you before the elders of my tribe. Can you walk?"

"Yes," said Cale.

"Can you climb?"

"With help."

"And she?" Muenda asked, nodding at Shamur.

"Like you would not believe," said Cale.

He suspected Lady Shamur was as nimble as Jak Fleet, though she appeared ill prepared for athletics in her current attire.

"What?" asked Shamur, noticing Cale's uncharacteristic smile.

"I realize it might seem improper," said Cale, "but you might want to slit those skirts."

Shamur didn't hesitate. With curt efficiency, she cut a line from just above her knees to the hem of her skirt, then shifted her dress and did the same in back. The mutilated garment gave her a wild look that reminded Cale of Tazi. The resemblance between mother and daughter was usually not so obvious, with their contrasting hair and eyes. Still, the two women shared an attitude of strength with a hint of mischief. Cale had rarely before seen the latter quality in Shamur. When she was done, Shamur offered the knife hilt-first to Kayin.

"I am sorry to have cut you," she said.

As Cale translated her words, the elf's face slackened with

surprise. He replaced the knife in its sheath and removed the sheath from his belt. Hesitantly, Kayin bowed to Shamur and offered her the knife and sheath together, along with a few words in his mellifluous language.

"What did he say?"

Cale translated: "'Thanks for not cutting deeper.'"

Shamur made a gracious curtsy and accepted the gift. Kayin shook his head in wonderment and bowed again, this time more deeply.

"Come with us," said Muenda.

The elves rose to retrieve their bows, but their relaxed gait reassured Cale of their armistice.

The elves led them a few hundred yards into the woods. With virtually every step, Cale noted another strange variety of flora. Tough gray vines stretched from trunk to trunk, and some mossy growth spread in patches on the ground. Giant yellow blossoms hung like bells from branches that sprung from two or three different types of tree, only to creep among the boughs and mingle with others of their kind.

"Here," said Muenda, indicating a gnarly trunk with many slender branches.

Cale and Shamur followed the elf up the woody path. As they entered the canopy, Cale wondered what sort of city the elves must have wrought among the trees. He was surprised when they emerged from the thickest foliage to see nothing but treetops in all directions.

"Where are your people?" he asked Muenda.

"They are almost here," replied the elf. "I summoned them when we first saw you."

He tapped the bone whistle that he wore on a thong around his neck.

Cale tensed as he felt a warm breeze and saw a shadow fall over the hilltop. He looked up, expecting to see the sun muted by a cloud. Instead, he saw a gigantic creature floating in the sky.

It was longer than three trade ships docked prow-to-stern,

and its shape was similar to that of the porpoises Cale had seen during his voyage across the Sea of Fallen Stars. Instead of fins, thousands—perhaps millions—of transparent flagella rippled in regular stripes along its flanks. The rest of its blue-green body was striped with narrow furrows that converged in a thick, hairlike mass near the center of its belly.

The gargantuan creature's slow descent gave Cale the impression that he was falling upward, toward a ploughed field with a thicket in its center.

Despite the animal's great size, Cale could see daylight refracted here and there through its skin. In some of those lighted spaces, the shadows of smaller bodies moved within the great creature. In other spots, chaotic patches of green moss dangled from its hide, and flocks of flower-birds nested in the crannies of its vast belly.

"Do not be afraid," said Muenda. "I am telling them we are at peace."

He put the whistle to his lips and blew, but Cale heard no sound.

The elves cocked their heads to listen to the reply, which was still undetectable to Cale's ears.

A moment later, Muenda piped again. He nodded as he listened to the reply.

"You are welcome in the village."

"Up there?" asked Cale.

Muenda smiled and nodded.

"You are the first humans to climb upon a skwalos in many years," he said. "You might find the experience startling."

Cale looked up and saw that the creature—the skwalos—had stopped its decent about fifty yards above the tree canopy. From the tangled mass on its belly fell what looked like half a dozen thick, black ropes. As they struck the branches nearby, Cale saw that they were as thick as his arms, and flat like noodles. Twigs and leaves stuck to the surface of the tendrils.

Nimbly navigating the slender branches, Muenda went to

one of the tendrils and wrapped it around his body. The tendril contracted snugly around his chest, waist, and thighs.

"See?" said Muenda. "It is easy. When you are ready, stroke its tongue, like this."

Tongue? thought Cale.

Muenda reached up and tickled the tendril with his hand. The elf began to rise toward the skwalos. The other elves watched him expectantly, as did Shamur.

"What did he say?" she asked.

Cale decided against a literal translation. Instead, he led by example, grasping one of the remaining tendrils.

"Like this, my lady."

The tongue—and Cale still wished Muenda had found another word for it—felt slightly warm and tacky, but not so sticky as he'd imagined. He wrapped it around his body three times and reached up to tickle it. When it squeezed him, Cale tried not to think of a constrictor snake.

Within moments, the tongue lifted him nearly all the way to the surface of the great beast's belly. He looked for Muenda but saw only hundreds of other tendrils. Some of them had withered to lumps, while others were kinked and curled close to the skwalos's translucent hide. He wondered how he would get from the belly of the beast to its back.

"Uh, oh," said Cale, as he realized the full implications of the term Muenda had used for the tendril in which he'd willingly placed himself.

He looked up to see the huge mouth of the skwalos open to receive him. Before he could call out to Shamur, the creature's great lips closed.

An instant later, the skwalos swallowed him whole.

CHAPTER 9

REVELATIONS

Twice more, Tamlin feigned sleep while his captives entered the prison to remove his bowl and replace it with another. The guards dared not approach the cage with the darkenbeast crouched atop it. Instead they snagged the old bowl with a fishing gaff and pushed the new one back from a safe distance. All the while, they whispered their fears over the botched kidnapping and argued about which of them would have to dispose of the transformed rodent when the order came to kill their captive.

The former rat was the size of a wolfhound.

Tamlin could hear the hunger gurgling up from its belly, but the creature obeyed its master's command and never left the top of the cage. Still, its jaws yearned down toward Tamlin, and hot drool dripped onto his face.

"Stupid rat creature," muttered Tamlin, grateful for the bars.

Feigning slumber was easier than actually sleeping. Naturally, Tamlin didn't trust his captor, but he couldn't imagine a sound reason for the man to lie about the death of his parents.

As the third or fourth wealthiest House in Selgaunt, and with political influence exceeding even that high station, the Uskevren were frequently the targets of scandal, intrigue, kidnapping, and recently even assassination. Because the Uskevren had so far, individually and on one glorious occasion as a group, defeated even the most powerful assaults, Tamlin had begun to think of himself as invulnerable.

Only last year he'd single-handedly defeated a troll. He'd every reason to feel confident that he would survive this trial and revenge himself on his captors. All he had to do was turn the tables on the villains, perhaps by luring a guard close enough to knock him senseless against the bars and take his keys and weapon.

That cheerful illusion dissolved in a stream of hot piss from the darkenbeast above. Tamlin barely moved to avoid the noxious stuff. After six days in this wretched captivity, he was beyond humiliation.

There was precious room to spare in the center of the cage, befouled with the darkenbeast's urine. He dared not lie too close to the bars for fear that the creature could reach him with its razor-sharp claws. Instead, he turned away from the filth as much as possible and hugged his knees to his chest.

When at last his aching body could relax enough to surrender to sleep, he escaped mercifully into his old dreams.

In a great castle filled with music and spring perfumes, Tamlin dances among his guests. The fairest ladies approach him one by one, and he favors each with a jeweled scarf. The price: a long,

melting kiss. If their consorts object, the men are too polite to show it. They smile and bow to their lord.

A commotion at the entrance, and the guests part. The Vermilion Guard drag a dirty elf into the hall. His rags are an offense to the fine attire of the nobles around him.

A disobedient slave, reports the captain.

You know my will, says Tamlin.

The captain draws his sword. The guards grasp the elf's hair and pull back his head.

An elven lady, the most beautiful woman ever to grace Tamlin's dreams, runs forward. She falls to the gleaming marble floor and throws her arms around Tamlin's knees.

Mercy!

Tamlin sneers at the word. He kicks away the pleading woman.

(Tamlin gasps at his own cruelty. He wants to apologize. He wants to take it back. He wants—)

The vanes! Commands Tamlin. He notices the approving nods among his guests. Out of the corner of his eyes, he sees the cruel, anticipatory smiles as his noble subjects hurry for a good vantage in the towers above.

The elf woman begs again, My lord, please. Remember—

Tamlin slaps her face hard enough to turn it away. He follows his guests, pausing briefly by his trio of elf concubines. They sit placidly in their tiny carriage, the fine chains that join their silver collars tinkling as they raise their faces to accept the strokes of his hand. With one hard glance back at the weeping woman, Tamlin raises his palms to the sky and rises up, up, and up. . . .

Tamlin awoke breathless. The ugly turn of his dreams shocked him, but he knew that some real sound had shaken him from the nightmare.

He thought he heard, from near the door, the scrape of leather on stone. At first it seemed to come from inside the prison, but he could see no one in the feeble light of the magic circle. He heard a familiar voice call from outside, at least two chambers away.

It was his father's voice.

"We have the ransom," called Thamalon. "Now send out my boy . . ."

Tamlin couldn't make out the rest of his words over the babble of his captors' panic.

"Impossible!" one of them shouted.

The rest was a clamor of slammed doors and heavy furniture shoved against them.

Tamlin strained to overhear more of their conversation, but he caught only phrases and curses.

". . . thought he was dead . . ."

". . . supposed to send anyone here, anyway!"

"Somebody had better tell . . ."

The door to his prison opened, and three men stepped in.

"Kill him if they get through," one ordered the others.

One of the remaining guards shut and barred the door, while the other watched the darkenbeast.

Tamlin squeezed the bloody fingers of his ruined right hand and prayed he could keep a fist with them. If he weren't already wounded, he might have liked his chances against a single opponent. Considering his state, he said a prayer to the Lord of the Dead.

"Dread Kelemvor," he murmured. "If it's not too much trouble, please take the other fellows first."

One guard stepped toward the cage, careful to remain out of range of the darkenbeast. Behind him, his fellow held the torch high.

"Listen," said Tamlin. "There's no point in killing me. That will only ensure your own death."

Both guards ignored him, their gazes locked on the monster perched over his cage.

"There's a good boy," the guard crooned to the darkenbeast, and he took a cautious step forward.

"Think of the reward you will have for turning against those criminals out there," Tamlin added. "I will personally see to it that—"

Tamlin spied movement behind the guard with the torch. Something dark wriggled out of a narrow coal chute and poured itself into the shadows. When the figure rose up behind the torch-bearing guard, Tamlin saw it was a young, leather-clad woman.

His sister, Tazi.

In the months since Tamlin had last seen her, she'd changed somehow. Even beneath the mask of coal dust, her face seemed different somehow—stronger, more angular, even dangerous. With her cool expression and her dark hair tied back in a simple knot, she looked somehow austere.

Not unlike our mother, he thought.

Tazi broke the illusion with an unsmiling wink at Tamlin, then she put a finger to her lips.

She clamped a hand over the torchbearer's mouth, pulled his head to the side, and cut his throat with one clean jerk. She sheathed her dagger and still managed to catch the torch before it fell. With her eyes on the back of the second guard's neck, she held the dead man's body until his death spasms subsided, then let it sink gently to the floor.

The effortless killing made Tamlin gasp. The joy at his sister's timely arrival mingled with sudden fear that she'd changed far more than her lean face revealed.

Oblivious to his companion's fate, the other guard raised his long sword for a strike against the guardian beast. Tazi caught his wrist.

As the man turned toward her, she smashed the burning brand into his face.

The man screamed.

Tazi dropped the torch, grabbed her dagger, and ended the man's noise with a quick thrust to his throat. His body fell to the side, removing the only obstacle between Tazi and the darkenbeast.

"Look out!" Tamlin called out—too late.

With a trumpeting shriek, the monster leaped at Tazi.

Tamlin lunged up to grasp the thing's scaly legs. The creature easily pulled away from his weak right hand, and its talons ripped his left to the bone.

Tazi raised her arms to defend her face, but the darkenbeast's buffeting wings beat them down. Its jaws snapped at her face. She slashed with her bloody dagger, severing the tendons of the creature's left wing.

The beast screamed again, but rather than retreat it charged at Tazi, climbing up her body with the hooks of its remaining wing and both talons.

The beast's scrabbling attack sent her staggering back. She stepped on the burning torch, and as it rolled she fell hard on her back. The monster scrabbled to stay atop her, shrieking and tearing. Fragments of Tazi's leather armor flew away like cinders from a bonfire.

Tazi stabbed at its throat, but the beast's jaws clamped shut on her arm and twisted, sending her weapon spinning to the floor.

"Tal!" she yelled. "In here!"

The only response was the screaming of men from the outer room and a deep, bestial roar that made the darkenbeast sound like a frightened mouse.

Tamlin reached for Tazi's dagger. Considering his recent run of bad luck, he expected it to lie a few inches beyond his reach. Much to his surprise, he grasped it easily. The problem was in gripping it in his ruined hands.

Tazi and the darkenbeast rolled over and over on the floor. For every precise fist, elbow, or kick Tazi landed, the monster scratched away a pound of blood-stained leather.

"Now would be a very good time!" Tazi yelled again to the outer room.

"Over here!" called Tamlin. "Roll this way!"

Tazi flung herself toward the cage. Her pernicious foe clung ever more tightly, raking and biting.

Tamlin tried to stab the thing in the spine, but the blow sent the knife straight through his feeble, blood-slicked grip. There was barely a scratch on the monster.

"Dark and empty!" cursed Tazi.

She slipped one hand up under the darkenbeast's jaws and pushed its head away.

"Sorry!" cried Tamlin.

He recovered the dagger and, gripping it so tightly he was sure his torn fingers would break off, he thrust the blade deep into the beast's neck.

The arterial spray was hot and sticky, but the creature continued to struggle. Tamlin pulled the blade out of the beast and stabbed again—and again the bloody knife slipped in his grasp.

Tamlin's injured hands were beyond agony, even numbness. All he felt at the end of either arm was a weightless fire flickering in the shape of his half-forgotten palms and fingers. He knew he couldn't hold onto the knife again if he tried.

If he could distract the thing even for a moment, Tazi might have a chance to wriggle free and get the knife. He grabbed for the darkenbeast's throat.

"Die, damn you!"

As Tamlin said the words, a jolt of energy thrilled his hands. A blue-white sheet of light coruscated over the monster's body, and Tazi yelped and leaped back.

Sparks shot from the creature's eyes and mouth, leaving steaming black lumps of ruined flesh behind. The darkenbeast thrashed once more, then lay still.

"What did you do?" said Tazi. Her hair had puffed up like the tail of an angry cat, and her face was red from the hot electrical flash.

"It wasn't me," Tamlin protested.

"It sure looked like it was you."

"Maybe it was the magic circle."

As he pointed at the arcane lines, he noticed a stream of blood running from his outstretched finger. He quickly tucked his ruined hands under his arms, squeezing them gently to staunch the bleeding.

Tazi looked down at the floor and quickly stepped away from the edge of the chalk circle.

"Don't do it again," she said. "I'm coming back over there."

Tazi knelt before the lock. She slipped a pair of picks from a pocket on her thigh and went to work on the lock.

Tamlin looked down at the corpse of the darkenbeast. He felt giddy triumph mingling with horror and a peculiar sense of pity at the sight.

"Sorry about that, old fellow. We had a few laughs, some good times, I know, but you left me with no—"

"Let's get out of here," interrupted Tazi, opening the cage door.

Tamlin stepped outside his prison, stood to full his height, and immediately wobbled. Tazi took him by the arm then put her own arm around his waist. Her muscles were as hard as packed sand.

"You've been exercising," said Tamlin. He felt increasingly dizzy.

"And you've been losing far too much blood," she said. "Don't talk."

She led him through a short, dirty hall to his captors' room. The corpses of two and a half of them were still there, along with the splintered remains of a stout wooden door. Tamlin's vision was blurring. He smelled blood and dung and seawater.

Soon they were in the slimy passages of the sewers, and Tamlin felt himself lifted in big, strong arms that carried him toward the daylight.

"Vox," Tamlin mumbled as he looked up into the dark, bearded face. "You're not dead."

"No," said Escevar, walking beside them, "but you might be if you don't lie still."

Amid the stink of the sewer, Tamlin thought he smelled

roses. Soft hands stroked his arms, and pleasant warmth filled his limbs. Feeling returned to his hands in the form of a dull tingling, which he recognized as powerful healing magic. It surged through every fiber of his flesh, knitting torn sinews back together.

"Hold him still," said a familiar, gentle voice.

It was one of the servants. He raised his head to look at her, but Escevar leaned over him, proffering a pewter flask.

"A little anesthetic?" he offered.

The open flask smelled of brandy, sweet and earthy rich. Tamlin felt a tickling at the back of his throat. His whole body craved a drink of the warm liquor.

"Great gods, no," he said with an effort. "That's exactly what got me into this mess."

Behind them, another roar echoed through the sewers, followed quickly by a pair of terrified screams.

"Somebody should go help him," suggested Escevar.

His tone made it plain that he was not volunteering for the job. To emphasize the point, he quickened his pace and led the way up to the street.

"It's probably better not to approach Tal in his present state," said the servant.

Tamlin looked up past the hands upon his arms and saw Larajin, one of the family's chambermaids—at least until recently.

It had been months since Larajin left Stormweather Towers, and she no longer wore the gold vest and white dress of the household maids. Instead, she had donned a plain, homespun smock and a dun-colored cloak. Russet hair spilled out from her hood, framing a fair face with hazel eyes so light they appeared almost yellow.

Those pretty features had been the object of much gossip from other servants who complained that Lord Thamalon favored Larajin more than was proper. There was even talk that Larajin was Thamalon's mistress, and some of it had reached Shamur. Perhaps the Old Owl had finally bowed to his wife's jealousy and married the girl off to some shopkeeper. That would explain why Tamlin hadn't seen her for months.

"It would be good to have one alive for questioning," said Tazi.

"No need," said Larajin, arching her delicate eyebrows. "I can question the corpses later."

"Larajin!"

"Look what they've done to him," said Larajin. "Look what they've done to your brother!"

Her hands moved from his arms to his forehead. They felt cool and soft, and Tamlin realized he was burning with fever.

"I know, I know," said Tazi. "It's just that I never expected to hear something like that from you."

"You have been away for a while," Larajin said as she continued her ministrations.

The pain was leaking away from Tamlin's body. Even so, he felt as weak as a kitten, and he was grateful when Vox lifted him up through the torn sewer grating and up to the streets. There was an Uskevren carriage, surrounded by men in blue livery, the gold horse-at-anchor ensign on their breasts.

"He should be all right, now," said Larajin. "I'll go back for Tal."

"Be careful," said Tazi, closing the carriage door. She called up to the driver, "Go!"

Tamlin squinted and smiled in a fashion he hoped looked brave rather than delirious. Tazi and Escevar smiled back at him from the opposite seat, but their expressions were tarnished with worry. Tamlin remembered then that he wasn't the only one in peril.

"They told me mother and father were—"

"Missing," said Tazi firmly. "Now that you're back, we'll search for them together."

Tamlin felt relief wash through his chest. He hadn't before realized how tense his muscles had remained those past, uncounted days.

Tamlin thought about what he'd heard during his rescue and said, "And in addition to his talent for imitating father's voice, Talbot has become some sort of monster."

"Well," she said. "In a manner of speaking, yes."

"And you've just returned from training as a master assassin?"

"That is *not* how I'd describe myself."

"Cat burglar, then. Just like mother."

"Well, yes. If you must be rude about it."

"And even the chambermaid has divine powers?"

"That's right," said Tazi. She glanced at Vox and Escevar as if considering whether to speak in front of them. Eventually she shrugged and said, "That, and she's actually our sister."

"Our sister . . ." Tamlin felt another wave of dizziness coming. He was saved by the absurdity of the revelations. "It appears that everyone I know has become some sort of storybook hero—" he sighed— "and all I can boast is 'most often kidnapped.' "

"Now would be a bad time to tell you about Larajin's twin brother?" Tazi asked. She raised a solemn eyebrow, but the quirk upon her lips was all mischief.

"Now you're making things up."

She kept smiling, but she shook her head.

"Next you'll tell me he's an elf."

Tamlin strove not to take offense at her wild laughter, even though it continued long after they turned off the streets of Selgaunt and rumbled through the gate to Stormweather Towers.

CHAPTER 10

THE SORCERER

On the morning after their emergence from the wood, the wagons waited at a rendezvous point. Within hours, Thamalon watched as eleven more small groups of wagons joined them. Some were similar to those Baeron commanded, while others appeared to be the more traditional sort of flat-bed conveyances piled high with crates and bundles. All were heavily guarded.

After all wagons reported to their commander, Baeron returned and ordered his men to resume their journey. Thamalon was glad to hear that his presence was still permitted, and gladder still that he remained with Baeron's team.

On his occasional business with dwarves, Thamalon found them blunt and predictable during negotiations. Only after a deal was struck did they relax and speak freely—and only after a few mugs of ale had loosened their tongues. At those times they could be the most ribald of colleagues, treating their business partners like decades-old friends if only for a few raucous hours.

In the three days Thamalon rode beside Baeron, he found the dwarf talkative even without benefit of ale. Once they were clear of the elven woods, Baeron became downright friendly, perhaps in gratitude for Thamalon's assistance during the ambush.

The dwarves had been traveling for over ten days, a period Thamalon knew as a "ride," the average length of a caravan journey. They came from their stronghold in the eastern mountains, avoiding elven territory as much as possible. As the Sorcerer's legions drove them farther and farther from Castle Stormweather, the elves retreated deeper into the forest, and the dwarf scouts were hard pressed to keep track of their shifting territory and avoid confrontations.

Curiosity about this other Stormweather rustled constantly in Thamalon's imagination. Had he come across the name in a history or heard that some lord in Waterdeep had named his mansion similarly, he might have smiled and forgotten it. To discover a fortress with the same name as his own holding after falling through an enchanted painting . . . that was a matter that deserved consideration.

Thamalon didn't much believe in coincidence.

Trying to keep his inquiries casual, Thamalon continued to press for more information on this Sorcerer and his Stormweather.

The dwarves made the perilous journey for trade with the Sorcerer's subjects, especially to buy their most precious commodity: throbe vapors. The armored wagons were actually huge tanks of the gas. They would return fully laden, each with enough of the vapors to fire one of their forges for months to come.

"Why did the elves attack you?"

"They object to the harvesting of throbe," Baeron explained, "and we bring weapons to trade with the Sorcerer."

"What is wrong with harvesting throbe?"

"The elves revere the skwalos," said Baeron. "They believe that the spirits of their ancestors reside in the animals."

"Skwalos?"

Baeron raised his bushy eyebrows, pointed upward, and asked, "What is your word for them?"

Thamalon looked up and saw a gray sky pregnant with rain.

"The clouds?"

"Ho ho!" Baeron punched his shoulder.

Thamalon realized it was a gregarious gesture, but it hurt. He rubbed his arm and wondered how many bruises this adventure would cost him before it was done.

"You do not jest?" the dwarf asked. "Look again."

Thamalon did so, scanning the clouds for a clue. After long seconds, he discerned vast, dark shapes cruising through the mists.

"The floating whale creatures?" said Thamalon.

"If 'whale' is your word for forest, then yes."

"Perhaps the comparison is not apt," admitted Thamalon. "How're they like a forest?"

"Is that a riddle?" asked Baeron, brightening.

"No."

"Oh," said Baeron, making no attempt to mask his disappointment. "Well, over time, the skwalos develop patches of fungus and moss. Some of the ancients eventually catch seeds on the wind and sprout flowers and even trees. My grandmother once told me of elf wizards who cultivated food upon the backs of the greatest skwalos, living in the sky with them to harvest their familiars."

"Harvest?"

"How do the wizards in your land do it?"

"Well, I know little about wizards, but I imagine they summon them with a spell."

"Things are very different here from your land?"

"Indeed. Almost everything here is somewhat strange. Except for you," he quickly amended. "You're very like the dwarves I have met. And the elves are not much different."

Baeron laughed as though Thamalon had made a great joke.

"How long have you been at war with the elves?" Thamalon asked.

"Us? We have had no war with the elves for centuries. Their foe is the Sorcerer. The elves attack only our throbe caravans, and we make an effort not to burn down their entire forest while fending them off. The elves protest and send their emissaries to pull at the king's ears, but they still buy our throbe-forged steel. Even the elves have their merchants."

Thamalon chuckled, for he found the remark more amusing than risible. While he was known as a merchant lord, he'd amassed his fortune primarily through land speculation before diversifying the family holdings into such areas as agriculture, craft ware, and investment in a dozen lesser merchants. The Uskevren and their subject interests launched as many as fourteen trade caravans throughout Sembia and neighboring lands each year. The only legitimate venture Thamalon consistently refused to enter was shipping, for the stink of piracy still lingered on the Uskevren name.

Before night fell, the caravan passed through the blackened ruin of a forest. Thamalon had seen such regions before, but rarely so soon after the wildfires had devoured the trees.

"The Sorcerer pushes them back," observed Baeron.

"He did this on purpose?" asked Thamalon. "I assumed it was lightning from a storm."

Baeron said, "Oh, that it was, Far-Traveler. That it was."

When they broke camp the next morning, Baeron promised they would soon enter the Sorcerer's territory. Thamalon was eager to see the lands surrounding the intriguingly named Castle Stormweather, but the sky had other plans. A steady drizzle dimmed the day, and the first sign of civilization was a muddy road.

A few miles later, Thamalon spied the first cultivated fields. He was somewhat relieved to recognize ordinary produce, but alongside the cabbage patches and barley fields he saw rows of huge melons with translucent husks. Perhaps it was a trick of the rain, but once or twice he thought he saw something stirring inside the big fruits. Whatever moved within them didn't alarm the workers who trudged between the furrows.

Thamalon noticed that those workers were elves chained neck-to-neck. Big men in red armor watched over them, spears in hand and lashes at their hips. Thamalon turned to Baeron for an explanation.

"Prisoners of war," he said.

"Slaves," Thamalon suggested with a frown.

"Best not to let the Vermilion Guard hear you say so," cautioned Baeron. "They are proud and quick to answer an insult."

"Does it not seem cruel to you?"

Baeron shrugged and said, "One does not prosper who makes war with the Sorcerer."

Despite the wonders he had encountered thus far, Thamalon began to think he'd seen enough of this strange land.

With each passing league, the caravan encountered increasingly frequent farmsteads. By noon they drove through a small village, where those few inhabitants who had to leave the shelter of their buildings waved at the travelers.

A few hours later, the villages appeared more regularly and converged so gradually that Thamalon realized they were finally within a city. This place was nothing like glorious Selgaunt, with its wide avenues and soaring temples. The place was a convocation of hovels, only rarely interrupted by a proper edifice whose barred doors were flanked by sentries in red armor. Even those buildings were bleak constructions, brick cubes and towers with little ornament. There were no horse-drawn carriages, only rickshaws drawn by pairs of elf slaves, chains jangling between their necks and wrists.

Thamalon noticed for the first time that he had seen no horses, no cattle nor swine—not any kind of beast other than the odd reptiles who drew the dwarven wagons.

They passed through a curtain wall under the scrutiny of more crimson-clad guards. They'd been expecting the dwarves, but they questioned their guest. Thamalon offered the same pseudonym he'd given the dwarves.

Inside the gate, the city began to resemble a Sembian town, with wide central streets and a veritable labyrinth of back avenues and alleys. Like the sprawling habitation outside the walls, the entire place seemed devoid of cheer—except for one peculiar sound.

Muted by the rain, a sweet melody drifted down upon the city from above. A woman's voice, without accompaniment, it was at once alluring and sorrowful. The wordless song moved Thamalon's heart to pity.

"What is that song?" he asked.

"Lady Malaika," said Baeron. "She calls the skwalos."

"She sounds so sad."

"Sometimes it takes tendays, even months to lure them here. The rain is a good omen. They will come soon."

Thamalon imagined what a sight that must be as he gazed around at all the sullen occupants of the city, their eyes cast down upon the rain-slicked stones and rippling puddles.

The caravan passed the last of the buildings and entered a vast plaza bereft of fountains, trees, statues, or any other common ornament of great cities. Instead, iron towers stood in ranks upon the stones. On their crowns were curved hooks and gigantic hollow spears from which ran long canvas hoses. Rust streaked every surface. Even the ground was stained red.

In the center of it all, looming high over the lesser towers, stood Castle Stormweather.

Thamalon couldn't discern its upper reaches for the rain, but the highest windows he could see were clearly higher than the tallest spire of the Hulorn's palace in Selgaunt. Unlike that garish monument, Castle Stormweather was a dreary fortress.

Its wet granite stones were almost uniform in shape, and no two were more than a few shades of gray apart.

While another wall protected it from ground assault, its upper reaches were even more fortified. Iron shutters were closed against the rain, and around every balcony were sturdy doors with arrow slits. Most of the ballista stations were far too lofty to fire accurately upon the ground.

This was a bastion that defended against the sky.

The dwarves turned over custody of their beasts and wagons at the inner gate, where four of the Sorcerer's guards awaited them.

"My thanks for the ride," said Thamalon. He grasped Baeron's arm firmly. "Good luck in your bargaining."

"Where are you going?"

"Perhaps I can find a map seller in the market," said Thamalon. "Or maybe a caravan master who has heard of my homeland, or at least some other region that I know."

"Perhaps," said Baeron, "but first you must present yourself to the Sorcerer. That is the law here."

Thamalon considered the prospect of meeting this Lord of Stormweather. He was very interested in learning more about this place and the man who ruled it, but he began to fear that meeting the Sorcerer might not be the best way to speed him home. The gloom of his city felt like the binder's glue in which careless flies were caught.

Thamalon longed for home.

Another city lay within the walls of Castle Stormweather. Every hall was an avenue bustling with courtiers and servants. Each antechamber through which they were escorted was larger than his own great hall.

The lavish furnishings of the guest quarters impressed even Thamalon, who was accustomed to the finest of Selgaunt's luxuries. Thick tapestries of exquisite design warmed the granite walls, and rich carpets softened the floors. Rather than candles or oil lamps, faintly hissing glass balls illuminated each room from brass pipes protruding from the ceilings.

Hot baths in deep oak tubs awaited the travelers. The dwarves murmured appreciatively as lovely elf maids stripped away their road-stiffened clothes and scrubbed their hairy shoulders. Thamalon might have surrendered himself to the pleasure, but the memory of the chained war slaves disturbed his thoughts as soft hands massaged the knots in his back. His troubled conscience wouldn't let him indulge his familiar instincts. Were these women servants or slaves?

Thamalon nearly changed his mind when he agreed to be shaved and his servant girl joined him in the water, straddling his lap to lather his face and scrape away his three days of whiskers. It would be no effort to seduce the lass, who seemed to expect and invite his attentions. Still, when Baeron and his fellows made quiet arrangements for their elves to join them in their chambers, Thamalon politely sent his away and retired alone.

He lay in bed restlessly, trying to ignore the sounds of carnal sport from the nearby rooms. In his younger days, his marriage vows had been no restraint to dalliance. His bastard twins were proof enough of that. Even apart from the question of the servant's consent, Thamalon felt a genuine desire to keep faith with his wife.

How strange, he thought. After all the years of clandestine escape from his unhappy union, he feared he'd become a romantic at last. He desired his wife in forfeit of all other women.

Thamalon slept, comforted by thoughts of returning to his beloved Shamur. He dreamed of her soft hair in his face, her breath upon his ear. When he awoke, it was with a cold feeling of doom and a fierce longing to see her one last time before he died.

His washed and mended house clothes lay upon a dressing table, but beside them were a pair of dark trousers, supple boots of a leathery fabric, a deep green tunic embroidered in floral patterns on the yoke, and a half-cape cut with dashing asymmetry.

Thamalon donned the unfamiliar costume and admired his reflection. An old man looked back at him, unsuited to the rakish attire. He smiled at himself, but the gesture seemed weary. Thamalon laughed at his own vanity, and the ghost of his youth laughed back at him. It looked something like his eldest son, and for a moment the image brought him joy before regret supplanted the feeling.

"Tamlin," he said to the mirror. "There's so much I have to tell you. I—"

Father?

Before he could decide whether he'd imagined hearing the word, Thamalon heard a servant scratching on the door.

"What?" he said.

"Sir," repeated the servant. He was a boy, not much younger than Tamlin. "It is time."

The lad led Thamalon toward the center of the castle and through a grand archway bigger than Selgaunt's Klaroun Gate.

On the other side was Stillstone Hall, a grand circular room wider than any cathedral. Its arched walls soared so high that their upper points faded with distance. They converged on a central dome through which gray light poured down on the throng below.

Hundreds of people filled the hall, most of them waiting their turn to appear before the lord of the castle. Their conversations were muted by the splashing of a great central fountain composed of huge, uncut slabs of colorful stones, the smallest larger than the dwarves' throbe wagons.

Two grand fireplaces blazed in opposite walls. Savory meats roasted on spits above the flames, and ranks of cauldrons bubbled with soups and some sweet, dark beverage. Servants tended the food and carried it among the crowd. To Thamalon, the place appeared like a cross between an Old Chauncel reception and the street outside of Talbot's playhouse, bustling with vendors.

At regular intervals along the walls stood the red-plumed, red-cloaked, and red-armored guards. More of them patrolled quietly among the throng, which parted respectfully—or perhaps fearfully—wherever they went.

On the far side of the fountain, upon a high dais smothered in carpets, the Sorcerer sat on a grand throne. His body was as lean and supple as a dancer's, and his tight-fitted breeches and jerkin showed off every sinew. Topaz and ruby glittered on the gold phylactery around his biceps, and the huge dark stones upon his bracers roiled with magic. From the sides of his crowned helm, gleaming brass bars curved over his cheeks, concealing his face from those he judged. As he pronounced his decrees, he held up a winged scepter embedded with a ruby the size of a man's eye.

The supplicants stood at the foot of his throne. To either side were elite members of his Vermilion Guard, their bright plumes spilling like manes upon their muscular backs.

Thamalon observed the Sorcerer dole justice to his people.

He resolved a matter of disputed property by dividing the territory in proportions equal to the evidence presented. Afterward, he sentenced one of his generals to public flogging for cowardice. Later, he granted a pension to a war widow and acknowledged the approving cheers of the courtiers.

At last he received the dwarf merchants.

After his chamberlain introduced the travelers, the Sorcerer cut straight to the matter.

"What does King Uldrim offer for this season's throbe?"

"Eleven coffers of gold," replied Baeron, "and the six finest sapphires of Glitterdelve mines."

He held up a platinum necklace in which the aforementioned gems shone, the smallest the size of his thumbnail.

The Sorcerer considered the offer, then said, "The king is generous to offer such an incomparable jewel. In these times of conflict, however, I have little need for ornament or coin."

The response didn't seem to surprise Baeron, who said, "Our liege commands me to say that the forges of Deepspire are at your service. Six hundred long swords, eight hundred hardened spears, forty suits of vermilion scale—"

"Throbe steel," insisted the Sorcerer.

Baeron bowed and said, "In that case, our liege offers two hundred swords, two hundred sixty spea—"

"Three hundred swords," said the Sorcerer, "and all forty armor. As for the spears and shields, one hundred each will suffice us until winter."

"Such quantities require more throbe," said Baeron. "Our yield will be diminished by at least . . . two wagons."

"Then you shall have two wagons more," said the Sorcerer. "Yet I wish a dozen greatswords, too, in the fashion of Warlord Krandar's famous blade."

"My lord . . ." said Baeron. Thamalon perceived that the dwarf was stalling for time, mentally calculating the cost versus gain for the additional weapons. "If your highness were to include a hundred yards of skwalos membrane. . . ."

The Sorcerer rose, leaving his voluminous cloak lying in his seat. He descended the stairs and reached toward the dwarf.

"Bargain," he said, clasping Baeron's forearm.

"Bargain," the dwarf replied.

Thamalon had seen far more complicated negotiations over much simpler exchanges, but still he sensed that he'd just witnessed a significant change from previous deals. Both the Sorcerer and Baeron seemed satisfied with the result, yet neither gloated in victory. Despite the disparity in their stations, they bargained fairly, as equals.

"Nelember Far-Traveler," called the chamberlain, a man whose pointed beard and winged hairstyle made him easy to recognize even across the hall.

Thamalon presented himself before the dais. The Sorcerer had returned to his throne, but he didn't sit. Instead, he drew his cloak over his shoulders and fastened its round clasp. On its boss were the crossed thunderbolts of Talos, god of storms and destruction.

"What mishap brings you to my demesne, old man?"

The Sorcerer's tone wasn't mocking so much as casual. His voice was familiar, too. Thamalon bristled at the appellation, but he sketched a courtly bow, ignoring the pain it brought to his still-bruised hip.

"My tale is strange even to me, so I beg your indulgence while I confess I don't understand it all myself. In short, some unknown enemy enchanted a painting to cast me magically across the world, so far from home that I recognize nothing here. The only boon I crave is that I may speak to your caravan masters and ship captains in hopes that one of them knows something of my home or some other land I know."

"What is it called, this land of yours?"

"Sembia, my lord."

"Sembia . . ." the Sorcerer said—slowly, as if savoring the word. Thamalon saw a faint twitching of the muscles in the man's neck. There was something the Sorcerer didn't like about its taste. "You say you are called Nelember?"

Thamalon couldn't think of an affirmative that wasn't a lie, and he didn't care to wager against the chance that the Sorcerer could detect a falsehood.

"It is a name by which I travel," he said.

"Nelember . . . Nelember . . ." The Sorcerer said the name as if he was tasting it, as he had "Sembia." At last, he said, "A wise man leaves old names behind."

Thamalon bowed. Was there some hint of mockery in the Sorcerer's voice? He wasn't sure, but he sensed the man was toying with him.

The Sorcerer removed his helm and passed it to his chamberlain before descending the steps. Once again, Thamalon struggled to conceal his emotion. The man's face couldn't have amazed him more.

The Sorcerer's dark beard jagged across his cheeks in a

savage pattern, so neatly trimmed that it looked at first like a dark tattoo. Prominent brows and a straight nose lent nobility to the natural beauty of his features. His was a face to make ladies swoon and men burn with envy. Most arresting were the man's emerald green eyes, which Thamalon had seen only a few hours earlier—in the mirror.

Apart from his exotic grooming, the Sorcerer looked identical in every respect to Thamalon's eldest son.

Tamlin.

Still, the man's face betrayed no sign that he recognized Thamalon as his father. He clasped Thamalon's arm and smiled easily, exactly as Tamlin greeted visitors to the Uskevren family home.

"Welcome," the Sorcerer said, "to Stormweather."

CHAPTER 11

BROTHERS

Radu grunted as he pulled himself onto the roof of the tallhouse. The action had been effortless the night before. The night before that, he might have leaped from the ground to the second-story eaves.

Chaney noticed Radu's strength wane steadily in the days since murdering Thuribal Baerodreemer. He hadn't been certain before, but it seemed obvious that the power killing gave Radu was fading faster with each murder. Perhaps there would come a day when Radu himself faded into a ghostly existence.

Chaney smiled at the thought.

While he hadn't been the most devout of men, Chaney prayed for his soul's release from the shackle of his killer. Even were the gods to grant him that wish, he feared his prospects for the here-after. His mortal life wasn't without blemish, so he shuddered to imagine just where his soul might be interred for all eternity.

Even more than the reckoning for his own relatively petty sins, Chaney feared that the unholy power binding him to his killer might also drag him into Radu's certain torment. Sometimes he bravely told himself that it would be worthwhile just to witness his murderer's damnation. At other times, he thought of perdition and shuddered.

To dispel the awful thought, Chaney focused on the object of his hatred.

Radu crept lightly across the roof, holding his scabbard up off the shingles with his hardened right hand. The assassin knelt beside the garret window. Despite the chill air, the shutters were open, and a long white curtain waved out like a flag. Inside, a pair of voices rose above a noisy fire.

Chaney looked past Radu's shoulder, into the tallhouse garret.

The unfinished room was filled with paintings. There were paintings on easels, paintings on the walls, paintings in stacks ten deep on the floor. Most of them were horrid, abstract landscapes. A few were barely recognizable as human nudes with black blots for eyes and raw scratches where mouths should be.

In one dark corner lurked a quartet of unfinished sculptures, abandoned on their pedestals. Crusty jars of dried clay rested beneath them, along with boxes of sculpting tools.

Frazzled brushes sprung like dead flowers from paint-stained vases in shelves to one side of a low fireplace. Palettes and paint pots, jars of gray water, trowels, knives, rags, bottles of linseed oil, charcoal sticks, and ragged sheaves of sketch paper littered the room. A sheet-draped stool and a low fainting couch crowded a small canvas stage.

On the other side of the fireplace was a messy nest of a bed smothered in dirty laundry, books, lithographs, and drawings. Next to the bed, a huge water pipe squatted on a low table. Upon its cap was a lascivious depiction of divine

Sune, her nude body entwined with that of a constrictor snake. Around the brass sheath of the pipe cavorted naked princes and virgins, while within its glass chamber steamed orange chunks of enchanted ice.

Chaney focused on the two men inside the room. With their high cheekbones, fair skin, and striking black hair and eyes, they were unmistakably Malveens.

Chaney barely knew Laskar. The man was almost as old as Chaney's father, and he'd been lord and master of House Malveen for as long as Chaney remembered. Twenty years past, that title meant power and influence. In the Year of Rogue Dragons, it meant nothing, and the sadness of that knowledge showed in Laskar's heavy eyes as he sat on the edge of the model's stage.

Pietro stood between a wet canvas and a pair of tall iron candelabra. He was the youngest, and as far as Selgaunt knew, the only other surviving Malveen male. Barely older than Chaney, he had already cultivated a reputation for degeneracy usually reserved for syphilis-ridden septuagenarians. Pietro stood a hand's width shorter than Laskar and Radu. His skin had an unhealthy sheen in the candlelight, and his teeth were stained from pipe smoke.

"At least consider the girls," said Laskar. He ran his ink-stained fingers through his thinning black hair, leaving a smudge on his temple. "Their prospects depend solely on the family reputation."

Pietro smiled at the blot on his brother's forehead but didn't point it out. Instead, he dabbed a richer shade of yolk on a jaundiced landscape.

"Your fat wife's the only one who complains that darling Gellie's unmarried. I doubt the girl minds much. She has no shortage of callers, even if none of the boys' fathers will consent to marriage. If you took your own sow to bed more often, she might squeal a little less about—"

In two long strides, Laskar crossed the distance between them and slapped Pietro's face. The shock of the blow sent the paintbrush tumbling through the air. It landed with a fat yellow skid mark on the bare floor.

Chaney heard the faint creak of leather as Radu tensed beside him. He wondered what emotions stirred beneath the killer's porcelain mask as he observed the confrontation between his brothers. Considering what happened the last time Radu quarreled with a sibling, Chaney fancied that he might just witness the end of the Malveen line then and there.

Two cheerful thoughts in one night, Chaney thought. How can I complain about this ghostly existence?

"I—I am sorry," said Laskar. He stared at his hand, still flush from the blow.

"You would never dare strike me when our brother was alive," Pietro said as he tenderly probed his mouth.

"I wish *you* were the one—!" Laskar choked off his retort.

"What? That I was the one who was dead?" Pietro laughed, showing his bloodstained teeth. "What a coward! You can't even say it aloud."

"That's not what I meant," said Laskar. He turned away from Pietro to stare at the fire. "I simply cannot bear your vulgar mouth. You may be my brother, but sometimes I could just . . ."

"We both know you will never cast me out," said Pietro. He retrieved his brush and swirled it in a dingy jar.

"I do not like these obscene . . . *things*. I like your selling them to Mad Andy even less."

"But you do not mind the commission they bring, yes?" Pietro said. He filled his brush with crimson pigment and slashed at the canvas. "Without Radu to help you squeeze the books, you need me—and my art."

"Andeth Ilchammar is dangerous, Pietro."

"You simply do not understand him. Your simple coin-counter's mind is incapable of real imagination. You know nothing."

"I know when I'm out of my depth," said Laskar, "and I know enough to stay clear of the Old Chauncel when they're spinning their webs."

They stood a while in silence, Laskar brooding, Pietro painting. Twice, Laskar's head rose as if he were about to speak, but each time the thought died silently in his closed mouth.

At last, Pietro said, "Why're you still here?"

Laskar squeezed a fist and bowed his head over it, but he kept his silence as he left the room.

As his brother's footsteps receded down the stairway, Pietro muttered, "Idiot." His eyes glistened as he stabbed again at his painting. "Weakling."

Radu was in the room before Chaney realized he had moved. His shadow fell across his brother's painting.

As Pietro turned, Radu plucked the brush from his hand and cast it into the fireplace. The flames leaped and popped as they devoured the paint.

"You shame us all," hissed Radu.

Pietro stepped backward, into his painting. The wet paint stuck to the back of his shirt, and he opened his mouth to call for help.

Radu's left hand clamped the artist's jaws shut.

"Quietly, little brother."

Radu watched as Pietro's expression shifted from terror to wonder. He released his grip.

"Radu?"

The mask rose and fell in a curt nod.

"But how . . . ?"

"Just listen, and obey. Laskar is the master of House Malveen."

"What, this shack? This tenement? House Malveen died with the fire—"

"Never say that," said Radu. "Obey Laskar. Help him. Together, you must rebuild the family's wealth, and its honor."

"Impossible! No one deals with him on fair terms. The Old

Chauncel take advantage at every turn, claiming they risk their reputations by dealing with the untrustworthy House Malveen, children of the great pirate queen. And Laskar, he smiles and bows and lets them have their way. He is weak, Radu. Not like you and Stannis." Pietro knit his brows as a thought unfolded in his mind. "I have not heard from Stannis since you disappeared."

"Forget him," said Radu. "He died long ago. Those were dreams you had, nothing more."

"No, he lived!" insisted Pietro. "He gave those glorious visions to me. They inspired all of this, all of my art."

"They draw too much attention," said Radu. "The wrong kind of attention. They hurt the family, Pietro. Get rid of them."

"Radu, you know I would do anything you say, but my patron—"

"He is using you," said Radu. "He is dangerous. Laskar is right."

"Even he agrees we need the gold. Since you left, I have had to help support the family."

Pietro lifted his chin in a haughty gesture that reminded Chaney of Radu before his disfigurement.

"Here." Radu put a pouch in Pietro's hand and said, "I am your patron now. Exclusively."

Pietro's eyes widened as he inspected the pouch.

"How did you—no, I know better—but how can I sell so many diamonds without drawing attention?"

"Cloak yourself and go to the Green Gauntlet," said Radu. "A man called Rilmark will find and instruct you."

"You do it," said Pietro, offering the pouch back to Radu. "You always took care of these matters before."

"I must not be seen," said Radu, drawing slightly away from his brother. "After the fire . . ."

"Nothing was proven!" protested Pietro. "The Uskevren met with the sage probiter, no doubt to bribe him, but nothing came of it."

"Only so long as they think me dead," said Radu.

"Why must we be the ones to crawl? If not for old Aldimar, mother would never have been captured. Stannis told me everything." A sly smile curled one side of Pietro's thin lips. "Once he even showed me how to hire an assassin to kill one of Thamalon's brood. It would have worked, too, if not for . . ."

"Stay away from the Uskevren," hissed Radu. "Revenge is for fools and weaklings. You and Laskar need allies, not enemies."

"But why? Why're we the ones who must hold out our cups like beggars? Stannis said—"

"Stannis is dead."

"How can you know that? *I* am the one he chose to receive his visions, not you."

"Those visions are gone," said Radu, "and they will never come again."

"How can you know?" cried Pietro. His defiant expression melted as understanding formed in his mind. "What did you do?"

"I protected the family."

Briefly, two bright blushing spots upon Pietro's cheeks gave him the appearance of a clown, then rage suffused his whole face. For a moment, Chaney hoped Pietro would strike Radu. He wondered happily how that might turn out.

Flecks of spittle flew from his purple lips as he hissed in rage, "The brother I knew would never hurt one of his own. How do I even know you are Radu behind that mask?"

Chaney could tell by his expression that Pietro immediately regretted the challenge. The blood fled his countenance as quickly as it had come. The brothers stared at each other for a moment, and Radu calmly flicked at a clasp to either side of his mask. He slowly lifted it away from his face.

Chaney had seen what lay beneath the blank white porcelain, so he wasn't surprised to see Pietro's face turn fish-belly pale at the sight.

Pietro uttered a weak yelp and stumbled backward, away from the horrible visage. He tripped over his paint box and scuttled crablike on elbows and heels as Radu came closer.

"This was the price of my failure," whispered Radu. He overtook his cowering sibling and knelt beside him. He grabbed his shirt and pulled Pietro's face close to his own. "If you fail Laskar, *I* will be the price of yours."

Before he donned his mask and slipped out the window, Radu slashed every painting and cast the brushes into the fireplace. He left Pietro whimpering in the corner.

"It warms the heart to see such fraternal love," said Chaney.

"Silence," said Radu.

He ran lightly across the rooftop and leaped to the next tall-house. Chaney ran after him, enjoying the brief flight between the tallhouse roofs. He'd experienced some limited success with directed flight, but he still preferred the comfortable feeling of walking on his own feet. The other phantoms flew after him in a dark cloud, their obscure faces hiding whatever emotions they still felt.

"That's the beauty of my situation," said Chaney. "I can say anything I want, and there isn't a damned thing you can do about it."

"You are mistaken," said Radu. "Believe me."

Chaney laughed and said, "Believe you? The way Stannis believed you? Believe a murderer who just threatened to kill his own broth— What?"

Radu stopped at the building's edge. He looked down past the yellow lamps of Larawkan Lane. Only a few hearty souls braved the bitter night air.

A couple of middle years strolled arm-in-arm down the avenue, while a trio of Scepters passed going the other direction. The lamplight glittered on the silver highlights of their boiled leather armor. The guardsmen saluted casually to the man, who touched his chest in acknowledgment.

"What're you doing?" asked Chaney.

Radu didn't answer. His eyes continued to scan the pedestrians.

Behind the couple followed a sulking teenage boy hunched low in his fur collar. He lingered behind just far enough to annoy his mother.

Radu stepped to the side and dropped to the alley the boy was about to pass. The three-story fall barely bent his knees, but it dragged Chaney through the stone roof and wall, leaving him squeamish and dizzy when he landed on the cobblestones.

Radu moved toward the alley's mouth.

"No!" shouted Chaney.

Behind him, the dark shades of Radu's other victims began to moan, low and anxious. They sensed even better than Chaney what was about to happen.

Radu reached out and grabbed the boy by the throat as he passed. He pulled him into the shadows and thrust him against the alley wall, squeezing tighter.

"You don't have to do this," said Chaney. "I'll shut up now. I believe you."

Radu continued pressing the boy's throat, squeezing harder and harder until Chaney heard a sickening crunch. Still Radu held the lifeless body against the wall. After long moments, the corpse crumbled to ash, and its spirit rushed into Radu's trembling body.

Chaney wept tearlessly, cursing himself for taunting the monster. He dared not turn around to look for the ninth dark specter standing forlorn and confused behind him.

"Now you believe," said Radu.

He leaped up, the new surge of infernal strength propelling him back to the rooftop and dragging Chaney's helpless ghost behind him.

◉ ◉ ◉ ◉ ◉

Radu looked down from his vantage atop the peaked roof of the Black Stag Inn. Chaney sat nearby, hugging his knees to quell the nausea he still felt after being dragged through two chimneys and an entire tallhouse—including a sleeping woman who suddenly sat up and clutched at her heart as the ghost passed through her.

Since Radu's demonstrative killing, Chaney was too stunned to keep up with the man's blinding run across the rooftops of Selgaunt. It couldn't have been only the stolen life energy that infused him with so much power. Chaney knew that something dangerous roiled beneath Radu's cool exterior.

The muted laughter of a hundred voices burbled up from the guest hall below. Were he not so preoccupied by his unwilling complicity in the boy's death, Chaney might have tried drifting down through the roof so he could hear the bard who so entertained the crowd. Perhaps it was a bard he'd heard before. He must have listened to a hundred different minstrels and storytellers in the years he and Talbot had spent in taverns and festhalls.

Instead, he sat silently as Radu held vigil over the spot where he'd agreed to meet Drakkar. More than an hour after the appointed time, he stirred at his post. Chaney rose to see what had happened in the street below.

Drakkar emerged from a dark alley and stalked impatiently out toward Sarn Street. His hasty gait was enough to show that he was extremely irritated.

Radu dropped to the ground and quietly followed the wizard. Chaney dived after him.

Drakkar turned west on Rauncel's Ride. Radu and Chaney followed him as he rounded the southwestern arc of the great encircling avenue. There they passed hundreds of houses "under the wall," those lower-class dwellings that seemed so rude and pitiable to the nobles who lived deeper in the heart of Selgaunt. Chaney had claimed a room in one of those buildings for a few months, until the landlord finally leased it to new tenants, who were none to pleased to find a squatter in the house. A speedy escape through the upper window had saved Chaney from a few more tendays in a jail cell. Had Talbot not returned from a visit to Storl Oak, his family's country estate, Chaney might have let the Scepters catch him. At least the city jails were heated in winter.

Drakkar paused a few times to look behind him, but Radu never left the shadows. Soon Drakkar left the main avenue and plunged north into the Oxblood Quarter.

Named for its slaughterhouses, the Oxblood Quarter was also home to other unsavory businesses. While there were festhalls throughout the city, those in the Oxblood Quarter were notorious for catering to the more demanding clients. The Scepters had recently closed one after the long-held rumors of slavery and torture were finally proven.

Drakkar looked around one last time. Satisfied that no one was following him, he slipped inside the plain side entrance of a nameless festhall. The location of such establishments were open secrets, but the absence of a sign or a popular name allowed upright citizens to ignore their existence while their neighbors and business associates paid a visit to their "trade concerns" in the Oxblood Quarter, insulated from scandal.

Radu leaped to the rooftop as nimbly as a cricket. Chaney had recovered enough from his earlier trauma that he anticipated the move and jumped just in time to ride his wake and avoid an unpleasant journey through the walls.

"Go inside," said Radu. "Tell me where he goes."

Chaney considered the consequences of refusing, but only for a second before he plunged through the roof.

It was much more difficult to will himself down than through a wall, and he wished that he'd practiced it more often. Passing through the roof tiles felt like thrusting his foot into a bucket of cooling tar. After the initial resistance, however, it was purely a matter of willing himself to sink.

Inside, Chaney found a small bedchamber lit dimly by the

banked fires of a pair of cheap iron braziers. The light barely illuminated the cheap canvasses tacked to the walls. The paintings were crude renderings of improbably proportioned satyrs and nymphs at a feast to Sune, goddess of beauty and love. The profound lack of either beauty or love in the lustful eyes of the satyrs and the fearful faces of the nymphs made Chaney doubt the clerics of Sune would endorse the work.

The door was ajar, its opening just wide enough for Chaney to slip into the hall without forcing himself through the heavy wood. Outside, the hallway floor was covered in thick, well-trodden carpets. Chaney imagined they smelled of pipeweed and spilled ale.

Chaney had never been inside the building, and he doubted he could sink down below the upper floor before coming to the end of the invisible tether that bound him to Radu, so he hoped Drakkar was bound for an upstairs chamber. His petty wish was granted moments later, as the cloaked wizard ascended the stairs, guided by a halfling in garish livery.

". . . instructed her before she left," said the halfling. "Rest assured, she will be the same as the usual girl."

The halfling led the wizard to the room next to the one from which Chaney had emerged. As they approached, the door opened, and there stood a pretty young brunette dressed in blue-and-white servants' garb. Tiny bells tinkled from her turban.

"The hair is wrong," said Drakkar. "I told you—"

"I beg your pardon, master," said the halfling, bowing.

"Easily changed, my lord," the woman said as she curtsied, her eyes at Drakkar's feet.

"Master," whispered the halfling from behind his hand.

The young woman's eyes acknowledged the correction. "Master," she amended.

Drakkar nodded slowly and said, "It will do."

He followed the woman into the room, and she shut the door. The halfling yawned into his fist and returned to the ground floor, scratching his round belly.

"Oh, no," said Chaney.

He'd recognized the woman's costume and had already formed a strong theory about the identity of the object of Drakkar's desire. He wished more than ever that he could somehow communicate with his old friend, Tal.

He returned to the roof, and Radu sensed his presence immediately.

"Where?"

"Here," he said. "On this side, toward the street. The room next door is unoccupied."

Radu leaned over the roof's edge. Looking over his shoulder, Chaney saw shadows moving behind the shutters.

"What did you see?"

Chaney considered the likelihood that Radu would break into the room to confirm his report. He thought of the dead boy and decided to tell as much of the truth as possible.

"He has a thing for chambermaids."

Radu considered that information for a moment then shrugged. He moved over the window to the unoccupied room.

"This one is empty?" he asked.

"Yes," said Chaney, hating himself.

He wanted to believe that he would be less helpful if Radu could hurt only him and not some innocent, anonymous stranger. Part of him was glad to think that Radu would kill more victims soon and thus more quickly burn out his own life. Chaney believed it was no crime of his own should Radu kill someone just to prove a point—but he couldn't shake the guilt. Would the boy's murder weigh on his own judgment when at last Radu perished and their souls were forfeit to the gods?

Radu slipped over the roof's edge and with his good hand grasped the bars that protected the shuttered windows. He curled his right arm around one bar to support himself, and he carefully peeled back the remaining iron shafts as easily as he might break the legs off a steamed crab. Radu broke the latch on the shutters and pulled himself inside.

He went immediately to the door, which he closed and latched, then he listened briefly at the wall. If he could hear anything, he made no sign of it. Instead, he laid his sword upon the bed and stretched his body out beside it.

The inky specters of his other nine victims gradually surrounded the bed and knelt at its edges, inclining their heads like mourners around the coffin of a beloved father.

On any other night, Chaney would have waited until Radu's eyes began to flutter with dreams, and he would scream to jolt the killer from his slumber. The howls of the other ghosts always followed soon after, and Radu rarely slept more than an hour before their only form of vengeance dragged him back to wakefulness.

"Watch them," said Radu with a nod toward the wall. "And watch the door. Wake me when he leaves or if someone comes for this room."

Radu closed his eyes, confident that he'd cowed his belligerent ghost to obedience.

Chaney hated him because he was right.

CHAPTER 12

THE DREAMING EYE

More dreams? Vox signed.

"Yes," said Tamlin from his dressing chair. His hands were busy lacing his codpiece, or he would have replied in the silent tongue only he and Vox understood. "At least I'm better rested after a few nights in a proper bed."

His bodyguard's question didn't bother him, but Tamlin realized he was in an irritable mood.

He hadn't slept well, and that had nothing to do with his health. Since Larajin healed him after his rescue, he'd remained under the constant attentions of Dolly, a housemaid with a profound affliction: absolute devotion to Tamlin. While in itself that wasn't an uncommon malady among the ladies of Selgaunt, it was an unfortunate predicament for a woman outside the noble caste.

Perhaps Dolly was the matter that gnawed at him.

As much as he enjoyed a tumble with the servant girls and tavern wenches, Tamlin knew perfectly well that he would never marry beneath his station. His father, while lacking in many other areas of paternal communication, had taken great pains during Tamlin's puberty to explain the facts of life as they applied to the men of Stormweather Towers. One should drink life to the lees, but never at the expense of the family reputation. Bastards were to be avoided or, failing that, contained with quiet payments on condition that the mother raise her children far from the legitimate family.

A second son or daughter might marry for love, but that was an indulgence not permitted to the head of a House.

Tamlin believed it was all wise advice, even considering his father's own indiscretion, incarnated as it was in Larajin—assuming that story was true. In fact, the thought that Thamalon had sired a pair of bastards after Tamlin's birth gave the Old Owl a rakish notoriety, at least in his son's estimation. A little tarnish made the aging relic that much more interesting.

Still, it didn't change Tamlin's opinion of consorting with the help—at least those who clearly doted on him. He had no qualms about seducing the willing, and he would gladly accept any invitation to an afternoon frolic, so long as the girl understood the limits. He would have no weeping drudges standing on the steps to his tallhouse, nor pestering his mother with plaintive letters.

And so, the problem of Dolly was no problem at all. Even when she looked up at him with such naked adoration while sponging his sweaty body or changing his bed linens while he lolled helplessly in a surfeit of sleep.

Still, she tried too hard to please, and perhaps that was the true source of Tamlin's ire. When he rose early that morning, he discovered a carafe of wine beside his bed and testily dismissed Dolly from the room. He'd ordered the servants twice before that he no longer wished to rise to an aperitif before breakfast. Dolly's disobedience angered him all the more because that morning he'd taken a sip out of habit before remembering his vow of abstinence.

They trouble you, said Vox.

"What?" Tamlin realized he'd been staring into space.

The dreams.

Vox looked at him querulously, but he didn't ask where Tamlin's mind had been drifting.

That was the reason Tamlin liked being alone with Vox. The mute barbarian had no compunctions about silently pointing at the obvious when Tamlin took every effort to elude it. At least with Vox, Tamlin didn't have to endure actually hearing someone state the matter he was avoiding.

"They're like the dreams I had as a child," he said. "The land there is unutterably beautiful, fantastic. Unlike anything you've ever seen, Vox, and when I'm there . . ."

Tamlin hesitated, realizing he was embarrassed to confess his childhood fantasy, especially since he was reliving it as an adult. He glanced at Vox, who looked back with an expression of honest interest, totally devoid of the snide skepticism of Tamlin's witty peers.

"In the dreams, I have powers," he said. "Magic powers. I can soar above the clouds, I can catch lightning and throw it where I will, and I can blow away the storm clouds before they burst into rain. At least, that's the way it was when I dreamed as a child. Since the dreams returned, they . . . well . . ."

Tamlin frowned, and Vox signed, *They changed?*

"Sometimes I do things I . . . I do despicable things, Vox. Really hideous stuff, like out of the worst ghost stories the meanest boys told around the campfires out at Storl Oak."

He shuddered at the memory of the executions on the high, revolving racks atop castle, the sycophantic clapping of his guests at the gory spectacle. Such grotesqueries drained him of the joy he felt at the return of his flying dreams.

Things you imagine doing for real?

"No! Absolutely not. In no way are these reflections of my own dark thoughts, my good fellow. And don't think I haven't given that possibility a great deal of consideration."

Vox nodded an affirmation. The gesture heartened Tamlin, because he knew his loyal bodyguard would never lie to him, even to spare his feelings. He needed that support, because, truthfully, he'd been wondering whether the dreams were some sort of window onto the darker regions of his subconscious.

Your dreaming eye is opening, said Vox.

"What?" Tamlin asked as he fastened the gold button at his collar.

The bearded man pressed a finger to his own narrow forehead then signed, *The door to dreams. Yours has been closed a long time.*

"Just because I drank a trifle too much?"

Vox shrugged.

"Nonsense," said Tamlin, but then he thought of the sudden lightning as he and Tazi fought the darkenbeast. At the time he imagined it had been some side effect of the magic circle around his cell.

Tamlin's heartbeat quickened at the thought that he might actually have some talent for the Art, but how was that possible? Even his childhood tutors had pronounced him hopeless, and they stood only to gain by tutoring the son of a wealthy merchant lord.

"That gives me an idea, Vox. Fetch me that poker."

Vox went to the fireplace and retrieved the iron rod. He handed it to his master.

Tamlin brandished it like a sword, though the weight was all wrong. He concentrated on the poker, willing energy to pass from his own body into the black metal. He couldn't be sure, but he thought he felt a faint warmth gathering in his palm.

"All right," he said, approaching the fireplace, "stand back."

He touched the poker to the metal.

Nothing.

"Drat it all," said Tamlin, turning back to look at Vox. The genuine surprise he saw on the big man's face made him laugh aloud. Even if Tamlin had his doubts, loyal Vox had nothing but faith in him.

"What a fool I am!" he said, tossing the poker back into its rack. He clapped Vox on one thick arm. "Letting you get me all worked up with childish fancies."

Tamlin returned to his dressing chair and pulled on his boots. Despite his self-effacing laughter, he couldn't shake the question from his mind.

"Just what do you know about this dreaming eye business, anyway?"

Not much, Vox admitted. *What the witches told me. An open eye can bring a man strength, power, or . . .*

"Or what?"

Sometimes impotence.

"Very funny."

Vox couldn't laugh, but Tamlin glanced at him to make sure there was a spark of mischief in his eyes. It was there.

Tamlin turned toward the full-length mirror and regarded his reflection.

His jacket was ivory white brocade with gold embroidery. Clusters of gold braid highlighted the Eastern cut of the collar, and a double-slashed pattern in the sleeves let the deep blue blouse peek through, completing the Uskevren colors. He wore the horse-at-anchor on a cloisonné medallion. The bejeweled hilt of a dagger protruded from one of his thigh-high boots.

On each hand he wore a pair of rings. Two of them were enchanted, one as a proof against poison, the other as a ward against mental assault. For physical threats, Tamlin would have to rely on Vox and his own sword arm.

But first . . .

"Would you check on my cape?"

Vox eyed Tamlin suspiciously.

"Come now, what harm can visit me in my own bedchamber?"

Vox reluctantly left the room. He had been loath to leave Tamlin's side since the kidnapping, for which the big man undoubtedly blamed himself.

Tamlin winced a silent apology for his deception, stepped behind the mirror, and pressed the floret that opened the secret door to his room. Quietly, he closed the door behind him.

In the darkness, he felt for the glass torch and whispered, *"Illumine."*

After its mellow light filled the narrow space, he wound his way through labyrinthine passages to his first destination.

Hidden within the walls of Stormweather Towers, Tamlin felt secure for the first time since his kidnapping nine days earlier. In the absence of his parents, he was the only one who knew the full extent of the network of secret doors and concealed passages throughout the mansion.

Oh, he suspected Tazi had found more than a few of them, or how else could she slip so easily in and out of the manor? Talbot was surely too dim to find them on his own, and lately he'd grown too big to fit through some of the narrower crannies.

Certainly none of the servants was aware of the hidden passages, except possibly for Erevis Cale—but the butler had vanished along with Thamalon and Shamur. Could the mysterious servant be responsible for the disappearance of Lord and Lady Uskevren?

Tamlin had mulled the thought like sour wine to make it palatable. No matter how long he stirred it, the idea remained unappealing. Despite the secret side to Cale's life, Tamlin didn't want to believe the man was capable of betraying his father. If a man couldn't depend on his closest servants, the world was a much darker place than Tamlin liked to think.

Before leaving the east wing, Tamlin paused. He pressed his hands against one of the many decorative bosses until he felt a slight shift, and he turned the concealed disc twice widdershins. There the wall opened to reveal another secret passage within the first.

The short hallway ended in yet another concealed door, this one to Thamalon's bedchamber. The servants had already searched the room, but what they sought was hidden more deeply than they knew. As Tamlin reached above the lintel for the keys he knew were there, he felt a sudden chill upon his neck.

Someone else was standing nearby.

"Father?" he said, heeding an intuition.

Tamlin listened for the scuff of a boot or the creak of a doorway—any indication of an intruder.

Nothing.

Tamlin shrugged off the eerie feeling and grabbed the keys.

He heard a tiny snap. In the gloom of the hidden passage, he could actually see the spark that leaped to his fingers. In the brief white flash, he saw a double shadow out of the corner of his eye, as if someone was standing immediately behind him.

He turned quickly, but there was no one else there.

"Hello?"

No one answered. He was alone in the passage.

He shuddered, and to dispel his lingering chill he said aloud, "I must have Escevar arrange for an exorcism."

He looked at the master keys. There were only seven on an undecorated electrum ring. Four of them, Tamlin knew, would together open all of the mundane doors to Stormweather Towers. Another unlocked the treasury, while the sixth granted access to Thamalon's desk in the library.

The seventh was the mystery key. Almost as long as Tamlin's hand, it was made of a purplish brown metal flecked with silver. Its three teeth seemed far too simple for a secure lock, and its size suggested a keyhole far too large to thwart a determined lockpick. As a boy, Tamlin had pestered his father about it, but the Old Owl had only shrugged. It had been dug up from the ruins of the previous Stormweather Towers, he'd explained, so whatever it had once opened must have perished in the flames. He kept it as a remembrance of his own father, Aldimar.

Far from answering his question, his father's explanation had only inspired his youthful imagination to a hundred doors and coffers the key might open. Did it lead to treasure? Monsters? An armory of enchanted dwarven blades? The bedchamber of a foreign princess?

Tamlin held the strange key and felt its peculiar warmth. Perhaps it was a charm to prevent keys from falling behind dressing tables, he mused. Or maybe the unique key was merely a token to facilitate a finding spell should the owner drop them while riding.

Alas, thought Tamlin, the truth to any mystery is always far less exciting than the speculation it inspires.

He left the passage to his father's room and secured the secret door before proceeding to his destination. Six turns, two more secret doors, and a short flight of stairs later, he arrived.

Tamlin checked the peephole to make sure the library was empty before he emerged from the secret passage. The entire household was awaiting him downstairs, but they could wait.

The secret door closed silently behind him as he went to the big desk. The burned rug had been replaced with a thick Calishite carpet, but the smell of lamp oil still lingered in the air.

Tamlin settled into his father's leather chair and surveyed the scene, trying to imagine how it had looked when the servants first entered the room on the night of the disappearance. Escevar had recounted their reports, but Tamlin still could make no sense of them. It was too great a coincidence that he would be kidnapped the same day his parents were abducted.

Or killed, he reminded himself.

The action he was preparing to take assumed that Thamalon the elder, at least, was dead. The clerics had been no help confirming the old man's death. Larajin claimed to have consulted her goddesses—Tamlin had blinked at the plural but he decided not to inquire further—but unfortunately, neither Sune Firehair nor Hanali Celanil would answer, or else Larajin exaggerated her powers.

Tamlin still doubted her other claims as well, despite Tazi and Talbot's corroboration. He had no illusions about his father's perfect fidelity, but yet another issue that put Tamlin at odds with his brother and sister seemed suspicious. Could Larajin be trying to drive a wedge between the siblings?

He wouldn't trust her until he knew more.

Tamlin had more confidence in the communion of High Songmaster Ansril Ammhaddan, at least if it was true that one received the value for which one paid. The services of the clerics of Milil didn't come cheap, but their services were praised as much for their efficacy as for their artistry. Ceremonies of Milil always included music, and the answers from their god came in the form of song.

"Look not for the owl in the forest night," sang Ammhaddan. "For far from this land has he taken flight."

There had been more, but most of it consisted of praise to Milil and his master Oghma, the Lord of Knowledge.

"What about Mother and Mister Cale?" Tamlin had asked.

The cleric's acolytes shushed him. The High Songmaster was not to be interrupted during a performance. Tamlin understood the unspoken meaning also. More questions would require more offerings. Under ordinary circumstances, Tamlin wouldn't have hesitated to pay. Until he had full legal control of the Uskevren House treasury, though, his resources were limited in the extreme.

In the meantime, the question of his father's disappearance continued to gnaw at him. He hoped to find some clue among Thamalon's letters.

There were none upon the table, nor anything extraordinary within the nooks and cubbyholes of the library desk. Tamlin checked the lower drawers but found they were locked. He also noticed a few fresh scratches near the keyhole.

Someone had been trying to pick the lock.

Tamlin immediately thought of his sister, but just as quickly dispelled the notion. If she had tried to pick the lock, he decided, there would be no such obvious signs.

He unlocked the drawer and opened it. Inside he found a sheaf of virgin vellum, a stoppered inkpot, a box of sealing wax, and a tiny jar of sand.

He removed all of these, sorted through the leaves of vellum, and found nothing unusual among them.

"Well, dark," he cursed.

If there had been any clue to his father's disappearance inside, then the anonymous lock picker had already stolen it.

Unless . . .

Tamlin felt around the bottom of the drawer, and ran his fingers along the seams.

Nothing.

Just as he was about to withdraw his hand, he noticed the distance between the drawer and the desktop was much greater than necessary. He felt around the top of the drawer cavity until his fingers found a niche.

"Aha!"

He pried open the false top and felt a bundle of pages slide out into his hand. They were letters, perhaps eighteen of them, each sealed with the crest of a noble family. Beneath them was a single sheet of folded vellum.

Tamlin opened it and saw familiar characters forming unintelligible words in a column, like a guest list or a shipping manifest.

"Some sort of code," muttered Tamlin.

He brightened at the intrigue, for he loved puzzles—at least, he once did. As a child he could spend happy hours pondering a clever problem posed by one of his tutors. As he grew older, he'd become less patient with such things, though he continued to find the idea charming.

He folded the list and slipped it into his boot before opening the first of the letters.

"Well, well, my darling," he said, "what tale will you tell me?"

"I've come to warn you I'm about to strangle your henchman," replied a deep voice, "and don't call me darling."

Tamlin dropped all of the letters except the one he was holding into the open drawer.

If there was one thing Tamlin disliked about his brother—and there were in fact dozens of things—it was that Talbot had been absurdly taller than his older siblings ever since puberty. Back then it had been fun to call him "the bastard child of a rampaging ogre," at least until Mister Cale had Escevar thrashed for the young master's offense. While that hadn't stopped Tamlin from taunting his "big little brother," as Tazi liked to call him, he abandoned that particular jibe after report of his offense reached his mother, and he saw displeasure crease her elegant brows.

For Tamlin, Shamur's disappointment had always been the worst possible punishment.

Tamlin smiled indulgently at his brother's jest, then he slipped the letter casually into his boot, snug against his thigh beside the vellum sheet.

"I suppose you're here to talk me out of the ceremony?"

"In fact, no," said Talbot.

He leaned forward to see what Tamlin was hiding behind the desk, but Tamlin shut the drawer with his knee to conceal the letters.

Tamlin had expected his brother to oppose his inheritance, especially since it required the legal declaration of their parent's demise. Surprisingly, Talbot had endorsed the decision on the grounds that it would make the search for their missing parents far easier once Tamlin could officially deploy the family resources. Once Thamalon returned, he could resume his former authority.

"I've come to discuss another matter."

"Oh?"

"Two things were missing from this room when I returned that night," he said. "One of them was a large sum of coin that belonged—"

"Yes, Escevar told me," said Tamlin, trying to keep suspicion out of his voice. "Are you quite sure the gold was here? It seems inconceivable that Father would fail to give you—"

"Don't you dare cheat me," growled Talbot. "We aren't children anymore, and this is a serious—"

"Then stop behaving like a child," said Tamlin. "What's important now is that we find out what happened to Mother and Father."

"You . . ." Talbot leaned across the desk, and for a moment Tamlin deeply regretted slipping away from Vox. Instead of grabbing him by the throat, however, Talbot struck the desk. "You're right," he said, "for once."

"It has been known to happen."

Tamlin smiled. On any of his friends, on any noble of Selgaunt, his smile was a balm to any quarrel. Talbot, unfortunately, was somehow immune to his charm.

"We will take this up again."

"Assuredly."

"And not through Escevar. Your whipping boy acts as if he runs this place," said Talbot. "He thinks he's Mister Cale."

"An hour from now, for all intents and purposes, he will be."

"That does not give him the right to talk to me as if—"

"Never mind him," said Tamlin. He tried to sound genuinely conciliatory. While he didn't particularly like or trust his brother, he knew he would need Talbot's support in the days to come. "Listen, no one wants Father back more than I do. You don't seriously believe I want all this . . . bother, do you?"

Talbot looked unconvinced, and he'd not forgotten about the other missing object.

"What do you suppose became of that painting of yours?"

Tamlin sighed. No matter how hard he tried to mend bridges, Talbot always found a way to tear them down again.

"I told you before," said Tamlin, "that painting was nothing more than a gift."

"One of those obscenities from Pietro Malveen? Hardly the way to impress the Old Owl."

"What do you have against the Malveens? They aren't the only House with a tainted past. In fact, Grandfather was the one who financed their earliest excursions."

Talbot glared at him and said, "How can you be so foolish?"

His gray eyes, which normally looked cool and bland, smoldered with hatred. Tamlin hoped it was all reserved for the Malveens.

"Pietro's a bit eccentric," Tamlin granted. "I'll be the first to admit that, but where's the harm in it?"

"He's barking mad," said Talbot. "Just like his brother."

Tamlin began to frame a joke about barking, then thought better of it.

"Don't be ridiculous. Laskar is as honest as bread pudding, and twice as boring, if you ask me. Despite his talent at fencing, Radu was every bit as dull . . . before he disappeared. That added a bit of mystery to him at least."

"You don't know what you're talking about," said Talbot.

"Then enlighten me," said Tamlin. "We're brothers, after all. Even if that bond embarrasses us both, we should trust each other."

Even as he said the words, Tamlin felt a twinge of guilt at his hypocrisy. He was asking Talbot to do what he would not.

"You already know my secret," said Talbot.

He held up a fist the size of a quart bottle and squeezed it tight. The hairs on the back of his fingers multiplied and grew thick. When he opened his hand, black claws jutted from his monstrous digits, each almost twice as long as before. The thick fur grew sparser along his forearm, and by his elbow the arm looked almost wholly human, as did the rest of his big body.

"That must come in *handy* when—"

"Shut up!" thundered Talbot.

Tamlin saw fierce canines protruding from his brother's snarling lips, and he clenched his jaw to prevent himself from flinching. It wouldn't do to show his fear. Instead, Tamlin stood his ground and returned Talbot's angry gaze with a steady stare. For long seconds they stood that way, locked eye-to-eye.

Talbot broke first. As he calmed himself, his face returned to its normal, human visage.

"Sorry," he said. "You sounded just like Chaney for a second. That was the kind of stupid pun he'd have made."

At last, Tamlin realized that his brother's recent brooding wasn't solely the result of sibling rivalry. Mangy gutterkin though he was, Chaney Foxmantle was as close a friend to Talbot as Vox and Escevar were to Tamlin. Perhaps Chaney and Talbot had been even closer. They'd been friends since childhood, and both of Tamlin's henchmen had joined the household as servants.

"No, I am the one who should apologize," said Tamlin. "If I have been short with you, it is because I resent the insinuation that I would do anything to hurt Mother and Father."

Talbot gaped at the uncharacteristic apology, and Tamlin remembered yet again why so many considered Talbot slow-witted. With his mouth open like that, he looked the perfect oaf.

"That's not what I was saying," said Talbot. "Pietro could have been using you—"

Tamlin held up a palm to stop Talbot and finished for him, "—as a dupe. I understand. I should resent that insinuation too, you know. I simply don't believe it. Pietro is utterly harmless."

"Tell that to Chaney."

"Are you suggesting the Malveens had something to do with his death?"

"We can't prove it," said Talbot. "Not without revealing what they did to me."

He shook his monstrous hand as if trying to fling some foul slime from it. In the blink of an eye it returned to its human form.

"I can't believe Pietro could kill anyone."

"He wasn't there at the time," Talbot said. "It was the other two, Radu and Stannis."

"But Stannis has been dead for—"

"*Un*dead," corrected Talbot. "Vampire."

Now it was Tamlin's turn to stare agape.

"Oh, please," he said. "Werewolf . . . vampire . . . ? Isn't it all a bit much? Next thing, you'll be leading us through the graveyards with torches and stakes, searching for the long-dead Stannis Malveen."

"He's already dead—again, I mean. Radu destroyed him to stop him from confessing."

"What happened to Radu?"

"If we're lucky, he died when House Malveen burned."

"And if we're *not* lucky?"

Talbot just looked back at him, letting Tamlin draw his own conclusions.

"We Uskevren certainly have no shortage of enemies," said Tamlin. He offered his hand to his brother. "It's up to you, me, and Tazi to ensure that those enemies all come from *outside* the family."

Talbot's eyes narrowed at the overture. Tamlin could hardly blame his brother for being suspicious, and he knew it would take far more than a handshake to mend their mutual distrust. What he wanted to learn was whether his younger brother would honestly rebuff him or play along at friendship until he had an advantage. Either way, Talbot would bear watching.

Before Talbot could respond, the library door opened, and

Escevar cleared his throat. Tamlin's long blue cape was folded neatly over his arm. Vox stood beside Escevar, glowering at his master.

"It's time, Master Tamlin," said Escevar. "Your guests are waiting."

CHAPTER 13

IT IS FORBIDDEN

To call Castle Stormweather large was a preposterous understatement. Thamalon had visited smaller cities. One could put the Hulorn's Palace and all its attendant buildings within the stronghold and still have room to cram in half the warehouses on the waterfront—and that was just the ground level.

The castle soared even higher than it sprawled wide, and Thamalon couldn't conceive of the miracles of engineering required to keep the place from collapsing. Once or twice in the past three days, he'd seen dwarves wearing the Sorcerer's crimson livery, so he supposed that the fabled craftsmanship of their people had much to do with the marvel. Still, he had to believe that the Sorcerer's magic helped sustain the titanic structure.

Since the castle's lord had granted him the full freedom of his abode, Thamalon had spent the past few days exploring the place. Walking was still mildly painful, but he thought it good to keep his injured hip limber. More importantly, Thamalon hoped to find some clues to the relationship between this Stormweather and his own—as well as to the uncanny likeness between the Sorcerer and his eldest son. He might have accepted the name of the place as coincidence, but the similarity between the Sorcerer and Tamlin wasn't just striking, it was utter and complete. They could be twins.

The thought of twins reminded Thamalon of his half-elf bastards, Larajin and Leifander. Briefly he wondered whether this Sorcerer could be another illegitimate offspring, but that made no sense. Only womb-brothers could look so much alike, and Thamalon had been present at Tamlin's birth.

Thamalon considered other possibilities that could be wrought only by magic. If the Sorcerer was an enemy, he could have enchanted himself to appear as Thamalon's son. He could be a magical construct shaped in the form of Tamlin. He could be a doppelganger employed by foes of the Uskevren.

Thamalon even entertained the fancy that the Sorcerer was Tamlin's wicked half, somehow separated years before from his gentler, weaker self.

Ridiculous, Thamalon told himself. Almost as ridiculous as being transported to this bizarre land through a painting in my own library.

He'd been certain that Tamlin had been an unwitting accessory of some hidden enemy. Thamalon had to consider the possibility that Tamlin and the Sorcerer were one and the same, and that his son was playing some inscrutable cat-and-mouse game with him. Even if Tamlin had successfully masked his hatred for his father over the years, could the careless dilettante actually manage to perpetrate such a scheme? Even if that was possible, Thamalon couldn't understand what Tamlin would have to gain by pretending to be a stranger to him.

That was the point at which all theories failed. No matter what the nature of the Sorcerer's resemblance to Tamlin, the real question was his motive. Why bring Thamalon there for some elaborate charade?

Thamalon couldn't question the Sorcerer even if he dared approach the matter bluntly. Since his audience with the Lord of Stormweather, Thamalon couldn't find the man even in his great hall. Instead, the Sorcerer's chamberlain assumed the seat beneath his lord's throne and dispensed petty justice, while all great matters awaited the Sorcerer's leisure.

Thamalon inquired of the servants and learned that their lord had gone *hunting*. They pronounced the word with a reverence unusual in a sport so common among the nobility Thamalon knew. Either it was a rare thing in those lands or else the Sorcerer's hunts were somehow exceptional.

His host's absence was as much an opportunity as a frustration for Thamalon. While waiting his chance to speak with the man, he could enjoy the hospitality the Sorcerer had offered. Perhaps he would learn something of the man by exploring his castle.

Soon he realized that that was a far greater quest than he'd imagined.

By the third day of his explorations, Thamalon had acquired a rough understanding of the main floor, with its great hall surrounded by guest quarters, shops, taverns, playhouses, and craft halls.

Since the rain had only increased since his arrival, Thamalon found the halls crowded with what seemed like thousands of people. Those who weren't hurrying to business were friendly and curious about the newcomer. Thamalon avoided those who seemed too inquisitive while seeking out gossips and tavern philosophers—those who would talk for hours with little prompting. From them he hoped to learn more about his host and the surrounding area.

Unfortunately, most of the talk concerned the politics of life within Castle Stormweather. Most of the lesser merchants chatted about improving their trade advantages, and Thamalon might have found those conversations more interesting in Sembia, where such matters affected his family. Members of the wealthier class were less inclined to associate with an unknown traveler, but Thamalon overheard enough of their buzzing to recognize the gossip of social adventure, petty and great. Count so-and-so had taken a second mistress but failed to keep that secret from his first; an old duchess had announced she was dividing her holdings among her three grandchildren, shocking the rest of her family who feared dissolution of the House; a sly merchant, hopeful of advancement in the court, had finally managed to place his comely daughter under the chamberlain's lecherous eye. . . .

Thamalon had heard it all, and none of it helped solve the mystery of his location or the coincidence of Stormweather and the Sorcerer's appearance. He retired to a tavern and sat a while sipping a strange, sweet mulled wine. There he met a man who smoked a long pipe and waxed poetical about the local wine and the Sorcerer's famous cellars.

That caught Thamalon's interest. Touring the Sorcerer's art galleries, his armory, and the water gardens had been acts of practiced civility. The prospect of inspecting his wine cellars was genuinely enticing.

Among his varied business ventures, Thamalon felt the most pride in his orchards and vineyards. Among his servants, there were few he held in greater esteem than his vintners. Thamalon visited his vineyards as often as he could justify the indulgence to himself. When selecting a new site for a vineyard, he loved to feel the grit and taste the soil as his master vintner explain how it was good, and in which ways it could be richer.

In summer he enjoyed picnicking among the vines with his wife and children, and at Higharvestide he would don homespun trousers and join the harvesters for an afternoon's picking. How long had it been since he felt the pleasant rupturing of grapes beneath his bare feet? The task had been an owner's indulgence, since it had been years since his vintners used anything but their efficient oak presses to extract the juice. They humored Thamalon's whim by providing him with an old-fashioned mashing tun, and he repaid the favor by keeping his visits short and infrequent so as not to slow their production.

Throughout the fermenting, filtering, casking, and aging, Thamalon always felt a sense of nurturing the raw produce of the earth into something far finer—something approaching art. While he didn't personally oversee the process, it was performed by his support and his will.

In a way, it was like raising children, but without all the bother. Should drought or excessive rains produce an inferior vintage, he had only to wait a year for another chance to get it right.

If only it were so simple to be a father. Unfortunately, in many ways Thamalon had approached parenthood as an owner rather than as a vintner, letting nannies, tutors, and whipping boys attend to the messy business of shaping a child into an adult. He sometimes regretted not tending more often to his children rather than leaving their daily care to his servants. He wondered how much they had suffered from his benign neglect.

The worse thought was that they'd turned out better for lack of his direct attentions. That idea injured his pride, but as one who'd single-handedly rebuilt the empire his father had destroyed, Thamalon believed a man was shaped most profoundly by the decisions he made *alone*.

Or perhaps that was only a feeble old man's excuse for spending too little time with his sons and daughter.

Thamalon tried to turn his thoughts back to the matter of the Sorcerer's wine cellars. What strange fruit did they harvest in this land? How might its yield compare to the vintages famous throughout the lands Thamalon knew? The pride of his own extensive cellars included racks of Arabellan Dry, Berduskan Dark, and Saerloonian Glowfire. He also reserved generous allotments of the finest domestic wines, including the famous House Ansril, House Beldraevin, and House Glaery. It was a source of great pride to him that House Uskevren also had its place among the most estimable vintages, as did his specialty wines, including the Usk Fine Old, Thamalon's Own, and the tart and fortified Storm Ruby.

Thamalon wished he'd been holding a bottle of one of them when he fell prey to that damnable painting. He would have liked to present it to his host, and perhaps the gesture would be enough to encourage the Sorcerer on to more speedy assistance in returning Thamalon to his homeland.

It was a fleeting, vain hope, but the wistful fantasy was enough to divert Thamalon from unhappier thoughts as he explored the increasingly lonely halls beneath the main floor of Castle Stormweather. Eventually, the tapestries and carpets withdrew to leave only flagstone floors and bare walls. Thamalon followed the trail of crackling torches in their iron sconces until he came to a plain iron gate.

On either side stood a pair of Crimson Guards. Those in front crossed their spears in the ancient gesture of forbiddance.

"Halt," said one. "It is forbidden to pass."

"I take it this is not the wine cellar?" said Thamalon amiably.

Beyond the gate he saw a large chamber. On the other side of its shadowy expanse was a heavy stone door embedded with river stones of blue and indigo and incarnadine. Between the gems, the stone curved and whirled in strange geometries that defied all symmetry. There were no recognizable characters among the arcs and spirals, but Thamalon sensed there was some foreign order among the chaotic lines.

"No," said one of the interposing guards.

He offered no further explanation, but since none of the

men seemed especially belligerent, Thamalon pressed another question.

"What is it there?" he said. "Some sort of—?"

"It is forbidden. Away with you!" said one of the guards. He turned his spear to point at Thamalon.

Thamalon bristled as much at the coarse rebuttal as at the threatening gesture.

"Your lord and master welcomed me as his guest. I doubt he would be pleased to hear that one of his—"

One of the other guards marked Thamalon's surprise and stepped forward. He lay a hand on the weapon to turn its point away from Thamalon's chest.

"You are the recent arrival?" he said. "The one they call Far-Traveler?"

Thamalon nodded curtly, holding his chin high.

The guard nodded back. He wasn't as unctuously accommodating as the upstairs servants, but he had none of the insolent tone of his fellow.

"The chamberlain must have been diverted by his scheduled visitors when you came to court. He is always distracted as the Sorcerer prepares to hunt. Otherwise, he would have told you that my lord invites his favored guests to enjoy all the chambers of his abode but one." He indicated the room behind him with a flick of his eyes. "The Ineffable Vault."

"I see," said Thamalon. He could practically hear the capital letters. He felt his eyes drawn inexorably toward the gloom-shrouded vault. "Had I known . . ." He raised his empty palms to the ceiling.

"If you wish, I shall escort you to the cellars. The sommelier would be pleased to show you the stores."

Thamalon followed the man away from the guarded portal. It was perfectly sensible for a man to keep visitors out of his treasury, but something about the unusual door made him think there was more than coin stored within.

Together they walked away from the gate, the hard heels of the guard's boots tapping a cadence on the stone floor.

Once they were out of hearing range of the other guards, Thamalon's escort stopped. He removed his helmet and turned to face Thamalon.

"If you please, sir," he said. He was a young man, and his cornflower blue eyes were wide with trepidation. "Allow me to report my fellow's insolence to our captain. I assure you he enforces strict discipline and will not overlook the offense."

Thamalon sensed the fear in the man's voice. A bead of sweat ran down the guard's cheek to vanish in his downy beard.

"Of course," said Thamalon. "I have no wish to trouble your master with such a trifle, especially since you have been so helpful."

The guard snapped his heels and bowed over his fist. "Thank you, sir."

As they continued their journey, Thamalon mused aloud, "I wonder what is so 'ineffable' about it?"

The guard cast a nervous glance at him and said, "I would not know, sir. No one ever enters it but the Sorcerer." After a few steps, he added, "On pain of death."

"I see," said Thamalon. After a few more steps, he ventured, "Surely you must have wondered."

"No, sir. It is forbidden."

"Where is the harm? I mean, why give it such a mysterious name if you don't want anyone wondering what's inside? Why block it with a gate that lets you see exactly what is being forbidden? Tantalizing, isn't it?"

The guard shrugged and kept his silence.

Thamalon tried not thinking about the mysterious vault, but of course the seed of curiosity had been planted, and his imagination fed it. He had a suspicion that the Sorcerer named his forbidden room exactly for that reason, and he remembered the old adage about the flying carpet that worked only when its owner did *not* think about elephants.

The past summer, Talbot's troupe had performed a play about a sorcerous queen who married a handsome but common man on the sole condition that he never open her wardrobe doors. Naturally, the man burned with curiosity about what his wife might be concealing inside that cabinet. One day, as his wife took her bath, he crept inside her bed-chamber and opened the wardrobe door—only to find her empty skin hanging there. When the fiend heard his screams, she emerged from her bath and gobbled up her disobedient husband.

Was this Ineffable Vault the Sorcerer's own test of his guest's fidelity?

Thamalon weighed his curiosity against his desire to be a good guest. In any other situation, he would never even consider snooping about his host's abode. The twin coincidences of the castle's name and the Sorcerer's appearance, however, tilted the scales toward impropriety.

Even as he considered where next to investigate his new surroundings, Thamalon couldn't dispel the memory of the guard's fear when he imagined the Sorcerer's displeasure. If insolence to a guest was so awful an offense as to set a young man to trembling, Thamalon didn't wish to learn what punishment the Sorcerer reserved for those who abused his hospitality.

CHAPTER 14

ABOVE THE CLOUDS

Cale watched Shamur lean into the wind, her eyes closed. The light of sunset turned her hair to gold as the wind lifted it up from her shoulders.

Fleetingly, Cale missed the feeling of wind combing through his hair.

Since a spell had rendered him permanently bald, he'd had few occasions to regret the loss of his distinctive red locks. In the years since, he had devoted himself so completely to service—first to Thamalon Uskevren, then to the Righteous Man, and finally to the Lord of Shadows himself—he'd rarely had time for mourning such petty pleasures such as the feeling of wind in his hair.

Besides, his baldness saved him the unpleasant task of washing skwalos mucous out of his hair.

When the creature's mouth had first shut upon

him, Cale thrashed against the suffocating enclosure. Not only did he fail to escape but he also managed to fill his nose with the faintly citric saliva that washed over him.

Before he was smothered, his fleshy prison convulsed and sent his body deeper into the belly of the skwalos. Cale felt himself squeezed upward, then to one side, then upward again. Each time he turned or paused, another titanic contraction of muscles sent him shooting in another direction.

For a frantic instant, he imagined the experience was not unlike birth. The life-affirming image did nothing to comfort him.

Cale's lungs craved air. He wished he'd taken a deep breath before entering the mouth of the skwalos. He wondered whether Muenda had failed to warn him out of spite or mischief. Perhaps he thought it best not to frighten his guests. Or perhaps, Cale mused darkly, Muenda hadn't warned him because he wasn't being welcomed but *eaten*.

Just as the throbbing emptiness in his lungs began to ache, the skwalos spat him out onto a soft, moist surface.

Cale had emerged into a cavernous room. Blue-green light filtered through the translucent membranes of the ceiling. A single round passage led from the room to a brighter chamber beyond.

Strong hands gripped Cale's arms and helped him stand.

"Fun, yes?" Muenda asked, smiling at him through a thick glaze of mucous.

Cale couldn't be sure whether his enthusiasm was genuine or a subtle form of mockery. He gave the elf the benefit of the doubt and didn't punch him in the mouth.

Shamur emerged moments later, smothered in pinkish slime. She waved away the elves who awaited her and rose with as much dignity as a woman dripping with sputum could muster. Wiping the stuff from her mouth, she gave Cale a few succinct requests she wished relayed to their hosts.

Cale translated them in more diplomatic terms than she'd employed, omitting certain emphatic adjectives.

Fortunately, the elves were accustomed to the bizarre mode of transportation, and Shamur's first demand was quickly satisfied.

The elves led them to the next chamber, the yawning mouth of which opened to the bright sky. There they found a natural pool in the surface of the skwalos. Without ceremony, Muenda and his companions plunged into the bracing rainwater. Cale and Shamur followed their example.

As they washed the slime from their bodies and clothes, Cale and Shamur gazed out over the broad back of the skwalos.

From this vantage, the place—Cale could still not think of it as a creature—seemed like a mountain plateau. It was as wide as Selgaunt Bay and four or five times longer.

On top, the creature's hide was almost entirely opaque except for a few wide patches on the side where thin membranes ballooned from its sides. Its surface was more rugged in a wide swath running ventrally from its blunt head and tail. From deep crags and furrows sprouted wild bushes and fruit trees. Among the flora walked elves with the same deeply tanned skin and black hair as Muenda. Some tended the plants, while others knelt over smooth patches of the skwalos, stroking its bare hide.

Almost without exception, the elves sang as they worked. Some of the lyrics were strange, perhaps in an ancient dialect peculiar to these elves. Some of them were more familiar. Cale heard invocations for spring rain, odes to elven beauty, and even a few old ballads whose lyrics had inspired a hundred legendary human bards across Faerûn.

Cale spotted five small circular tents scattered over the length of the skwalos. When Muenda noticed the direction of his gaze, he said, "When the moon rises, you will talk with our elders."

In the hours since, the elves had left Cale and Shamur alone to explore their fabulous conveyance. They went to the farthest edge of the creature and found a ridge of hard, gnarly thatch that marked the safe margin of the skwalos' flat back. From there they looked down on the land. The deep green forest sprawled to each horizon. A few meadow clearings dotted the expanse, rare and lonely among the uncountable trees. To the northeast, Cale spotted the mountains he'd seen earlier. South of them, a flat blue crescent curved toward them from the horizon, a vast lake or sea.

Cale and Shamur scanned the landscape for any sign of human habitation, but they saw none. The skwalos rose into the wispy clouds, and the fine mist briefly invigorated their tired bodies. When the creature emerged into the naked sky, fatigue gripped them at last. They left the edge of the skwalos and climbed to a higher vantage point upon the rugged spinal ridge. There they rested as the breeze dried their bodies and their clothes.

Several times they repeated their respective stories of the previous night, speculating on which of the Uskevren's enemies was behind the latest assault. The Talendar and Soargyls were obvious candidates. Their wealth and enmity for the Uskevren were almost without limit. Shamur favored the former House, assuming they wanted revenge for her killing Marance Talendar. Cale pointed out that the surviving Talendar had equally good reason to thank her for ridding them of their undead ancestor.

Shamur suggested the possibility that their rivals had joined forces, as they'd done so long ago to destroy Thamalon's father. Cale allowed that it was possible but reminded her that the Talendar and Soargyls hated each other even more than either of them hated the Uskevren.

They considered other political permutations. They considered the thieves' guild. They considered personal vendettas. Everything seemed possible. Nothing seemed likely, much less certain.

Eventually their conversation dwindled with the daylight.

As the last embers of twilight faded in the west and the skwalos drifted south with the breeze, Cale was fretting uselessly about not feeling the wind in his hair.

In any event, it wasn't his long-lost hair or even his brief spate of vanity that troubled him.

It was the night sky.

Cale knew the constellations as well as most any man, and he recognized no pattern in the emerging stars.

"Look," said Shamur. She pointed to the horizon. There rose the crescent moon, lonely in a sky of distant stars. At a glance it appeared normal, but its attendant shards were missing. "That is not Selûne."

"The stars are wrong, too," said Cale. "I think we aren't only far from Faerûn but far from Toril."

To Cale's surprise, Shamur nodded as if she had already been thinking of that possibility.

"The journey through the painting," she said, "reminded me of a time I traveled to another plane of existence."

Cale felt an eyebrow rise at her remark, but Shamur didn't seem to notice. Cale was beginning to understand that she hadn't revealed all of her secrets. Not by a long shot.

Shamur sighed and leaned into the oncoming breeze.

"In other circumstances," she said. "I might have enjoyed this strange journey."

Cale knew how she felt, but he kept it to himself. Rarely did he question his continued service to the Uskevren. Since the death of the Righteous Man and the revelation of his own role as the Shadow Lord's favored servant, Cale had wondered about his purpose. It was becoming increasingly difficult to believe that his masquerade as a servant among the nobles of Selgaunt had any great purpose.

Perhaps it was only sentiment that had kept him there so long. For years, he'd dedicated himself to serving the Uskevren family without becoming a part of it. No matter what affections he held for them, he remained a favored servant—separate and unequal.

Even in the familiar halls of Stormweather Towers, he knew, Cale had no home in Sembia. In his heart, he felt his destiny lay elsewhere, as yet undiscovered.

All he needed was a sign to know it was true.

"It has all the makings of one of Tazi's 'wildings,' " said Cale.

Shamur turned her head to him.

Cale didn't meet her gaze. Instead, he affected not to notice how much his comment had surprised her. In truth, he'd surprised himself with it. He had sometimes wondered whether Shamur suspected his affection for her daughter was more than protective. The constant spats between Tazi and Shamur were sparked not by their differences but by their sameness. Cale was certain of it.

So, too, was he certain that if anyone in the Uskevren household could guess his love for Tazi, it would be Shamur. To provoke her on the issue, however subtly, was undoubtedly dangerous.

Cale felt Shamur's studious gaze on his face. He continued to stare at the horizon, where the moon and the stars suffused the clouds with gray light.

Eventually, Shamur spoke.

"When I was Thazienne's age, I believed I was free. My brother would inherit, and my sister would marry well, leaving me to follow my heart. And so I did, both in love and in adventure. If you think these wildings of hers are something, it is only because I have not told you all of *my* stories."

Cale smiled at her and said, "I should like to hear them one day, my lady."

Shamur didn't return his smile.

"My first lover gave me two gifts," she said. "One was a magical sword. It was keen and fast, and it made my feet lighter than down. With Albruin in hand, there was no height I couldn't climb, no leap I wouldn't dare."

Then she did smile, a wistful expression of sorrow long ago distilled into wisdom.

"What was the other gift?"

"He left me," she said. "He knew what a young girl I was, how easily I would become attached to him, and he knew—even as I did not—that my 'wildings,' as Tazi calls them, would someday end. No matter how far I chased through the Dales and along the Moonsea coast, one day I would have to come home.

"I didn't believe him, of course. I believed my entire life could be one long adventure, that I would be forever free of family bonds and obligations, but one day I did come home, and it was to take my niece's place as Thamalon's bride. I did not love him, then, nor did I relish the prospect of becoming a lady of the Old Chauncel, and yet I loved my family. I wouldn't buy my own happiness with their ruin. I sold Albruin and put aside my wildings with no more thought of my youthful lover or our adventures."

Shamur stopped speaking and looked at Cale.

"Thazienne has been away for a long time," she said, "but soon she will come home."

Cale considered her words. There was little doubt in his mind that Shamur understood his feelings for Tazi, and less still that she didn't condone a prospective relationship between her daughter and a family servant.

He knew he should resent her intrusion, but the matter wasn't that simple. Even if he believed Shamur's mores were the shallow bigotry of the noble class, there were other, far more compelling reasons he shouldn't pursue his love for her daughter—reasons Shamur could never imagine.

Before he could formulate a polite continuance of their conversation, the elves rescued him from the uncomfortable silence.

"Erevis Cale," called Muenda. "Shamur Uskevren. The elders will speak with you."

They followed him down the skwalos' spine and across the tangled woods upon its back. Muenda led them to a tent illuminated from within.

Inside, a lantern glowed with enchanted light and warmth. Blankets covered the floor except beneath the bare legs of the tent's three inhabitants.

Two were female elves so old and frail they might have been skeletons wrapped in blankets. The third was an ancient male elf with more flesh on his small, round belly than on all the rest of his body. Their skin was the color of old oak, their hair as white as ash. One of the women beckoned them to sit.

"I am Rukiya," she said. "This is my sister, Kamaria, and her worthless husband, Akil."

Cale inclined his head, uncertain of their custom. Shamur did the same.

"You have come far from your home," said Rukiya. Her voice was as clear and as strong as a girl's.

Cale replied that it was so before quietly translating for Shamur.

The woman nodded and said, "The children sing of a strange human man in the forest this morning. He helped a throbe caravan escape our blockade."

Cale considered defending Thamalon's actions as those of a man unfamiliar with the local conflict, but he decided the elders had already considered the point.

"Is he safe?"

Rukiya said, "He went south with the dwarves—" her expression turned grave as she added— "into the domain of the Sorcerer."

"Your enemy?"

"Our mortal enemy," she agreed.

"It was not always so," added Kamaria. Like her sister, she spoke with the voice of youth. "As a young man, the Sorcerer was a friend to the elves. Even now, my great, great granddaughter remains at his side. The foolish girl."

"She would not stay if there was no hope," Akil said.

"Be quiet, you old fool," said Rukiya.

Cale sensed a warm sentiment beneath her scolding words.

"I merely say what no one else wishes to remember," Akil replied.

"We wish only to find my master and return home," said Cale.

"How will you find your way, shadow walker?"

At first, Cale thought perhaps he had misunderstood her words, but Rukiya's eyes glittered with mischief. They saw more than he realized.

"I do not understand."

"Your master whispers your name to us," she said. "Yes, his shadow falls upon our land as well as yours. He tells us what kind of man you are. A killer."

"Assassin," added Kamaria.

"A righteous man," said Akil.

"Silence, you useless bag of bones," Rukiya scolded.

Cale didn't like what the elves were implying, but he couldn't mistake their meaning.

"We didn't come here to kill the Sorcerer," he said.

"And yet," said Rukiya, "you require our help."

"I see," said Cale.

"What are they saying?" asked Shamur.

Cale didn't answer. Instead, he looked back into Rukiya's eyes for some sign that she was testing him. Was it failure to refuse or to accept?

His voice reedy and high, Akil sang,

"I forbid you maidens all,

"Who wear gold in your hair,

"For to go to Stillstone Hall,

"For young Tam Lin is there."

"What was that?" insisted Shamur. "Is he singing about my son?"

"Never mind Akil," said Rukiya. "He dreams when he is awake."

"Why do you sing that song?" Cale asked.

"Pay him no mind," said Kamaria. "The song is forbidden in the Sorcerer's demesne, for it contains the name that must not be spoken. To utter it there means death."

"Why?"

"For once, before he buried it with his soul, Tam Lin was the Sorcerer's name."

CHAPTER 15

THE BURNING CHALICE

Dolly held the crystal decanter and poured the mead, careful to avoid touching the Quaff of the Uskevren. She spared only a quick, blushing glance up at Tamlin. He noticed her hopeful look but didn't acknowledge it. Instead, he stood upon the dais where his father's chair usually sat and watched as Escevar lifted the silver tray and bore it to the presiding cleric.

Standing beside High Songmaster Ammhaddan, Tamlin smelled the sweet, musky bouquet of the honey wine. His mouth watered for a taste. For the second time since his kidnapping, he was about to violate his oath of abstinence. This time his excuse was that such a solemn ritual shouldn't be sullied with a base substitute.

Not with most of the Old Chauncel looking on.

The feast tables had been pushed to the walls to make room, and the hall was filled to capacity with members of all of Selgaunt's noble families, great and petty. Among the hundreds of visitors were faces Tamlin knew well: Baerent, Toemalar, Baerodreemers, and Foxmantles. Soargyls and Ithivisk mingled with the Karns, Mandrales, Elzimmers, Malveen, and Kessyls.

In the nearest row, seated comfortably in places of honor, were the most prominent and powerful lords of Selgaunt. Tamlin listened to the High Songmaster's evocation and smiled at those he counted most dear—and most dangerous.

Fendo Karn smiled warmly back at Tamlin. His loyalty was all but assured by blood, for he was cousin to Shamur Uskevren. Beside him sat Saclath Soargyl, the fat and sneering son of a man whom Thamalon counted as one of the family's deadliest enemies. Next was the honorable Ansible Loakrin, Lawmaker of Selgaunt, who had a reputation for impartial justice.

Conspicuous among the merchant lords was the Hulorn himself, Andeth Ilchammar. While many, including Tazi, joked about the man's eccentric tastes in art and opera, Tamlin enjoyed the lord mayor's generous galas and his devoted patronage of the arts. The nobleman returned Tamlin's gaze with a courtly nod.

Beside the Hulorn sat the elegant Presker Talendar, head of the oldest noble House in Selgaunt. The man's silver-shot hair was always perfectly coifed, and his glittering emerald eyes never failed to capture the attention of those who looked his way. That day, however, Presker had an even more arresting feature.

Upon his finger was the very ring that Tamlin had seen on his kidnapper's hand.

Presker smiled warmly and gently pressed his hand to the crest over his heart: the black Talendar raven, its sharp beak dripping with a single crimson drop. The gesture was Presker's habitual greeting, a friendly if not particularly warm acknowledgement of a peer. Tamlin realized that the same gesture could be a private threat.

Tamlin thought, What a brassy, bold bastard!

He smiled and nodded at Presker even as his mind spun through the possibilities. He couldn't for an instant imagine that the cunning lord was so careless as to reveal such a distinctive jewel while in disguise.

He must have wanted Tamlin to recognize the ring. Tamlin was certain of it.

But why?

Moreover, Tamlin wondered how the devil Presker—or whoever had arranged to enspell the painting he'd given his father—had managed to remove it from the house. Barring coincidence, it had to be the same person who'd removed the coin Talbot left in the library. Unless the wards had failed completely with the death of Brom Selwyn, nothing should be able to leave or enter the mansion magically. That suggested a thief.

Or else a traitor within the house.

Before he could ponder the matter further, Tamlin heard the descending notes that signaled the conclusion of High Songmaster Ammhaddan's evocation.

"By the grace of Milil, I anoint the cup," sang the cleric.

He took the Quaff of the Uskevren in his hands and raised it high. Flames erupted from the cup. Tamlin could feel the heat and knew that Ammhaddan's hands would have been seared had he not already cast protective spells upon himself.

"The Quaff of the Uskevren," declared Ammhaddan, "rejects the alien hand."

Ammhaddan returned the cup to its platter, and the flames subsided before the heat could boil the mead. He nodded to Escevar, who bore the cup to Tamlin's siblings.

Since Tamlin's rescue, Tazi had undergone a transformation no less astonishing than Talbot's shapeshifting. She'd shed her leather armor in favor of a sculpted green bodice with cascading silk skirts. Gems glittered at her ears and about her neck.

Beside her stood Talbot, who wore a white blouse big enough to serve as a sail on a small fishing boat. Golden studs running down the front of his blue leather doublet completed the house colors.

A few paces behind him stood Larajin.

Even though she stood on the floor and to the side of the dais, Tamlin had no doubt that Larajin's beauty arrested all attention. A resplendent, ruby red gown accentuated every curve of her slender body. Its plunging neckline wasn't unusual at a Selgauntan social affair, but some quality of light drew Tamlin's eyes inexorably to the fair white flesh of her throat, where the golden medallion of her goddesses hung upon a velvet choker.

Before he could mask his expression, Tamlin realized he was frowning at Larajin. Until the revelation of her parentage, Tamlin had never given the woman much thought. Since then he'd realized she could pose a threat to the family's reputation—and perhaps even to his inheritance. She looked a few years younger, but as a half-elf she might well claim to be older than Tamlin.

There was no question of her legitimacy—not so long as Shamur lived to defend her children's rights. With both Shamur and Thamalon missing, the question could be stickier. Even if she didn't seek a claim on the family fortune, could her years of servitude in the house of her own father have led her to seek revenge? Her demeanor had never suggested malice, but Tamlin knew how changeable appearances could be, especially among the nobles of Selgaunt, legitimate or otherwise.

Larajin's curious form of worship was also troubling. Tamlin had asked Escevar to inquire about her curious medallion. On one side was the face of Sune, goddess of love and beauty. On the other was a golden heart, symbol of Hanali Celanil, elf paragon of those same ideals. The Uskevren traditionally worshiped all of the major gods in their temple gallery. In Stormweather Towers, not even bright Waukeen, merchant's friend, held a position of superiority over the other divinities. While High Songmaster Ammhaddan most frequently presided over family ceremonies, that was a matter of personal friendship with Thamalon rather than any mark of Uskevren allegiance to a single deity.

Should Larajin insist on Uskevren sponsorship of her own sect, the social scandal would be nothing compared to the potential for backlash from the established temples of Selgaunt. The clerics of Sune might brand her a heretic and bend all their considerable power to thwarting her family.

After the rescue, Tamlin commanded Escevar to deliver Larajin a reward for healing his injuries. The payment came promptly back, along with a polite note declaring that Larajin could never accept payment for helping her own flesh and blood.

There could be no clearer warning that she intended to press some issue to him soon.

Escevar brought the Quaff of the Uskevren to Talbot. Upon its silver tray, the metal mead goblet looked plain indeed, yet—apart from the House crest, the horse at anchor—it had gradually become the most famous symbol of the Uskevren clan.

Years past, Phaldinor Uskevren tasked his wizard with creating an enchantment to prevent his guests from stealing his favorite mead cup. Helemgaularn of the Seven Lightnings had done at least that much, for ever since then the Quaff of the Uskevren had been not only a family heirloom but also the test by which one could prove blood relation.

It had proven that ability just over two years earlier when a pretender in league with Uskevren rivals—including Presker Talendar, Tamlin reminded himself—had come to Stormweather Towers claiming to be none other than Perivel Uskevren. Within the family chronicle, Thamalon's elder brother was a nigh legendary figure—indeed, Talbot seemed to have adopted him as a sort of patron saint. Still, Thamalon had been certain that Perivel had fallen in defense of the original

Stormweather Towers, long before Tamlin was born.

As Thamalon told the story to Tamlin, enemy wizards had somehow enchanted the Quaff to reverse its original power. Thus, when Thamalon grasped the goblet, it falsely blazed to mark him as a pretender to his own bloodline.

That trick might have snatched away Thamalon's claim to the family holdings if not for Larajin's seemingly innocent intervention. When she touched the enchanted cup, it remained quiescent. The attendant witnesses, never imagining she was Thamalon's child, considered this their proof of the pretender's trickery.

When Thamalon confided the story to Tamlin, he'd omitted the reason why Larajin's touch didn't activate the Quaff. Twenty-six months later, Tamlin understood the incident for what it meant. Larajin's claim was certainly true.

Talbot took the Quaff from the tray and drank a lusty draught. Briefly, Tamlin feared he'd drained the cup, which would require the embarrassing extra step of refilling it before it came to Tamlin. Worse, instead of passing the cup to Tazi, as he'd been instructed, Talbot paused to look back at Larajin.

Talbot had always treated Larajin as a sister, even long before he learned the truth of their relation. Tamlin hoped his affection for the girl and his scorn for his elder brother wouldn't urge him to make a scene. Simply by passing her the Quaff of the Uskevren, Talbot could prove Larajin's legitimacy without Tamlin's consent. Such an act might be grounds for casting him out of the household—but only after Tamlin was installed as lord of the house. With the succession moments away, Talbot could dash it all to pieces.

Escevar cleared his throat—Tamlin thought his henchman was becoming quite good at that essential butler's trick—but Talbot ignored him. Instead, he looked back over his shoulder at Larajin. Tamlin couldn't see his brother's expression, but he imagined some conspiratorial exchange between the two.

For a moment, Tamlin considered sending Vox over to take the goblet from his brother. The resulting conflict might be an even worse spectacle than Larajin's unwanted revelation, and it would put the brother's dispute firmly in the public eye.

"Tal," whispered Tazi.

He turned back to face her, an easy smile creasing his lantern jaw, then he passed her the goblet with a courtly nod. As Tazi accepted the cup and drank from it, Talbot smiled past her at Tamlin. He winked.

Beneath his fraternal smile, Tamlin seethed. He could take a jest as well as anyone, but Talbot was trying his limits in front of all the family peers. He would never have shown such insolence to their father, Tamlin was certain. It was an ill harbinger for the days ahead of them.

Tazi sipped from the cup and passed it to Tamlin. He accepted it, noting that there was still a dram or two left. Perversely, he was grateful that Talbot had left him so little mead—not that his brother had meant to do him a favor.

Tamlin turned to the audience before raising it high. He paused, knowing that his stillness would draw all eyes to him. It was an actor's trick he'd learned far better than Talbot ever could.

"This House is bound as I bind it," said Tamlin. "Its coins flow as I bid, and as I speak, so shall the Uskevren stand."

With that oath, he drained the Quaff. He raised the goblet high, displaying it to all present.

The vessel flared with light and rose out of his hand. It floated a few feet above him, tilting slightly to send a shaft of golden light both through the stained glass window on the upper gallery and down upon his face.

A murmur of surprise rippled over the crowd. Tamlin could hear every whisper as clearly as if the speaker's lips were upon his ear.

"How gauche!" said one of his Karn cousins.

"This did not happen at his father's oath, I wager."

"Look at how handsome he is in that light!" whispered a young woman.

Tamlin glanced at her where she stood with her father at

the back of the crowd. It was Gellie Malveen, a sweet lass who would never find a husband so long as Laskar struggled with debt and his younger brother's notoriety.

"It is a portent of great fortune!" called High Songmaster Ammhaddan. "Look how Waukeen illuminates him with her golden favor. From this day, House Uskevren will flourish as never before."

A bit much, thought Tamlin, but at least he's earning his pay.

Still, he had no idea the Quaff of the Uskevren would respond in such a manner. He wished for the thousandth time that his father were there and he could dispense with this entire ceremony.

The newly anointed Captain of the Guard rapped his staff of office upon the floor.

"Long live Thamalon Uskevren!" he shouted.

The house guard added their voices to the second call. With the third, the entire assembly raised their voices as one.

"Long live the Lord of Stormweather!"

CHAPTER 16

THE HUNT

Thamalon leaned heavily upon the marble railing, panting in the rain-cooled evening air. His heart galloped in his chest, and he was fairly sure that some of the lightning he saw bursting against the night sky was a reflection from within his pounding head.

What was I thinking? he berated himself silently—because he had no breath to speak aloud. *I didn't think I was too old for this.*

For a man of his years, Thamalon considered himself fit and hale. He still enjoyed a long stroll or a vigorous ride on horseback. While his weapons of choice were the contract and the ledger, he had lately proven that he could still wield a blade with the best of them when necessary.

But there he was, about to expire from climbing a long stairway.

Earlier in the evening, Thamalon heard the same haunting tune that had welcomed him to the bleak streets surrounding the castle.

"What is that song?" he'd asked a servant.

"Lady Malaika calls the skwalos."

"But where is she?"

The servant pointed upward and said, "She sings from her observatory in the uppermost chamber of the west tower."

The guards at the base of the stairway didn't turn him away, as Thamalon had half-expected. Instead, they suggested he take advantage of the mechanical litter attached to the railing. At that moment, Thamalon considered the device the sort of novelty reserved for invalids and ladies who avoided any risk of perspiration. When he spied a faint smirk upon the lips of the servant who offered him the conveyance, pride demanded he refuse it.

Soon he felt the smug guard had outwitted him, and a mere flight of stairs threatened to do what none of his enemies had yet achieved with assassins, poison, and magic.

Thamalon didn't much appreciate that irony.

Somewhat defensively, he noted that there was nothing "mere" about the titanic stairway. He must have climbed more than twice the height of the tallest tower in his own home, and still he'd arrived only at the *lower* balconies of Castle Stormweather. Even from that height, he could barely perceive the giant bonfires that sizzled to either side of the grand entrance to the stronghold. From the balcony, they looked like fireflies drowning in a murky pond.

Another wave of thunder rolled in and broke against the castle walls. Thamalon felt the vibration in the air. The wind swept the rain into the sheltered balcony, and Thamalon stepped back. A sudden vertigo swirled in his head, and he nearly stumbled as he reached out to lean against the wall.

"Father?"

He turned around but saw no one else standing on the landing. Torchlight danced upon the wall stairway walls. On the wall opposite the balcony, a long tapestry stirred in the breeze. Upon its rippling fabric, elves danced among deerlike creatures while strange birds and colorful jellies floated in the trees above.

"Who is there?" Thamalon said.

The voice had sounded like the Sorcerer—or Thamalon's own eldest son.

Lightning briefly illuminated the dark corners of the landing. Still, Thamalon saw no one.

"Hello?" the voice called.

It seemed to emanate from behind the tapestry. Thamalon looked for some signs of a lurker—a bulge in the fabric, a pair of boots protruding from the bottom—anything—but there was nothing.

He pulled back the tapestry and put his hand to the wall. Lightning flashed again, banishing the shadows for an instant.

Still, Thamalon saw nothing behind the tapestry.

He hesitated for a moment, then he glanced up and down the stairway. No one was coming.

He felt the cool stones, pressing and pulling here and there. On the eighth try, the stone he pressed sank several inches into the wall, and a secret door groaned open to reveal a dark, narrow corridor.

The mechanism worked almost exactly like those governing the hidden passages in Thamalon's Stormweather. He hoped that was yet another proof of a purposeful connection between the places, and not an indication that the design was common. He hated to think that any of his guests might snoop around his home as easily as he was about to do there.

Checking once more for intruders on the stairs, Thamalon took a torch from the wall and entered the secret passage.

Inside, he located the counterweight and closed the secret door.

He followed the passage barely more than ten feet, where it ended at an oak-and-bronze portal of unmistakably dwarven craftsmanship. Set in the wall beside the door were a similarly ornate bronze lever and wheel crank.

Spotting no handle nor lock on the door, Thamalon tried turning the wheel. It remained obstinately fixed. The lever rose as he lifted it, snapping into place directly perpendicular to the wall. The burring of gears emanated from beyond the door.

Thamalon hoped it made no greater noise elsewhere in the castle, especially near suspicious guards.

Never mind the guards, he thought. Worry about the Sorcerer.

Seconds passed like minutes, until finally the muted clamor ended with an emphatic *clunk* behind the door. When nothing else happened, Thamalon tried the wheel once more. It turned smoothly, and the two halves of the door parted to the perfect cadence of metal gears.

Beyond the door was a small room, no larger than a privy. Its walls were lined in red velvet. A hundred pewter studs cast gentle light from the walls and ceiling. In either of its far corners was a tiny seat, and upon its inner door were smaller versions of the lever and wheel.

Before entering, Thamalon set aside the torch. He might need it to navigate another secret passage, but he was wary of setting fire to the pretty little room.

Thamalon had already divined the chamber's purpose. He'd seen a much cruder version of the mechanical lift in the warehouse Presker Talendar reserved for the most precious of his imported porcelain, jade, crystal, and similarly fragile objects. Thamalon knew that the fantastic device cost Presker far more than it saved in labor expenses. Still, it was the talk of the town for a tenday, and tours of the new wonder gave Presker a fine excuse to curry favor with prospective partners.

The lever inside the lift jutted straight out from the wall. Thamalon pushed it upward, found it stuck fast, then wheeled the doors shut before trying again. As he'd predicted, the lift began to rise.

As he ascended, Thamalon thought on Presker Talendar and his many other rivals in Selgaunt. They'd fought each other for decades, sometimes in the pursuit of the most beneficial trade concessions—and sometimes to the knife over ancient feuds. In that time, Thamalon had thwarted dozens of attacks on his businesses, his reputation, and even his life and the lives of his wife and children.

He wasn't above retribution. He had not fingers enough to count the Talendar and Soargyls he'd ordered murdered in dark alleys. He regretted none of them, for each had a hand in the deaths of his father and brother, or else they'd actively strove against the life of an Uskevren.

Even so, Thamalon remained proud that he never allowed his wrath to descend to the level of petty vengeance. No one had died upon his word for an idle threat, nor for a mere insult. Indulging one's ire was a quick path to damnation, he believed. That was one of the lessons he feared he hadn't imparted to his sons—and he'd lately added to his prayers a plea that they not murder each other.

The gods smiled upon the Uskevren, at least so far. While a few dear friends and several key members of the household had perished in defense of the family within the past few years, none of his kin had fallen to an assassin's blade.

Thamalon meant to keep it that way, and for the past ten months he'd been working secretly, tirelessly to that end. If only he could complete the negotiations he'd so carefully crafted, then he would go gently into his final slumber, knowing that his sins and those of his father could be washed from the hands of his children. If he succeeded, he need no longer fear that the lives of his sons and daughters would end upon a rival's blade.

What infuriated him was that only when he was so close to achieving that goal, one of his foes had hurled him a thousand miles—if not farther—from where he needed to be.

The rattling chains slowed, and the lift chamber came to a gentle halt. Thamalon listened for a commotion on the other side. If he heard voices, he planned to descend again and hope investigators could not arrive before he fled.

He heard nothing, so he opened the door. Beyond was a passage similar to the one he'd entered below, and he immediately spied the lever operating what must be from the outside another secret door. He closed the door to the lift behind him and turned the lever all the way down, sending the lift back to its original place.

The second secret door also opened behind a tapestry. Thamalon blessed his luck that he remained concealed, for he heard sobbing from beyond the fabric. He lay down to peer under the tapestry.

The room beyond was unlighted, but the moon shone through a breach in the storm clouds and filled the glass chamber with silver light. It curved around the tower to either side from the central spire. Flowers overflowed their vases on low tables between an intimate trio of couches. To one side of them was a small round dais on which stood a stringed instrument that must have been a harp, despite its improbable geometry. On the other side of the furniture was a basin carved of a seamless chalcedony.

The chamber's sole occupant was a slender elf woman. He knew at a glance that the woman had been starved by illness, or more likely by despair.

As Thamalon spied upon her, the woman heaved a sigh and sat up. With an economical swipe of her handkerchief, she dried her cheeks and assumed an imperial composure, head erect, eyes firmly forward, focusing on nothing. With a fine brown hand, she replaced the coal-black tresses that had spilled across her face.

Unveiled, her face was even more youthful than Thamalon had imagined. She appeared even younger than his daughter, except for those wise, dark eyes. She might be twice or thrice Thamalon's age, he reminded himself.

After a moment, the elf rose and went to the basin. With an arcane pass of her hand, she evoked an image in the air.

Miniature clouds formed above the basin, and wild lines of electricity arced between them. Simultaneously, lightning flashed above the dome.

As the woman observed the image of the sky, Thamalon left the secret passage. He closed the door just as the thunder crashed over the tower, then he slipped out from behind the tapestry.

In the silence between the thunder, he cleared his throat.

The woman looked at him, one fine black eyebrow arched.

"If I am disturbing you, my lady . . . Malaika . . . ?"

She didn't reply, but Thamalon took the slight raising of her chin as acknowledgement of her identity.

He waited a moment more for an invitation to stay. He didn't wish to take her silence for consent, so he tried another tack.

"Then, alas, I shall have to await rescue. I am afraid I depleted my supplies on the second day of the climb, and my guide perished not five hundred steps below the summit."

A flicker of concentration smothered Malaika's smile before it could form. Still she didn't speak. She turned back to observe the image she'd conjured.

As Thamalon approached, he noticed that the woman was even smaller than he had realized. Her thin body gave her only the illusion of height. The crown of her head didn't reach the height of his shoulders.

Thamalon joined her at the basin. A dark, rippling liquid filled the bowl. Motes of colored light rose and popped like bubbles on its surface.

Thamalon looked from the clouds above the basin to those outside. They looked identical in every way but scale.

Turning back to the basin, Thamalon saw something new. A vast shadow floated through the clouds. Its tip pierced the foggy shroud at last, and vapors trailed from the ridges of its body as it emerged into the clear sky.

From their vantage, the creature looked less like a whale

than a perfectly symmetrical island. From its back sprouted a veritable forest from which glowed tiny red fires. One of the fires winked out, and a barely visible orange thread ran out from the greenery. As the line grew longer, it curved back in the wake of the monstrous creature. A few seconds later, its leading point exploded into a ball of flame.

"The fools," whispered the elf, her tone urgent and pitiful.

Before Thamalon could ask a question, lightning leaped from a point near the fireball to strike at the spell's origin. A few seconds later, a nearly identical bolt struck the same spot.

The elf reached to the basin and plucked at the image of the soaring creature. With her gesture, the vision grew larger. Thamalon could see a tiny image of the Sorcerer, his crimson cloak snapping in the wind. He gripped his winged scepter in one hand. In the other he held a fiery blue ball of spitting lighting. Beside the gargantuan creature, he appeared no larger than a gnat.

"What is that?" Thamalon asked.

He pointed to a long green shape emerging from the forest atop the skwalos. From its hunched back rose a pointed fin, beyond which a flatworm of a tail tapered to a ragged little fluke. Its yellow wings were wider than its body was long, and its hind claws were enormous even for the creature's great size. A fleshy, spiral horn sprang from its long skull. The faintest aura of witchfire played along its length.

"Yrthak," said Malaika.

Trepidation soured her dulcet voice, and Thamalon wondered whether she feared more for the Sorcerer or for his foes.

The yrthak cupped its wings and floated steadily down toward its prey. Its eyeless head was split with a crocodilian smile. Between its yellow teeth, its tongue curled up to form a fat pink knob. The creature held its mouth open, as if tasting the storm.

"He doesn't see it," said Thamalon.

He watched as the Sorcerer flew toward the surface of the skwalos. From his outstretched fingers, five dazzling sparks raced toward unseen targets beneath the tangle of flora upon the back of the creature.

The elf's fingers danced above the image, evoking quick views of each successive target of the Sorcerer's spell. Two of the magic missiles struck and slew elf archers crouching amid the shelter of the foliage. Another wounded a white-haired elf and shook him from the concentration of his own evocation.

Another wave of thunder broke over the tower, shaking the metal casement. A sympathetic vibration set the glass humming all around Thamalon and Lady Malaika.

The place is called Stormweather for a reason, Thamalon told himself. Still, he counted the paces between his position and the relative shelter of the stairs.

"No!" Malaika cried.

She gripped the edge of the basin as the yrthak folded its wings and dived toward the Sorcerer. Even before it reached him, an invisible force shook the Sorcerer's body and tore the cloak from his shoulders. Thamalon heard nothing except the wind and rain, but his teeth ached as if someone had scratched fingernails across a slate.

The Sorcerer's great helm buckled beneath the force, and his limbs trembled as if in seizure. For an instant, his muscles strained against the attack, but then his arms and legs went slack.

The Sorcerer fell, and the yrthak dived after him, jaws agape.

Thamalon felt a grip on his arm. Malaika didn't look at him, but her tiny hand squeezed tighter as they watched the Sorcerer plummet.

The Sorcerer's arm reached out in a gesture so casual that Thamalon wasn't sure whether he was conscious of it. Then came a dark, flapping blur, and the crimson cloak few back into its master's grip. With a dancer's graceful flourish, the Sorcerer rolled his shoulders back into his mantle. In the instant he fixed the clasp about his throat, the shapeless fabric billowed out in the fullness of its enchantments.

The Sorcerer stopped falling so abruptly that the yrthak plunged past him before realizing its prey had recovered. As the creature spread its wings, the Sorcerer was already unleashing a hail of white fire. Fierce meteors shot through the yrthak's wings and tore black rents along its flanks.

The creature flailed helplessly. Before it could turn its tumble into a glide, a lightning bolt flew from the Sorcerer's fist and sheared away one of its crippled wings.

The Sorcerer started to pursue his fallen foe, but then he paused and looked all around. He spotted two more yrthak descending from the skwalos. He flew up long before they could reach him, flinging white beams of lightning and red balls of flame at his opponents. One of the fliers blackened and fell, while the other turned its seared back to its foe and plunged into the obscuring clouds.

Triumphant, the Sorcerer turned back to his original prey. He mirrored the course of the skwalos, shocking its enormous flank with lightning to spur it closer and closer to Castle Stormweather.

When Lady Malaika looked up through the ceiling, Thamalon followed her gaze to see the terrible silhouette of the skwalos through the glass. He discerned the Sorcerer's location by tracking the white streaks of energy he cast.

Thamalon turned back to the basin for a better view, hardly noticing that Malaika withdrew. He saw the Sorcerer shake his scepter at the skwalos. From its bright ruby shot a barbed spear. The weapon sank deep into the creature's hide, and immediately a ribbon of red lightning shot down from the wound to the ground. The crackling light persisted even after the initial flash, coruscating in a constant line between earth and sky. It wriggled and contracted, tugging its skyborne prey toward the ground.

The Sorcerer raised his scepter, and in a hot red flash, another spear appeared above the pulsating ruby. He flew to the other side of the skwalos, alert for further defenders.

None came.

He cast the second harpoon, and another red line of energy bound his prey to the ground. Slowly, the skwalos began sinking below the clouds. The Sorcerer followed until Thamalon could see neither of them through the basin's cloudy image.

He spared a glance through the ceiling windows, but all he could see were dim eruptions of red light through the clouds. The thunder began to subside, leaving only the sound of steady rain upon the glass.

Malaika sat beside her harp, head bowed as she leaned upon its neck.

"It's over," he said, thinking it might console the lady.

"No," she said. "It is only beginning. Soon my lord's servants will catch it with their flensing hooks." Malaika looked at Thamalon as if seeing him for the first time. She said, "You are the traveler."

"You may call me Nelember," Thamalon said, making a courtly bow.

"Yet that is not your name."

He repeated his bow, this time with an apologetic hand over his heart. He didn't question how she perceived his obfuscation.

She gestured an invitation to sit, and he obeyed, then she rose to stand close to him, looking down into his face. Her eyes searched his features for long seconds. She touched his brow and ran a finger down the straight line of his nose.

"What secret do you keep from my lord?"

Thamalon smiled at her remark. He affected a casual tone and said, "What makes you think I have a secret from him?"

"Because everyone has a secret from the Sorcerer," she said. "That is his curse."

Where she had seemed at first frail and frightened, she was transformed into a daunting inquisitor. Thamalon feared that she might be the more dangerous of his hosts.

"What secret do *you* keep from him?" he countered, already regretting the bluntness of his riposte.

"Not a one," she replied. "That is *my* curse."

"Does he know you weep for his enemies?"

"Rather say, 'for his victims.' Yes, he knows. Nothing pleases him more than forcing me to call the skwalos, then to watch as he enslaves and butchers them."

"Are you his prisoner?"

"No," she said.

"Then why do you endure it?"

"Because I remember him as he was," she said, "as a boy whose heart was filled with dreams. You know my curse. My blessing is that I can still remember him as he was, and I can hope that he will become that boy again. Perhaps you will succeed where I have failed these many years."

"What possible influence could I have over—"

"You are his father, are you not?"

Her words came as no surprise to Thamalon, and more than ever he accepted the likelihood that this Sorcerer was the dark reflection of his son, just as Castle Stormweather was a vast shadow of his home. It was a simple puzzle on its face, but he still had no idea of its key.

Thamalon began to suspect that the woman was somehow reading his thoughts.

"Did he tell you so?" he asked.

"No," said Malaika. "I believe he suspects it but is not certain. You humans change so quickly over so short a time. Still, I see you in him. He has your eyes."

"He does look very much like my eldest son," admitted Thamalon. "They could be twins, but he's not Tamlin."

"Hush!" Malaika glanced urgently at the stairway and said, "Let no one hear you say that name."

"Let me guess," said Thamalon. "It is forbidden."

"It is no matter for jest. You have not yet seen what he is capable of doing to those who displease him."

"Even one he suspects could be his father?"

"*Especially* to him. The Sorcerer guards his power jealously. He keeps it secure in a vault beneath the castle."

"Keeps what secure?"

"His dreams," she said. "Once constrained, they gave him the power to hunt the skwalos and destroy all who would oppose him."

"I assure you, I have no designs on his dreams, my lady," said Thamalon. "All I wish is to return safely to my own home and my own family. What possible reason would I have to offend my host by disturbing his precious vault?"

"Because it is the gate through which he first came to our world," she said, "and opening it is the only way for you to return home."

CHAPTER 17

ALLIANCES

Escevar pinched his nostrils shut with a blood-stained handkerchief.

"I warned you not to broach the subject so soon," said Tamlin. He suppressed the laughter, but his amusement obviously showed.

"It's not funny, Deuce," said Escevar. "I think she broke it."

"Did she at least give you an answer?"

"She said if you like Brimmer Soargyl so much, you should marry him."

"Did she like any of the other prospects better?"

"She refused to hear of them. I think her words were, 'I will not be married off like so much decorative chattel.'"

"Well, we knew she wouldn't care for the idea.

Perhaps she still fancies that Steorf fellow. Give them a few more months, and one of them will tire of the other. Still, now is a much better time. Did you speak with Talbot?"

Escevar glared at him over the handkerchief.

"All right, all right," said Tamlin. "Much as I dread the thought of what offspring the great brute might produce, I'll make some time to suggest it to him myself."

"You had better invite the entire house guard to that conversation. If you can put a leash on him first, so much the better."

Tamlin sighed. He'd known his siblings wouldn't welcome the thought of socially advantageous marriages, but he'd hoped they would at least consider the idea. It wasn't as if he was unwilling to do the same to ensure the continuance of House Uskevren. Most of his peers had already produced at least an heir and more often two or three. More than ever, it was imperative to show stability, and marriages were the easiest way to reassure the rest of the Old Chauncel.

If Tamlin could establish a few new alliances along the way, so much the better.

"Here," said Escevar, who had put away the handkerchief and revealed his swollen pug nose. He laid a sheaf of parchment atop the books Tamlin had been reading. "These need your signature."

Tamlin glanced at the new documents—land leases, transportation bonds, pay releases, bills of sale—all of them were important if boring, but they irritated him all the more because they were distractions from his more crucial work.

"You already balanced these against the treasury?"

Escevar grimaced and said, "We cannot pay out more until we've received the balance of this month's income, but these are the most urgent issues."

Tamlin signed them one by one. Impatience turned his usually elegant signature into a ragged scrawl. When he was done, he reached for the sealing wax and nearly knocked over the candle.

"Here," said Escevar, removing the documents and taking away the candle. "I'll take care of that for you."

"Remind me to give you a raise," said Tamlin.

"I gave myself one this morning."

He wiggled his thumb and pointed to the Uskevren seal on Tamlin's hand.

"You're the very model of efficiency," laughed Tamlin. He removed the seal from his thumb, but he hesitated before passing it over. "You didn't actually . . . ?"

"Hopping Ilmater, Deuce! It was just a joke."

"Sorry," said Tamlin, surrendering the ring. "I guess the lack of sleep is making me jumpy."

"If you wouldn't insist on having the servants wake you so early, you might get a good night's rest."

"I know," said Tamlin, "but even with your help, there is still so much to do. Somewhere among these letters must be the clue to my father's disappearance."

"You still think he's alive somewhere?"

"Maybe," said Tamlin. "Yes. He must be. And I must find him."

"And give up all this?"

With an awkward wave of his own laden hands, Escevar indicated the stacks of documents on Tamlin's desk.

Such clutter was a new phenomenon in Tamlin's receiving room. Adjacent to his bedchamber, the place usually projected the false impression that Tamlin was meticulously tidy in his business pursuits. The fact was that he'd spent most of his life avoiding exactly such endeavors, so he rarely had any use for the chamber's exquisitely carved writing desk or its bookshelves stocked with histories of the Dalelands, Cormyr, Sembia, and all the most significant states bordering the Moonsea. Except once or twice to pretend he had been engrossed in one of the books before a surprise visit from his father, Tamlin had never read so much as the preface to what he presumed was desperately dry reading.

Those same shelves overflowed with texts on elementary trade practices and folios of laws and regulations by state. While he needed them for reference, Tamlin had been finding that he remembered far more of his father's business instructions than he could have hoped. Still, he left the day-to-day administration to Escevar, who'd paid far better attention during those tedious meetings.

Tamlin's real interest resided elsewhere. Open on his desk and on the shelves all around were tomes and librams and codexes—not mere books. These were the repository of arcane knowledge, secret lore, and chronicles whose narratives were merely a disguise for the power that lay beneath them.

"What do you hope to find in all these spooky old books?" asked Escevar.

"Perhaps some clue about magical paintings," said Tamlin.

That much was true, but he left unspoken his other reason to investigate matters arcane. Just before Escevar's arrival, Tamlin had discovered a most intriguing account of his own grandfather's startling display of magical powers in the moments before his death.

"Has Pietro replied to your invitation?"

"He begged off," said Tamlin, "but he said he would look for me at the Soargyl affair."

"Suspicious, that."

"Perhaps," said Tamlin. "Talbot likes the Malveen for this, too. Still, I find it hard to imagine Pietro conspiring to harm me. We have always gotten on so well, and he has never shown the least political inclination. And don't suggest Laskar is up to any tricks. The man would give you a straight answer to a 'Where's Elminster?' riddle."

Escevar shrugged an affirmative.

"No, I think our enemy lies elsewhere," said Tamlin, "and I think he's using magic."

"Like the Talendar did last year," suggested Escevar.

"Yes, but we put an end to that, didn't we?" Tamlin still looked back on the fight against Marance Talendar with pride.

He still kept the ugly hand axe that had proven so lucky in his several battles against conjured monsters. "That reminds me, have you heard from the guild?"

"Yes," said Escevar reluctantly. "It will cost more than the entire month's warehousing fees, but they're willing to send one of the wizards you requested. She will arrive at dusk."

"Helara?" Tamlin remembered the blond, red-robed wizard as both competent and easy on the eyes.

"No, the gadget-mage," said Escevar.

"Magdon! But she's only an apprentice."

"Apparently she graduated to journeyman wizard since you last saw her. Besides, after the trouble of your promissory note last time, they insist on payment up front, and we simply do not have enough ready coin to entice a senior—"

"All right, have done," said Tamlin, waving him down.

Having been responsible for the family treasury the past few days, he was beginning to understand why Thamalon had always been angry at his spendthrift ways. Being wealthy didn't always mean having coin on hand.

"It matters little to me which wizard they send, as long as she can shed some light on our current predicament."

"And on those dreams of yours?"

Tamlin felt a pang of guilt. He should be concentrating all his efforts on finding his parents, not the meaning of the return of his childhood dreams. Still, he couldn't resist the hope that the two events were somehow related.

"Perhaps," he admitted, "but only after she helps us determine what spells have operated in the house on and since that night. Maybe she will even find that painting, or the stolen gold—just as she helped us find those odd coins before. Probably they'll turn up in some footman's locker."

"Are you sure of that?" Escevar frowned. "Mister Cale is scrupulous in selecting the servants."

"And where is he now?" said Tamlin, stroking his chin. "What do we really know about good old Mister Pale, anyway?"

Escevar tried and failed to smother a smile.

"What?"

"You look just like your father when you do that," said Escevar, imitating the chin stroking. Usually comparing Tamlin to Thamalon was enough to provoke the younger Uskevren, but this time it only made his expression that much more severe—and that much more like his father's. "What I meant was, your father trusts Cale."

Tamlin appreciated Escevar's use of the present tense. Despite his legal assumption of his father's mantle, Tamlin still couldn't bring himself to believe his parents were dead.

"True enough," he said. "Still, the fact that he too is missing troubles me."

"Does it have to have been a servant?"

"I think it had to be someone inside the house," said Tamlin. "Barring an intruder, that leaves the servants and my siblings."

"But they're the ones who rescued you."

"Yes, yes, but something about the way the kidnappers behaved made me suspect there had been a change in plans. Or perhaps the one who hired them planned all along to rescue me, and—"

"What better alibi than to be the one who saved you?" Escevar completed his thought. "I see what you mean."

Tamlin rose to pace around the desk. Escevar finally tired of his master's restlessness and sat down beside a bust of Helemgaularn of the Seven Lightnings. Tamlin had had the statue moved into his office in hopes that the old wizard's wise eyes and fabulously braided beard would act as inspiration in his own magical investigations.

At last, realizing that Escevar wouldn't be the first to cast such black suspicions on his family, Tamlin voiced his own uncomfortable thoughts.

"It seems awfully convenient that Talbot killed the two kidnappers who ran."

"He must have known you would have a cleric question their

spirits," said Escevar. "Besides, they knew nothing of use."

"But that cleric was Larajin. She and Talbot have always been close. How do we know she told us the truth?"

"Well, she wants your support for this new shrine of hers," suggested Escevar.

Tamlin had been giving serious consideration to Larajin's petition for funds, but the heretical nature of her worship troubled him. The Sunites would resent competition of any sort, especially from a sect that reduced their deity to a human reflection of the elf goddess of love and beauty. While Thamalon and Shamur had raised their children to reject bigotry, too many of Selgaunt's rich and powerful disdained anything to do with elves.

"It's not really Larajin who worries me," Tamlin said by way of dismissing the troublesome matter, "but Talbot. I'm afraid he's always hated me."

"He's your younger brother," observed Escevar. "It's practically his duty to hate you."

"Well, if he's not behind this intrigue, then whoever is gave him yet another good reason to hate me. He thinks I've stolen his coin."

"You're sure he actually left it in the library?"

"The lack of a receipt is strange," allowed Tamlin. "Still, what a clumsy ploy that would be. It's easier to believe he's telling the truth. What really bothers me . . ."

Tamlin didn't complete the thought. He'd told no one about the mystery correspondence he found within his father's library desk. He still had the vellum sheet of code and the one letter that he'd slipped into his boot, but he had found the others missing by the time he returned to his father's library.

What troubled Tamlin about their speedy disappearance was that Talbot had been the only one to see him handling them.

"Maybe there is no enemy inside the house," said Escevar, rescuing Tamlin from his unpleasant reverie. "Even without magic, a very good thief might have slipped out with a painting, or your brother's coin."

"A hundred-pound coffer of coins?"

"Well, maybe a very strong thief. Or one with a magic bag of holding-absurdly-large-objects, like that one you almost bought from that warlock at the Black Stag a few years ago."

"I see your point," sighed Tamlin. "Still, the thief angle troubles me, too. If it had happened at any other time, I might suspect Tazi was playing a prank on Talbot or me or both of us."

For a while, he stood silently by the window. Outside, the courtyard was sheathed in ice after the previous night's hailstorm. Four of the groundsmen had finished cutting away the upper half of a tree that had broken under the weight of the ice, and they were chaining it to the harness of a draft horse that stamped and blew plumes in the cold morning air.

"Well," said Escevar, rising from his chair. "I'll leave you to your contemplations."

He made a cursory bow and slipped out into the hall.

Vox entered and shut the door behind him before taking up his place beside the fireplace. He stood there as still as a statue, his big hands planted firmly on the butt of his great axe.

Since Tamlin's escape through the secret passages, the bodyguard had refused to leave him alone in a room. There was no point in arguing with him, for Vox could pretend to be as deaf as he was mute when Tamlin gave him orders he didn't like.

Tamlin returned to his desk. He set aside the books he'd been studying and removed the coded list and the letter from his sleeve, along with a copy he'd been annotating. Since the disappearance of the other letters, he didn't trust any locked drawer to keep the clues safe.

At first glance, the letter he'd saved from the thief disappointed Tamlin. It was full of insincere thanks for a singularly dull Eventide feast that Thamalon had hosted over a month earlier. Tamlin didn't remember any of the banal entertainment to which Gorkun Baerent referred, but that was hardly surprising considering that he'd insulated himself against the dreary festivities with a little party of his own well before the guests began to arrive.

Thinking back on the event with a clear mind, however, Tamlin instantly realized that the anecdotes and remembrances must have been invented. He was sure, for instance, that he would have remembered a dozen halfling women juggling flaming pins over a bridge of ice conjured by a Thayan wizard—no matter how drunk he'd been at the time.

Obviously the letter was in code, and if Tamlin's guess was right, the vellum page held the key to breaking it.

He'd tried holding the page to a mirror, reversing each individual word, reading only the first letter of each word—only the second, and the third letters. He'd tried reading it backward and vertically, but none of those simple variations unlocked the secret of the scrambled words.

Until that morning's news that Tazi was angry with him, Tamlin had considered asking his sister for help. She was clever with such things, but he feared she would be more likely to push him out a window than help him crack a mysterious code.

Tamlin needed a break. A nice stroll might be just the thing to stir his imagination toward a solution to the problems he faced. Unfortunately, the only way to get away from all distractions was to take that walk within the walls of Stormweather Towers.

The secret passages had been calling to him ever since he'd fetched his father's master keys. Perhaps it was the return of another childhood phenomenon, like his dreams, but Tamlin felt a strong desire to retreat into those secret avenues. There he could travel without escort, without distraction, without any impediment to his whim. If he wished, he could emerge from behind the kitchen ovens and surprise a scullery maid with a pinch. If he was very quick, he could vanish as quickly as he'd appeared, as if by magic.

That's why he liked the secret passages so much, he realized. There he could travel unseen throughout the mansion, emerging when and where he wished and vanishing just as quickly.

Like a wizard.

Tamlin looked over at Vox, whose black stare had never left his master since he entered the room.

"You realize," Tamlin said, "there's really no safer place in Selgaunt than within the secret passages of my own home."

The barbarian's gaze did not waver, but his scowl deepened.

Your father is not the only one missing lately.

That was true, thought Tamlin. Both Thuribal Baerodreemer and Gorkun Baerent had vanished in the days following the disturbance at Stormweather. In both cases, the nobles had disappeared without a trace, and no amount of divination magic could conjure an explanation from their spirits.

"I'd bring you along, really. It's just that irksome 'secret' clause."

Where are you going? signed Vox.

"I just wish to walk about the house, unseen. Perhaps I'll visit the wine cellars."

You want a drink?

"No, no, I assure you. It's just so cool and dark down there. I like the quiet."

Maybe you want to sleep?

"If I wanted a nap, I wouldn't be going for a walk."

When you were little, and your nanny found you had left your bed, you were sleeping in the cellar. Remember?

"No. How absurd!" said Tamlin. Despite his objection, he half remembered being lifted from his blanket on the cool stone floor. "Why would I do such a thing?"

Try as he might, he had no clear memory of such nocturnal visits to the wine cellar. Apart from the obvious appeal of its stores, he didn't know exactly why he found the dank chambers so soothing, yet he did. Casting his mind back to childhood, he could conjure only a vague recollection of dozing among the casks.

"Dreaming eye, eh?"

Vox nodded. *It may be.*

"I think you're on to something, Vox, old boy. A stroll in the cellars is exactly what I need."

A visit to the wine cellars held many simple pleasures. One of them was an excuse to carry a real torch. There was no logical reason why Thamalon should forbid the continual flames lamps from the cellar, but Tamlin realized the Old Owl had done it to enhance the atmosphere.

He had succeeded.

A black path ran along the bare stone ceiling above the route most commonly used by Thamalon and his guests upon visiting the cellars. As Tamlin and Vox followed the trail, cobwebs fluttered in the corners—for the servants were under strict orders not to dust there.

The narrow passages between casks the size of carriages gave the place a claustrophobic air. In winter, the wine cellar felt only slightly cooler than in summer. All it needed were a few well-placed skeletons set into the walls, and one might mistake it for a catacomb.

For one who had enjoyed its stores so freely, Tamlin had seldom visited the wine cellars—at least not since he was a child. He remembered hiding among the casks while Escevar and Tazi searched for him in a game of hide-and-seek. He could also recall at least one occasion on which he'd precociously dared the pretty young daughter of one of the cooks to explore the place with him. He'd hoped to kiss her, but instead he ended up leading the hysterical lass back out of the darkness after she glimpsed a big yellow spider.

The more he struggled to recall these childhood memories, the more strange it seemed that he'd avoided the place throughout his teens and twenties. Whenever Thamalon had invited visitors on a tour, Tamlin had found a reason to beg off. On those rare occasions on which he wanted a specific vintage from the cellars, he'd never thought twice about sending Escevar or another servant to fetch it rather than entertain his guests with an excursion into the fabled depths of Thamalon's cellar.

Whether it attracted or repulsed him, the cellar had spoken to Tamlin all his life, and he had never realized it.

"Feel anything?" asked Tamlin.

Vox signaled a negative. His torch sizzled as the flame touched a patch of moisture on the low ceiling.

"Neither do I," said Tamlin. Disappointment hung heavy on his words, but he shrugged it off as he spied a familiar feature of the cellars.

Opposite an iron rack devoted to bottles imported from the farthest reaches of Faerûn was the wall of ancestors, or "the rogues gallery," as Tamlin liked to call it. From Phaldinor all the way down to Thamalon, the heads of House Uskevren and their immediate families were preserved in fresco.

Thamalon's painting was a striking likeness, but Tamlin suspected the others were less accurate. Indeed, they were rendered in the classical style that loved grace more than realism. Most of their contemporary portraits had perished in the fire that consumed the original Stormweather Towers, but on occasion Tamlin had seen a surviving etching or cameo of one of these ancestors. All of them displayed the strong Uskevren brow and nose. Those who lived long enough for their hair to turn snowy reassured Tamlin that he would likely keep his full head of hair even in his dotage—should he live long enough to reach it.

"Remember this?" Tamlin ran his fingers across the face of Roel Uskevren, his great uncle. Despite diligent but careful scrubbing, the faint image of a mustachio curled up from his lip to his cheeks.

Vox made the simple gesture for "ouch."

"Poor Escevar," said Tamlin. "I felt just awful about the beating he took for that one."

He felt worse, signed Vox. He pointed to the motto at the top of each portrait's border: *Too Bold To Hide*.

Vox had made it plain long ago that he found the tradition of a whipping boy both unfair and unmanly. In his opinion, he who made the offense must be brave enough to own up to it. Allowing another to take his place didn't speak well of the young man whose family motto praised courage and accountability.

Thankfully, Escevar hadn't served in his original function for over a decade, and he seemed no worse for the punishment. In fact, his endurance had paid off far sooner than he could have imagined. He was chief among the Uskevren family servants.

Tamlin ran his fingers along the carved letters. Something about them disturbed his thoughts. It was more than just a guilty conscience over daring Escevar to the vandalism and the hundred other offenses that had earned the servant a hiding. Nor was it his own lingering sense of uselessness since and even before his father's disappearance. He felt that he was on the verge of some revelation, but he couldn't put it into words.

Vox touched his shoulder. *What is it?*

"I'm not sure," said Tamlin. "Something about this place... about these portraits. Don't you feel a little strange down here?"

Vox thought about the question before answering, *I do now.*

"Sorry, old chum. I didn't mean to give you the ginchies, but you made me think of something . . . I've got it!"

Tamlin snatched the vellum page and the Baerent letter from his sleeve. He opened the letter and ran his finger across the words.

"Yes!" He tapped the word "bold," then "hide" a few lines farther down. Together, they appeared a total of eight times in Gorkun's note. Tamlin's excitement began to fade almost as quickly as it had arrived, for despite the unusual frequency of these words from his family motto, they revealed nothing in themselves.

Still, they marked the beginning of some pattern.

Vox touched Tamlin's arm and again signed, *What is it?*

"So far, it's proof that my father was sending secret messages to the families listed on this page," said Tamlin. "Once I've finished decoding it, I'll know whether this is a list of our friends or a roster of our foes."

CHAPTER 18

KILLING TIME

Radu caught the edge of the fountain before he could fall to the ground.

Chaney looked for a loose stone or an unexpected step in the courtyard, but he saw none on the moon-dappled ground. The only obscuring shadows were those formed by the inky bodies of the other ten ghosts, who shuffled silently in a circle around the fountain. The usually nimble Radu Malveen had merely tripped over his own feet.

"You don't look so good," said Chaney. "Maybe you should go lie down for a while."

In the four days since Radu's cruel demonstration of his ire, Chaney felt his former antagonism returning. He told himself it was because no matter what he said, Radu would do as he pleased. In truth, he just couldn't stop himself.

Radu coughed, harsh and wet.

His expression was unreadable beneath his mask, but his breath steamed above his high collar. When he tugged loose the laces and pulled the collar open, Chaney saw blood on the mask.

"Nasty cold you have there."

Radu sat on the edge of the fountain. Even on that cold Alturiak night, water cascaded gently over the lips of the successively larger basins that rose above the reservoir. The enchantment was limited to the fountain, for the trees in this interior garden were nude with three months of cold Sembian winter. Lady Stellana Toemalar was famously stingy, so Chaney wagered himself that the spells that kept the water flowing were ancient remnants of a previous Toemalar's fancy. Perhaps in its youth the magic had kept the entire garden alive throughout the bitter season.

The entire courtyard was barely wider than an alley. While other families kept entire manor houses in Selgaunt to remain closer to their businesses, the tight-fisted Toemalar saw maintaining an additional household as an extravagance. While their holdings outside of Selgaunt were considerable, they maintained only a large tallhouse within the city. In fact, the edifice consisted of seven smaller, adjacent tallhouses forming a horseshoe around the center courtyard.

Radu unclasped his mask and set it aside. He tugged his glove off with his teeth and wet his bare hand. He flicked cold drops on his shadowed face and carefully wiped the blood from the remains of his upper lip.

"I know what you're thinking," said Chaney. "You're thinking, 'Damn and dark, but I wish I'd taken that wizard up on his offer to spirit me into the house.'"

Radu spotted Chaney's rippling image in the water.

Chaney grinned at him.

"Actually, I don't blame you on that count. Magic hasn't exactly been the boon of the Malveens, now, has it? Imagine how differently your life might have turned out if not for black sorcery."

Radu feigned interest in his toilet. He smoothed back his long, black hair.

"Seriously, imagine it," said Chaney. "Think of what might have been had you got rid of Stannis years earlier."

The remark jolted Radu into looking up where Chaney's face should be. Moonlight reflected off the sharp, bright fragments of the bone blade that still jutted from his cheek and brow.

"You know nothing."

"No?" said Chaney. "Still, there's no harm in speculating. What if you had managed to restore the family wealth? What if you had never invited that mad pack of wolves into your old house? Do you think you would be killing old women for gold now?"

"Be quiet, or else—"

"Ah!" said Chaney. "That's the thing, you see. I've been giving your 'or else' some thought. No matter what I do or say, you're still killing the innocent."

"Not the innocent," said Radu. "Not unless you disobey me."

"Yes, yes. That worked on me before, but not again. I'm already dead. I'm a dark and empty ghost, by Kelemvor! What use is pity to me? Why should I feel any worse when you murder some useless boy than when you kill the grand dame of the Toemalar? Nothing I do will stop you from killing *someone*."

"Perhaps next time I will choose a target more dear to you. Perhaps a friend."

"I would like to see you try that," said Chaney. "The only friend I care about is the one man we both know can defeat you—just like he did before."

"He did not defeat—"

" 'I've got one hand,' " said Chaney, waving at Radu through the fountain. " 'Not to mention this fashionable mask. I meet clients in the sewers because I enjoy the ambience, and if I dare not let anyone know I'm alive, it's because I enjoy the air of mystery.' "

Radu sat silently. At first, Chaney thought he was seething with anger, then he saw that the man's body was perfectly relaxed. He looked so still that for a moment Chaney thought he might have died, then he saw the faint plumes of breath appear before the ragged holes that were once his nostrils.

"Sorry, my old fellow. My point is not simply to mock you—though that has been a great comfort to me—it's to help you."

Radu stared at Chaney's reflection.

"I know, I know, I'm too kind. Forgiving. Paragon of mercy and all that. Actually, it's more a matter of necessity. You see, I think your injury has affected your ability to reason. Do you think part of that knife got down into your brain, perhaps?"

"What?"

"You must admit, the choices you've made these past months have been questionable to say the least. How do you expect to achieve the things you desire this way?"

"What do you know of my desires?"

"Stop me when I go wrong. You want your crazy brother Pietro to stay clear of the Hulorn and all the inter-family plotting among the Old Chauncel. Instead, you would like him to help big brother Laskar with the family business—and preferably not the kind of family business you and the late, unlamented Stannis were conducting. You would much rather they be legitimate, unimpeachable . . . honorable."

Chaney paused to watch Radu's expression. Unfortunately, he'd lowered his face once more into the shadows.

"You have done some damned wicked things, Malveen. There's little doubt you're bound to crawl through steaming dung in the Barrens of Doom and Despair when you die, but the last thing you want to do is drag the rest of your family down there with you. By the way, I notice you haven't stopped me yet."

Radu didn't reply. His gaze shifted from Chaney's reflection to his own. It was only a black shape, but the ragged edges of his right cheek marred his silhouette. When he spoke at last, it was in a clear, soft voice.

"What do you know about me?"

"I saw your nasty little dungeon," said Chaney. "I saw those pathetic wretches you murdered for your pleasure."

"They were warriors. Each of them had a chance to defeat me."

"After starving for how long under the care of that wretched eel you called a brother?"

"They were recovering their strength befo—"

Radu coughed again. As the spasm subsided, he lifted his mask, turned away, and spat something red.

"Pretty," observed Chaney.

Radu wiped his shadow-shrouded mouth with his sleeve. He turned back toward Chaney's reflection.

"You think you know something of the city because you slept in the gutters for a few nights," said Radu. "You have never seen its heart."

"Is this where you tell me how cruel Stellana Toemalar once had a girl beaten for bringing her cold tea? Or perhaps that you butchered Thuribal Baerodreemer because he irritated you, but that's all right because he tortures house pets? Bugger all that. It doesn't matter who you kill or what kind of people they are. You kill for sport. You kill for coin. The gods built whole worlds of pain for people like you."

"Have you considered the likelihood that your soul goes where mine does?"

"Indeed I have," said Chaney. "The way I see it, there are two possibilities. One, our souls go their separate ways when you die. That's the one I prefer, naturally. Two, we go screaming down into the Abyss together. That one is not so appealing."

Radu made a harsh little sound. It was like a laugh, only with a little spray of blood.

"So you hope to persuade me of my evil ways and set me on the path to redemption?"

"How callow do you think I am?" Chaney replied. "Great gods, no. You're a black-hearted beggar without the slightest hope of salvation. I have no doubt of that."

"Then what are you trying to accomplish with this insipid talk?"

"Maybe I would like to see Laskar rid of you. He never did me any harm, and I hate to see a decent bloke burdened with the Malveen family curse. That's you, by the way—a curse on all those you love." Chaney watched for some sign that his words had stung Radu, but he saw none. "Or maybe I'm just sick of having no one else to talk to. You're a rotten conversationalist. No doubt you've heard that before."

"Once or twice," said Radu.

Chaney nearly choked in surprise. For an instant he thought Radu had made a joke, then he realized that the long solitude must have affected Radu as well as him, and the man had simply answered out of habit—with no trace of irony.

"It seems to me you should reconsider your present course. Your problem has never been gold. It's reputation. Now that you've scared Pietro into obeying Laskar, the only lingering blot on the family honor is you, my friend. I know it's too much to ask that you fall on your sword, but you should at least leave Selgaunt. If you need a little boost of energy before you go, I don't think many would miss Drakkar, or Mad Andy."

"We made a bargain," said Radu.

"A deal with a couple of murderous maniacs hardly counts. To them, you're nothing more than another monster they conjure for their sick little games. Where's the honor in that?"

"You know nothing of honor."

"Well, I know that you're dying," said Chaney.

"Nonsense."

"Oh? Then have we been sitting here because you so enjoy my company or because you wanted to enjoy the lovely flowers? You're unraveling, old son, and it's getting faster with each killing. You can't tell me you haven't noticed."

Radu put the glove in his teeth and slipped it back on his

hand. He replaced the mask with its steel cap and raised the collar of his cloak above his chin.

"If you murder this woman tonight, you'll only hasten your own demise."

Radu rose, weak but steady as he walked away from the fountain.

"Then to the Hells with me," he said. "To the Nine Hells with us both."

Twenty minutes later, Radu paced back and forth before an open window in the bedchamber of the late Stellana Toemalar. Apart from the moonlight, the room was dark.

Chaney stood before a wide vanity mirror. Behind him, almost indistinguishable from the gloom, stood the shadows of Radu's other victims. The beak-nosed Stellana Toemalar had joined them, as had the chambermaid with the unfortunate duty of sleeping at the foot of her mistress's bed that night.

The shades kept their eyes on the floor, but Chaney heard their ghostly voices and knew why they clustered behind him instead of their killer. He felt a cold trickle of guilt running down the hollow interior of his ethereal stomach.

He nearly leaped when a bat suddenly flapped into the room.

The creature alighted on the edge of the bed. As Radu and Chaney watched, it quickly grew tall and shifted shape, transforming into a familiar human form. After a few seconds, Drakkar sat on the edge of Stellana's disheveled bed. He tapped the foot of his staff on the floor, and faint red light began radiating from its head.

He touched the bloodstain on the pillow with the tip of his middle finger, and he wiped his finger on the sheets.

"I hope the old harridan was not too much trouble," he said. "What a fierce one she was, especially to the gutterkin who played too close to the walls. The children of Selgaunt would thank you, if they only knew."

"Ask him why he wanted her killed," said Chaney.

He tried not to think about the phantoms at his back. Their urgent moaning felt like a pressing need to urinate.

Radu ignored him.

"Don't you want to know the reason why you're killing these people?" Chaney asked.

"No," snapped Radu.

"I beg your pardon?" Drakkar said.

He rose from the bed, holding his thorny staff before his body. He kept his distance from Radu and glanced around the room suspiciously.

"Do you have a partner?"

Radu drew a long breath, and Chaney could practically feel the heat of his ire. It pleased him to think he'd gotten under the man's skin, even as he was flush with power.

"I work alone," said Radu.

Drakkar looked unconvinced.

"Have you found the letters, then?"

"I told you—" began Radu.

"I know, I know," said Drakkar, waving down Radu's words. "You are not our fetch. No, you are far more valuable than that. Part of that value lies in our trusting your discretion."

"He's calling you a liar, you realize," said Chaney.

Radu didn't rise to the bait. Instead, he merely inclined his head.

"Are you sure there is no one else here with us?"

Drakkar withdrew a forked twig from a pocket inside his robe. He plucked a thorn from the head of his staff and held the two objects between his thumb and little finger.

Radu parted his cloak with his stony right hand, exposing the hilt of his blade. He made no move to draw the sword, but Drakkar noted the gesture.

"Have no fear," he said. "I cast no enchantment on you. It is merely a spell to locate that which I seek."

"He's impugning your honor, man! How can you let such an insult pass unanswered?"

Chaney laughed, as much at his futile attempt to bait Radu as at the man's earlier involuntary outburst. Chaney wouldn't trick him again any time soon, but he'd scored a coup—and Radu knew it.

Drakkar set his staff against the bedpost and pulled a folded letter from his robe. He held it with the broken seal facing upward, then he rubbed the thorn and twig together above it while intoning an arcane phrase.

Chaney moved closer to the wizard and looked down at the seal. It was the horse-at-anchor, emblem of the Uskevren.

The twig wriggled between Drakkar's fingers. At first it looked as though the wizard was twisting it. Soon Chaney saw that it had a mind of its own, turning this way and that as it sought some desired object.

Drakkar followed its urging. He took three steps across the room and turned toward the fireplace. He walked closer, turned aside a step, and turned back, frowning at the twig.

"How could she be so careless?" Drakkar asked.

He reached toward an ivory coffer upon the mantle, then thought better of it and withdrew his hand.

Instead, he bit off one of the thorns and crushed it in his teeth. He blew a whispered word and a sparkling red cone of glittering dust out upon the mantle. As the motes gradually vanished from sight, Drakkar smiled as though he saw something the others didn't.

"Not bad," he commented.

He cast a third spell, this time plucking a thorn and casting it at the mantle with a few words of power. Chaney saw a rippling in the air, as if Drakkar's thorn had been a stone thrown into a still pool.

Drakkar casually flipped open the lid of the coffer and peered inside. He turned it over to spill a mass of jewelry onto the floor. He made a satisfied grunt as he set the coffer aside and felt the mantle where the box had been.

His fingers traced simple shapes against the stone, and Chaney knew he was feeling for some secret catch. On a whim, he reached out and touched the stone with his own ethereal hand.

He didn't feel it so much as sense its shape as his fingers passed through the surface of the stone. He pushed them into the solid surface and wiggled them in what he sensed was a hollow chamber beneath.

Drakkar's searching fingers passed through Chaney's forearm. The wizard started, briefly withdrawing his hands, then he looked around and shuddered.

"Hmm."

Chaney saw that Radu had also noticed the wizard's surprise.

Drakkar resumed his search.

"I wonder . . ." said Chaney.

He poked a finger through Drakkar's shoulder. The trick had had no effect the last time he tried it, but maybe he'd been doing it wrong.

"Take . . . that . . . you . . . unctuous . . . little . . . pervert!"

He punctuated each word with a jab to Drakkar's shoulder. He looked back to grin at Radu, who cocked his head in a silent threat.

Chaney kept prodding the wizard's shoulder.

"Ah!" exclaimed Drakkar.

Chaney triumphed for an instant before he realized that Drakkar had found the loose tile in the mantle. It slid aside to reveal a pin. Drakkar pressed the pin, then pushed the tile the rest of the way aside.

In the hollow cavity of the fireplace mantle was a stack of folded vellum. As Drakkar removed the documents, Chaney saw the Uskevren seal on the first folded letter.

"Ah, the late Thamalon Uskevren," mused Drakkar. "What trouble his schemes have wrought."

As the wizard rifled through the rest, Chaney saw that not all of the correspondence was from the Uskevren. He also noticed the bloodbeak insignia of the Talendar, the cockatrice of the Karns, and the three watchful eyes of House Foxmantle.

"Must be quite a party."

Chaney whistled to mask his concern. While he had not been on good terms with his parents since he was a boy, he hoped neither of them would be scheduled to receive a visit from Radu Malveen.

"Someone must be angry that he didn't receive an invitation," the ghost added.

"Yes," said Drakkar as he skimmed the contents of one of the letters. "Just as I thought!"

"What is it?" asked Radu.

Drakkar smiled slyly. Chaney recognized that look and knew the wizard was glad to have piqued the assassin's curiosity.

"To us, it is evidence of treason," said Drakkar. "To you, it is security of employment."

"How does it feel to be the lackey of a lackey, Malveen?" asked Chaney.

The taunt didn't even register on Radu. His eyes were fixed on the sheaf of letters and their seals.

Drakkar saw the object of Radu's interest. He chuckled in a fair imitation of warmth.

"Whom shall we visit next?" he asked, as he shuffled through the letters.

"Done," he said, flipping past the horse-at-anchor.

"Done," he dispensed with the Baerent flame.

"No need," he said as he placed the letter with the Talendar crest to the back. "Ah, no matter. It is a decision my patron will be sure to make soon."

Drakkar began to stuff the letters inside his robe, but Radu reached for them. The wizard anticipated the action and stepped away.

"Tut, tut, my good fellow. What is the matter? Perhaps you regret not agreeing to fetch them yourself? Then you might have pored over them at your leisure. Is there a name in here that interests you?"

Radu regained his composure and said, "No."

"That is well," said Drakkar. He secured the letters beneath his robe and strolled casually to the window. Once there, he extinguished the light on his staff and turned to face Radu. "We are friends, so I will tell you something to set your mind at ease. I have found the names of nine noble Houses in these treasonous letters. Three of them have already been punished. That leaves six more visits for you to make, six more fortunes for you to receive, not to mention the favor of my master, whose memory of friends is twice as long as his memory of his enemies."

"That's because he kills his enemies, Malveen," said Chaney. "Don't listen to him."

"Even a man like you," continued Drakkar, "might have qualms about striking against certain old families of Selgaunt. Perhaps there is one that you favor, hmm? Perhaps one that has been unduly punished for old, forgotten crimes.

"To be plain," said the wizard, "the Malveen crest does not appear on any of these letters. Even should one appear, I think, it could be overlooked."

Drakkar twirled his staff as he watched Radu's masked face for any sign. There was none to see, but the wizard nodded anyway.

"Be assured, my anonymous friend, that we can safeguard your secrets . . . just as long as you continue to keep ours."

CHAPTER 19

TRAITOR

"**M**y Lord Uskevren," said Escevar from the doorway. He cleared his throat for the second time.

"Wait a moment," said Tamlin. "Wait! Wait . . . Oh, bother."

Tamlin's concentration teetered when he first heard the door open, and he struggled to remain focused on the puzzle before him even through the interruption. Unfortunately, his thoughts were balanced on a most precarious problem, and at last they fell into complete disarray.

For hours he'd been annotating a copy of the Baerent letter, by turns transposing words and individual characters. The clue of the family motto had proven true, but it was only a means of organizing the rest of the cipher. Of that much he was certain.

The rest remained guesswork and supposition, but Tamlin had a working theory. Based on the names mentioned in the seemingly innocuous letter and the frequency with which usually staid nobles made trifling jests and relayed dull anecdotes about their pets, Tamlin was beginning to believe his father was gathering support for some political action.

If remarks involving a dog meant agreement and those about cats or foxes meant opposition or neutrality, then Gorkun Baerent at least was conspiring in alliance with Thamalon.

That made sense to Tamlin, because Gorkun disappeared under similarly mysterious circumstances. There had been no reports of thunder in Sundolphin House, where the head of the family had been last seen. However, Dolly reported hearing from the domestics' grapevine that Gorkun had recently received a gift the size of a painting.

Tamlin would have paid good coin to know the identity of the artist.

Unfortunately, Stellana Toemalar, whom Gorkun reported as telling a rather dry fable about a fox and a hen, was famously uninterested in art in general and that of Stannis Malveen in particular. Even assuming Thamalon's enemies were attacking those loyal to his plan, why eliminate Stellana if she weren't clearly in the loyal camp?

The more difficult problem came with Thuribal Baerodreemer. The man was simply not mentioned in Gorkun's missive. Either his death was unrelated to the list, or the letter simply didn't mention every member of the scheme.

The most intriguing element was the mention of Presker Talendar boasting of his new hunting dogs. That made sense only if he'd feigned alliance, only to turn on the others. The man had done worse things to the Uskevren in the past, so that seeming discrepancy only strengthened Tamlin's confidence in his developing theory.

Tamlin needed to see more of the letters before he could finish solving their riddle.

"What is it now?" he asked.

Realizing how testy he sounded, he threw a weak smile after the words by way of apology.

"The mage has finished preparing her devices," replied Escevar. Vox stood behind him, having risen from his chair just inside the door. "She awaits your pleasure."

"I thought she was meant to arrive at dusk."

"It is an hour and a half past, my lord."

Escevar smiled as he intoned the formal address, but the playful glint in his eye dispelled any notion of disrespect. Obviously, he enjoyed playing first-among-servants to a master who'd inherited power before his time. He'd already donned the dark livery of butler, though he cut a distinctly different figure than had the tall and gaunt Erevis Cale before him.

"Ah, very well then," Tamlin replied. He clapped his ink-stained hands, gathered up the coded list, the Baerent letter, and all his notes into a calfskin portfolio, and tucked it under his arm. "Let us go down at once."

They hurried across the east wing and into the library.

The servants had cleared the area around Thamalon's desk. On its surface rested a fantastic contraption resembling a metronome smothered in a collapsed house of gold foil cards over which someone had sprinkled the contents of a six-year-old boy's vacation treasure chest. Tamlin spied an owl's skull and a cork—two fetishes he'd seen on the previous contraption Magdon had devised for him.

The wizard stood behind her work. She had changed considerably in the time since Tamlin had first met her. She was no taller than Escevar, but she'd shed a stone or two in weight. She was still no nymph, but the word "ample" was more accurate than "chunky." Her hair and skin were both as white as chalk, with a faint pink blush at her lips, nostrils, and eyelids. Instead of her apprentice robes, she wore a long coat of deep burgundy. It had enough pockets to store the entire contents of an alchemist's shop.

She bowed as Tamlin approached and said, "My Lord Uskevren."

He nodded back at her and said, "Escevar has told you of my needs?"

"He has," she said with a brief glance at the butler.

For an instant, Tamlin imagined some conspiratorial message pass between their eyes. He wondered briefly whether she was flirting with Escevar.

Well, he thought. Good for him if so.

"You wish to detect any lingering indication of powerful magic," she said. "Specifically, teleportation spells."

"Yes," agreed Tamlin. "That's my principal interest. However, I have recently noticed certain . . . *manifestations* that seem to indicate I might have some sorcerous abilities of my own."

Magdon grimaced at his words, as if expecting but dreading them.

"My lord," she said, "I inquired of the archives before leaving the guild hall. You have been tested before, both for proficiency at wizardry and innate talent."

"Yes, yes," said Tamlin. "I realize this. It's just that these dreams I have been having suggest otherwise, and on one occasion I seemed to produce some sort of lightning effect while fighting off a darkenbeast."

Magdon nodded, as if she'd heard all that before.

"Fortunately," she said, "we can perform both tests with this array. Still, I must caution you against investing too much hope in success. The proctors at the guild have never yet failed to detect signs of the natural Art."

"Do they often try again after rejecting a candidate?"

"Well . . ." said Magdon.

"There it is, then," said Tamlin. "We will be the pioneers who confirm or refute their reputation. Exciting prospect, isn't it?"

"Very exciting, my lord," Magdon said dryly.

To her credit, she didn't roll her eyes. Tamlin thought she must have had some experience in the past year indulging the whims of wealthy but untalented nobles.

"What do I do, then?" he asked.

"First, set aside any enchanted items you're wearing. Keep them well away from the desk. I will activate the array and ask you to approach."

Tamlin nodded, handing over his rings and charms along with the portfolio to Escevar, who remained near the library door with Vox.

Magdon uttered a few words and tapped the inverted pendulum at the heart of her magical construction. The dozens of paper-thin gold sheets rose to form an irregular sphere around the center post. At every vertex between them hovered some fetish object: a bit of mirror, a wad of tar, a dog's tooth, a tiny doll made of hair.

On the side where Magdon stood, a deep indentation formed in the sphere. As she walked away from the device, the dent bulged back outward, forming a perfect sphere once she was more than ten feet distant.

"Now approach the sphere," she said.

Tamlin did as she bade, slowly walking forward. With each step, his imagination wrestled with his reason. His mind said it was preposterous to think he had some dormant talent for the Art. His heart told him there was no other possibility, for his dreams were undeniably true visions.

Three steps away from the globe, Tamlin realized he was holding his breath. The golden ball remained perfectly spherical. When he released his breath, the leaves fluttered briefly but returned to their places.

"Closer," said Magdon.

The encouragement in her voice sounded genuine, but Tamlin's hopes had already begun to fade.

He took another step and saw no change in the globe. He looked back at Vox and Escevar. The big man was also holding his breath, and Escevar looked as anxious as a mother watching her child approach a scorpion.

"You can do it, Deuce," he said. "I mean, my lord."

Tamlin realized then how he must look, and he felt a blush

of shame rise to his cheeks. He quickly took the last two steps and stood inches from the magical globe.

The foil leaves shuddered in the faint breeze his approach created, but they soon resumed their positions.

The result was obvious even to him. There was nothing remotely magical about Tamlin Uskevren.

"Sorry," he said. He refused to look back at the disappointment he knew had crossed Vox's face. He suspected Escevar was suppressing a smirk, and he had little use for that, either. "I know how ridiculous I've been about this. Let's pretend it never happened and turn to the serious matters at hand."

"Aye, my lord," said Magdon. She returned to her contraption and brushed its base with a feather. "This is a more complex version of the compass spell I made for you last time. Instead of harmonizing with an object, it seeks out sympathetic patterns in the Weave, the very fabric of magic."

Tamlin remembered the terms from his childhood lessons, even though they had been of no practical use to him since then. He tried not to feel envious as he watched Magdon sculpt her creation with a few graceful gestures of her white hands. At her unspoken command, the foil globe refigured itself into the shape of a cone rotating smoothly on its invisible axis. It rose to float independently of its base.

"You may take your things back," she said. "This spell will seek only the residue of the most powerful magic, and only that derived from translocation spells."

Tamlin watched as the gadget-mage spoke the words of spellcraft and sprinkled what looked like amber dust over the hovering cone.

Magdon completed her evocation with the command, "Seek!"

The cone flexed and turned like a hound's snout seeking the spoor of its prey. It rotated halfway around the library before darting to a point only a few feet from its original position. Orange light emanated from the space within the floating gold leaves, and the radiance burst into a ragged cloud with

206 • Dave Gross

trailing tendrils. Rather than dissipating, the magical light remained in place about three feet above the floor.

"There," said Magdon. "The marker shows that there was definitely some sort of translocation event at that point, and recently."

The cloud looked to Tamlin like the afterimage that formed on one's eye after looking directly at a bolt of lightning. Even as he stared at it, another burst of light created a second cloud over the first.

The quivering pointer floated a few feet toward the desk. Its radiance burst again, creating a third lingering mark in the air.

"That means three separate events," said Magdon. "Judging from their consistent size and brightness, I'd say they all occurred within the period of an hour or two."

"Father, Mother, and Mister Cale," replied Tamlin. "But where did it take them?"

"The spell is not capable of showing us . . ."

Magdon's words trailed off as she watched the spinning cone begin to turn on its vertical axis. Its frail leaves began to flutter, its fetish objects rattling in an unseen turbulence.

"What is it?" demanded Tamlin.

"There must have been more than one powerful translocation spell connected to that spot," said the mage. "It is still seeking."

Her magical compass point trembled as its rotation came to a stop. It pointed down at the floor at an angle, then shot downward as quickly as a diving sparrow. The compass's fragile body smashed itself flat upon the floor, sending a spray of shattered glass, ceramic, and bone in all directions.

"Where was it pointing?" asked Tamlin. "Did anyone mark the spot?"

"No need," said Magdon. "Look there."

From each of the three cloudy markers emanated a ragged beam of light. All of them slanted down, through the floor, at the same incline.

Down, toward the center of Stormweather Towers.

"Follow me!" called Tamlin.

He rushed out of the library and sprinted toward the grand stairs. He took the steps three at a time and slid across the polished marble floor of the foyer before recovering his footing enough to run east toward the feast hall.

"There!" he said.

A pair of porters had almost dropped their burden as they stared at the three glowing beams descending from the ceiling, passing through the cabinet they carried, and disappearing into the wall beside them.

"Out of the way!" cried Tamlin.

He shoved one of the men aside to get through the door the porter was blocking.

Vox finally caught up with his errant master, and Escevar and Magdon appeared behind him, panting.

"It goes through to the kitchen," Tamlin said, leading the way.

The kitchen staff stood against the farthest walls, their gazes locked on the magical beams that had suddenly appeared in their midst. The three lines passed through the huge central oven and into the floor below.

"The cellars," said Tamlin.

They crossed through the pantries to the cellar stairs, pausing only to light torches before plunging into the dark corridors below.

"I don't see anything," complained Escevar.

"Keep looking," urged Tamlin.

He tried to estimate the angle of the beams in comparison with the relative positions of the cellars and the kitchen. Unless he was grossly mistaken, they should have arrived . . .

"Here!" called Magdon. "Under here."

Tamlin crouched to peer beneath an enormous empty cask that Thamalon kept only for show. Over the years, visitors to his cellars had seared their names into its face with a brand. It was the Old Owl's version of a guest book.

Beneath the gigantic barrel, the beams of light passed through it and down into the ground below.

"The source of the spell must be below this room," said Magdon. "What's down there?"

"Nothing but the foundation," said Tamlin.

He thought about the secret passages in Stormweather Towers and wondered whether or not Thamalon had shown him everything after all. He resented the idea that his father might have considered him unworthy of his full trust—despite the fact that Tamlin knew how often he'd disappointed the Old Owl—but then another thought rescued him from those futile recriminations.

The house was built on the foundation of the original Stormweather Towers.

Even if the Old Owl had kept no secrets from Tamlin, who was to say that Thamalon had known all of Aldimar's secrets? Was Thamalon not just as much a disappointment to his own father, who'd expected the elder Perivel to lead the family after his untimely death?

"Summon the gardeners," said Tamlin. "Have them bring their picks and shovels. I want to see what lies beneath these stones."

The magical light of Magdon's spell had already faded before the gardeners arrived with their tools. The men took one look at the floor and reported it would take hours just to pry up enough stone to make room for digging. Tamlin dashed their hopes of postponing his orders commanding them to fetch help from the stables. He would have set the entire house guard to digging if there had been enough room in the cellar.

Next, he sent Escevar to escort Magdon back to the library, where she could retrieve the remnants of her magical contraption and return to the guildhall. The mage made no attempt to disguise her curiosity about what lay beneath the wine cellar, but Tamlin had already decided that he would keep any discovery a family matter until he knew he needed more help from the wizards.

Soon, the cellar rang with the sound of picks on limestone. Tamlin watched anxiously as the men cracked apart the floor and pulled it away in chunks.

This will take time, signed Vox.

"I know," said Tamlin. "I know. Still, there's nothing else for me to do except . . . Where's my portfolio?"

He realized he hadn't taken the slipcase with his father's correspondence and his notes on the cipher with him during the excitement of Magdon's spell. He must have left it in the library.

"Wait here," said Tamlin. He looked to see that the men were all engrossed in their work before stepping behind a large cask and pressing the stone that revealed a latch to the secret door. The secret paths of Stormweather Towers reached even there, below the ground floor.

Vox glowered at his master. He knew he wasn't welcome in the secret passages, and he obviously hated letting Tamlin out of his sight.

"Don't fret, you mother hen," said Tamlin. "I'll be right back, and none will know I've left, so long as you stand here."

Vox shook his head in a weary and practiced expression of exasperation.

Tamlin closed the secret door behind him and found the spiral stairway that led directly to the second story. From there it was two turns and a pair of secret doors to the library. When he arrived, he checked the peephole before entering.

Magdon was the room's only occupant. She knelt on the floor, gathering the crushed foil of her magic-detecting apparatus.

Tamlin entered the library and closed the door silently. He moved well away from the secret door before coughing to avoid startling the wizard. It hadn't happened to him, but he would never forget the story of the three days Uldir Foxmantle lived as a Chultan tree frog after surprising his house mage in his study.

"My lord Uskevren," said Magdon.

The albino tried to rise and bow at the same time, managing to perform neither gesture very well. Tamlin remembered that his first assumption upon meeting Magdon and her sister was that they were peasant girls indentured to the wizards' guild.

You can take the girl out of the country, he thought.

"Oh, do not let me disturb you," he said, looking around for the documents he'd left. "Where's the portfolio I left here?"

Magdon replied, "My lord, I could not say."

"Could not," said Tamlin, feeling a sudden rush of anger, "or would not?"

Forgetting the danger of frightening a wizard, he stalked toward her. He paused before closing the distance and veered toward her satchel of materials on his father's desk. A glance told him there were no pages inside. Still, he knew a mage could render things smaller, or transport them with a spell.

"My lord, I promise you," she protested. "I took nothing."

"Who else was in here with you?"

"Only your man, Escevar," she said.

Relief washed over him then, followed by a sharp pang of chagrin.

"I beg your pardon, mistress. I hope you can forgive my intolerably poor temper. Since my father's disappearance, my manners have suffered. Escevar must be looking for me downstairs even now."

"Yes, my lord."

Tamlin was inclined to stay and apologize further—one never knew when one might need a favor from the wizards—yet he was anxious to recover his one tangible clue to his father's disappearance. He sketched a courtly bow, a gesture far out of proportion to Magdon's station, and turned to leave.

"My lord?"

"Yes?"

"It is I who owes an apology," she said. "I have deceived you."

Dark and empty, thought Tamlin. Here it comes, and me without so much as a smatchet.

While he was far more proficient with a long sword, Tamlin longed for his lucky axe. The weapon had saved him from a rampaging troll. Perhaps it would help him cut down the wizard before she transmuted him into something wretched.

Rather than raise her hands to conjure something out of the empty air, Magdon said, "The spell I cast for you was a ruse. There is no spell to show whether a person has magical potential."

"What?" said Tamlin. "Why would you do such a thing?"

"He said it would relieve your mind," said Magdon.

"Who?"

"Your man, Escevar. He said you were fraught with worry, and performing that charade might help you sleep better."

"That idiot," said Tamlin. "Even if his intentions were benign, how dare he . . . Wait a second. Do you mean to tell me that I am even now digging up a perfectly good wine cellar because of a mummer's trick?"

"Oh, no, my lord. That spell was genuine. I would not accept payment for a mere ruse. As things stand, I should return my entire fee. If you wish to complain to my mistress Helara, it would be only fair."

She removed a pair of coin purses from her satchel. Tamlin noted that they must contain at least twice as many coins as she had demanded for her services.

"We shall speak of this another time," said Tamlin. "Until then, I hope your penance shall take the form of the utmost discretion about this evening's events."

"Certainly, my lord."

"And keep the gold," he said. "One day I may come to you for a service."

She made a deep curtsy and kept her eyes on the floor as he turned and left the room.

Forgetting his promise to Vox, Tamlin dashed down the steps, retracing his earlier path when following the beams of light from Magdon's spell.

He paused in the grand foyer and asked the doormen, "Have you seen my butler?"

"Yes, my lord," replied one of the men. He stood straight at attention. "He went to summon a carriage for the visiting mage."

"How long ago?"

The guard frowned and said, "At least ten minutes ago, my lord."

"Dark!" shouted Tamlin. "Find him at once. Bring him back here, and make sure he has a leather portfolio with him. No one may look inside it but me. Do you understand?"

The guards snapped perfect salutes.

"Send a double guard to take your place here," Tamlin added, then spun on his heel and ran down to the cellar.

Vox nearly leaped at the sight of his master returning from a path other than the secret passage. Before he could sign a complaint, he saw the deep scowl on Tamlin's face.

"Bad news, Vox," he said. "We've found our traitor."

CHAPTER 20

THE INEFFABLE VAULT

I'm getting too old for this.

The thought kept returning to Thamalon's mind like some refrain from one of the operas Shamur adored so much. He hoped his predicament would turn out better than it did for the characters whose tragedies were sung in the amphitheater of the Hulorn's Hunting Garden.

He pressed his ear against the door and listened— yet again—for any sounds of inhabitants in the room beyond. He'd been doing so all morning at dozens of secret doors, and each time he heard voices or footsteps nearby, his heart skipped a beat.

It was only a matter of time before he blundered into the wrong room and revealed that he'd been skulking through the Sorcerer's no-longer-completely-secret passages.

Apart from the incredible difference in scale, the hidden corridors of Castle Stormweather were remarkably similar to those in Stormweather Towers. They weren't exactly the same, but they reinforced Thamalon's notion that this grand bastion and his own relatively modest manor home were fraternal if not identical twins.

How he could accept those similarities and deny the likely relationship between the Sorcerer and his son, Thamalon did not know. Nor did he care to examine the question too closely. It was a matter of faith and intuition, and Thamalon preferred to leave it that way.

Thamalon heard nothing beyond the door. He estimated that he'd wound his way through the servants' quarters and was near a kitchen or one of the lesser feasting halls. He sniffed for some smell of roasting meat or baking bread, but either he'd misjudged his direction or else the secret door sealed too tightly to allow odors to pass through.

He searched briefly for a sliding panel that might reveal a peephole. There were many such devices in his Stormweather, some of which had proven quite useful in spying on those who awaited his arrival before a trade meeting. Thamalon felt utterly no guilt in the subterfuge, which he assumed his competitors also employed. To his way of thinking, anyone so foolish as to discuss trade secrets in his rival's home deserved what he got.

Unfortunately, Thamalon had found precious few spy holes in the monstrous reflection of Stormweather Towers. Perhaps they were simply impractical in walls more often constructed of granite than of wood. Or maybe, Thamalon thought, the Sorcerer had other means of spying on his guests.

Thamalon felt exposed. He wondered whether the Sorcerer was even then observing his guest's ostensibly clandestine explorations.

He put his faith in the hope that the Sorcerer's resumption of his hunt would keep him sufficiently distracted throughout the afternoon. The man had already brought down two of the great skwalos, but Thamalon's dwarf friends had told him to expect no fewer than six catches before the Sorcerer gave up his slaughter. If catching them was as demanding as the contest Thamalon had witnessed the night before, he felt reasonably sure the distraction would prevent the Sorcerer from scrying through a basin like the one Lady Malaika used to observe his hunting.

Satisfied that the room beyond was unoccupied, Thamalon raised the brass latch and eased the door open a few inches. The room was bare of furnishings, and Thamalon realized it was a continuance of the secret corridors of Castle Stormweather. Inside he found two more latched doorways and a spiral staircase descending below the ground floor.

At last, Thamalon thought.

He'd been hunting for a passage down to the wine cellars, and to the chamber below.

The Ineffable Vault.

He'd not yet decided what to do when he reached the forbidden chamber. He'd questioned Lady Malaika on its function, but she claimed to know its powers only because the Sorcerer had told her of them long ago, when they were young and shared all their secrets. She had no first-hand knowledge, and no further advice except to caution Thamalon against detection.

That was superfluous advice.

The stairs led to another chamber on what Thamalon judged must be the level of the cellars. The Vault was at least another twenty feet down, yet the stairs descended no farther. He found another door, listened for voices, and carefully went through.

Thus he continued through the cellar level of the castle until at last he heard the sound of human voices.

Screaming.

His first instinct was to retreat. After his initial panic, Thamalon realized that there were other kinds of places traditionally lodged underground. Aside from treasure vaults and wine cellars, after all, there were dungeons.

The Stormweather in which he'd grown up had included such a place. Its six cold cells were reserved for drunks and brawlers among his father's guard. Thamalon smiled at the memory of his own brother's brief incarceration in the dungeon. Perivel had staggered down to the prison to impress a couple of wenches he'd lured home. The big man was drunker than he realized, for the doxies locked him into one of the cells and demanded he pay bail to be released. Once he handed over the last of his coin, the women blew him a pair of kisses before running back out to spend their new bounty. Luckily for Perivel, Thamalon had been the first to hear his hoarse bellowing the following evening. Had their father discovered how easily his eldest son had allowed himself to be tricked, he might have left him in the cell for another tenday.

When Thamalon rebuilt Stormweather Towers years after the rest of the Old Chauncel razed the original, he saw no reason to restore the dungeon. Any offense worthy of confinement called for dismissal, in his opinion. Anything less could be left to the discretion of the captain of the guard.

Thamalon never thought his father cruel for using the cells—his dungeon was simply a prison. No one ever suffered more than mild privation and bland food in the dungeons of Stormweather Towers.

Not so in the castle.

The sounds Thamalon heard through the walls were a melody of pain. The staccato cracks that punctuated the screams could be only the rhythm of the lash. Thamalon had heard such sounds before, in public punishments for crimes of property and contract. Witnessing those that crossed on Uskevren business was his repellent duty. Unlike some of his peers, he had never developed a taste for human suffering, however deserved.

Revulsion wrestled with his curiosity. As was becoming typical for him, wonder prevailed. Thamalon moved slowly toward the horrid sounds.

He came to an alcove much like an opera box with four chairs situated on steps before three shuttered windows. The sounds of torture came from beyond the louvered panels.

Thamalon tried to swallow away the disgusting taste that came to his mouth as he considered the implications of the viewing box.

He knew he should leave immediately, but he felt the compulsion of one who passes a horrible spectacle in the street and cannot resist turning to watch it. Thamalon lifted one band of the shutters just enough for a peek into the yawning maw of the Abyss.

The Sorcerer's dungeon was the size of Talbot's playhouse. Like the Wide Realms, it was a circular structure with stepped rings descending to a central platform. Dozens of cells surrounded the theater in stacks five high. Inside more than half of them lay dirty, naked humans and elves. Five or six more prisoners hung limply in spiked cages dangling from the ceiling.

The torturers were brawny men wearing red cowls over their heads. They moved methodically among the screams, like battlefield surgeons undaunted by the chaos around them. One drew the lash over the red back of an elf chained to a bloody frame. Another pressed a glowing brand shaped like a lightning bolt into the armpit of another big man—perhaps a recalcitrant member of the Vermilion Guard. Two more turned the wheels on a rack that stretched an elf until his shoulders popped out of their sockets. The elf didn't move or speak. Thamalon guessed he was already dead.

He closed the shutter.

Perhaps there were more clues to be gleaned by spying on the place, but Thamalon could bear to see no more of it. He endorsed discipline and punishment, but this was wicked work.

The nasty taste in his mouth had trickled into his stomach. He felt queasy for a moment, then suddenly much better. Whatever guilt he'd felt about betraying the Sorcerer's hospitality had evaporated. All that remained was a fierce desire to escape that infernal place and return home. If that meant harming the Sorcerer by opening his precious vault, then that was only added value.

CHAPTER 21

BETWEEN THE WALLS

The hairs on the back of Tamlin's neck stood up as straight and as hard as sewing needles. He turned around to see nothing behind him but the bare wall that concealed the secret door to the cellars. Even so, he felt the strong sensation that something was coming through that passage, toward him.

The sound of picks and hammers on the stone floor resounded in the cool chamber. He briefly considered ordering the workmen to pause in their labor, but his desire to see what they would find beneath the foundation was too great. Already they'd uncovered an arc of granite stones that formed a partial archway. Inside the frame they formed, a weird blue stone plugged the gap that should have provided a passage.

He didn't know what it was, but Tamlin knew as

sure as the stars shone on a clear night that the uncovered artifact was a clue to his parents' disappearance. He would do nothing to delay its excavation.

"Put your backs into it, men."

Tamlin smiled in what he hoped was a beneficent manner as his men glanced up at their master. They hadn't understood his insistence about digging up the floor, and they understood even less what they saw there.

"Tamlin?" called a voice from behind him.

Tamlin turned, but there was nothing there but the wall— and the unseen secret door within it.

"Wait," said Tamlin. "Stop digging. Listen."

The hammering subsided, and the voice called again.

"Tamlin? Is that you?"

The voice sounded exactly like his father's, and it was definitely coming from behind the door.

"Talbot?" Tamlin called. "Is that you in there?"

His brother's talent for mimicry had often amused Tamlin, even before it played a role in rescuing him from the kidnappers. Under the present circumstances, however, it was a jest in very poor taste.

"No," replied the voice, this time more assured, as if the speaker had been initially dubious of Tamlin's identity, "it is your father. Where are you?"

Tamlin paused before answering, "I'm in your favorite room of the house."

Talbot would probably know the answer to his brother's simple test, but an outsider posing as his father would not.

"The wine cellar," he said. "Good!"

"Father! Where in the Nine Hells are you? I can barely hear you."

"Within the walls," he said.

"Wait," said Tamlin. "I'll follow your voice. You sound like you're in . . . You men, go up the stairs and tell Vox to double the guard, then come back here and resume the dig."

After the workmen had gone, Tamlin slipped through the

hidden door and called, "All right, I'm in the secret passage. Where are you?"

They called back and forth, each seeking the source of the other's voice. Thamalon heard his father's voice more clearly, but no matter where he went, he remained alone in the secret passages.

"I think this is as close as we can come," said Thamalon.

"I still can't see you."

"Well," said Thamalon., "I think I know the reason for that."

They exchanged their stories of the days since Thamalon disappeared from the library. Tamlin was both astonished and relieved to hear of his father's transportation to another world, and Thamalon's voice turned cold and hard after Tamlin reported that Shamur and Cale had also vanished.

"Let us save the details for later," said Thamalon. "For now, the most important thing is keeping you and your siblings safe. The first thing you must do is to have yourself appointed as head of the family. I realize you may not feel entirely comfor—"

"Already done," said Tamlin.

"What? You mean you had me declared dead?"

"Weren't you just proposing I do exactly that?"

"Well, yes, naturally. I just didn't expect . . ." The idea that Tamlin had done something before being told to do so was slow to sink in. "What I mean, son, is well done."

"Thanks," said Tamlin, sounding more perfunctory than grateful. He was grateful for the praise, and normally he would have beamed and crowed about it, but this was a time for business. "Unfortunately, I'm having a beggar of a time decoding those secret letters of yours. I understand that you have been rallying other families in a concerted action, but I can't for my life figure out whether it's to establish a new trade consortium or an attempt to marginalize our worse rivals among the Old Chauncel."

Thamalon didn't respond for so long that Tamlin began to

think their line of communication had broken.

"Father? Are you all right?"

"That was some good work, Tamlin. Now, if you compare the letters more closely, you should note the progression of dessert items actually spells out . . ."

"I had only the one letter, Father. The others were stolen."

Again, Thamalon paused before answering, though Tamlin suspected he was less surprised at his son's competence than at the ramifications of the theft.

"That means one of our enemies got into Stormweather."

"Or else he was already here," suggested Tamlin. "I have identified a likely traitor among the staff. Unfortunately, he escaped with the remaining letter before we could question him."

Thamalon sighed and said, "Then it's good you didn't finish decoding the letter after all. Perhaps the stolen letters will tell our enemies nothing."

"He also stole your cipher sheet and my notes on decrypting it."

"Blast," said Thamalon. "That makes it much worse."

"Naturally," said Tamlin, "all this would have been much easier if you'd taken me into your confidence before they got to you."

He immediately regretted the petulant words. They were useless and childish. Before Thamalon could chide him or even apologize, though, Tamlin spared him.

"I must admit, I don't blame you for that. I have been a bit of a gadabout, I know. Once we get you safely home, I promise I'll be of more help."

"Never mind that for now," said Thamalon. "Beware the Hulorn. He must have learned at least something of our designs."

"You meant to circumvent him on some approaching issue?"

"No," said Thamalon. "We mean to remove him entirely."

Tamlin whistled and said, "That is . . . rather a bold endeavor, wouldn't you say? Even if the other families do not agree with him, everyone wants a figurehead through which to advance their concerns and thwart those of their rivals."

"Agreed," said Thamalon, "but removing *this* Hulorn is necessary."

Tamlin had never really discussed Andeth Ilchammar with Thamalon, but he knew of his father's disdain for the eccentric lord mayor of Selgaunt. Tamlin had always found the man amusing, if not truly admirable among noble society.

"For far too long," Thamalon added, "Ilchammar's caprice has been an impediment to the prosperity of Selgaunt. Most do not know it, but he still nurtures the blackguard who nearly put us to war with the Tangled Trees last year."

"That wizard who offered to buy my half-sister from you last year?"

"Drakkar," agreed Thamalon—then a beat later, he blurted, "Half-sister?"

Tamlin suppressed a chuckle. He enjoyed letting the Old Owl know he had learned a secret or two in his father's absence. In other circumstances, he might enjoy watching him wriggle a while longer before letting him off the hook, but there would be time for that later.

"Four of your correspondents have been murdered since you vanished," said Tamlin, returning to business. "Stellana Toemalar was the latest."

"All the more reason to guard yourselves," said Thamalon.

"We'll be better prepared with you returned home," said Tamlin. "This vault of yours must be similar to what we're unearthing in the cellar. They must be two sides of a magical gateway."

"But who put it there?" countered Thamalon. "If it's buried beneath the cellar, it had to have been there since before you were born. How could our enemies have possibly placed it there?"

"You built the house on the site of the original Stormweather," offered Tamlin.

"What are you getting at?"

"Since magic was obviously involved in your disappearance, I've been doing a little reading," said Tamlin. He wasn't yet ready to admit that he'd hoped to prove he himself had sorcerous powers. The thought seemed almost too fanciful to repeat. "I wonder about your father's sudden display of magical power when your foes brought down the first Stormweather. What other secrets might old Aldimar have kept from you?"

"He was using wands," said Thamalon. "He never showed any other ability to hurl spells."

"Still, to employ such things well requires some knowledge or inherent power. Where did Aldimar get his?"

"Hmm," considered Thamalon. "Perhaps the gold I spent on your tutors was not entirely wasted."

"Not all of it," agreed Tamlin. "Once we've finished unearthing this gate, I will have Magdon figure out how to activate the thing."

"In the meantime," said Thamalon, "I must find your mother and Cale."

"No," said Tamlin, "first we'll get you back here, then we'll look for them together."

"You might be the *temporary* head of the household, but I am still your father, and I say . . ." Thamalon's voice was building to the familiar crescendo of irrefutable orders before it trailed off uncharacteristically. "Well, dark and damnation. I say you are right."

"What?" said Tamlin.

"I said, 'You are right.' "

"Careful," said Tamlin, "if we keep agreeing people will think we're both imposters."

"By the same coin, you must promise me that you will place the safety of the household above my rescue."

"Very well, but—"

"Including your brother's."

"Now you're just trying to vex me . . ." said Tamlin, "but I agree. I shall see to Stormweather first. It's settled then. Can you stay safely where you are?"

"Not for long, I fear," said Thamalon, "but perhaps I can return. My host should be back from his hunt soon. I-expect he'll go out again in the morning."

"Judging from what you've told me, you've been away for only eight days?"

Thamalon agreed it was so.

"Fourteen have passed here since you vanished."

It was Thamalon's turn to whistle appreciatively.

"Why could you never pay such careful attention during our trade conferences?" he asked.

"Such dull stuff, don't you know," said Tamlin. "Actually," he continued in a more serious tone, "I suspect I have a knack for this magic business after all."

"As well you might," said a third voice—a voice that sounded very much like Tamlin's, "but I am not prepared to relinquish my legacy just yet."

The passage shook, and Tamlin almost fell to the floor. He held onto the wall for support as thunder rolled through the secret passage. A flash of white light blinded him for an instant, and he heard his father shout a curse that disintegrated into a scream of agony.

"Father! What's happening there? I just saw—"

"You were such a timid boy," boomed the other Tamlin's voice. "From your brother I might have expected such willful abuse of my hospitality, but from you, Thamalon, you bookworm, you coin counter—" the man's laughter was full of mock admiration— "I expected much less."

For a moment, Tamlin thought the patronizing voice was addressing him, then Thamalon spoke again.

"Father! How did you . . . ?" the Old Owl managed to say before his voice failed.

Tamlin had only seen the flashing light, but he feared his father had felt its full power.

"Whoever you are, release my father at once!" demanded

226 • Dave Gross

Tamlin. He gripped his sword, wishing he could thrust its point through the worlds and into the heart of the villain who tormented his sire. "Return him now, or suffer the wrath of the Uskevren."

"Brave boy!" the man's laughter boomed even louder. "I *am* the wrath of the Uskevren."

Then, with a shock of thunder and another blinding flash, the stranger severed whatever tenuous link had held the two houses together.

CHAPTER 22

"Here they come!" shouted Muenda.

Cale watched the southern horizon. A dark wedge of clouds swept toward them like a vanguard. Lightning flashed deep within its roiling mass.

He looked to either side, where the other skwalos soared beside their own. Their line stretched from east to west in a graceful arc, each within range of the next one's archers for mutual defense.

In the days since they'd joined the elves, more of the gargantuan creatures had joined their southward trek. Cale noticed the first at dawn after their first night upon the skwalos. Throughout that morning, one or two more appeared each hour. By noon, they began combining with larger groups until they formed an armada over one hundred strong.

Before long, Cale realized that the skwalos they'd

"boarded"—he couldn't avoid sailing terms when describing the creatures—was a small specimen. Whole villages, and even thorny fortifications hung from the trees, sprawled on the backs of the greater skwalos. From aeries in the immense dorsal ridges of the largest skwalos flew elves on the backs of fantastic creatures that might have seemed gigantic if seen apart from their enormous hosts. Some were winged reptiles with great horns upon their skulls. Others looked more like bats the size of a mainsail, except for their many eyes and their three beaked mouths. One that glided down to perch upon a distant skwalos could only be a blue dragon.

"Do you see anything?" asked Shamur.

The willowy Lady Uskevren had tied her ash-blond hair in a tail that whipped behind her head like a war banner. The shreds of her skirts flew back as well, revealing strong legs that would have made a woman half her age envious. She gripped an elven bow with an arrow already nocked, and she wore a quiver of long arrows on her hip.

The elves had trusted them with weapons in return for their oath that they would defend the skwalos so long as they remained aboard. Cale had accepted a bow and arrows as well as a long, sharp spear. He would have preferred a sword, in case the attackers managed to board the skwalos.

"There," said Cale, pointing to a spot above the storm front. A line of nine flyers in wedge formation emerged from the obscuring clouds. Aquiline heads, talons, and wings merged with muscular leonine bodies: griffons. Had they not been arrayed in an attacking force, Cale might have been glad to see a creature more familiar to the lands he knew.

The griffons were uniformly huge, even larger than the pair Cale had glimpsed at the Talendar stables a year before. Each bore two riders clad in bright armor and scarlet cloaks. One of each pair held the reins in one hand and a long needle of a lance under the other arm. The second perched atop a higher seat in the saddle and wielded a recurved bow.

The elves sang to each other from the backs of their

skwalos. Their ululating calls passed from east to west, then back again. Cale translated the salient portions for Shamur.

"The Vermilion Guard," he said. "Elite soldiers."

Even as he spoke, four more groups emerged from the nearby clouds. Shamur's gaze never left the approaching griffons.

"I have an idea," she said.

When she relayed it to Cale, he could only groan.

"Even if we can gull them," he said, "what makes you think we could control one?"

"Trust me," she said.

"My Lady . . ."

"Call me Shamur," she said, turning a confident grin on him. It didn't assuage his concern, but its determined beauty had a stifling charm on his protest. "At least until we return to Stormweather."

Cale sighed and said, "Yes, my lady Shamur."

"Come on," she said. "We might not have chosen this adventure, but we can at least enjoy it."

"We should wait to see what the elders do," said Cale.

He strongly suspected that Rukiya, Kamaria, and Akil were powerful wizards. The old elves had spent the morning preparing harnesses of mystic tokens and materials for their spells. A few of the younger elves had done the same, but they'd intoned songs of flight and flown to the other skwalos hours earlier, leaving the defense of their home to Muenda and the other scouts.

Cale realized that Shamur might not be the only one who intended to lure the Vermilion Guard into assaulting their skwalos. The gambit was already working, for the first squad began diving toward them.

A flight of arrows heralded their arrival. None of the missiles found an elf target, and if they pricked the skwalos to irritation, the great beast displayed no ire. As the bowmen reached for their second volley, the griffons swooped low across the surface of the skwalos. The lancers raked the elders' tent, which immediately blossomed into a fountain of flame.

The lead rider and his first two wingmen escaped the explosion, and the two in the rear veered away in time, but the four griffons between them screamed as they emerged from the sudden fire. Their wings trailed smoke as they bore their scorched riders up and away from the skwalos.

Cale noted with a little disappointment that none of the men had fallen from their mounts. Either they were bound to their saddles, or they were very elite indeed.

The leader and his first two wingmen kept low, the bowmen picking out targets of opportunity while the lancers sought out elf archers. Arrows struck at them from every shelter among the brush, and a pair sprouted from the flank of one of the griffons, one to either side of the lancer's thigh. The creature screamed its anger, but it remained in formation.

Shamur shot at the lead lancer, a captain judging by the long orange plume on his helmet. The arrow missed him by feet, but his bowman spotted the attack and pointed to Shamur. The captain shouted a command and steered his griffon toward the strange humans among their elf foes. His wingmen followed in tight formation.

"Ready," called Shamur.

Cale disliked her plan, but to abandon it would only endanger her further. He raised his long spear as if to throw it, while she crouched beside him and aimed another arrow at the rider to the captain's left.

The lance came speeding toward Cale's heart. Just before it reached him, he thrust the butt of the spear against the "deck" and braced it with his foot. The griffon-rider pulled back on the reins but kept the point of his lance steady. Cale deflected it to the left and ducked low to avoid the griffon's talons. At his right, Shamur dropped her bow and leaped at the griffon. She grabbed its harness and clung tight to the creature's feline body as the attackers swept past.

"Shamur!" cried Cale.

This was *not* the plan she had described.

Cale raised his spear to hurl it at the back of one of the other riders, but before he could throw it a powerful blow sent him tumbling to the deck. A griffon screamed triumphantly as its shadow passed over him, and a bright ringing filled his head as he turned the fall into a roll.

Back on his feet, Cale cupped the back of his head to feel the deep talon wound. His hand came back smothered in blood. A wave of vertigo rose in his skull, and he fended it off by sheer force of will.

He crouched and looked high for the griffon on which Shamur had pounced. The attackers' once-regular chevron formation had scattered in disarray, but it still wasn't hard to spot the flyer with Shamur attached. That one tumbled in its own exceptional sphere of chaos.

The bowman had already fallen from his high saddle. Tymora smiled on him, for he landed upon the surface of the skwalos and rose stunned but alive. Beshaba took her turn with him next, though, and a cloud of elven arrows descended on the dazed man. He fell again, and this time he did not rise.

Up on the griffon, Shamur and the captain struggled for control of the reins. The man was almost twice Shamur's size, but she had thrust his helmet forward and held it there with her left hand, covering his eyes as she unbuckled his sword belt and slung it over her shoulder in a motion worthy of a prestidigitator. Rather than draw the blade, however, she unfastened leather straps that secured him to the saddle. She released her grip on the captain's helm and grabbed the reins in both hands as she rose up to stand on the griffon's back. The man pushed back his helmet just in time to see her leap up and kick him with both feet. Shamur fell to the side, holding desperately to the reins as her weight pulled the griffon's head down. The captain plummeted from his seat.

He did not land on the skwalos.

Cale ran back to his bow and nocked an arrow, looking for

any target that threatened Shamur as she struggled to regain the saddle. He wasn't well practiced with the weapon, but he could at least serve as a distraction. If he could get his hands on a blade, and the attackers landed on the skwalos. . . .

Cale sprinted to where the bowman had fallen, for the man had been wearing a short sword at his hip. Cale's vision faltered, and his legs wobbled beneath him. He'd lost more blood than he'd realized, and he knew he must tend the wound on his scalp. He found shelter beside a thicket. Kneeling there, he glanced up to see whether or not he had attracted the attention of the remaining griffon-riders.

The surviving bowmen concentrated their fire on the elf archers aboard the skwalos, while their lieutenant rallied them back into formation. Before they'd regrouped, two of the burned griffons had already turned back, and a third fell to elf fire.

A flash of blue light overcame even the bright sunlight. Cale blinked away the temporary blindness and saw Akil levitating above the smoldering ruins of his tent. The old elf cackled with glee as he flicked his fingers for a second time and sang out a staccato phrase, scoring a black line across one of the attackers and sending his helmet flying. The man lolled insensate in his saddle as his bowman reached forward in a panic, trying to catch the reins.

"Stop wasting your strength, old fool," called Rukiya. Cale could hear her with perfect clarity, even though she hadn't raised her voice. "You tell them too much! This is only a probe of our defenses."

"She is right, my husband," called Kamaria. Her voice was similarly enchanted. "Save your strength for the Sorcerer. Look, the enemy is repelled."

Cale donned his black cloth mask and said the prayer of healing. He'd performed the ritual often enough that he found the cool trickles of divine power a familiar sensation as they surged through his arms to his fingers. He pressed them against his injured head and felt the tingling sensation of healing flow into his skin, through his veins, and down to the bone. In moments, he felt only a faint line where the open wound had been.

Cale shook his head to dispel his dizziness. Evoking divine power was at once draining and exhilarating, not unlike a vigorous fight. He liked the feeling.

Cale put away his ceremonial mask and located the fallen bowman, or what was left of him. It appeared that every elf on the skwalos had put an arrow through his body. Cale took his sword belt and secured it to his own waist.

He looked up to see the last five griffons retreating, while one flew back toward the skwalos. Shamur sat confidently in the front saddle, grinning like a child on her first horseback ride. She guided the griffon toward a spot near Cale. The creature landed with feline grace, apparently undisturbed by the exchange of its rider.

"Let's go before our hosts decide to stop us," said Shamur.

Cale glanced back at the three old elves hovering above their sparsely defended home. None of them looked in his direction, and Cale knew they were purposefully ignoring their guests. They were giving them their chance to leave, thus sealing their agreement.

Cale hesitated before mounting the griffon. The thing was the size of a grand carriage, and he couldn't see how to climb onto its back.

"The other side," said Shamur.

Cale walked around the enormous beast to find a sort of leather ladder built into the griffon's harness. It trailed down from the saddle, between the creature's wing and flank. At Cale's touch, the griffon raised its wing in a well-trained gesture allowing him access.

Cale passed his bow up to Shamur and clambered into the seat behind her. Even before he could secure the straps to his waist and thighs, she slapped the reins and clucked. The griffon responded like an old, familiar mount. It leaped into the sky once more, its beating wings deafening both its passengers as it rose up from the skwalos. When it flew above the clouds, the griffon spread its great wings and glided southward.

"We're free!" shouted Shamur.

"Which way are we headed?" yelled Cale over the sound of the griffon's wings.

"Where else?" Shamur shouted back.

"But how will you find it?"

"I'm hoping Ripper Junior here will know the way back home."

"Ripper Junior?"

"Remind me to tell you the story some time," Shamur said.

Her laughter rang out even over the wind. Cale had never heard her sound so full of glee. Even in the face of peril both to her and to Thamalon, she couldn't resist the thrill of danger. After hiding so long beneath her own mask as a society matron, at last she could return to the adventures of her youth.

Cale had no wish to dispel her cheer. Thus, he didn't tell Shamur of Rukiya's demand, the condition by which Cale had sealed their alliance with the elves. He didn't know how the ancient elves spoke to the Lord of Shadows nor why Mask would tell them of his servant, Cale. All he knew was that the elves had foreseen the arrival of one who could help end their war with the Sorcerer. While their airborne armies assaulted Stormweather Castle, they wished to send an assassin past the Sorcerer's defenses. No elf could pierce the veil of suspicion and fear that separated them from the Sorcerer's people. Only a human assassin would do.

When Shamur learned the Sorcerer's youthful name was Tam Lin, she dismissed the similarity to her own son's name, despite the added coincidence of Castle Stormweather. Even if the place was a reflection of her world, it was nothing more. She couldn't accept the possibility that any part of her own son could be a hated tyrant.

Or so she'd said to Cale. For years she had pretended to be something other than she was, wearing the visage of a severe and stately society matron over her true self. Cale wondered whether her brave and mischievous laughter was yet another mask.

Either way, he couldn't stop thinking how much her wildness reminded him of her daughter, the woman he loved. The thought made him dread their final destination all the more. If he had to choose between saving Thamalon's life and sparing the Sorcerer's, he knew already where his loyalties lay. Even if this Tam Lin was some dark reflection of the scion of the Uskevren.

Yet what would Tazi think of Cale if he fulfilled his promise to the elves? If the Sorcerer was, somehow, her elder brother, Cale couldn't imagine that Tazi could ever forgive his murderer.

CHAPTER 23

POSSESSIONS

"They'll kill you, you know."

Radu leaped from the wall of the Hunting Garden to a third-floor balcony of the Hulorn's Palace. Still flush with energy from his most recent killing and heedless of detection by the Hulorn's guard, he had no need of spells.

"Obviously they suspect you've been spying on them. Why else would Drakkar tell you to meet him at the gallery of his patron without revealing the man's identity? When you arrive, you simply prove that you've been there before."

Radu leaped up to a window ledge on the fourth floor.

When Chaney flew up to join him, Radu said, "Why are you waiting for an answer if you can read my thoughts?"

"I can't read your thoughts," said Chaney, "and thank the gods for small favors. On the other hand, I did overhear that sending from your master."

"*Employer*," hissed Radu.

"Touchy. That veneer of yours is peeling away by the hour. I suppose I would be a bit testy, too, if I were about to seal my family's doom."

Radu clutched the balcony rail hard enough to crack the marble.

"On the other hand, if you were to kill Drakkar and the Hulorn while you have the chance. . . ."

"Save your breath, phantom. You cannot manipulate me."

Chaney laughed and said, "Perhaps if I still needed breath, I would take that advice. Still, you can't say you haven't considered cutting their throats to insulate your remaining family from their schemes. Can you?"

"My brothers will be safe."

"Oh, so this Rilmark character you sent Pietro to meet is an upstanding citizen, good contact among the Old Chauncel, the very model of a—"

"Enough. I apprehend your meaning."

"Your problem has always been bad associates, you know. Come to think of it, that's what my father always said to me. Look how I turned out."

Radu made a derisive snort and said, "We are nothing alike."

"Not yet," said Chaney, "but you will die soon, and we'll see what sort of ghost you make."

Chaney received no reply, as expected. After a few more leaps across improbable distances, Radu came to the balcony where he first spied upon the Hulorn.

"Welcome," called Andeth Ilchammar.

The lord mayor wore his public disguise and stood amid the gently floating artwork in the very center of his distorted chessboard floor. Drakkar stood beside him, and between the wizards stood a red-haired man whose freckles and pug nose made him look younger than he probably was.

Chaney recognized him at once as Escevar, Tamlin Uskevren's constant companion. His presence there could only mean one thing.

"You don't want this job," said Chaney. "This could be your last chance to kill these schemers and save your family."

Drakkar beckoned to Radu. "Come," he said. "Allow me to introduce you to my master and another of our associates."

The wizard smiled knowingly, and Chaney felt vindicated in his earlier warning. He wished only that he could convince Radu of the danger and persuade him to turn on the wizards, but he knew the assassin resented any influence—especially since they both knew Chaney would say anything to deflect the assassin from Talbot Uskevren's family.

"Recent events have required an acceleration of our previous schedule," explained Drakkar. "Now that we have proof that Thamalon Uskevren was the principal conspirator against the lawful government of Selgaunt, his lands and holdings are forfeit to the Hulorn. Unfortunately, his heir has proven more difficult than we had anticipated. In the interest of putting this ugly chapter in our fair city's history behind us, it would be well if he were eliminated. To that end—"

"No!" protested Escevar. "That was never the deal. You promised to support—"

"You came to us," said the Hulorn. "We promised you nothing."

"I only wished to—"

Drakkar snapped his fingers, and a red thorn flashed from his hand to Escevar's cheek.

"Silence, you mollusk," the wizard said. "If you held any sway with us, it vanished when you destroyed the painting."

"Yes," drawled Andeth, turning to Escevar as if in sudden memory of a past slight. "That was ill done. I should have liked to have hung Thamalon Uskevren's grave in my collection."

Escevar clawed at the tiny wound on his face. The thorn burrowed beneath his flesh, wriggling its way up toward his ear. He grimaced in an effort to keep his tongue still.

"That's what you get, you bloody beggar," said Chaney.

He felt a surge of heat fill his immaterial body, and he kicked angrily at the traitor's leg.

Escevar cried out, falling to one knee.

"I said *silence!*" screeched Drakkar, raising his hand for another spell.

The Hulorn put a hand on his arm and shook his head.

"We still have need of him," the lord mayor cautioned.

"Oh, most excellent!" shouted Chaney. He could hardly believe what had just happened. The ghost raised his foot and stamped hard on Escevar's thigh. "Take that, you rat!"

With a grunt, Escevar fell to the floor, clutching his leg.

"The razor," Andeth chided Drakkar. "Not the club. How many times must I tell you?"

"It was only a cantrip . . ." murmured Drakkar, seemingly mystified by the potency of his own spell.

Chaney could tell by the angle of Radu's head that he suspected the ghost was responsible for Escevar's discomfort. If nothing else, he must have wondered at Chaney's exclamation, but he dared not speak to him in front of the others. Instead, he remained silent, as usual—and, as usual, his silence began to make the other men fidget uncomfortably until they returned to the matter at hand.

"This man will lead you to Stormweather Towers and let you in," said Drakkar. "There, find Tamlin Uskevren and put an end to him."

"The Uskevren are exceptional targets," said Radu.

"You'd better believe it, Malveen," said Chaney. "You go in there, and I promise you won't be coming back out."

Drakkar looked to Andeth, who frowned but bobbed his head.

The Hulorn said, "Perhaps a fifty percent increase in your usual fee?"

"Triple it," said Radu, "and pay me now."

"Surely you jest," said Andeth. "For that sum, I could hire a small army."

Radu shrugged and turned to leave.

"Wait," said Andeth. "Double it is, then. Half now, half on compl—*wait*!"

Radu had one hand on the balcony rail.

"You drive a hard bargain," said the Hulorn. "Triple it is. Drakkar, fetch my butler."

Drakkar gaped at his master's offhanded dismissal, but he obeyed.

"Such a sum should do much to improve Laskar's circumstances," said Andeth. Chaney saw Radu stiffen, but only because he was watching for a reaction. So was the Hulorn, apparently. "Who knows how far the Malveen star could rise with your continued service to the city."

As the trio approached Stormweather Towers, Chaney continued to test his newfound power. It failed more often than it succeeded, but he learned that he could inflict at least an annoying injury on the frightened Escevar if he struck while angry.

The problem was that he was more fearful than angry. He knew Tal had little love for his older brother, but he was fairly certain he wouldn't take pleasure in Tamlin's death.

"Don't do anything foolish," said Radu, "lest I act beyond the purview of my employ."

Escevar bobbed his head in tepid agreement, but Chaney suspected the words were actually meant for him.

Chaney feared that Radu relished the thought of facing Tal. No other swordsman had come so close to Radu's skill, and Tal had done so largely by dint of his supernatural strength and resilience. Radu's new, unholy powers more than made up for the advantages of a werewolf.

Werewolf. . . .

The thought gave Chaney an idea. Just as Tal's affliction had been both a curse and a blessing, being a ghost provided certain advantages. Chaney had devoted himself to tormenting his killer with nothing but words, but he had at least one other weapon at his disposal, providing he could learn how to use it in time.

Yet Chaney wondered what else he could do. If the stories were true, then perhaps he could do more than smite a living man with his rage.

Chaney reached into Radu's body. He clutched for his heart and squeezed.

Radu didn't even break his stride.

Dark, thought Chaney.

He tried again with both hands, to no better effect.

Despite the failure to hurt Radu, Chaney did feel something. It was like the physical sensation of slipping on a pair of gloves.

Hopeful, Chaney thrust his arms into Radu—one down each of the assassin's own arms—and he stepped into the living man's body.

Chaney felt like a child struggling with a shirt his nanny was trying to force over his head. He felt the weight of limbs and torso begin to form over his own ethereal body. Cold surged from the place his heart had been and ran through a network of veins he no longer had.

Radu stopped walking. He shook his head violently then he turned around to look behind him.

Ahead of him, Escevar stopped and looked back, puzzled.

"What is it?" he asked.

Chaney felt Radu's body shiver and his muscles grow taut.

"Stop it!" hissed the assassin.

Chaney could no longer stifle his laughter.

"Why didn't I try this months ago?"

He kept shrugging his arms and legs into Radu's body, trying for a comfortable fit. The cold he felt did not subside. Instead, it grew sharper.

Radu clenched his fists, and Chaney felt the unutterable pain as the hardened sinews of his right hand ground and popped.

He felt the molten agony of the bone shards still embedded in his face, even as the rest of his skull felt as cold as ice.

"What?" repeated Escevar, his voice a whisper, as he backed away from Radu.

"Relax," said Chaney.

He heard the trembling in his voice, even as he tried to sound nonchalant. Stinging hot tears welled in his eyes, but the cold in the rest of his body continued to intensify. He wanted to laugh, to mock Radu, to shout out in triumph, but the words were frozen in his mouth. The pain continued to grow until at last all Chaney wanted to do was scream, but he couldn't even breathe.

Get out!

Chaney fell to the ground in a thousand shards of shattered ice. Above him, Radu Malveen staggered briefly, then he stepped briskly away from the spot where he'd been momentarily rooted.

"Try that again," said Radu, "and I will kill every living thing within those walls."

"But I did—"

"Silence," Radu cut off Escevar. "I was not talking to you."

Escevar led the rest of the way in silence. Radu followed from a safe distance, keeping to the shadows. Chaney limped along behind him, still shuddering from the pain of being ejected forcibly from his first attempt at possession. It felt like a combination of a severe beating, a heroic hangover, and an infernal case of frostbite.

"What in the Nine Hells is inside of him?" Chaney asked himself, then he realized he'd probably answered his own question.

At the gate to Stormweather Towers, Escevar balked at the sight of a doubled guard. They saluted when he came into the torchlight and they recognized the master's butler.

"What has happened?" said Escevar.

"My lord requests you attend him at once," said the guard.

As two of the guard's comrades flanked him, Escevar realized his peril. He said nothing, however, as the guards removed his sword and took him by the arms.

The moment they entered the herald's door, Radu struck.

To Chaney it appeared that Radu's blade had merely caressed the first guard's neck before thrusting forward to stab up into the second man's jaw. They fell forward simultaneously, as if stumbling over the same unseen obstacle.

One of the men holding Escevar released his captive and reached down to catch one of his companions. He saw the dark shape of Radu's coat flap toward him, but before he could open his mouth to shout an alarm, his eyes became the mouths of twin streams flowing down his cheeks.

The fourth guard had time to draw his blade, but he made the mistake of using Escevar as his shield.

Radu lunged forward, transfixing both men through the heart.

For a moment, all five bodies remained intact. Radu ran past them as steam rose from their open wounds into the chill night air, then, each within a second of the previous, the bodies crumbled to white ash and flowed after their killer.

The assassin was already running toward the house, so the pale essence of the dead men swirled behind him like the foamy wake of a black ship.

Guards shouted from the grand entrance to Stormweather Towers, "Who's there? Stand and unfold yourself!"

Radu veered away from the main entrance and ran through the garden. The wisps of his victims continued to trail behind him like smoke from a burning man.

Chaney saw a pair of guards at the kitchen door. They arched their necks to peer west through the shadows of the garden, but they didn't see Radu sprinting through the shadows. Chaney knew what their fate would be when the killer reached them. If he had a voice to warn them, he would . . .

Before he could reconsider his sudden inspiration, Chaney flew toward one of the guards—astonishingly, even faster than

Radu. His ghostly form entered one of the guards. After an instant of quickly smothered confusion, Chaney felt the night air on his face, warm woolen clothes upon his body, and most amazingly—the body that housed his spirit.

"Over here!" yelled Chaney, pointing toward Radu. "Over here!"

The other guard drew his sword and peered where Chaney pointed, but he saw nothing.

"Run!" advised Chaney. "You can't stop him!"

The guard turned to question his companion just as Radu emerged from the darkness.

"Sorry," said Chaney.

He stepped out of the possessed guard's body just as the man's partner felt Radu's blade sever his spine.

The guard Chaney had inhabited shook his head and blinked at the sight of his fallen companion. He raised his sword to defend himself, but Radu beat it aside effortlessly. The assassin's blade dipped neatly into the man's throat.

Chaney knew he'd given the guard no time to escape, even if he could apprehend his peril in the second before his death. Still, the ghost didn't want to find out what would happen to him if he was in the man's body at the moment of death. Perhaps nothing, since he was already dead and bound to Radu. He wanted time to give the matter more thought before he dared to experiment.

Chaney consoled himself in the knowledge that his shout had started an alarm all around the house. First a chain of voices, and a rapid, resounding bell alerted all within Stormweather Towers to the danger.

"Now you're well and truly buggered," said Chaney. "No point in going on, now that the entire house is alerted. Maybe you could take a nice holiday along the southern Moonsea. You could use some sun."

Radu ignored both Chaney's jibes and the disintegrating bodies of the guards and pulled on the kitchen door. It remained firmly shut.

"I'm guessing about now you're wishing you'd taken his keys before killing your guide," said Chaney. "Let's get out of here."

The vapors of his victims finally caught up to Radu. They rushed over his body, then into his face, through the holes in his mask, and finally—Chaney imagined—into his mouth and nostrils.

Radu gasped at the massive influx of power. It wracked his body and threw the sword from his hand.

"Oh, dark and empty," gulped Chaney.

An instant later, the magical feedback reached him, too. It blasted the very memory of substance from his mind, unraveled all his reason, and scrubbed the vision from his eyes. For an eternity or a second, all he knew was a universe of white screams.

When reality returned, it was a sensation of motion. Radu dragged Chaney by his invisible leash through the splintered kitchen door. The staff had long since gone to bed, except for Brilla, the chief cook. She clutched a trembling knife in one hand as she pressed her plump body against the far wall. Chaney remembered the woman fondly, for she'd always been kind to him even as the other servants avoided young master Talbot's scurrilous friend. He was glad to see Radu had wasted no time for killing her before he sought his target.

He felt the tug and got his feet beneath him. He ran to catch up to Radu, but something blocked his way.

Chaney realized he could still hear the screams from the recent influx of life. Barely visible, even to his sight, the ghostly images of Radu's victims huddled all around him. They clutched at Chaney's clothes and hair like palsied beggars craving a coin. One of them grasped his knees in the ancient gesture of petition. Chaney looked down at the demented face of the man he'd possessed. Confusion and betrayal swelled in his eyes.

Those damnable eyes. They would not stop looking at him.

"All right," he said. "All right. I'll think of something."

The phantoms released him, and Chaney ran out of the kitchen.

He found Radu in the long passage between the feast hall and the kitchens. Radu stood near the center of the corridor, crouched in a swordsman's guard. A white halo blazed around his head as the surplus of unholy energy burned from his saturated body.

Radu put his back to the huge oaken feast hall door. To either side and across from him, ranks of mounted armor lined the walls, each beneath the personal insignia of its former owner. House guards stood before either end of the corridor. They held their target shields before them, edges overlapping to form a wall over which they thrust the points of their swords. With the help of the empty armor, they surrounded the intruder. Slowly they marched toward the center of the hall, hedging him in where he had no escape.

Radu spun around and kicked the feast hall door. His foot shot through the thick wood, creating a hole just large enough to reveal the ranks of house guards already waiting behind it.

Chaney allowed himself a brief smile of satisfaction at seeing his nemesis cornered, then he sank into the body of one of the house guards, careful not to take one from the front ranks. Merging with the man's body felt like forcing himself into a pool of cool mud. It was more difficult than possessing the guard at the kitchen door but far easier than forcing his way into Radu Malveen.

"He means to kill Tamlin!" shouted Chaney. "Be careful, he's inhumanly strong and deadly with that blade. Take him down with spears!"

A man wearing a sergeant's braid looked incredulously at Chaney's host and said, "How do you—?"

"Oops," said Chaney.

He stepped out of the guard's body into the sergeant's, earning an instant promotion.

"Do it!" said Chaney with his new authority. "Summon reinforcements with spears."

One look at the cornered assassin told him that Radu

had heard his command and understood its true source. He glanced up to see the higher reaches of the grand stairway.

"Look out!" shouted Chaney. "He's—"

Radu had already leaped fifteen feet up to the second floor. He ran toward the east wing—

Toward Tamlin's bedchamber.

"That's a stroke of luck," said one of the guards near Chaney.

"What do you mean?"

"The master is still down in the cellars, overseeing the—"

"Oh, dark," said Chaney.

The ghost had long feared that he and Radu each heard what the other did, as demonstrated by his own recent "eavesdropping" on the message Drakkar sent the assassin. Before he could say anything else to the guards, Chaney felt himself pulled from the sergeant, toward Radu.

On the lower floor.

Even amid the shouts and alarms throughout the house, Chaney heard the constant moaning of his spectral choir. They floated all around him, no longer content to lurk in the shadows. Something had stirred them. Chaney wondered whether there was a limit to the number of souls Radu could contain. Or perhaps the ghosts sensed something Chaney himself could not, some dread oracle of disaster.

Chaney willed himself along the tether that bound him to Radu. The motion carried him through the marble tiles, past the stone foundation, and into the rocky soil beneath. At last he emerged in a stairway of unadorned stone. There, Radu fought a hulking figure in Uskevren livery.

Chaney recognized Vox, Tamlin's voiceless bodyguard. Because his friend Talbot had always hated the brute, so had Chaney. Old rancor was nothing compared to their current, common purpose.

The big man fought a holding action. He'd already dropped his big axe in favor of a pair of heavy, notched knives—sword-breakers. Each time his foe's blade thrust toward him, Vox parried in an effort to catch Radu's slender blade in the teeth of his own weapons. Even if he were not aware of the horrid effects of death at Radu's hand, Vox was taking no chances. That he was fighting in pure defense suggested that he expected help from above.

Unfortunately, the mute couldn't call for help.

Possessing the man would only distract him and hasten his death. Trying to do the same to Radu had already proven futile. Chaney simply didn't have the power to overcome the assassin's implacable will, especially when the man was so fully empowered by the spirits of the dead.

The same spirits that circled Chaney, moaning and pulling at him. What were they trying to tell him?

"Blast me for an imbecile!" Chaney cried.

He had failed to possess the assassin, but he'd tried it alone, without the obvious help that surrounded him. Chaney beckoned the other ghosts to follow him. As one, the wave of souls rose above Radu Malveen, and plunged into his body.

It felt like diving into churning ice water, but this time Chaney wasn't paralyzed. Rather, he could feel his own touch on Radu's arms and legs. It was like grasping the limbs of a life-sized marionette.

Except this puppet fought back. Chaney felt a black force struggling against his own will. It wrestled him for control of Radu's limbs and sought to thrust him from his body.

He tried speaking through Radu's mouth, but the most he could evoke was a low gasp. Instead, he jerked the man's sword arm out of his defensive line.

Vox hesitated, apparently sensing a trick.

"*Doo iiitt . . .*" croaked Chaney through Radu's mangled throat, then he kicked out, tumbling Radu's body down on the stairs.

He looked up at Vox, imploring him with his borrowed eyes to strike before it was too late. The barbarian squinted, and for a moment Chaney thought Vox could see through Radu's mask, even through his skull, into the ghosts that lay beneath the flesh.

The barbarian inverted his sword-breakers and plunged them into Radu's belly. One of them sank so deeply that it bit hard into the stone stairs and stuck fast.

The twin wounds were exploding stars in Chaney's brain. The pain threatened to overwhelm his will, to force him to retreat from this agonized body. He felt his hold on Radu wavering, but he struggled to hold fast. For an instant, he had never felt so powerful, so certain of his success. He watched through Radu's eyes as Vox pulled free one of his sword-breakers and raised it for the coup de grace.

All at once, the other ghosts fled, leaving Chaney helpless and alone within Radu's body.

"Cowards," spat Chaney.

Radu's lips didn't echo his sentiment. Instead, he kicked Vox in the chest with such force that the big man flew backward into the slanting stone ceiling.

Even within his prison of bone and flesh, Chaney could hear the horrible crack of Vox's skull against the stone—first against the ceiling, then again upon the stone steps. There he lay, as still as death.

Realizing he'd lost what sway he'd held over Radu's body, Chaney tried to follow the treacherous ghosts in their escape. To his horror, he found he couldn't move, nor could he exert the slightest influence over Radu's movements.

He was trapped inside.

Radu gripped the sword-breaker that pinned him to the floor. With a grunt, he pulled it from his body. Chaney felt the nauseating agony of the aggravated wound. An instant later, he felt an infernal heat fill the cut, burning it away. The pain lingered, but Radu rose to his feet.

As he stepped over the body of his fallen foe, Radu sketched a quick salute with his blade. In the years Chaney had spent at Master Ferrick's academy, he'd never seen Radu make such a gesture to a fellow student. In truth, none had ever come so close to stopping him.

Radu entered the cellars. He passed through the iron

racks and beyond the tasting room, then he came to a room lit by torches.

Inside, all the casks had been moved away to make room for a freshly dug hole. The excavation had revealed a stone archway inscribed with arcane symbols. It surrounded not an empty space but a great plug of blue stone with veins of many colors. Before it stood Tamlin Uskevren, and before him stood a team of six men holding picks and shovels, who stood defensively before their lord.

Chaney had known Tamlin Uskevren since he was a boy. He'd last seen Talbot's older brother almost a year before. Since then, Tamlin's handsome features had grown leaner. He had been a youth prone to slouching, and leaning on mantles and in doorways, but he stood tall as he faced the intruder. His eyes were as hard and as brilliant as emeralds.

"Please, my lord," said one of the workers. "Flee, while we hold him off."

He was a young man with a face still too smooth to want shaving. He watched Radu Malveen's slow approach, and his hands trembled upon the haft of his weapon.

Radu nodded toward the lad in acknowledgement of his brave speech. Chaney knew he would be the last to die, after he had seen the fate of his fellows.

"No," said Tamlin. He drew his sword and raised it to a steady guard position. In his left hand he fiddled with a ring of keys, rubbing one of them like a prayer bead. His gaze never left the assassin's eyes, and his expression remained assured. "Stand down. No one else will die in my place tonight."

"But my lord!" the young man protested until one of his elders drew him away by the arm.

"Run, you idiot!" Chaney screamed.

He knew perfectly well that no one but Radu could hear him, but he couldn't bear to remain both useless and silent.

"Leave us," Tamlin ordered. "I presume our visitor has no objection?"

Radu nodded. He stepped to the side, allowing the workers

to pass. They filed out slowly, past the assassin, then they beat a hasty retreat.

"Well spoken, Lord Uskevren," said Radu. His voice had faded to the rustling of dry leaves. He bowed slightly and raised his blade.

"Who sent you?"

Radu cocked his head in a disapproving gesture.

"It was worth a try," said Tamlin, "but I see you're a professional. I don't suppose you're open to a counter offer?"

Radu took a step forward and raised his sword.

Tamlin stepped to the side, holding his guard high and to the center. When Radu mirrored his motion to cut him off, Chaney suspected Tamlin had been attempting to run past, toward the wall. Perhaps there was a hidden escape there.

Too bad Radu wouldn't let him try it.

Tamlin made a shallow feint toward the intruder's thigh. The trick didn't fool Radu, and his guard never wavered.

The assassin attacked. His first feint lured Tamlin's guard outside, and he thrust again. Tamlin barely recovered from the first false thrust in time to parry the second—at a cost of a searing cut on his shoulder.

Tamlin retreated a step, then two more. The man followed him, maintaining their distance with a dancer's grace.

"At least let me lead," quipped Tamlin. "It's my house, after all."

The assassin replied with another attack, this time beating Tamlin's blade before cutting under his guard and pinking his thigh.

Tamlin fell back, stumbling over the loose stones of the excavation. His opponent allowed him to recover before advancing once more.

"Don't you dare toy with me, you beggar!" Tamlin bellowed.

Briefly, Chaney thought of Talbot's mocking imitations of the boys' father. In anger, Tamlin sounded much the same.

Radu and Tamlin heard the clamor on the steps at the same

time. Help was coming, and the assassin could no longer afford to taunt his prey. Tamlin knew it, and he made a hasty retreat—right into the open hole.

He fell hard on his back, the air whooshing out of his lungs. To his credit, he held his blade firmly upward, anticipating Radu's leap after him. He even kept the keys in his hand, and Chaney saw a blue gleam from the largest one.

Tamlin's defense was far too weak. Radu beat the blade aside as he landed lightly atop the unearthed archway. In the same motion, he thrust his blade neatly through Tamlin's heart.

Chaney winced as he felt the slight grating of stone as the blade passed through Tamlin's body and chipped the stone plug beneath. Blue light surged up from the buried artifact, so bright that Chaney could see Tamlin's skeleton beneath his flesh. In the next instant, it wiped away his sight, and a high keening took away his hearing. He felt a flash of agony so brief it might have been ecstasy.

Then he felt nothing at all.

CHAPTER 24

THE VANES

Sunlight gilded the crests of the clouds, yet the black belly of the storm still rumbled after each flash of lightning. Everywhere they flew, the storm rushed toward them.

"Castle Stormweather," said Cale.

He spied the titanic edifice at the very heart of the storm. Its massive cluster of gray spires pierced the clouds a few miles away. Above them wheeled griffon-riding sentries.

Shamur nodded grimly and urged their mount lower until the griffon's wings brushed the clouds. Her cheerful mood had waned during their flight from the elven armada, and neither of them had spoken since their departure. They were saving their strength for what lay ahead.

Once cloaked by the mists of the storm, Shamur

gave Ripper his head. The griffon dived into the clouds, plummeting so quickly that Cale briefly feared the creature meant to kill itself and its riders. The wind pressed him into the high back of his saddle. He felt the flesh on his face rippling as they fell ever faster through the darkness of the storm.

Just before Cale thought he might lose consciousness, the griffon veered to the left, gradually decreasing the angle of its descent. It dived briefly once more, guided by instinct, and quickly rose up, flapping its wings to brake its speed. They emerged from the cloud cover, and Cale caught his breath as he saw how close they had come to the castle.

Ripper dropped easily onto the roof of one of the stronghold's spires. In the center of the landing stood a stable with a peaked roof. Even in the high wind, Cale could smell the musty odor of a bird coop mingling with the musk of big mammals.

A pair of attendants in heavy padded armor ran out to take Ripper's reins. When they saw who had returned the griffon, they reached for their truncheons, hesitating only when they saw Cale pointing an arrow at them.

"Tether the griffon, but don't alert the others," said Cale in the common tongue.

The men understood and obeyed.

Once Shamur had dismounted and stood behind the men with a drawn blade, Cale climbed down and removed the attendants' weapons, keeping one and throwing the other over the roof's edge.

"Who else is up here?" he asked.

"Four wounded from the harrying teams, along with two guards," reported one of the men, nodding toward a stairway adjacent to the stables.

"Anyone else?"

The man shook his head.

"Where is Thamalon Uskevren?" demanded Shamur.

The attendants looked back blankly.

"A stranger to these parts," said Cale. "We know he's here."

One of the men nodded in comprehension then grimaced. He glanced back over his shoulder, toward the highest of the castle's spires.

"The . . . Vanes," he said reluctantly. "You'll never make it up there. Only the Vermilion Guard is permitted—"

"That's enough," said Cale. "Can you take care of these two?"

Shamur nodded and said, "First let's feed Ripper, boys, then let's find some rope."

Despite her cavalier tone, Shamur's eyes were lined with concern. She hadn't liked the sound of these "Vanes" any more than Cale had. She prodded one of the men with the point of her sword.

"Back here in fifteen minutes," said Cale.

The attendants had answered quickly enough and seemed frightened enough to be telling the truth, but Cale couldn't count on that. Cautiously, he descended the steps to the guardroom. Lying on the stone steps, he crept down far enough to peer into the room below.

He saw two guards, both of whom had doffed their helms and set aside their breastplates and pauldrons. One of them sat at a table along one wall, rinsing bandages in a basin. The other carried a hot cauldron carefully into another room. Through the open door, Cale saw three occupied cots and inferred that there were at least three more in the room.

He got back to his feet and considered the two weapons in his hands. The sword was more certain, and he didn't have time to waste. Still, neither of the men was his assigned target, and he had no reason to believe that either of them was particularly despicable. Seeing them tend the wounded only aggravated Cale's qualms about killing them.

He made his choice and slipped quietly down the stairs, pausing only for an instant to scan the rest of the room. Satisfied that it was empty except for the men he had seen, he stepped behind the guard with the bandages and rapped him sharply on the head. The man fell forward, his arm knocking the basin off the table. Cale lunged forward and caught it just before it would have shattered on the floor.

"You all right in there?" called the other guard.

Cale heard the man set his cauldron on the floor and begin returning to the room. He stepped to the side of the door and pressed his back against the wall. When the guard came through, Cale shut the door behind him with one hand while raising his truncheon to strike.

The guard was no mere stable hand, however. Sensing the motion behind him, he ducked his head forward and kicked backward, striking Cale in the hip and groin. He spun in the same motion, reaching for his sword as he opened his mouth to shout for help.

Cale thrust the truncheon into the man's open jaws, choking him and smothering his alarm. The unorthodox attack shocked the guard into clutching for Cale's weapon rather than using his own.

Cale pushed forward, forcing the man's head back as he reached for his sword arm. He caught the man's wrist and twisted, turning him to face the ground, and removed the truncheon in the same motion. The man coughed and gasped for breath. Cale knelt on his back and rapped his head once. The man stopped moving, but his breath continued to come in struggling little wheezes.

Satisfied that the two men would remain unconscious a while longer, Cale bolted the door to the sick room, and he turned to his main task.

A little less than three minutes had passed since he'd left Shamur.

"You're late," said Shamur. She stood beside the same griffon. Cale knew there hadn't been time to remove the beast's saddle, but the lather had been wiped from its tawny coat.

"I had a hard time choosing the right color," Cale replied.

Shamur looked at the bright red armor Cale had lugged up from the guardroom and laughed. Cale wasn't sure whether she or he was more surprised at his banter. It was a great relief to jest after all his brooding on the journey to the castle, and it reminded him again of his friend Jak Fleet. The wise-cracking halfling always helped Cale shed some of the gloom that naturally gathered around him.

"At least this way they won't shoot us down on sight," Cale said.

He began putting on the armor and immediately realized it would never look convincing on his tall, gaunt frame. Even had it been made to fit him, Cale thought he would never prefer metal armor to his familiar black leathers. At least in them he felt he could breathe.

Despite her height and her decidedly feminine shape, Shamur looked far more convincing as a Vermilion Guardsman once she tied her hair back and donned the helmet.

They finished their disguises by securing the long capes to their shoulders. Cale added the short sword to the long sword at his weapon belt. Once they found Thamalon, he wanted his master to be armed.

"Ready?" asked Shamur.

Cale nodded and said, "Are *you* prepared? This Sorcerer sounds even more dangerous than Marance Talendar."

"Wizards fear me," said Shamur. "Just don't get between us."

"If he is there, my lady, perhaps it would be best—"

"Shamur," she corrected him.

"Shamur," he said. "Let me deal with the Sorcerer. If Thamalon is up there, he will need you."

"Yes," she said, "that would be best."

Cale was surprised that she didn't argue the point, but he didn't wish to question this small good fortune.

They mounted the griffon and took to the sky. Shamur urged Ripper to climb, and they followed a rising spiral up to the central tower of Castle Stormweather. They spied three other griffon-riding teams circling above the high tower, and Shamur kept a safe distance from them.

A dozen or more courtiers stood upon the tower surface, their fine clothes damp from the surrounding storm. They held palms over the mouths of their goblets to protect them from the drizzling rain. Servants coursed among them, refilling cups and offering hors d'oeuvres. Despite the weather, they chatted cheerfully as they observed the spectacle above them.

Ugly posts of rusty iron rose from the edge of the tower at the four corners of the world and their children. At each of the eight points swung the metal blades of a gigantic weather vane, each facing the next as the wind swirled around the tower. Beneath each vane stood a red-armored guardsman, a sword at his hip and a long spear in his hand.

Strapped to four of the wheels were corpses, one so long rotting that its body flopped where its arms had pulled away from their sockets. Bound to a fifth was an elf whose brown skin had burned to gray flakes in the wind and sun. Two of the wheels were empty, but lashed to the last of them was Thamalon Uskevren.

He couldn't have been on the rack for more than a few hours, a day at most. His eyes were closed, but his head lolled against the spinning of the wheel. The cold had drained the color from his face, and his clothes were damp with rain and sweat. Except for the blood at his wrists, where his wire bonds chafed his skin, he appeared unwounded but for profound privation and the torture of the elements.

"I changed my mind," shouted Shamur. "Leave the Sorcerer to me!"

"It would be better if we concentrate on—*ulp*!"

Shamur leaned forward to send Ripper plunging toward the congregation among the torture wheels. The diving griffon sent the courtiers and their servants scattering to the edges of the tower, their fine goblets crashing to the stone floor behind them. The guards raised an alarm before gathering near the center of the tower to form a unified defense.

"Get ready to jump!" Shamur yelled above the cacophony of terrified courtiers and the screaming wind. She pulled Ripper's neck to the side to force a tight turn and dived toward the tower again. "Get him down from that thing!"

"This is not the best way to—" Cale gave up trying to persuade Shamur of a less direct attack. The sight of her tormented husband had driven out any lingering inclination toward subtlety.

He gripped the back of the saddle with one hand while unbuckling the straps with the other. Shamur brought the griffon in close to the vane on which Thamalon slowly spun. Too late, Cale realized how hopeless it was to leap from the flying animal to the wheel. He had no choice but to jump anyway.

He hit the sheet metal blade hard enough to make a Cale-shaped dent in its surface. He grabbed for the rigging with both hands and held fast with one. Fortunately, one was enough to let him swing around and catch hold with the other. He might have climbed the blade as nimbly as a spider were he not hindered by the vermilion armor, yet he took one glance down at the spears of the guards and was glad for the protection.

The shock of impact stirred Thamalon to wakefulness. He craned his neck to see Cale clinging to the vane above him, then beside him, then below him as the wheel turned in the wind.

"We've come to get you out of here," said Cale.

"Oh, good," said Thamalon thickly. He sounded drunk, more like his wastrel son than himself.

Cale felt a sudden thickness in his throat. Like Shamur, he felt a rising fury against the man who had set his master upon this torture device, but even more he felt the sour tang of guilt that he'd failed to protect Thamalon.

"Let's get you off this thing."

"The guards," murmured Thamalon.

"Shamur is keeping them busy."

"Where?" Thamalon asked. He lifted his head, blinking through his grogginess.

Ripper screamed as Shamur brought him in for another pass over the Vermilion Guard. Cale hoped she stayed out of range of their spears and that the flying guards who circled the tower hadn't yet arrived. He put his trust in her and concentrated on freeing Thamalon.

"Hold still," said Cale, "this is going to be tricky."

He cut the wires binding Thamalon's right wrist to the blade. Thamalon's arm fell limply to his side, all sensation long since squeezed out of the limb.

The heavy armor made it difficult to maneuver on the spinning vane, but Cale thrust one foot between the frame and the metal blade. Wedged there, his leg gave him an anchor. He unclasped his weapon belt, looped it through Thamalon's belt before securing it once more, and freed his master's legs.

Awkwardly, Thamalon put his limp arm around Cale's neck. Cale felt a feeble strength in his embrace and hoped it would return more quickly once he got Thamalon down.

"Hold on," he warned Thamalon. "Go limp, and make sure to stay above me."

He cut the remaining bonds, then kicked away to fall to the tower floor. The impact knocked the wind from his lungs, but the ill-fitting armor at last proved useful as more than a disguise.

Thamalon rolled off of Cale and lolled on the stone roof. Cale rose to a crouch and drew his long sword. To his surprise, none of the guards approached him.

The courtiers and servants had already fled the roof, and the guards had withdrawn to the far side, near the stairs. They held their spears up at attention and watched the sky above.

Cale looked up to see Shamur and Ripper circling the tower, waiting to land near Cale and Thamalon. She looked down at her husband lying on the ground, struggling to rise to his hands and knees as Cale stood protectively above him.

She didn't see the Sorcerer rising in the sky behind her.

"Shamur!" cried Cale. "Look out!"

She turned just in time to see the man shake his winged scepter at Ripper. A spear of red lightning shot from the scepter's giant ruby to plunge into the griffon's back, straight through the archer's seat in the double saddle. Sparks from the scintillating shaft ignited Shamur's red cloak. As the griffon fell onto the tower floor, she threw herself to the side, rolling to smother the flames. They had spread from the cloak to the long plume on her helm.

Ripper's body rolled until it hit the low wall at the tower's edge. Its impact sent half a ton of stone tumbling from the tower's edge, but the creature came to a halt, its wings splayed horribly as its leonine legs twitched for a few seconds before going limp.

"How many more uninvited guests must I endure?" bellowed the Sorcerer.

To Cale's ear, the voice sounded like Tamlin imitating his father. He couldn't see the man's face within its barred helm, but he feared he already knew whom he would resemble.

Shamur whipped off her flaming helmet and cast it away. She drew her sword and glared up defiantly at the Sorcerer.

"We are the death of you," she said, "if you don't allow us to leave here with my husband."

The Sorcerer laughed and glided slowly down to her.

"What a fierce one you are! Lady Uskevren, is it? However did mild Thamalon win you over with his ledgers and abacus? Let me have a look at you."

Cale saw her frown in puzzlement at the Sorcerer's words. Perhaps she was beginning to recognize his voice as well. Cale hoped that wouldn't cause her to hesitate at the wrong moment.

"Can you stand?" he whispered to Thamalon.

Thamalon rose to his feet, but he stood hunched painfully,

his arms hanging in simian fashion at his sides.

"Barely," he said, raising one hand to receive the short sword Cale passed him. He held it gingerly but with the unconscious grace of a practiced swordsman.

Cale doffed his helmet and pulled open the straps on his pauldrons, letting them slip to the roof.

"Stay here," he said, before circling around the tower.

All eyes were on the Sorcerer and Shamur, so he felt he had at least a slim chance of closing with the man should he land.

The Sorcerer remained carefully out of reach of Shamur's sword. He lowered his scepter and gazed appreciatively at the woman.

"I can see the resemblance in your eyes," he said. "I suppose I should be grateful."

"Reveal yourself," Shamur shouted. "Show me your face!"

"With pleasure, my dear girl," said the Sorcerer.

He lifted his helm and tossed it to his soldiers, who fell over themselves to catch it before it struck the floor.

Shamur grimaced at the sight of her son's face.

She snapped at him, "What have you done to Tamlin?"

The Sorcerer flinched.

"Do not speak that name," he growled. "I will not tolerate—"

The tower shook as thunder rumbled up from the castle's foundation—exactly as Cale had felt at Stormweather Towers twice before falling into the strange alternate plane. He'd made it halfway around the tower's edge, slightly behind the Sorcerer. It was still too far, and the man still floated too high above the tower roof. Cale crept ever closer, praying that none of the guards would notice him and cry out a warning.

"Who dares?" said the Sorcerer, shooting a glance at Thamalon and dropping slightly closer to the tower floor as he did so. He seemed surprised to see his guest was still present. "How—? Who else have you brought here?"

"Tamlin!" cried Shamur. "Where is he?"

"Of course," the Sorcerer said. "He would be able . . . But that means . . ."

Cale sensed that the man was about to flee. He would have no better opportunity than this one. He ran at the Sorcerer.

"My lord!" shouted one of the guards.

Shamur spotted Cale at the same time. Her gaze flicked uncertainly from the Sorcerer to Cale.

"No!" she shouted. "Wait!"

But Cale knew that to hesitate would mean their deaths, not to mention thousands more when the elves arrived. He leaped while still two yards behind the man, thrusting at his spine.

The Sorcerer turned just enough to elude instant death. Cale's blade sank deeply into the man's back, piercing his lung.

Despite her uncertainty, Shamur pounced upon the wounded Sorcerer. Shocked by his wound, he sank to the floor as she pulled him down. Cale had already withdrawn his sword and pressed it to the man's throat. He pinned the Sorcerer's left arm to the roof and kicked away his scepter.

"Don't kill him," hissed Shamur. She knelt on the man's right arm, though not too heavily. Her expression flickered between mistrust and wonder. "He could be . . ."

She didn't finish her thought.

"Don't worry," said Cale. He shouted at the approaching guards, "Stand back!"

At the sight of the blade to their master's throat, the guards withdrew a few steps.

"Drop your weapons," said Cale.

They grudgingly complied, throwing down their spears and unbuckling their sword belts.

"Idiots," grunted the Sorcerer.

His handsome face was twisted in a rictus of pain and annoyance. He twisted his pinned arms to press his fingers to Cale's leg, and he spat out a word of Art.

Even as Cale drew his blade across his enemy's throat, an

electric jolt snapped his spine like a whip and blinded him with a flash filled with green afterimages. His body jerked in uncontrollable spasms, and the Sorcerer pushed him away. Cale fell back on the roof. As the Sorcerer rose painfully to his feet, Cale saw Shamur twitching on the roof beside him.

The shock passed in mere moments, but that was all it took the guards to recover their weapons and form a line between their master and his foes. Cale rolled slowly to his side and seized the sword he'd dropped.

The Sorcerer looked up at the sky.

"You!" he shouted, shaking his fist at the heavens. With a gesture that left incarnadine trails behind his fingers, he waved away whatever vision only he had perceived then he snapped to one of his guards, "Take me to the Vault!"

The Sorcerer leaned heavily on the man's shoulder, and Cale saw he was leaving a trail of blood. Perhaps he would die before he reached his destination. Cale thought a prayer to Mask that it would be so.

Before descending the stairs, the Sorcerer paused to give his men one last command.

"Take these interlopers. When I return, I want to them all spinning on the Vanes."

CHAPTER 25

PASSAGE

After the blinding light and the horrid keening sound, Tamlin floated in a white abyss. He'd lost both his sword and the mysterious key that had pulsed in his hand as they uncovered the gate. His hand went to his breast. Not only was the flesh unbroken by the wound he was sure had killed him, but it was also bereft of clothing.

As the light receded to a comfortable level, Tamlin saw that he was completely naked.

Also, he was flying.

Tamlin floated in the center of a high hall. Its ceiling soared so far above him that he could barely make out its vaulted arc. He looked down to see that the floor was a distant shadow. All around the curving walls were doors and windows, crooked passages and candlelit promenades, half-balconies and flights of stairs that rose up past balconies of mirrors and portraits, only to turn and end abruptly in midair.

The room looked like a jumbled jigsaw puzzle of Stormweather Towers stacked four stories too high, with pieces lost from a hundred other puzzles mixed in. There stood a gigantic suit of armor that Tamlin's uncle Perivel had once worn. Upon a flight of stairs was a painting of his mother as a young woman, but Tamlin had never seen the portraits to either side of her. One of them was a green-faced lion-woman.

Tamlin was fairly certain he would have heard of such an unusual ancestor.

"Where in the world . . . ?" Tamlin let the question melt away.

"Beats me," replied a voice behind him.

Tamlin tried to turn around, but he managed only to squirm where he hovered in the air.

"Just think about it," said the voice. "Not, 'I'd like to turn around now.' That's not the way it works. Instead, just imagine that you've already turned."

Tamlin did as the voice instructed. His body responded instantly to his will, turning him gracefully around.

"You're a natural!" said the man who floated before him. "It took me hours to figure that out, and a tenday to get good at it."

Apart from the floating, the other figure differed from Tamlin in two significant ways. First, he was fully clothed. Second, he was very nearly transparent.

"Chaney Foxmantle!"

"In the ectoplasm," said Chaney.

"You're a ghost?"

Chaney lifted the collar of his shirt and peered through it at Tamlin.

"Either that, or I've got one hell of a complaint for the girl who does my wash."

"Very funny," said Tamlin.

"I see something funnier," said Chaney, smirking.

Tamlin covered himself with both hands. Scowling at the ghost, he said, "This is no time for jokes."

"Trust me," said Chaney. "There's never a better time for a few laughs than after you've just been killed."

"You saw what happened?"

"I had a box seat," said Chaney. "It's a long story, but you'd better hear it all."

Tamlin listened in wonder as the ghost relayed his tale. By the time he was finished, Tamlin felt a heat for vengeance rising in his heart. He couldn't decide whom he wanted to murder first, but the Hulorn was a favorite for when he was next in a betting mood.

"Not only was I *not* inducted into this ghostly procession of yours," said Tamlin, "but somehow you and I both ended up in this strange place. It looks a bit like Stormweather here, doesn't it?"

"I was just thinking the same thing. That looks like the banister Tal and I used to slide down when we were boys."

"What do you suppose happened to the other ghosts? Were they destroyed?"

"I don't think so," said Chaney. He pointed to an open hallway lined with windows. "Look there. Can you see it?"

Tamlin saw a shadowy figure lurking by one of the windows. It pressed its smoky hands upon the glass as if trying to escape.

"And there," said Chaney, pointing to a door far below them.

Tamlin saw a pair of dark specters tugging at the latch of a portal that looked exactly like the kitchen door at Stormweather Towers. Despite the shadows' efforts, the latch remained stubbornly fast.

"Why're they here?"

"It must have something to do with that big stone block you dug up. What was that thing?"

"I'm not certain," said Tamlin, "but I suspected it was a

secret relic of my grandfather's. Also, it might be the key to my parents' disappearance."

"How so?"

Tamlin told Chaney his story since the kidnapping. While he'd never known his brother's friend very well, he decided it was safe to confide in him. After all, Chaney was already dead. He wouldn't be spreading much gossip in the Green Gauntlet.

"So this portal somehow intercepted them from being trapped inside a magic painting? If so, they must be in here somewhere," suggested Chaney. "Maybe this is some sort of magical family mausoleum."

"I hope you're wrong about that."

"Sorry," said Chaney. "Never mind me. Sometimes I say ridiculous things."

"My bet is that it's some sort of otherworldly hiding place, like the secret passages in Stormweather Towers."

"That makes sense if your grandfather had some secret magical powers," agreed Chaney. "After all, you aren't dead. I mean, you don't *look* like a ghost."

"And my wound is healed," said Tamlin. "If old Aldimar had some contingency spell that could be triggered only on his death, then it must also be designed to heal him of the wounds that killed him."

"Too bad he didn't spend the extra coin on the clothing spell."

"At least I wouldn't be caught dead in those threadbare rags," Tamlin shot back. "I would make a far more fashionable corpse, I assure you."

He meant it as a friendly jest, and he was glad to see Chaney took it that way.

"You see? It's all much easier when you don't take it too seriously." He stopped laughing abruptly and said, "Hey, how did you do that?"

Tamlin was fully dressed in his favorite attire: a green and blue quilted tunic threaded with gold and pearls, russet velvet trousers held with a jeweled belt, and thigh-high boots made of black leather so supple it might have been silk.

"I need a sword," Tamlin said, and his favorite blade appeared at his hip."

"Nice trick," said Chaney, appreciatively. "Can you get me one?"

Tamlin smiled and buffed his fingernails upon his chest.

"A blade for my friend, if you please."

A short sword appeared in Chaney's grasp. His triumphant grin transformed into a frown as the weapon fell through his intangible hand and down to the distant floor.

"Dark," said Chaney.

"Enough of this. That murderer is still in my house. We have to go back and stop him."

"You mean go back and get killed again?"

"I won't make the same mistake again, I promise you. This time I'll fetch the archers and have him perforated from a distance."

"Not bad," said Chaney, "but how will you get back there?"

"Good question," said Tamlin. "This place is full of doors. What do you say we open a few?"

They flew down. When Tamlin set his feet to the floor, he felt vaguely disappointed as weight settled once more around his shoulders. He willed himself to levitate once more, and he rose a few inches in the air. Satisfied that he'd not lost this miraculous power, he settled down, once again obedient of gravity.

"Nice trick, isn't it?" observed Chaney.

"Somehow, I feel I could do anything here," he said. "It's as if all the powers of my dreams were suddenly real."

Tamlin approached the two dark specters. They withdrew slightly at his approach, but still their hands scrabbled uselessly at the edges of the door. Their faces turned to him hopefully, and they moaned like dogs begging for their supper.

He recognized one of them as the ghostly remains of Stellana Toemalar, a shrewish old widow with a notorious dislike for children and an insistence on hideously complex contracts. Tamlin still hadn't relinquished his own childhood resentment for her scolding ways, but he felt more pity than anything else to see her reduced to a mute and desperate phantom.

"Here," he said, pulling at the latch.

It opened easily, revealing an endless expanse of clock-work machinery—not just a room, but an entire world of gears and pistons and wheels. Cogs and levers formed the plains and mountains, even the seas and clouds of the mechanical world. Tremendous clusters of pulleys and chains floated above the land like clouds. Everything was the color of metal: dull lead, bright brass, deep copper, black iron.

The moaning of the specters turned to a regular pulsing sound as they drifted out through the door. Tamlin watched their bodies transform into solid matter as they came ever closer to their destination. Before they were too distant to see, Tamlin thought he saw them transforming into simpler, puppetlike shapes.

He shuddered and closed the door.

"What in the world . . . ?" he asked, though he felt he knew the answer already. "Another world entirely. Another plane."

"Was that their afterlife?" asked Chaney.

"Perhaps," said Tamlin. "The other specters seem drawn to different doors. Let's have a look."

Tamlin released another phantom into a world of lush forests and prowling beasts. He fell to the grassy ground in a hunter's crouch, his body solidifying into a younger, stronger version of Gorkun Baerent. Tamlin knew him as a fair-dealing man who loved hunting far more than managing his shipping affairs. A feral smile formed on Gorkun's lips as he realized the nature of his new surroundings. The man looked back at Tamlin with a joyous and grateful expression. Tamlin waved to him as he closed the door to the arboreal world.

He tried another door, slamming it almost immediately after the specter lingering at the portal slipped through, falling down into a mass of fighting bodies. The clamor of the place, the screams of triumph and agony, were deafening and repulsive.

"What *is* this place?" asked Chaney.

"Some sort of nexus of worlds," speculated Tamlin. Even as he said the words, he heard their ring of truth. "The ghosts seem drawn to particular worlds, perhaps their just rewards . . . or torments."

"Then why don't *I* feel drawn to any of them?"

Tamlin shrugged, then said, "Wait a moment."

He closed his eyes and tried to feel any attraction to a particular door. Soon he realized he was merely listening rather than extending any intellectual or emotional sense. Still, he imagined he could feel currents flowing through the weird house, invisible avenues running from door to door—or to the windows and chimneys, and up and down the stairways.

"Are you getting anything?" asked Chaney.

"Something, yes . . . but I still don't know what it is. Let's try some of those windows."

Together, they flew up to a high balcony housing six windows. The glass appeared clear from their side, but all they saw beyond was starless night.

Tamlin opened one.

The smell of autumn leaves rushed into the room, and the breeze chilled his body. Beyond the open portal, clouds rushed across the full face of Selûne and her attendant shards. Far below, the moonlight illuminated a grassy plain where hundreds of wolves loped toward them. Their pace increased as they strove to keep up with their leader, a naked, hirsute brute whose dark hair whipped back like a war banner. He raised a sword the size of a wagon axle and lowered its point toward Stormweather, and all the beasts swarmed down from the hills.

Tamlin slammed the window shut. Cooling sweat chilled his hands. He looked at Chaney.

"Did you see that?"

"Uh huh," said Chaney, still staring at the window. "It looked like Talbot."

"What do you think it means?"

"I guess it means you should stay on his good side."

"No chance of that, eh?"

They looked at each other dubiously.

"Maybe it's just a warning of what *could* be," suggested Tamlin. "It doesn't have to happen."

"You're probably right," offered Chaney. "Still . . . You want to look through another window?"

"No, thanks," said Tamlin. "Maybe later."

"Then it's back to the doors."

"No," said Tamlin. "I just. . . ."

He pictured his father and mother, and as an afterthought Mister Cale. Closing his eyes again, he willed himself to see where they were. Gradually, he felt drawn to another window. He followed the lure across the room and down a level.

When he opened his eyes, he was hovering before a stained glass oval with no latch or sill.

"Do you have to break it?" asked Chaney.

"I don't think so."

Tamlin reached out to touch the surface of the glass. It became clear, and he looked down from a great height at the top of a tower encircled by giant weather vanes. On the roof between them, his mother and Erevis Cale lay stunned on the ground. Nearby, his father slumped over a sword he used as a cane to keep himself from collapsing on the tower roof.

Behind a screen of guards, a man in a scarlet cloak looked up at the window. Except for his beard, the man looked exactly like Tamlin.

You! he said.

Tamlin sensed the word rather than heard it.

With a gesture, the other man dispelled the vision. Tamlin stared at the stained glass window.

"What was that?" asked Chaney. "He looked just like you."

"I think we'll know soon," said Tamlin.

A few minutes later, a fine network of lightning flashed from window to window, and thunder shook the place between the worlds. Tamlin pushed off from the floor to hover in the air, as if by some forgotten instinct. Chaney followed his example.

"Here he comes," said Tamlin.

"How do you know?"

"I can feel it."

"You!" thundered a voice from high above them. Tamlin looked up to see the bearded image of himself standing before a glowing portal at the end of a floating stairway. "You should not have come here, boy."

"Uh, oh," said Chaney, fading back from the impending conflict.

"Who are you?" demanded Tamlin.

This was the other self he'd seen in his slumbering visions, the cruel avatar of his dreams. He flew up to face his double, and the man flew down to meet him in the center of the hall.

"Don't you recognize me?" his doppelganger sneered at him, but Tamlin perceived a shadow of fear in the man's emerald eyes.

"You are no part of me," said Tamlin. "Somehow you've usurped my dreams, I know that much! And this place, it belongs to my family. You have no right to be here."

"That is where you're wrong, boy. I am the *only* one who has a right to Stormweather. I'm the one who built it."

"Aldimar," said Tamlin. "Grandfather?"

"Right, and right," said his double. "You are clever enough, if weak and ignorant. No doubt you have a hundred questions for me. If you were anyone else, I might indulge your curiosity. However . . ."

He shook his fist at Tamlin, then splayed his fingers wide as he shouted a word that had eluded Tamlin in all his half-remembered dreams:

"Anabar!"

Lightning shot from Aldimar's palm, straight toward

Tamlin's body. It cascaded over him like cool water, and he jerked in surprise. An instant later, he realized the energy had washed over him harmlessly.

Tamlin had never before been able to trap one of those arcane words in memory. The language of wizards and sorcerers was slippery to the mundane mind, but this one fetched up in his brain.

Anabar, he mused. What other words have I forgotten from dreams?

"What?" roared Aldimar. Tamlin hated the way the man's expression turned his own features into a cruel visage. "What trickery is this?"

"Oh," said Tamlin. The bluff was his favorite gambit among his admittedly limited arsenal of negotiating tactics. "I know a thing or two. Nothing to boast about, mind you. Perhaps I'll trade one to you for your history of the portal and this . . . nexus."

As Tamlin had calculated, his insouciant bluff irritated his nemesis. Aldimar plucked a bit of black goo from a little pouch in his harness, balled it in his fist, and flung it toward him.

"Effluvaen!"

Tamlin tried not to flinch as the ball of flame rushed toward him, exploding in his face. He felt a warm tingling as the fire burst impotently around him. Not so much as an eyebrow had wilted in the holocaust.

Hearing another arcane word started a miniature avalanche of memories. Half a dozen more magical triggers sprouted in his fallow memory. He *did* know magic after all—or at least he once had, as a boy, in dreams. Almost two decades later, in a world between worlds, he could evoke them once more. He would need the raw materials to cast the spells himself. As he thought of them, he sensed their scant mass appear in the pockets of his belt. He knew at once this sort of instant summoning was a trick that would only work there, in his home.

His *true* home, he realized. The Stormweather between the worlds.

"Come now, Grandfather," Tamlin said, surreptitiously

touching the conjured items in their pockets. Less a bluff than an educated guess, he revealed his greatest secret hope. "Surely you realize the futility of using my own power against me?"

With that he threw back the fire and lightning, along with a clap of thunder for showmanship.

Aldimar cringed at the first blast, but he held fast against the bolt and the thunder.

"It is true that you were born in the radiance of the Vault. That might give you more natural affinity for its gifts, but I have had decades to learn its power."

"The decades since your *death*, old man," shot back Tamlin. "What kept you here, when you should have gone on to your just reward?"

"That is the price, lad. See how much you haven't learned? The Vault demands servitude for its gifts, and I would still be its damned gatekeeper if your dreams had not given me a way out. Why should you mind? They were nothing to you but sleeping fancies. For me they were salvation. They were *life*."

Aldimar flew toward Tamlin, pausing only after he'd come within a yard of his grandson, his identical twin. Tamlin could see the sweat on his neck.

"I have seen what you did with them," said Tamlin. "You corrupted everything I ever dreamed of."

Tamlin pushed a finger into his grandfather's chest and felt a satisfying solidity there. He kept the smile in his heart from reaching his face as he realized how he could end the stalemate.

Aldimar shrugged and said, "Your pubescent fantasies were hardly the sort of world in which a man should live. I made something worthy of them. I built a nation. I became a *king*!"

"A tyrant, actually," said Tamlin, "but what's the point of quibbling over terminology? Even if I could overlook the rest, I saw what you were doing to my parents. In my opinion, that more than justifies a spot of grand-patricide."

He drew his blade.

"Foolish whelp," said Aldimar. "What makes you think you could match blades with me?"

Aldimar conjured a blade to his own hand and rushed forward in a flying lunge.

"Well," said Tamlin, neatly parrying the attack, "judging from what I've read about your life, you were never the keenest swordsman. Besides, I suspect you have had little opportunity for practice over these past decades, relying as you have on the power you stole from me."

"Don't count on it, child." Aldimar attacked his legs, and Tamlin barely flew back in time to avoid a dire wound.

Despite his bravado, he knew he was at a disadvantage off the ground. He flew to the floor and turned to receive Aldimar's charge. His wily opponent circled to the left and above him, refusing to join Tamlin on the floor.

"Fledgling!" he cried. "You can only dream of flying. Surrender and let it end swiftly, or watch as I return to the Vanes and finish off your parents."

"No!" Tamlin flew up, furiously beating his opponent's blade to create an opening. "You're *never* going back there."

Aldimar laughed as he retreated up toward the door from which he'd arrived. Despite all the power of his will, Tamlin couldn't match his speed. Aldimar had his hand on the door as Tamlin landed on the high stairway.

"And how will you stop me?" Aldimar taunted as he pulled on the door latch.

It didn't budge.

"Well," said Tamlin, relief giving him new strength. "I suppose I could refuse to open the door. Among the many things *you* don't know is that I died to get here. I'm thinking that makes me the gatekeeper now, and that means you're going nowhere."

Aldimar fairly snarled as he glowered at his grandson, then he forced a laugh. Tamlin heard its falseness.

"I wonder what will happen when I kill you here," Aldimar said, "in the seat of our shared power."

He made a savage ballestra down the stairs, slashing at Tamlin's head.

Tamlin stepped away from the cut and riposted at Aldimar's wrist as the Sorcerer tried to recover. His blade slipped off the man's bracer and barely grazed his thumb. Still, Aldimar hissed like a man long unused to pain. He retreated to the top of the stairs, his back against the unyielding portal.

"I hope my father wasn't unduly fond of you," said Tamlin. "It would seem not, since he hardly ever mentions you. But then, my father is never one to dwell overmuch on failures."

He parried every attack with as much nonchalance as he could muster, grinning up at his counterpart with a cool facade despite the fear that churned in his heart.

Aldimar grew more frantic with every attack, slashing wildly at Tamlin's head and arms, and abandoning the use of his blade's point all together. Tamlin recognized the flaw in his attack and exploited it with quick, short thrusts after each parry, pinking Aldimar's thigh, then his shin and his foot. The tiny wounds did little harm, but they enraged his opponent beyond the last bastion of reason. Tamlin watched for the inevitable rush.

It wasn't long in coming. Aldimar bulled his way down the stairs. Tamlin immediately retreated, crouched low, and thrust up into the man's belly, just below the sternum. His blade sank deep into Aldimar's body, stopped briefly as his heart contracted around the wound, and pressed in inches farther as Tamlin renewed his thrust. He bent his elbow and followed his sword upward until he was face-to-face with the man who had stolen his appearance, his power, and his dreams.

"That's all for you, old man."

CHAPTER 26

"That's the third or fourth spookiest thing I've ever seen," said Chaney.

"Indeed," said Tamlin.

It gave him the chills to watch his own body dissolve at first into a transparent image of itself, then to a smoky shadow that slunk its way down the stairs. Tamlin watched it creep along until it came to a wide pair of doors that reminded him of those that lead to his mother's solar.

"What do you mean, 'third or fourth'?"

"Malveens," said Chaney. "Extra spooky."

"Ah."

"Where do you suppose those doors lead?"

"I have an idea . . . Someplace hot? With brimstone and pools of lava," ventured Tamlin.

He'd thought he might experience mixed emotions

after the death of his grandfather, but his feelings remained refreshingly clear. The old pirate deserved a long draught of the torment he'd visited on others.

"Shall we take a peek?" asked Chaney.

"Why not?"

Tamlin joined the shade at the doors and opened them. Contrary to his guess, this particular hell was cold and dry. Aldimar fell howling into the ice, where his body melted into the shape of a fat, white, sluglike creature before it froze again, stuck to the windswept plane.

Tamlin closed the door behind him.

"Whew," said Chaney. "Sort of makes you want to go out and do good works, doesn't it?"

"Yea, verily," agreed Tamlin, with an inner earnestness that belied his flippant tone.

"Listen," said Chaney, "while you were busy dispatching your evil twin, I was doing some thinking. You found a window that showed your parents, right? What about your brother and sister?"

"Of course!" said Tamlin.

Even before he closed his eyes, he felt the thread of his desire coursing through the jigsaw Stormweather. He followed it to a skylight window. At Tamlin's touch, it showed an image of the solar back at Stormweather Towers.

"There," he whispered.

Talbot and Radu Malveen fought beneath the great blue stones of the waterfall. Their blades flashed faster than the eye could perceive, and Talbot's white shirt was already streaked with blood. Radu seemed untouched, except for a wide swath missing from his cloak.

A dagger whirled down from the top of the waterfall stones, toward the assassin's face. With a twitch of his blade, Radu deflected the missile effortlessly, without even glancing up at Tazi perched upon the rocks. Ignoring her, he pressed the attack on Talbot.

"Kill 'im, Tal!" Chaney shouted at the window. He looked

at Tamlin. "We have to go back!"

"But I'm dead there," said Tamlin. "Even if I can open the door, won't I vanish for good if I try to go back?"

"I don't know," said Chaney, "but they need help."

"You're right, of course," said Tamlin.

He thought of home and followed the alluring path to a trapdoor at the base of the weird hall. Tamlin lifted it by its round iron ring, revealing the same strange blue stone that plugged the gate he found under the cellars.

"Uh oh," said Chaney. "I hope you don't need that key to get through."

"Me too," said Tamlin. "Maybe my blood is what activates it."

He cut the heel of his thumb with his sword and pressed the wound to the stone.

Nothing.

"Wait a second," said Chaney. "Aldimar was dead when he was trapped here, but somehow he had a body in that other world. That must have been *your* body, the one your dreams created. All along, you existed both in Selgaunt and in that other world—at least until he took over that one."

"Sure, but I just killed him . . . *aha*!"

"Exactly," said Chaney. "Your body here and your body there—they could be two separate things. When he came in here, he must have left it behind. Or in transit . . . or something like that."

"To get back home, I have to go to the other world first," concluded Tamlin.

He glanced back at the window to Stormweather Towers. Tal had just shattered Radu's blade, but the assassin caught the following cut between his left palm and his petrified right hand. He wrenched the sword away and shot a hard kick into Talbot's chest. The blow sent the bigger man flying across the wide room, out of range of the window.

Radu looked up at Tazi, who threw another knife at him. He blocked it with his ruined hand and poised to leap up at her.

"Hurry!" urged Chaney.

Tamlin flew to the portal through which Aldimar had appeared.

He blew a kiss to the ceiling as he opened the door and said, "Tymora, smile on me."

White radiance spilled out, blowing back his hair and conjured clothing even as it drew his essence out into another world.

Tamlin fell to the ground. An aching pain burned deep within his chest. He rose to his knees and felt his back. His hand came away bloody.

"My lord!" called a guard in red armor. "Please, now that you have quelled the Vault, won't you allow Lady Malaika to tend that wound?"

Tamlin allowed the man to help him walk out of the dark chamber, past a set of sturdy gates. He looked back to see the now-familiar gate, without the blue seal that blocked passage from Stormweather Towers.

He was wearing Aldimar's clothes, and the men around him were Aldimar's soldiers.

Yet they had no idea that Aldimar was dead.

"Yes," said Tamlin. "Send her to the tower. I return there immediately."

"My lord," said the guard. "Your scepter."

Tamlin nodded as he accepted the heavy wand with its winglike blades. At its touch, he knew its power to drive his own spells and transform them into greater, more varied incarnations. He uttered the words to his flying spell as he touched the feather token on his harness. He knew it would be there, for he remembered all his old dreams. Despite his terrible wound, for the first time in his life he felt complete.

Likewise, he knew the way out of the basement, through

the great Stillstone Hall, and up to the highest tower. Seeing the places around him, concrete and real, brought back a flood of assurances that his forgotten dreams had never been dreams at all.

Malaika.

Something about the word was a charm to speed his remembrance. Strangely, he couldn't hold an image of the woman in his mind.

Everywhere he flew, the inhabitants of Castle Stormweather scurried out of his way, falling over themselves to make obeisance to their master as he hastened to the defense of the fortress. At last, he surged up through the central tower and flew up above its roof. Desperately, he searched the battle-churned scene for his parents.

Dead guardsmen lay scattered over the roof, and among their bodies a score more fought on. Their opponents were elves armed with spears and swords. More of them descended from long dark ropes depending from an enormous creature floating overhead.

Skwalos, Tamlin remembered. Those are their tongues.

Beside the dangling tethers hovered more elves hurling magic down at the human defenders.

Another wave of elves joined those on the roof, but they were still outnumbered by the armored humans. Among the elves, Shamur fought shoulder-to-shoulder with Erevis Cale. Between them lay the slumped and bloody figure of Tamlin's father.

"No!" Tamlin screamed. Then, to his soldiers, "Stop! Fall back at once!"

No one heard his cries amid the clashing blades and exploding spells. He calmed himself and thought of the spell to enhance his voice. He spoke the word and blasted his voice to all within sight.

"Cease fighting! Fall back now! I call for truce!"

The warriors were slow to respond, but gradually they backed away from the elves. Tamlin looked all around to see that everyone was staring at him.

He felt highly vulnerable. Before he consciously decided he needed protection, his fingers were already tracing the glyphs and his lips already forming the arcane words.

He finished the spell just in time, as a pair of lightning bolts shot through him from points near the dangling tethers from the flying creature. He felt the hair on his neck rise, and his eyes burned from the flash, but he was little worse for the attack. Apparently the invulnerability he enjoyed in the Stormweather nexus was considerably less potent outside its walls. He followed the lingering afterimage of the bolts back to their origin, where an old elf woman and a younger elf man gestured toward him.

"Wait," he called. "Truce, I say. Let us hold a while and speak of terms."

"Never," shouted the young wizard who had attacked him. He pronounced his words precisely, as if they were the few he knew in the common tongue, and he'd practiced them often. "We will never surrender to you."

"Listen to him!" cried a sweet voice from below.

On the rooftop, amid the smoking carnage, stood a lithe brown elf with hair as dark as a still pool on a moonless night. She must have arrived by magic, for heaps of bodies blocked the path from the stairs.

Malaika, thought Tamlin. That's your name, but who exactly are you?

"I call for truce, not surrender," called Tamlin, wresting his gaze away from the beautiful elf. "Come, let us each tend to our wounded, and let us meet and speak of peace."

The elves hesitated, suspicious of a trick. One of them barked out a laugh so harsh that Tamlin couldn't imagine the sound emanating from an elf. Considering the cruelty Tamlin had witnessed in his dreams—or visions, as he was coming to think of them—he could hardly blame them.

"Here," he said, holding the winged scepter out before him. In it, he knew, lay the greater store of his warlike power.

Without it, he could still hurl spells, but not endlessly. "I offer this as a token of good faith."

"Beware," warned the old woman mage.

Despite her warning, the younger wizard flew forward, hesitating only as he drew near his sorcerous adversary. Tamlin met the elf's gaze with his own, trying to show his honest intentions without seeming overeager. The young man snatched away the scepter and flew back to hover near the old woman, holding the weapon as triumphantly as if he'd wrested it from the foe. The old woman gazed curiously at Tamlin.

"We will recover our dead and tend our wounded," she said, "until the hour when we parlay. Name it."

"Dawn, two days hence," he said. "A time of new beginnings."

The Vermilion Guard lowered their weapons and turned to gape up at their master, allowing the elves to place their fallen on the long fronds from their creature-vessels. As the elves retreated, Tamlin flew down to his parents. Malaika met him there.

"My lord," she said. "You are wounded."

"Tend to my father first," he said.

Malaika started at the word "father." Her hopeful eyes lingered on Tamlin as she knelt beside the fallen man. She looked to his several wounds and pressed her hands upon the horrid sword-cut in his breast. She closed her eyes and raised her voice in song.

Tamlin moved to kneel beside her.

Shamur blocked his way, and a glowering Erevis Cale raised his sword to Tamlin's breast.

"Tamlin?" said Shamur. "How do we know it's really you?"

Tamlin struggled for a proof. "I don't know, Mother," he said. "Do you have any suggestions, Mister Pale?"

Cale shrugged and lowered his sword.

"That is good enough for me," he said, then he muttered something with the word "impudent" in it.

Shamur raised a hand to Tamlin's face and said, "When did you—?"

"I will tell you everything later. Now, we must look after Father and get back to Stormweather."

"He is dying," said Malaika.

"No," said Tamlin. "He can't be."

"He was wounded before the fight. His heart is failing."

"You must save him," said Tamlin.

"I cannot," she said. "Not here. He has the blood. You must take him back inside."

"What?"

"Do you remember where we met?"

"I don't . . . *Malaika*. It is you, isn't it? That's why I can't remember you."

She nodded sadly as she rose and put her hands to the wound in his back. She sang the ragged edges back together as he cast his own spell, conjuring a levitating, concave disc to convey his father down to the portal between the worlds.

Tamlin gestured to Cale to help him lift the Old Owl gently into the concave disc.

"What are you two talking about?" insisted Shamur.

"Mother, meet Stormweather. Stormweather, this is my mother. Now, let us hurry."

"Where is the elf woman?" asked Shamur. She looked around the Stormweather nexus with a disappointing lack of awe. Everyone except Malaika had arrived through the gateway in the Ineffable Vault and stood within the strange version of the mansion they called home. "I thought she was right behind us."

"She's here," said Thamalon, gazing around the nexus with an expression of curious familiarity. "She's always here."

Since passing through the gate, he appeared completely healed of his wounds. Tamlin had enjoyed a similar anodyne, but both Shamur and Cale still bore the wounds of the battle atop Castle Stormweather

"I feel it, too," agreed Tamlin.

"Not that I feel ungrateful," said Cale, nodding at his injured shoulder, "but perhaps she could lend my lady and I a little aid."

"Sorry, old chap," said Tamlin. He was beginning to enjoy being the one who knew more than everyone else around him. "We've always loved you like an uncle, but you aren't actually blood now, are you?"

"What is that supposed to mean?" said Shamur.

"No, he's right," said Thamalon slowly, as if gradually coming to understand the nature of the place. "Neither of you is an Uskevren."

Shamur began to sound impatient. "Would one of you please explain—Look out!"

She crouched low and whipped her sword from its sheath.

"Don't worry," said Tamlin. "That's just Talbot's old pal Chaney.'"

Chaney waved and sketched a poor imitation of a bow.

"Sorry, my lady," the ghost said, "I didn't mean to startle you."

"But he's dead," Shamur protested, refusing to address the spirit directly. "Isn't he?"

"Aye, a ghost," said Tamlin, "but that's nothing. Wait until I tell you about some of Talbot's *other* friends. But never mind that for now. I have to go pull the children out of a spot of trouble."

"We'll come with you," said Shamur resolutely.

"No," said Tamlin and Thamalon together.

Shamur looked ready to argue with her son, but then she turned to her husband, surprised at his complicity.

"I . . . I still feel weak from the passage," Thamalon explained. "I would only hinder you. Cale, go with him."

"My lord," nodded Cale.

"Shamur," Thamalon added, almost timidly. "Would you remain with me a while?"

"But . . ." Shamur hesitated, torn between her desire to return and help her children and the lure of her husband's curious tone. "Of course," she said.

When she reached for his hand, Thamalon withdrew.

A terrible understanding chilled Tamlin's body as his gaze met his father's. Through their green eyes, they forged a wordless bond.

Not yet, they said. This is our secret.

"Father," said Tamlin. "We will return for you."

Thamalon stepped forward as if to embrace his son before thinking better of it.

"Hurry," he said.

Tamlin kissed his mother and led Cale to the base of the strange hall, where he lifted a trapdoor. When he saw the bright radiance surge up from its aperture, he stepped back before its magic could draw him through.

"You were right!" said Chaney, hovering just beside his shoulder. "Now that you're whole, you can return."

"See you on the other side?" asked Tamlin.

"I don't know," said Chaney reluctantly. "Back there I was bound to that miserable beggar. It's boring here, but at least I'm free of him. I don't know whether I should take the chance that I'll be stuck to him again."

"All right, then," said Tamlin. "We'll likely do well enough without your help. I'll tell Talbot you're safe."

"Bastard," muttered Chaney. "All right then. I'm in. What do we do? Just jump in?"

"I think being close is enough," said Tamlin. "Just in case, take my hand."

He did, as well as a ghost could, and so did Cale. Together they stepped toward the portal.

The white rush and thunder took them, and they tumbled out of the world and into the one they knew. They emerged in the deserted, excavated cellars of Stormweather Towers.

"Chaney?" Tamlin called. "You here?"

Tamlin no longer saw the ghost, nor did he hear a reply. He hoped the trip between the planes hadn't dissipated the spirit. He'd been hoping for some supernatural assistance in the fight ahead. He moved toward the stairs.

He flew beside Cale, soon passing him. He rushed out of the cellar steps, into the grand foyer, and up the grand stairway. There he turned west, toward the solar and the sound of battle.

The once fine double doors had been smashed to flinders and shards. Inside, countless paths had been torn through the foliage, and two of the trees had been knocked completely over. One of the towering stones from the waterfall lay upon the ruins of a row of shelves and the crushed flora they once held.

Tamlin heard only the sound of running water and heavy breathing. He followed the latter sound to its source. Before he reached it, he found the slumped bodies of three of the house guards. He frowned at the sight of them and continued to find the source of the panting.

Tazi lay back against the remaining half of a huge, crushed pot. Her left jaw was already blackening, and blood streamed from her nose and mouth. She held her left arm close to her ribs.

When she saw Tamlin, her eyes widened.

"Ruh!" she whispered, slurring her words through puffy lips. The blow that blackened her face must have made her bite her tongue as well. "He things you deh!"

Tamlin heard a small choking sound deep within Cale's chest. The tall man knelt beside Tazi, cradling her head in one arm while holding a blade in the other.

Tamlin felt his bravado dissolve once more into fury. He struggled to contain the wild emotion as he stroked his sister's battered cheek and falsified a smile for her.

"Don't worry, little sister. This time, I'm here to rescue *you*."

"No," she insisted. "I thing he kill Dal alrea'y. Ruh!"

The practiced smile trembled and fell away from Tamlin's face. He looked to Erevis Cale and said, "Guard her."

"With my life," promised Cale.

Tamlin flew up off the ground and soared across the ruins of the solar. He saw no sign of movement until he heard a low growling in the far corner. There, making a round trail of bloody footprints on the floor beneath the sun window was a black wolf the size of a pony. It bled from a dozen wounds and held its hind leg up protectively. Nearby, a maimed guard cowered from the beast, trapped in the corner by his own fear.

"Malveen!" bellowed Tamlin. "Where is he?"

The guard looked up at him with mingled hope and fear. Still too cowed to speak and draw the wolf's attention, he pointed with his chin toward the pond.

Tamlin flew back to the waterfall, careful not to come too close to the obscuring clumps of foliage. Water sprayed in an arc over the carpet, where a colossal blow to the fountain had uprooted its plumbing. Its cascade left ripples across the water, which remained murky with blood.

Tamlin flew closer, seeing a figure lying beneath the surface of the water, unmoving. Cautiously, he approached.

It was Radu Malveen, his mask shattered during the fight with Tazi, Tal, and the house guard. Fragments of porcelain still clung to his cheeks, attached to posts bonded through his flesh to his skull.

The reflection of another face rippled in the water above Malveen's. It was Chaney, waving frantically and mouthing words. Tamlin had no talent for lip reading, but he peered closer to make them out.

"What are you saying, man?" said Tamlin. " 'He . . . is . . . faking . . . !' "

Tamlin flew up to the ceiling just as Radu Malveen surged out of the water, his sword extended fully and pointed once more at Tamlin's heart. The point pierced Tamlin's leather jacket, pricking his chest just above the nipple as Radu's leap carried him high. Just before Tamlin's back hit the ceiling, the inhuman assassin fell back into the pond with a crimson splash. There he crouched for an instant, preparing for another leap.

"*Anabar!*" shouted Tamlin, thrusting his hand at his enemy.

The lightning formed a thick column all around and through Malveen, cascading down into the pond and leaping back up into his body, its power spread and magnified by the water. For an instant, Tamlin saw the man's skeleton, black against the white outline of his flesh. Jagged spikes protruded from the face of his skull and the bones of his right arm.

The assassin fell motionless into the water.

Tamlin kept his distance, looking around for a mirror. He hoped Chaney could relay some confirmation of the kill. At last he found a basin and looked into it, searching for the ghost's reflection.

Chaney arrived an instant later, grinning and mouthing the words, *Out cold.*

"My lord," cried a guard from the solar door. Six other men crowded behind him, anxious for battle. "The reinforcements have come with spears."

"No more need," said Tamlin. He turned to see Cale standing with Tazi in his arms. "Send a runner to the House of Song. We have need of healers, but don't wait for them—see to my sister's injuries immediately."

"Aye, my lord," the guard said. He delegated the orders to one of his men, who immediately ran out of the room, then he turned back to Tamlin. "What of the wolf?"

"Leave him to me," said Tamlin.

One look at the snarling animal told him it would be no easier to subdue his brother than it was to neutralize Radu Malveen. He thought of his vision in the Stormweather nexus. Talbot's death was the one sure remedy to the dire prophecy he'd seen. Tamlin might never have a better chance to remove his dangerous brother from the family.

No, he decided. Should the vision prove true, he would deal with it when the time came. He wouldn't stoop to preemptive fratricide, no matter how dangerous Talbot might someday become.

"On second thought," he said. "Send for Larajin, and let no one else near him until she arrives."

He uttered the words to another spell and reached into the pond with his magic. Radu's body floated up from the water, his head lolling to one side, his lips and eye sockets pink and swollen. The faintest movement of his chest showed that the assassin still lived.

"What shall we do with this one?" asked the guard.

The man did a credible job of retaining his composure in the face of his young master's sudden demonstration of sorcerous powers. Tamlin decided to keep an eye on the fellow for future advancement.

"What's your name, man?"

"Kainan, my lord."

"Well, Kainan, fetch me some shackles," he said. "Heavy ones, and plenty of them. Post a double guard in the big workshop downstairs. Clear out the furniture. I will desire some privacy during our conversation."

CHAPTER 27

PRIDE OF THE LION

"I still say this is too dangerous," said Talbot.

"Too late to back out now," said Tamlin. "If you're so frightened, you should have left with the servants."

Talbot growled at him and said, "I'm thinking about Tazi. You saw how she looked last night."

"Speak for yourself, big little brother," said Tazi. "Underneath that pelt of yours, you were plenty bruised."

"I didn't mean anything by it," said Talbot. "I was just concerned about putting you and Larajin in dan—"

"You are my dearest friend, Tal," said Larajin, "but do shut up."

"Now, now, children," said Shamur. Her voice carried far more authority since it came from everywhere and nowhere. Tamlin might have enjoyed watching the effect her disembodied command had on Talbot and Tazi if he didn't already know her reasons for speaking to them from the Stormweather nexus. "Stop your quarreling and listen to Tamlin. He is head of the family, now."

"That's another thing—" began Talbot.

"Son," interjected Thamalon. Like Shamur, he spoke from the refuge of the nexus. His voice was hale and warm, belying the truth that only Tamlin knew. "Remember your promise to me."

Talbot sighed and said, "Yes, Father."

"What promise?" asked Tamlin.

He'd hoped that his father's confidence in him meant that no more secrets would be kept from him. Apparently, that had been a vain hope.

"They're here," said Cale.

"How do you know that?" demanded Tamlin, dimly aware that he'd been purposefully distracted from his question.

"My lord, it is my duty to know."

Tamlin thought he heard his father chuckle. He sighed.

"Places, everyone," he said. "Is our guest comfortable up there?"

The guard Kainan leaned over the rail of one of the balconies on the second floor. He waved and nodded before glancing back at the unseen occupant of the seat behind him. Tamlin sketched a salute, and Kainan faded back into the shadows.

Larajin and Tazi took their spots beside Tamlin at the head of the table. Talbot leaped up to the balcony overlooking the feast hall, fifteen feet above the floor. He landed as lightly as a dancer, but the balcony creaked under his weight. Cale simply vanished.

A few moments later, the herald announced that the guests had arrived. Tamlin nodded his permissions back to the man. As the first of the visitors filed into the hall, he flicked a speck of imaginary dust from the arm of his chair. He affected an air of boredom as the Talendar, Karn, and Baerent representatives filed into the feast hall and stood behind their places. Uskevren servants held their chairs for them as they sat.

A few of them cast inquiring glances at Tamlin's odd appearance. He'd briefly considered shaving the strange beard his grandfather had left him, but ultimately he kept it. He'd also retained Aldimar's vermilion cloak as well as a wide belt of pouches and pockets full of spell materials and foci. Alas, none of the new affectations was particularly fashionable.

Presker Talendar cast an inquiring glance toward the head of the table. The normally cool nobleman appeared anxious, and he fidgeted with his great emerald ring.

Tamlin retained his disaffected attitude until Saclath Soargyl arrived with his nephew Brimmer. As they entered the room, Tamlin fairly bolted from his seat, grasping their hands in both of his as each party raced to bow lower over the other's hands. It all ended messily in a series of awkward embraces and how-good-of-you-to-comes, then there was an icy moment in which Brimmer lurched forward to kiss Tazi's hand. Tamlin watched the vein pulsing under her eye as she suppressed her own urge to throttle both men.

At last, the heads of the Old Chauncel took their places. Andeth Ilchammar made his entrance with his familiar Drakkar at his side and a trail of guards in black tabards. By custom, no noble House carried weapons into the hall of its host, the exception granted only to the Hulorn. His men took positions on either side of his seat at the other end of the table. Behind him, a wide alcove full of windows looking out onto Selgaunt Bay was shrouded in draperies. No one from outside would spy on the day's proceedings.

"Welcome, my lord mayor," called Tamlin. He raised his goblet to toast the guest of honor. "May Waukeen bless our proceedings, and may Helm keep all good folk from harm so long as they dwell within our walls."

Tamlin tasted the ceremonial mead, careful not to drink more than a sip. He'd been so fraught with adversity the past tendays that he had no time to appreciate the distractions from his longing pangs for a drink. He had to make an effort not to drink deeply to calm his nerves. His plan for the coming meeting was far from infallible.

His guests murmured their approval of his toast. When they set their cups down, the business began.

"Our convocation today—" began Tamlin. He wasn't the least bit surprised when the Hulorn stood to interrupt his speech.

"Our business here is treason," said Andeth Ilchammar, throwing his cape off one shoulder in a dramatic flourish. "Or rather, the rooting out of traitors in our midst. We come here to judge an accusation so dire that only the sage heads of the Old Chauncel can condone its measure."

Tamlin watched to see which of the "sage heads" nodded approvingly of the Hulorn's words. Fat Saclath was the loudest, which was no surprise. Brimmer looked confused and stupid, which was no great feat.

Presker and the heads of the other Houses on Thamalon's list of conspirators cast their eyes at the head of the table. Tamlin wondered whether they were looking for a savior or a scapegoat.

"I have here a list of names," cried Andeth, receiving a scroll from Drakkar. "Names of those who would seek to undermine the lawful order of the city of Selgaunt in its charter from the Overmaster of Ordulin— What? What do you think you're doing?"

Tamlin had leaped up from his seat and stood upon the long table. The cloak that enhanced his flying spells billowed up to give him a grace and drama far beyond Ilchammer's flamboyant gestures.

"Alas," said Tamlin, adopting Ilchammer's officious tone, "I suffer from an unfortunate incapacity to endure transparent attempts to obfuscate the efforts of a corrupt functionary to subjugate the will of the rightful leaders of Selgaunt."

The Hulorn gasped, but at the same time his face brightened in an expression of delight and admiration. He looked like a man who'd just learned that the entertainment he was about to enjoy was in fact his favorite opera.

"What brave talk from the son of the man who engineered the very sedition we have come to consider here today."

"Spare us, Mad Andy," said Tamlin. The assembled nobles gasped at the young man's audaciousness. "I grow weary of your nattering. You know as well as anyone how easily bored I am, especially at so shallow a charade."

Drakkar choked so hard that Tamlin expected to see one of the man's eyes pop from its socket.

"How dare you speak to me in such a manner!" blustered the Hulorn.

Despite himself, he couldn't keep the smile from his face. Tamlin could see that he was enjoying the play. Unfortunately, the rest of the Old Chauncel took umbrage at the young upstart's blatant show of disrespect. Only a few kept their emotions in reserve, while the rest babbled on about insolence and respect for one's elders. Even some of those whom Thamalon had entrusted with his scheme turned coat to back the stronger horse. Tamlin silently noted them for future consideration while the Hulorn shook his scroll at him.

"I have evidence!"

"You do," said Tamlin. "I concede it. My father plotted to have you removed from office, confident that the city would prosper in your absence."

Andeth stared down the table at Tamlin, astonished. Tamlin winked at him. Let him wonder what that meant.

"Then you must realize," interjected Drakkar, "that the penalty for your father's treason is forfeiture of all Uskevren holdings and properties."

The wizard turned his head in a dramatic gesture indicating all of the trappings of the feast hall, but everyone could see that his eyes lingered longest on Larajin. She returned his gaze with a steady stare of her own, one that promised a response to his leering threat, and not the one he craved.

"I realize that is the price of an *unsuccessful* coup," replied

Tamlin, "and thus, I am moved to call for an immediate vote among the assembled body. I move that the Hulorn, Andeth Ilchammar, Lord Mayor of Selgaunt, is unfit for office on grounds that he has employed assassins to murder members of this very assembly."

The silence that followed Tamlin's declaration was heavy enough to push Drakkar and his master down into their seats. It lingered for long seconds after Tamlin stopped speaking.

Presker Talendar bolted up from his seat and said, "I second Lord Uskevren's motion and demand an investigation into the Hulorn's contacts."

Andeth cocked his head at Presker, his narrowing eyes promising that Tamlin wasn't the only one marking adversaries this day.

"You have no evidence!" barked Drakkasr. "There is no evidence!"

"Ah, I was hoping you would say that," replied Tamlin. He walked to the center of the table and gestured up to the balcony. "Master Malveen?"

Pietro Malveen rose timidly from the shadows, trembling either from the effects of his drugs or else from fear to see such august company assembled below him. He clutched the railing to steady his hands.

"It is true," he said. "Ilchammar commissioned me for those paintings he had sent to the ones who disappeared. I did not know he had them enchanted to trap—"

"Hearsay!" shouted the Hulorn. Still he couldn't keep the wild grin from his face. He'd never seemed so full of glee and life, not during his most antic introduction of a queer new opera nor a distressing gallery of avant-garde paintings. "Balderdash, of course. It goes without saying. These are groundless accusations, inadmissible in any court. Who can testify to seeing any such 'magic paintings?' "

"I can," called Thamalon's voice. "For I fell victim to one and would remain trapped if not for the valiant efforts of my son."

"So can I," added Shamur. "If our sworn testament is insufficient in your judgment, we have also identified the ghost of a man slain by the Hulorn's own assassin. The clerics can compel him to bear witness to the schemes of Andeth Ilchammar and his minion, Drakkar."

"I am not a *minion!*" snapped Drakkar.

"Oh, bugger it all," laughed Andeth. "It looks like a fight after all, doesn't it?"

As one, the Old Chauncel pushed back their seats and stood away from the table. To either side of Andeth and Drakkar, the Hulorn's guards drew their weapons and formed a defensive line around their charges.

"Where are you going?" asked the Hulorn. He drew a twisted wand from inside his cloak and waved it at the assembled company. "You pretentious fools don't really expect us to let you stand aside while we resolve this issue, do you? You have your part to play, even if all you ever do is talk, talk, *talk!*"

Drakkar was already chanting his own spell as the Hulorn spread his foul magic across the hall. A ghastly green vapor coalesced in a line from the Hulorn to Tamlin's seat. It rippled along the table, spilling over to either side to touch the assembled nobles.

Tamlin flew up to the ceiling to avoid its effects, noting that Tazi had already faded into the shadows, and Larajin raised a warding hand before her face as she clutched the two-faced medallion of her goddesses.

On the floor, the noblemen began to melt, their bodies sinking like collapsed tents over their suddenly disjointed bones. Their flowing flesh melded and mingled, leaving behind their garments as a snake might shed its skin.

Throughout the horrid transformation, their mouths continued to shriek, their eyes rolling and their teeth gnashing as they bit and spit at one another. Only Fendo Karn and Brimmer Soargyl scurried backward unchanged, apparently protected by hidden talismans.

Tamlin whistled low and long.

"That was a dirty thing to do, Mad Andy. It will take us days to get that out of the carpet."

He flicked his fingers at the Hulorn, sending five crimson darts at the man's face. Ilchammar dispelled them with a dismissive wave of his hand. Upon one of his fingers, one of a ring of six topazes flashed and turned dark.

"Witty," the Hulorn replied. "If I had known you would prove so amusing, Thamalon the *Lesser*, I would have invited you to join my little coterie long ago."

From the floor in front of Drakkar, a night-colored stallion rose from a ring of fire. The conjured horse-fiend reared and stamped at the gibbering mass of mouths and eyes upon the floor.

Drakkar pointed at Tamlin, and the nightmare leaped upon the long table, leaving burning hoofprints in the polished oak surface. Before it could rear up to strike at its hovering target, a huge figure leaped down upon its back, gripping its fiery mane and pulling its head back.

"You told me he was dead!" Andeth spat at Drakkar.

"So I was informed," protested the wizard.

Astride the nightmare, Talbot hissed at the burns on his hand and legs, but he raised a gigantic sword and struck a glowing wedge out of the creature's neck. Molten blood oozed from its wound, and the demon horse stumbled off the table, falling into the hungry mouths on the floor. Talbot leaped clear with an actor's flourish and turned to hack at the fallen nightmare before it could rise again.

Andeth had produced another wand, this one garnished with bits of fur and scaly hide. He thrust it like a sword, and a dull glob of matter shot forth to stick on Tamlin's right arm. He tried to shake off the offending mass, but it spread instantly up and down his limb. Tamlin felt a momentary numbness, and he watched as his arm transformed into a huge black viper.

"How striking!" called the Hulorn. "You shall be the envy of Selgaunt with so daring an ornament."

The snake's head hissed and rose to strike at his face, and Tamlin fleetingly wished he'd taken Aldimar's helm as well as his cloak. He tried to grab his treacherous limb, but the snake writhed away from his grasp before rising to strike again.

Across the room, Talbot knocked down the Hulorn's guards two at a time. When one of them flanked him and raised his sword, his eyes grew wide and he let out a little choking sound before dropping his blade. As the guard fell to the floor, Tamlin briefly glimpsed Tazi moving on to another unwitting target, deftly avoiding the writhing mass of flesh and mouths that had been the Old Chauncel.

He wanted to help them, but it was all he could do to evade the attacks of his own venomous arm. At last he slapped it and spat out the syllables that sent a sheet of lightning coursing through the snake—and his own body. He shuddered and grimaced through the self-inflicted agony, but his reward was that the rebellious arm hung limp.

He looked up to see that Cale and Vox were leading the house guard in an attack on the Hulorn's men. While the soldiers clashed, Cale dashed through them, ducking under swords and between shields, leaving a trail of falling foes in his wake. He cut himself a path straight for the enemy wizards.

The Hulorn's laughter degenerated into an uncertain cackle. He and Drakkar hadn't been idle during Tamlin's struggle. A purple sphere shimmered around the Hulorn, and a wall of flame leaped up to block Cale and the Uskevren guards—no matter that its sudden appearance immolated a few of the Hulorn's own men. Their screams rose higher than the maddening chatter of the gibbering mouther that still crept over the floor.

The wall of fire ignited the hall's tapestries, and flames crawled up toward the ceiling. Tamlin had a sudden vision of Stormweather Towers falling to cinders all around him, just as the original structure had done years before at the hands of Uskevren foes.

"No!" he cried to everyone and no one in particular.

Nowhere in his restored memory was there a spell for extinguishing fire. All he could do was wreak more destruction, so he turned his attention back to his foes.

"*Anabar!*" he cried, hurling a stream of lightning toward Andeth.

The white energy dissipated as it struck the Hulorn's magical shield. Andeth laughed all the more.

"You rank amateur!"

"Mistress Thazienne!" cried Brimmer Soargyl. He stumbled away from the gibbering mouther, barely escaping its snapping teeth. "Let me convey you to safety. None of this madness need interfere with my proposal."

Tazi spared the man only a brief, incredulous look before pushing him back into the sprawling monstrosity on the floor. There he howled and screamed as dozens of jaws nipped at his ample flesh.

"Your suit," she said, "is refused."

Tamlin hurled fire, lightning, and pure energy at the monsters Andeth and Drakkar summoned, but the wizards conjured the creatures far faster than he could destroy them. Soon, the Uskevren guard was outnumbered by a small horde of rats, a trio of blubbery demons, and some hideous, floating, spidery sack of flesh that dipped its long claws down into the fray to suck at the combatants.

Cale maneuvered his way behind Drakkar, grabbed the man's chin, and cut his throat. The knife's edge barely scratched the wizard's skin, leaving a mark like a chisel's scratch on granite.

"Drakkar!" cried Larajin. Her arms were raised in an evocation of divine favor, and the smell of rose petals filled the room even over the acrid stench of burning wood and fabric. She held out her hands toward the mage, and golden light radiated from her palms. "The goddess can no longer abide your wickedness."

The wizard jerked as he felt the effects of Larajin's spell strip away his magical protection. Cale's fingers dug into his face, and his knife cut Drakkar a new, wider grimace.

"Dark and empty!" cursed Andeth, seeing his most powerful ally slain.

He backed into the dark recess of the draped alcove. With a wave of his conjuring wand, he summoned a cloud of tiny bats to swarm above him, blocking Tamlin's line of fire. He began shaking yet another wand.

"Cover me, men!" he ordered. "This is not over, Uskevren. Not by any means!"

"Tamlin!" cried Larajin. "He's getting away!"

Tamlin shook his head and smiled back at his half-sister.

"Can you put out that fire?" he asked.

"Yes, but the Hulorn!"

From the obscuring darkness of the alcove, Andeth screamed, "You! But why—?"

Whatever words he might have spoken next exploded in white radiance that scattered the bats and set the gibbering mouther to screaming even louder than before.

"Not to worry," said Tamlin. "He just met our new associate. Now, let's clean house."

EPILOGUE

Shamur's face was composed as she embraced Tazi and Talbot, but Tamlin knew she'd been weeping. He stood with her as his siblings went to their father, knowing they were saying their farewells. Tamlin had prepared them before they left home. He'd feared they would blame him for failing to save Thamalon. Instead, Talbot had turned cold and silent, Tazi turned to Steorf for comfort, and Larajin took Tamlin's hand to comfort *him*.

When they were ready, he led them through the gate.

"When did you know?" asked Shamur.

For a moment, Tamlin feared she was asking how long he'd kept the secret of Larajin from her, then he realized that she and Thamalon had spent almost a day together, and they'd already put that issue to rest. Shamur wanted to know when Tamlin realized when his father had died.

"As soon as we came through the gate, I had a feeling," he said. "When he wouldn't touch us, I realized why."

"He is a ghost."

"No," said a soothing voice. Malaika appeared beside them, her sad eyes somehow less tormented than Tamlin had seen them before. "Not a ghost."

"What have you done with my husband?" demanded Shamur.

"Only what he wished of me," said Malaika. "I have kept him awake here long enough for him to bid farewell to you and his family."

"I *am* his family," insisted Shamur.

"But not his blood," said Malaika. "To Aldimar was I secretly wed, and upon his death betrothed to his progeny. For years I waited, buried under the ashes of his home, until at last Tamlin came to me in dreams."

"I remember," said Tamlin, smiling wistfully, "but then the dreams stopped."

Malaika nodded and said, "Aldimar lingered within me, unwilling to travel on to his fate."

"I saw his fate," said Tamlin. "I wouldn't want it, either."

"It was far worse for him after the years he spent usurping your place. He was hard before, and greedy, but then he turned wicked and cruel."

"But my father," said Tamlin. "He won't face the same sort of . . ."

"See for yourself," said Malaika, gesturing toward Thamalon.

The others had left him and returned to Shamur. Talbot had one big arm over each of his sister's shoulders, and Tazi wiped at one eye with her wrist. Larajin looked cautiously toward Shamur, reluctant to approach.

Shamur regarded her husband's bastard through eyes so hard and gray they might have been river stones. For a moment, Tamlin feared she might slap the girl. Instead, Shamur opened her arms and welcomed Larajin into her embrace. The gesture set Talbot and Tazi both to weeping, and Tamlin made his escape before he lost the last fragments of his composure.

Thamalon smiled warmly at him as he approached.

"Well met, Lord Uskevren."

"Don't call me that," said Tamlin. "Not you."

"It makes me proud to know you are the one who carries on my name," said Thamalon. "You did well with the Hulorn. Perhaps you could have spared the house another scorching, but. . . ."

"You always find something to criticize."

"I'm joking, Tamlin."

"I know," he said. "I know. I just wish you could . . ."

"I know. So did I, at first, but now that I've spent some time here, now that I've seen you and your brother and sisters fighting side by side instead of toe-to-toe, I know it is time."

"But there's so much you could teach me."

"I've taught you everything you need to know."

"But I wasn't listening!"

Thamalon laughed and said, "No, you weren't. Still, you heard enough of it. I'm tired, ever since coming to this place, wearier than you can possibly imagine. I need you to open a door for me."

"Which one?"

Thamalon looked up, toward a half-gallery upon one wall.

"That one feels right," he said. "I've said my good-byes, and I cannot bear to say them again without being able to hold your mother in my arms."

Together they flew toward the door. Its oak surface gleamed as they approached. When Tamlin opened it, he smelled summer grass and grape leaves. Sunlight poured down upon arbors and vineyards nestling between hills of deep green forest.

Thamalon sighed and drifted toward the fields, his sorrowful smile turning ever more content as he slowly twirled down into eternity.

❧ ❧ ❧ ❧ ❧

The cold wind whipped the Uskevren banners as the moon gleamed on the gold thread on the horse-at-anchor. Tamlin closed his eyes as he faced the wind. After a moment's reverie, he turned back to his lone companion on the rooftop.

"Where will you go?"

Radu shrugged and said, "East. Perhaps across the Moonsea." His uncovered face looked like a hideous mask, with sharp fragments of the bone blade that had crippled him jutting from his cheek and brow. "I will abide by our compact," he said.

"Stay well away from Selgaunt," said Tamlin, "and for the gods' sake, never let Talbot learn of our arrangement."

"So long as you continue to foster Laskar and Pietro."

"They shall be as cousins to the Uskevren, living here, within the halls of Stormweather."

"Then I shall never need to return."

Tamlin nodded to acknowledge the unspoken threat. He'd known his bargain with Radu Malveen would require that he allow the assassin to live and thus ensure that Tamlin would uphold his promises. In return, Radu had agreed to invoke his peculiar powers one last time. With the escape of his ghosts at the moment of Tamlin's death, he might have escaped his inevitable disintegration, but he'd willingly accepted it once more.

Tamlin felt a surprising admiration for the man who had killed him. He didn't like Radu Malveen, but he couldn't deny that the assassin had been faultlessly loyal to his family.

Together they looked out over the moonlit roofs of Selgaunt, Radu for the last time. From the vantage of Stormweather's highest tower, Tamlin could see the entire city from Mountarr Gate in the west to the farthest tower south of Selgaunt Bay. To the northwest, the Hulorn's weird palace looked unusually serene in its mantle of snow.

Who would reside there next was an issue the Old Chauncel

had still not resolved. After their ordeal in the recent spell duel, they were even more fractious than usual. It could take months before a new candidate emerged for approval—assuming that Thamalon's proposal to eliminate the office entirely was dismissed. Without his personal efforts, Tamlin feared, it soon would be, then it was only a matter of time before a new Hulorn was chosen.

"Can he communicate with you?" asked Tamlin.

"He never stops," Radu said.

Tamlin suppressed a smile. It was hardly a humorous subject, but the thought of Chaney Foxmantle choosing to remain with his killer even after the Stormweather portal freed him from his leash amused Tamlin to no end. It also made him sad to think that Chaney could not bear to reveal himself to Talbot for fear that he would lure his friend to vengeance against a foe who might well kill him.

Tamlin said, "Actually, I meant Andeth."

"He is even worse."

"Serves you right," said Tamlin, who could only imagine the bitter ravings of the man called Mad Andy. Even if Tamlin couldn't punish Radu personally, it pleased him to think that someone would. "Now, get out of my city."

They watched as the last of the wounded skwalos slowly rose above the bloody cobbles of the flensing grounds. It was a mere child, no larger than a trading cog. Its immature body was still as translucent as a wine bottle, and its membranous skin caught and refracted the sunlight to cast rippling patterns over the crowd, making the elves and humans alike appear to be standing fathoms beneath the waves.

"Don't look so sad," said Larajin. "Everyone is looking to you for strength."

She held onto Tamlin's arm, weary from exhausting her magic to heal the surviving skwalos. Even all of her divine powers had been barely enough to allow the crippled animals to return to the sky.

"You are the one they should thank," said Tamlin. "All I've done is repeal a few of my grandfather's most egregious dictates. It will take much more than a few merciful gestures to repair all the harm he has done."

Tamlin was surprised by both his strange sense of responsibility for the evil committed in his guise and his acute sympathy for the skwalos. The slaughter of a stag or boar hunt had never given him qualms, but these creatures were mined for their flesh and vapors while still alive. It was all he could do to keep his expression stately and assured before the Vermilion Guard. The elite soldiers were already suspicious of the sudden changes in their master. Tamlin knew there were whispers that the elves had somehow managed to possess his body during the brief, aborted war. He hoped he would not have to electrocute a few would-be assassins to retain his authority.

Across from his honor guard stood the elves, who watched Tamlin every bit as carefully for any sign that his promised concessions were a ruse to buy time. Among the emissaries dispatched to ensure that he fulfilled his promises of the tentative truce were three ancient wizards, two women and a man. Beside them stood Malaika, her dark eyes full of mingled hope and caution. Tamlin had wanted to stand with her, to ask her a thousand more questions, but he knew that standing among the elves would only undermine the already crumbling loyalty among his men.

"I just wish everyone knew I wasn't the Sorcerer," he said quietly.

"Some know already," said Larajin, nodding toward Malaika. "Until the rest are ready for the truth, they need to believe their leader is still with them."

"For now, perhaps, but I can't keep trying to lead both our household and this . . . this *dreamland*."

"It isn't a dream, you know."

"I know," agreed Tamlin. "It just doesn't seem as real. It doesn't seem as *important* as . . ."

"Home?" offered Larajin.

"Home," he agreed. "Speaking of which, it is almost time to return. I promised Tal that I would write him a receipt for the gold we found hidden in Escevar's chamber."

"I think your word might be good enough," she suggested. "It's time you and he learned to trust each other."

"Perhaps," said Tamlin, "but Father would have wanted me to write a receipt anyway."

Larajin smiled wistfully and said, "No doubt he would. While you're at it, don't forget to talk with Thazienne about that Soargyl business. She still seems angry with you."

"I haven't forgotten," sighed Tamlin. "I just hope she doesn't punch me in the nose before I can finish explaining."

"Well, if she does, I won't be able to heal it until tomorrow."

"In that case, perhaps it is time I began to practice that stoneskin spell."

Tamlin was overseeing the repair of Shamur's solar when he received the news of Tazi's departure.

"She didn't even say good-bye?"

"No," said Cale. His normally sanguine tone was replaced by a curtness that verged on the offensive. Tamlin was almost afraid to broach the subject of Cale's continued service, and something told him that the man had already made a decision to leave Stormweather Towers. "Not even a note."

Tamlin had known his sister was upset at their father's death, but he hadn't expected her to leave home again so soon after such a long absence.

"Perhaps we should go after her," said Tamlin.

"No," said Talbot. He stood knee-deep in the dirty water of the solar's pond. After the workmen had failed to set the tumbled fountain stones upright, he had shed his shirt and waded in to help them. After a few mighty heaves, they'd restored the great blue stones to a semblance of their former positions. "She wants some time alone."

"She told you she was leaving?" asked Tamlin.

"Not exactly," said Talbot, "but I had a feeling."

"Leave her," said Shamur.

She stepped carefully over a puddle while holding up the edges of her black skirts. Even in mourning clothes, she remained one of the most elegantly attired ladies of Selgaunt. She held her head regally high, her eyes barely dimmed by the grief she kept inside. Tamlin barely recognized her as the wild warrior who'd fought beside Thamalon and Cale on the tower of Castle Stormweather.

"But now is when I need her help the most," said Tamlin.

"She needs her freedom, little big brother," said Talbot. "Besides, it's better she's out of sight while Brimmer Soargyl is convalescing from those bites."

"I told him Larajin would heal those for him," said Tamlin. "After all, we are funding that shrine of hers. That's got to be worth laying hands on a Soargyl for a few moments."

"He won't go anywhere near an Uskevren woman these days," said Talbot. "He's still scared."

"As well he should be," added Shamur.

Tamlin flinched when he realized how casually they'd been discussing Larajin in front of Shamur. Despite their fears that their mother would resent the constant reminder of her husband's infidelity, she'd treated the girl with surprising warmth since Thamalon's death. Even before Tamlin could broach the subject of acknowledging Larajin publicly, Shamur had made the suggestion herself, explaining that it would do much to soothe the injured feelings of the clerics of Sune, who could attribute to nepotism the Uskevren's impolitic support of Larajin's heretical philosophies.

"Now," Shamur said, "leave this mess to the servants and come to dinner."

Tamlin offered Shamur his arm. As they departed the solar, Vox silently followed. When Tamlin glanced back at him, the mute barbarian touched his forehead and unfolded one fist in a gesture like a blossoming flower.

Yes, Tamlin signed back. *My dreaming eye is open.*

ACKNOWLEDGEMENTS

Sincere gratitude to my fellow Sembians: Phil Athans, Lizz Baldwin, Richard Lee Byers, Clayton Emery, Ed Greenwood, Kij Johnson, Paul S. Kemp, Lisa Smedman, and Voronica Whitney-Robinson. Without the loan of your wonderful characters and keen advice, this would have been a short story. Especial thanks go to Phil, Ed, and Paul for inspiration and support above and beyond the call.

JEAN RABE

THE STONETELLERS

"Jean Rabe is adept at weaving a web of deceit and lies, mixed with adventure, magic, and mystery."
—sffworld.com on *Betrayal*

Jean Rabe returns to the DRAGONLANCE® world with a tale of slavery, rebellion, and the struggle for freedom.

VOLUME ONE
THE REBELLION

After decades of service, nature has dealt the goblins a stroke of luck. Earthquakes strike the Dark Knights' camp and mines, crippling the Knights and giving the goblins their best chance to escape. But their freedom will not be easy to win.

VOLUME TWO
DEATH MARCH

The escaped slaves—led by the hobgoblin Direfang—embark on a journey fraught with danger as they leave Neraka to cross the ocean and enter the Qualinesti Forest, where they believe themselves free. . . .

August 2008

VOLUME THREE
GOBLIN NATION

A goblin nation rises in the old forest, building fortresses and fighting to hold onto their new homeland, while the sorcerers among them search for powerful magic cradled far beneath the trees.

August 2009